BROTHERS FROM ANOTHER MOTHER

One for All? Always?

K. B. Pellegrino

Livres-Ici
PUBLISHING™

Brother from Another Mother

Urban Dictionary - submitted by Elmer, January 20, 2005
A term used to describe a good friend that you have known almost your whole life. The word 'brother' is used because the friend is extremely close to you to the point that he is almost like your brother – but from a different mother. And that rhymes…

CONTENTS

1

Interrupted Game

Attorney Norberto Cull, western Massachusetts famous defense attorney, had planned a day at home without the kids hoping to catch a Patriots game in quiet. He watched Tom Brady, bad finger and all, attempt to move the ball in the AFL championship game against Jacksonville. So far, no dice! He groaned loudly enough for his wife of over twenty years, Sheri, to look up from downing a bowl of freshly made chili-onion dip and tortilla chips and shake her head in mild disgust. Norbie glanced in her direction and laughed.

"Sheri, Oh Cheri, Cheri, my darling," he said, "You're not too glamorous when you eat Mexican; slow down, or I'll tell your mother you're eating carbs en masse." He ducked as a shower of tortilla chips came his way. "Hmm," he said, "You want to play" and he dove toward her thinking, *Hell, no need to dwell on Brady when Sheri is being playful.*

Norbie and Sheri were madly removing their sweats when the doorbell rang. Norbie swore. *Can't be the kids. They're with their cousins and won't be home until nine tonight. Fuck, no need to answer!* But the bell rang and rang and rang ending with a pounding on the door.

"Norbie, constant bell ringing is not an aphrodisiac in anyone's book. I'll get the door." Sheri started to dress.

Norbie heard muffled voices; Sheri's and another unknown one. A tall, imposing man with a ponytail shuffled into the living room with Sheri. Norbie thought he looked vaguely familiar, but when the familiar face spoke, he then knew the voice; from way back as the guy said, "Well,

1

I'll be damned, Bro, how the hell are you?"

"Sheri, meet Candido Rodriguez again, an old friend from the Springfield Boys Club who now sports a pony tail. How the hell long has it been? I've only seen you sporadically over maybe thirty years and I don't remember the new 'do'?"

Candi appeared nervous, looking at Sheri.

"Sheri, I would never barge into a family Sunday afternoon, but, forgive me, my needs at this moment are so overwhelming that I simply am not able to wait until tomorrow."

He apologized to her for intruding, not to Norbie; no, he would never apologize to Norbie. "I need Norbie's advice now. I need help now."

He turned to Norbie and said, "Brother from another mother, you have to help me. The police may be at the door any second now. Perhaps that beautiful front door should be left open a bit so the police won't feel the need to break it down."

Sheri did not need a blueprint for action. No one was going to break down her front door; that beautiful antique oak, custom-made door with wavy grey stained-glass inserts must be protected at all costs. She'd had to practically arm-wrestle with her carpenter to get him to order it; he said it was overpriced, beautiful but overpriced. She bolted to the front door; a testament to her regular yoga and physical training and opened it as two state troopers, two West Side uniforms, and West Side Detective Ash Lent approached on the stone walkway. She saw a handsome black Mercedes sedan that wasn't hers parked in her driveway, along with two cruisers and another car with their blue lights flashing.

She thought, *Hell, my mother will hear about this, and then I will hear about this again; and the kids. They'll be furious they missed all the fuss. Thank God for small favors. Our boys would think it a blast, and our girl would be petrified thinking that it must mean they were all going to jail.*

"Good morning, Detective Lent and gentlemen of the police. Please come in. Norbie and Candido are waiting for you."

Norbie thought, *Damn, Sheri's learned some discretion; it's always important to act as if everything is as it should be. Sort it out later, in private.*

Norbie welcomed the police in, directed them and Candido to his study, and shut the door on Sheri, knowing she would try to listen to their conversation. Ten minutes later the police walked out with Candido, not in cuffs. Norbie went into their bedroom and changed clothes, only to leave without an explanation, just a kiss and "I'll be home later. Don't wait up for me, Sweetie, it may be an extended conference."

He did not miss the annoyed look on Sheri's face.

Sheri searched her brain trying to figure out who this Candido Rodriguez could be. She knew if she had met him sometime before, that it was maybe at some event. She had been in Norbie's life since her freshman year in college. He was a junior then leaving over twenty years of his associations unconnected to her. For some reason that seemed important now.

I was married at twenty-five, she thought. *We have four children together. There should be no secrets. What has he told me about his childhood? Did he ever mention Candido to me? No, not by name, but he often spoke of experiences at the Boys Club he believed shaped him for his life today. Maybe I didn't listen carefully enough. They were important to Norbie.*

The trouble with marriage is that we each have our own agendas for moving forward. I didn't think what Norbie experienced before I met him could possibly be that important, really! Maybe thinking that way means I'm as narcissistic as some of the murderers he's represented.

With a sigh, Sheri entered the kitchen to clean up and plan for dinner, alone again.

Norbie entered the Major Crimes Unit conference room in the West Side Police station shortly after his new-almost client and the police arrived. In addition to Detective Ash Lent, Captain Rudy Beauregard was present. The Captain and Norbie acknowledged each other with a handshake and a courteous nod. The old friends had gone head-to-head on many a case. Their history involved the cagey tortoise and facile hare scenario, evolving into situations where they both worked for moral reasons against the establishment's mandates, often to their own surprise. No one ever doubted who was who. Beauregard reminded folks of the tortoise with his slow gait, while Norbie's reaction time was that of an athlete's at the starting gate.

Norbie requested some time with his new client before the Captain could make an arrest and also asked just why was his client being arrested? "Captain, just what is the charge against Candido Rodriguez? I need to understand why there were State Troopers outside in their cars along with your detective and the uniforms."

Captain Beauregard responded in a most serious tone, "Cull, I let your client come into the station without cuffs and without immediately arresting him in deference to our history together. The press would have loved reporting a person of interest in a serial murder was arrested at the beautiful estate of Norberto Cull Esq., known for his charitable contributions to all kinds of non-profits. But don't get me wrong, kindness ends right after your conference with your client. You understand? CPAC has jurisdiction over these murders," he added, using the acronym for the state's Crime Prevention and Control unit.

Knowing what the involvement with CPAC meant, Norbie asked, "You mean you're charging Mr. Rodriguez with serial murder?" Norbie was taken aback, perhaps not shocked because his line of work had made him immune to shock. But charging Candido Rodriguez with murder did not fit with his experience of his old friend and sometime adversary.

Norbie thought, *I'm fortunate with Beauregard. Wouldn't happen with another police department! Still, if Captain Beauregard had the goods on Candi, even he wouldn't be so gracious. His demeanor, however, doesn't inspire any comfort; looks as if Candi is in serious trouble. I don't love representing clients who are my friends; albeit from over 30 years ago. And he is now a client. I'm totally screwed here. Candido and I, and my five other friends from the Springfield Boys and Girls Club; well we were like brothers, and brothers stick together.*

Alone at last in the uncomfortable physical space of an interrogation room, complete with one desk, three chairs, and a large mirrored wall, Norbie sat opposite Candi.

"Do you want to tell me what you know; and don't bullshit me, Candi. Remember, I may not have seen you often in over thirty years, but I know you and know you well."

For a moment, Norbie remembered one of the more memorable times he had seen Candido when Norbie was busy saving the tall skinny kid's ass from a beating. *Candi was a notorious ladies' man even at the age of twelve. I, at the time, looked six years old, while Candi looked seventeen; and Candi used his mature profile to hook up with any available, well-developed girls.*

One young lady's brothers had caught up with him, and it took all of my skills in negotiating to remind them we were on the front lawn of the Boys Club, and if the director saw them fighting, they would all be thrown out. That was important because the next night was Golden Gloves night and the other boys were scheduled to fight.

They knew if the director saw them, then they would not be fighting. They left, promising to catch up with Candi at another time. That wouldn't happen if he saw them first, I knew. Candi could run like a gazelle.

"I've only heard of three unsolved murders in the area, Candi, and although they are all women, they've all been found in different towns and maybe have different MOs. So, I'm surprised that they would be called serial murders. Is this what Rudy's talking about; that he thinks you're connected?"

"Norbie, I killed no one. I love women and always have; you know that about me. The cops are crazy. Even when my first wife Sally deliberately damaged my new BMW, I didn't do anything; I knew I deserved it. I have a great job, good job history, two grown daughters who love me, two grandchildren, and have lived a model life for the last fifteen years; maybe not before that but now, absolutely a model life."

Norbie did not see Candi as a murderer and certainly not of women. He was never a fighter; he was a lover, a runner away from fights, and one who sometimes suffered from verbal diarrhea, but not a fighter. Norbie concluded that Candi thought fighting might damage his pretty face.

They talked for an hour, and all Candi could tell him was that he knew all three murder victims, had been their therapist ten to twelve years before, and had attended two of the young ladies' weddings. He was as surprised as anyone he would be suspected of killing them. He said that all three had called him a day or so before their deaths and asked for help. In each case, Candi called the local police.

Candido relayed he had a friend in the District Attorney's office whom he had helped get on his feet years ago; a man who believed that Candi had saved his life and who had in return called and told him he was being arrested. Candi then headed right to Norbie's house, located in West Side, the town where he and his wife also lived. "I knew you lived in West Side, Norbie; everyone knows this is your home. I live only half a mile from here. Apparently, the police were watching my house, knew about the impending arrest, and made the call that I was on the move. That's how they got to your home so fast; I knew they were right behind me. I had been told they were coming to arrest me during the game because they knew I'd be tied to the television. You see I have a whole set-up in my house; you know one of those home theatres and I left seven guys watching the game and my wife in the kitchen making guacamole and salsa. I didn't tell Heather where I was going. She'll kill me later, but I'm not telling her until I know what I'm up against."

"Candi, just what is your work history? Are you a therapist or a social worker?"

"I'm both, Norbie."

"If so, why haven't I seen you around? I thought I knew everyone in the field through some of my clients. Tell me about these women."

Candi described a career consisting of several positions, each one leading to a better one. He worked for the State Division of Youth Services after graduating from Boston College as a social worker. He learned to write grants and was successful in doing so for several state agencies.

He moved to non-profits as a grant writer and picked up his Master's degree in clinical social work from an area college. He had also written programs for the disabled in Massachusetts for the Bureau of Substance Abuse Services, Department of Mental Health and Human Services, Division of Youth Services, and many programs for alcohol education and drug recovery for both public and private agencies. He'd had a long history of working successfully with clients pursuing alcohol and/or drug-related recovery, stemming both from a personal desire to change and/or court requirement. His grant writing paid the big bills.

"Clinical counseling, while personally rewarding, drained the psyche and was not a way to get rich," Candi said.

"Norbie, I have money; good money. There's enough to pay you for any fee; I trust only you. You'll believe in me. If I am charged, my professional life and maybe even my personal life will be ruined."

Norbie brushed aside Candi's comment. "There will be time enough to talk about the business side of this. We don't quite know what 'this' is, yet, do we?"

Candi's knowledge of each of the victims murdered was dated. He had not seen any of them in the last few years but said he received calls from all of them a day or two before each died saying they were being stalked. One of the calls left a message; only two had he spoken with, and those two were scheduled to meet with him the next Monday afternoon following their deaths. Neither one showed. The third one was dead before he could speak with her.

"Candi, what kind of issues do you think they had; I mean how were you certain they were being stalked, or better yet, how were each of them certain? They must have been experiencing some trauma in their lives to even think about being stalked. Someone could be following my wife for weeks, and she wouldn't notice.

"So, don't you think unless the person doing the following was really acting weird, that the ladies noticing the stalking required their being sensitive to something especially negative in their lives?

"Another way to think about it is; being followed is one thing; being stalked is quite another. You're smart, what made you believe they were being followed and did you only believe it after the first one was murdered?"

Candido's face was being supported by his hands in a stance that screamed of defeat. Norbie had never seen him looking that way; even when it looked as if he was having the shit kicked out of him at age twelve. But, he knew, now was not the time for sympathy for his old friend; now was the time to ferret out information from a clearly traumatized client.

Candido said, "I don't know how to tell you why I believed them. You know when you've worked as many years as I have in the field of counseling and especially in substance abuse counseling, you become insulated from falling for dramatic statements, tears, and recriminations. It's not that you've lost your sensitivity; it's just you see through their false dramas, lack of self-awareness, and in some cases, their deliberate avoidance of accepting the truth about their situations.

"No, Norbie, I'm a pro at behaviors; but again, as you know, no one's a pro when it comes to dealing with a sociopath. So, even I am able to be manipulated, but only in the short-term. Over time the best manipulator's behavior is visible to most."

"Candi, I don't need a lesson in your insightfulness, we only have a short time before you are charged. You understand you're being charged? Tell me about each of the three women and everything you know or think you know before Captain Beauregard comes in here. Remember each murder was in a different town so three different police departments will be involved as well as the Hampden County District Attorney and the state police. Tell me in each case, if you are able to remember, what officer you spoke with and what did you say?"

2
Remembering

The first lady killed was Tonya Brown.

"Tonya was about thirty-five years old when she was murdered. I guess it's all right to tell you, Norbie, because I'm defending myself. When I knew her, she was a self-described drop-dead beautiful supposedly black woman who was in the midst of some serious marital problems. She had two little boys at the time when she came to me for counseling."

He went on saying that her husband was white, as was her mother, but that her partial black heritage was important to her. Although she looked Caucasian, she identified as black. She would never use the term Afro-American because she didn't think her heritage was from Africa but from the Islands.

"Tonya believed this despite the fact her mother could not remember, just who, among the many, was her father.

"Her mother was a recovering alcoholic; dry for over thirty years and Tonya was attending AA at the time she came to see me. In her phone call that evening before her death, she said she never relapsed and I believed her. In fact, I don't think Tonya was an alcoholic. I think she just had a few bad nights acting out, and blaming alcohol for her actions was easy. So, AA was a first step in examining her behaviors and history."

When Candi originally met Tonya, she said her marriage was problematic mainly because her husband Danny was insanely jealous. Tonya told him, "Maybe his being jealous is not without some reason."

In therapy, Candi discovered that Tonya had an early history of using pretense to get what she wanted; mainly attention. She would constantly say her relatives and friends were jealous of her and they created difficulties because of their jealousy. It had taken a long period of counseling before Tonya was able to discover for herself the dangers of using jealousy as a strategy.

"Tonya, like many beautiful women, had difficulty separating attention from meaningful relationships," he said. She wanted the easy way out. It had always worked before, but at that point in time her strategy had been used too often, and she now thought it was too late to save her marriage and family. She loved her two little boys, and they were losing a father.

"Tonya realized she didn't want that, thinking their father was a good man. He needed counseling; they both needed counseling. Unfortunately, her husband Danny was killed in a construction accident in the midst of my work with Tonya. As a result, Tonya was a mess; loaded with guilt, trying simultaneously to address her alcohol abuse, grieving, and coping with her boys' care."

"I treated Tonya for a long time through my employment with two different mental health vendors and for a period when I had my own clinical practice; the first agency was a crisis vendor, and the other was an agency supporting troubled single mothers with multiple problems."

He reported he liked her; that when she finally addressed her issues, she did it with honesty. At the end of her treatment, she had reconciled with her husband's death and was happily looking forward to a better life. He heard she had remarried.

Tonya was found early on Sunday morning, October 29, 2017. She lived in Monson and was found dead near the waterfront of an empty cottage on Lake George, Wales, on the day after her call to him.

Norbie asked about the last phone call.

"Tonya left a hysterical message," Candi said. "'I know someone's following me. It's the same car out there no matter where and when I leave my home or work.'" She said she was the office manager for a wholesale auto parts distributor in Palmer. In Palmer a smaller city, she thought it was easy for her to spot being followed.

When Candido spoke to Tonya on the phone, she said that she maybe had a photo of the guy but it was only a profile, and she didn't recognize him. He drove a dark grey or black Nissan, but she was uncertain about the model. He had her cell phone number, and she was getting frequent calls. At least she thought the calls were from him. The message was always the same: a mechanical voice repeating three or four times, "You can't run away, Tonya, you can't run away, Tonya…"

Candi said he read that the police had not found any identifying information on or near the body. Her mother, not a husband, identified Tonya's body only a few hours after she had not returned home.

As to the officer in Wales that Candi spoke with, he said, "I don't remember his name. It may have been the chief for all I know. I may have it in my notebook. I still use a notebook rather than my cell. I regularly lose my cell phone, and if I had notes on clients on the cell; well that would present problems for me."

The two, knowing their conference time was limited, talked about the next victim, Janice Shaunessy. Candido was visibly moved by her death; her uncle was a close friend of Devon O'Brien from his and Norbie's Boys Club days.

Devon O'Brien had originally requested Candi intervene in Janice's out of control life. Janice was a born party girl, and her uncle thought it had gone on too long. She had one little girl whose father was unknown. He said she was his friend's only niece, in fact, she was the only daughter on his friend's side of the family.

Devon candidly told Candi, "The family members all gave her too much attention. They, including me, took her everywhere and spoiled the hell out of her. Christ she's gorgeous and a target for all the wrong guys."

Norbie interrupted when Candi took a breath. "You mean our Devon O'Brien; our buddy?"

"Yeah," Candi answered, "who else? He says he sees you sometimes. Let me finish."

Devon said that Marti, Janice's daughter, was being well taken care of because Janice could always rely on her family to pick up the pieces when she went off the radar. Devon thought that, from his perspective, Janice was what he'd call 'a situational alcoholic.'

Devon brought Janice to Candi after she returned home from a two-night stay somewhere and couldn't remember where she had been. In the past, Janice had not been willing to talk to someone; now she was frightened and actually thought she may have been raped during the unknown weekend. Candi connected her with a rape counselor and to a very good therapist. She insisted, however, that Candi continue counseling with her. He discussed it with her therapist, and the woman thought it was more important that Janice work with someone she trusted. She suggested that Candi be the therapist; and with Janice's permission, she would consult on her case, when it was needed.

Janice did very well in therapy and attended AA meetings and related counseling during the approximately two years she was in treatment with Candi. During that period, Janice met a very nice man who owned three small retail malls in the area. Janice married Ben Bianchi three years after Candi first met her.

"It was one happy wedding I tell you. Janice's daughter was then about seven and was in the wedding party. I truly thought, Norbie, that this was one of my success stories. And then she gets murdered. Again, found on a Sunday morning, December 31, 2017, on the shores of Lake Lorraine.

"The news reported there's a private road off Page Boulevard in Springfield that gives access to the lake and was where her body was found. You remember the road, Norbie, we used to swim up there."

"Tell me about the phone call she received the night before she died and if she stated any reason why she would call you rather than her uncle, or Devon, or her husband Ben," Norbie asked.

"Norbie, I asked her that question, and she said, 'Candi, I don't know if this guy following me is from my past. He knows where I am all the time. I've tried out-maneuvering him when I'm driving, but he gets to my destination just minutes after I arrive. I get calls that hang up and some that leave weird messages: "Janice, there's always pay-back. Janice, there's always pay-back… over and over."

"She said it was unnerving, but her life was so normal now that this had to be from her life before. I agreed to meet her the next day, New Year's Day, but she didn't show. I called her cell, but it clicked off immediately; I couldn't even leave a message. Then the news came on. Again, there was no identification on the body, but I just knew it was her and I immediately called the police and told them about her."

Norbie was not comfortable, not even a tad bit comfortable with Candi's rush to call the police. *Candi calls the police to be helpful and because he's worried about Janice not showing up. Doesn't everyone who watches television know the police look seriously at anyone who shows too much interest in a crime? And in this case, the interest is immediate, even before the body is even identified? Candi's call probably helped them ID the body. Hell, can't I get clients who are smarter. These social workers think that every good turn by them will be interpreted in the same context by others. Wrong, wrong, wrong, so fucking stupid!*

"Candi, who in the Springfield Police Department did you call? I know you know most of the cops there. Was it someone we know?"

"Yeah, well I first called Jack Ladd. Remember him from the club. He used to be a cop. I see him once in a while at the YMCA. I have his cell number, because he's helped me get some clients into rehab. Sometimes if the cops bring the client in, there's less paperwork; you know, help us out kind of thing. Everybody in my industry wants to know a cop to call in a crisis. Jack was always amenable to helping my clients.

"So, I called Jack, who then connected me to Joe Stellato in the Crimes Unit there. He couldn't understand why I was calling, and then I told him I was certain that the body was Janice's. It took a lot of explaining, you know! Some cops don't bring the job home with them like we social workers tend to do. But I know others whose noses are always in everyone's business wanting to know what's going on everywhere; so, I don't' understand why Stellato thought it was a big thing."

He's clueless about investigators' minds, Norbie thought. *They're not looking at what's important to Candi; they're looking at everyone in sight as a candidate to charge.*

No matter how he tried, Candi couldn't add any more information on Janice Shaunessy. Norbie did have a question.

"Candi, Jack Ladd's not on the force now; he owns a bunch of bars in the area; a couple high-end ones. So why would you call him for a name on the police force?"

"Norbie," Candi replied, "who's in the know in the area: cops, defense attorneys, bar owners and druggies, they're knowledgeable. I knew Jack as a former cop would point me right for Springfield, and I didn't ask you because you ask too many questions, and I wasn't ready for them then. I thought the two murders were just a coincidence, then."

The two then discussed the third murder victim, Lisa Moliano, who was found on Sunday, January 14, 2018 down on the Connecticut Riverfront behind the mall area in West Side.

"Lisa was exotic and charming. She turned heads wherever she went. She walked into my practice one day when I was covering for a social worker who had the flu. I was doing crisis duty for the agency. She was weeping, and I'm telling you if it had been earlier in my career before I straightened out, I would have brought her home. You won't believe her reason for being there. Her husband had just left her for another woman. Couldn't imagine leaving that girl! They had no children. She said they were waiting another year to get 'fiscally sound;' her words not mine.

"They'd been married for three years, had built a new home, and were busy furnishing it. Lisa discovered her hubby had been with this other woman and maybe a second woman for most of her marriage. It was unimaginable to her that her ever so solicitous husband was lying through his teeth throughout their marriage and maybe their courtship too.

"I worked with her for about a year. She was solid; just had the misfortune of falling in love with a completely self-absorbed asshole. He inferred it was her fault; that she didn't understand him and never would. Well, she took care of that. She divorced him quickly and got the house, unfortunately with the mortgage."

Candi said that about four years later he was urged to attend her second marriage to a neurologist who practiced in Worcester. She had moved there with him, and they became the parents of two children. Lisa's name before she married Dr. Moliano was Lisa Flaherty. Her maiden name was Lisa Talbot.

"I remember all that," he said.

"I also recall she was a linguist and spoke what she called 'The Irish,' which I would say was Gaelic. I remember her giving me a lecture about Scottish Gaelic and the 'Irish.' She said, 'We Americans get it wrong because we simply don't understand any language but English; we also view "The Irish" as non-relevant because there is such a limited number of people speaking it. We don't understand that language is about the connected society and its history; it's always relevant.'"

Norbie had himself attended some lectures on the 'Irish' speakers with his wife after he was entranced by the signage he saw in southwest Ireland, English and Irish on the same signs. But now it was not 'The Irish' that tickled his fancy. He wanted to know if Lisa lived in Worcester now, why was she found on the West Side part of the river edge?

Candi hung his head. "I never talked to her. Maybe she came to Springfield to see me; and if that's so, I feel guilty I didn't answer that call. It wasn't local, so I thought it was some crazy sales call. I, normally, only answer calls I recognize, or are, at the very least, in the same area code. I listened to it the next day, and that's when I called the police. That's three, Norbie, it's why they're looking at me. I called Jim Locke who's a licensed psychologist and used to be in Major Crimes Unit over here at West Side. He called Millie, the MCU Admin person over there, who took my statement over the phone. That's the last I heard until today."

He mumbled, "I was in bed all those Saturday nights alone. My wife Heather takes care of her eighty-nine-year-old grandmother Caroline on most Saturday nights. She does an overnight there, taking turns with her two sisters and one sister-in-law. Heather's parents are both dead, and her grandmother is the only one left on both sides of the family of the two generations above her.

"I wanted her to have Caroline live with us, but Heather is not Latina, and her family responds differently than mine would to the care of an elder relative. Caroline wants to live alone until she's ready to die. Her kids cover the weekends during the day and overnight and have a graduate student stay over on weeknights. On weekdays, Caroline attends some center for the elderly. My Abuela would never want strangers staying in the house for whatever reason. Different rules, I've learned!"

Norbie was not at all satisfied. "Candi, there has to be another reason why they're looking at you. Did you ever have a personal relationship with any of these women, or does anyone think you've had a relationship with them? What about your history with any of your agencies? Have you ever been spoken to about getting too close to female clients? What about the families of these women? Do they see you as having helped or do they see you differently from that? And do you know of any evidence that has been in the news connecting you to the crimes?"

Candi, whose whole persona screamed speed, answered, "No, no, no, no and maybe." Norbie was now having difficulty not losing his cool. He knew that under stress, Candi would revert back to the streetwise-guy attitude he had perfected and stay there unless forced to face his fears.

"Cut the smart-ass talk, Candi and tell me what's behind the 'maybe.'"

Candi told him he'd heard the news report state that a newer style, black SUV was seen near two of the crime scenes at Lake George in Wales and Lake Lorraine in Springfield.

"Norbie, I have a black 2017 Toyota Rav4 SUV, but I tell myself the Rav4 is one of the most popular cars out there and that they can't use it against me. But I am afraid."

"Where has your car been lately, Candi, near any lakes or dirt roads?"

Norbie asked "I mean Lake George or Lake Lorraine or the river? The police will grab your car and test it. Have they any evidence the women were killed where they were found or were they moved there?" *Just how many details about these crimes do you know, Candi? Do you know too much? Could you be guilty? Shit, sometimes I hate this job.*

"What the hell do you mean, Norbie?" Candi snapped. "If you don't believe me, no one will. You do believe me? You know me. You have to believe me. You're my lawyer."

Norbie then explained to Candi that his job as a criminal defense attorney meant he had the obligation of giving the best defense he honestly could, but based on the facts of the case and his client's wishes. His belief in their innocence was not a requirement, but a plus.

"Candi, I don't see you, based on our history as kids together, as a murderer. However, I have learned over the years that even ordinary people can be moved to violence during specific times in their lives. I could give you a hundred examples based on passion, addiction, sleepwalking, etc. I haven't seen you in over thirty years. I don't know what's important to you today, but I'm willing to defend you. I don't believe you are a serial killer. That will have to be enough for you now. Get another lawyer if it's not enough."

There was a knock on the door, and Captain Beauregard entered the room.

3

Enterprising Wife

Heather was having a difficult time making up excuses as to why Candi left all his friends alone with her and the food. He said he had big troubles and would explain later. She didn't know where he went, why he left, and to make matters worse, he was not answering his phone. She finally decided to tell her guests that a client was in crisis which was her favorite excuse whenever they were late for an event.

His friends finally left; it took longer than it should have. Most people would not delay their visit if their host disappeared. Not Candi's friends, oh no; they would stay until the last beer was gone. She thought, *Two-thirds of the group today was Latino; not all Puerto Rican, but a mix including Cuban, Mexican, and non-Latino. The Cuban, Puerto Rican and Mexican guys have an excuse for staying, it's their culture not to leave until way after the party's over, but what about the other one third, it's just free beer?*

The house phone rang, and she ran to answer hoping it was Candi but knowing he would only call her on her cell. A woman named Martina was on the line, and she was crying and very emotional as she spoke.

"I need to speak with Candido Rodriguez, please, it's important. I'm being followed and getting phone calls."

Heather explained Candi wasn't there, but she would have him call her in the morning. Martina was not to be put off and asked for him to call her no matter what time he came in. She wanted his cell phone, but that was a no-no. Candi generally did not give his cell phone out to clients, and Heather believed Martina was a client or a former client.

"Martina, may I have your name and number please?"

Martina said her full name was Martina McKay and gave Heather her cell number.

"Candi left his cell here so you'll not be able to reach him that way," Heather said. "I'll have him call you. Meanwhile, why don't you have a family member stay with you until Candi reaches you?"

Martina thanked her and clicked off, but not before Heather asked her how she had their telephone number which Heather thought was unlisted. Martina answered.

"This has always been Candi's home number."

Heather was not one to let others make decisions for her. If she were, she would not have married Candi. Her parents certainly didn't approve of her choice of a husband. They thought their daughter was beautiful, smart, and talented, and didn't for a minute believe she should marry a divorced man with two grown children, who was ten years older than her and was not of her heritage. She used to laugh to herself that her parents had not entered the twenty-first century. Her mother even said that the fact that Candi was Catholic didn't count at all despite both families shared the same faith.

Mrs. Lafferty said, "Candi's a divorced Catholic; he may as well be from the Church of the Latter-Day Saints. And what kind of name is Candi, anyways? It sounds like he's selling drugs."

Heather used to be amused by her family's characterization of Candi. But both her parents were now dead, and all she had left in the world were her sick grandmother, siblings and Candi, and his children. Now she was afraid, and when Heather was afraid, she knew her personality would react with a call to action. Action was the only method of smoothing the fear that gnawed at the pit of her stomach; she was swimming upstream and losing the battle.

She felt she was being pushed backward, or heading toward an unknown catastrophe. She'd had therapy before to treat what her therapist called anxiety. But her conclusion was she needed to control herself.

I can't take that feeling that my world may be spinning out of control. I have to do something. I will be lost if I don't do something. After all, didn't I want him because he was so good with women, so smooth that I couldn't control myself? All women love my Candi.

One of the first decisions she made to assuage that horrible feeling of no control was, at the first opportunity, to change their home telephone number. Why should they be bothered with clients from his past? Her second decision was to do exactly what Candi would do. She remembered when he called his old friend Jim Locke.

They had attended Jim's wedding to Detective Petra Aylewood. Petra and Heather saw each other regularly at the West Side 'Yoga for Living.' Jim was the right contact; she was certain. He had just recently left the West Side Police Department, so she believed he would know the ropes for sharing information. Jim could take it from there and make sure this girl was protected. She made the call, and Jim was at home. He listened carefully and told her to have Candi call him when he returned home.

Heather emphasized to Jim, the importance of Martina getting immediate help, carefully explaining previous calls from the other three women. He promised he would call the police and give them Martina's number to follow up.

Heather tried to watch television, though not the 'after the game'. She was streaming a series about a father and son private investigator team located in Newfoundland, which she hoped would calm her down.

It didn't do the job. She thought, *If I'd only been honest with Candi. If I'd only told him about the first call from the second woman, it would be all right; but I didn't.* She prayed for God to forgive her. *Guilt, guilt, I was raised on guilt. If I'd told Candi about the call right away, he would have called Janice immediately. Maybe she'd be alive today. I thought I was so savvy. Why didn't I tell him; don't I trust him? Well, I guess I don't.*

Doesn't ten years of loyalty from him count for anything at all? Apparently not, at least not in my mind! I know I was just jealous. I saw Janice's wedding pictures with her arm draped around Candi kissing him. She was gorgeous. Would any wife want her husband receiving calls from such a knockout?

I was jealous, filled with petty jealousy. And now she is dead. I didn't like his association with old clients, especially since one had already been murdered at that time. I only thought about me; about me and my situation. Is that why I married a social worker; to make up for my lack of involvement with others' problems?

Heather entered Candi's office at the end of the family room. Yesterday she had planned to go through some of his stuff; he'd left a mess which from her perspective limited the value of the room. She never brought visitors in there because of Candi's lack of containment. Heather had even bought a good-looking wall storage armoire thinking it could hide at least eight big storage boxes. It was large and contemporary in style; but attractive enough, not a monstrosity. It had taken her two days to put the thing together.

She thought, *All the advertising on television which show the delivery of goods ordered shunted right into the buyer's room. Nowhere do we, the customers, see the effort we will have to invest in unboxing the damn item, cutting up the boxes for recycling, and putting the thousand pieces together based on instructions probably translated from original Mandarin to Pidgin English.*

Her original plan was to throw each of Candi's piles of folders in a separate box and then store the box on a shelf in the armoire. But now, she knew she would go through some of the old files, those relating to young and beautiful women. Maybe she'd find the files on the four women who had called him.

She thought, *There has to be something there. It's eight to fifteen years later, and Candi gets calls from them; all four of them? One was married to a doctor. She couldn't find better professional help for her problems than a social worker from the past? I just don't buy it.*

Something's there. I'll pull all the files he kept on young women for that period and go from there. No, I'll pull all young people who were his clients. Bet there are not many men. No, women were probably his client base in those days.

Heather worked diligently into the night, sorting, storing, setting aside file after file. She was left with a waist-high pile of folders to go through, while all the others were stored away. She found a great deal of satisfaction when she viewed the room's design finally prevailing, again allowing her eye to find comfort. But she had foolishly done the mindless work first. Now, when she was tired, she was faced with seriously going through the pile of files on the floor before her husband came home. *And just where is my husband?*

It took two more hours for Heather to scan the papers in all the files on the floor and take relevant notes. Heather was a pro; every folder had a photo of the client. She sorted out the elderly and the very young women. She kept all the men. Unlike Candi, Heather knew she had some personal bias about violence.

She thought, *Maybe some guy liked all these women and met them in Candi's office when they were getting therapy. I have access to the files. I know on television, the cops have to have a warrant to see therapy files, and maybe they never can. Even if they were able to get the dead women's files, they probably couldn't get the other patient files. Well, I have access, and nobody will ever know what I find, if I find anything relevant.*

Heather's experience as a private secretary for a CEO of a large realty management group was useful. She knew from reading her boss's correspondence and watching his decision making, just how to sift through papers and find what's important. The first collection of data she found important was that all four of the women were Candi's clients in the three years before she and Candi were married; that all were beautiful, noticeable from the little two-by-two photo attached to each file.

She found three other beautiful young women who were clients during the same time period as the three women who were murdered and Martina McKay. She put all the other women's files alphabetically in the storage box for that time period. Next, she sifted through all the men's files looking for those seeking therapy during the same time period. She found ten files and stored the others.

Heather listed the names on all the kept files; and she was surprised she had heard a few of the men's names before; Jack Ladd, Myron Hicks, Devon O'Brien, Vic Cramer, and Gerry Valle. It was not that she knew the men personally, remembering only having met Myron, but she was certain Candi had repeated their names several times calling them old friends and she remembered they may have been at her wedding; it was too long ago to be certain.

She knew of Vic Cramer, who was a well-known realtor and who dabbled heavily in politics, putting money in where it would do the most good. She had also met Jack and Devon several times. It surprised her that Candi treated these men because she thought therapists normally tried to hand friends needing therapy off to colleagues. She reviewed the selection of male files whose names she didn't recognize and only kept two of them.

Now, I think I'm a professional detective or psychologist, she thought, *that I know by looking at a picture who could be a murderer. Well, I can only go by my instincts, and these are my choices for possible culpability.* Thinking she heard a car outside, Heather put her choice files in her own briefcase and filed the others. She would read more tomorrow.

Jim Locke and Martina McKay were greeted by MCU Detective Petra Aylewood-Locke. Petra had gone to the station earlier, despite not having duty on this Sunday evening, to assist with the potential arrest of Mr. Rodriguez and was now preparing a proper reception for Martina; and the reception included Captain Rudy Beauregard and Detective Ashton Lent. It was a very busy Sunday night for Major Crimes. Detective Mason Smith was working on some draft questions to ask Candido Rodriguez that would be shown to his attorney, in the hopes that Mr. Rodriguez would talk to them. The draft was written earlier, before Candido was brought to the station, therefore requiring much revision if there was the slightest chance Mr. Rodriguez's attorney would allow them to be answered.

Petra thanked her husband Jim for bringing Martina to the station, but her body language informed him he could leave now. *I'm barely out of the MCU, and now I'm just an errand boy,* he thought. *No one is irreplaceable; that's what they say. I guess it's true.*

Damn, I wish I could sit in on this interview. This is the part of the job I miss. Although I bet I got more info from her on the ride over than they'll get in an hour, I'll let Petra work for that info later. She'll know I questioned Martina. Let's hope Martina doesn't remember everything she told me. Jim left experiencing only a fifteen-minute conversation with the desk sergeant.

Martina McKay entered a small interview room with Detective Aylewood who offered coffee, tea, and an assortment of pastries. Petra normally brought pastries in when she worked on a Sunday. She would pick them up from the nearby Italian bakery. If she had to work on a Sunday, then she would eat holiday, high-caloric food to make up for it. For all her nervousness, Martina seemed very grateful and asked for coffee with no sugar or cream.

"I know good cannoli when I see them," she said. "I'll forgo sugar and cream in my coffee any day if I can have a cannoli with my coffee."

Petra certainly agreed with that dietary concept; Martina's logic seemed reasonable to her.

When Petra returned to the interview room, she noticed that Martina's hand was shaking as she moved the pastry from her napkin to her mouth. Petra put her hand on Martina's shoulder, placing the mug of coffee on the grey metal table.

"Martina, we're here for you. You're safe. Please take a moment to relax before the Captain comes in to talk to you. He's the best. You can tell him anything, but please tell him everything. Now is not the time to hold back." Just then Captain Beauregard entered the room.

After introductions, the Captain made small talk while Martina McKay finished her coffee and cannoli. He then asked her to tell him what had been happening. Martina said, "Captain Beauregard, for the past two weeks, I have been followed by a black SUV; a pretty big one. I can't identify the model, and in fact, I think there may be two different model cars, but both are black. Now, I don't know cars well. They're not important to me, but I know size and one SUV is bigger than the other; that much I'm sure of.

"I know it sounds crazy to think someone would follow me and probably even crazier to think two people are following me. But I am being followed. Believe me, Captain, I am being followed!"

Captain Beauregard asked if she knew what times in the day and was it every day that she saw that car. Also, did she walk rather than ride at times and if she did, whether she saw a person following her.

"Captain, I only walk when I'm at a mall shopping. I do shop at the Holyoke Mall at Ingleside, at the Longmeadow Mall, local grocery stores, and sometimes in downtown Springfield. I've never actually seen a person, but a black SUV is often near me. I've tried to get a plate number. One day the SUV came close, but the plate was covered in mud. I saw one number, the last number, and it was a two.

"I first notice, every day, the SUV is there about fifteen minutes after I leave my condo by the West Side Country Club; actually, after I leave the country club access road to the condo. I've told a couple of my friends in the other condos, and they are all on the look-out. I have to be careful what I say. People will think I'm crazy. I'm not. I'm not crazy." And Martina started to cry. Her shoulders shook.

Captain Beauregard was assessing Martina McKay as a witness as he did with all witnesses. Did he think she was honest? Did he think she was reliable? Did he think she was reasonable? He thought, yes, was his answer to all three questions. Most importantly, he deduced she was a most frightened woman. He surmised that Martina was not a woman who needed drama in her life.

I need more information about her. My gut says Martina wants a quiet life now. She's tired. I see the strain around her eyes and mouth, despite her taking good care of herself. She is one good looking woman. I figure she's maybe in her late-thirties or younger. She is well-dressed, and I can see she could turn a man's eyes. Why did she call Norbie's client Candido Rodriguez before calling the police? Why did she call Jim Locke?

And so, Captain Beauregard verbalized some of his ideas in questions to Martina. His final question was, "The two on the number plate of the car. Was it on the bigger of the two SUVs?"

Martina was calmer now. She remembered Detective Aylewood's words. Despite her difficult experiences where she learned disclosure could be dangerous, she decided she would tell the truth, the whole truth because she was so distressed.

Except she said, "Captain, No one ever tells the complete truth because the truth is variable, changed by the lens of the person speaking. I'll do my best to tell you everything. I've not slept well for the last week, and it's taking its toll. I know in my heart I'm in jeopardy.

"I'll answer the last question first. The two on the license plate was on the bigger of the two cars. Captain, I lead a simple life now, but I have not always. I was an ambitious woman, working for a B.A. in History for two years at Harvard when I fell for a kind of charismatic anarchist who encouraged me to involve myself in some pretty hairy situations, all with good intentions on my part. All actions were to help animals who were being maltreated, make changes in our poisonous environment, and picketing every food manufacturer, importer, and distributor that our group could identify. In the beginning, we were honest; fearless of the establishment but honest. I was so involved.

"My parents' direction for us did not involve interest in helping others. Our family's values were focused on taking care of our closely-knit family. My parents felt that loyalty to our family was enough work for anyone in life. In retrospect, both my parents suffered from chronic health conditions and my two brothers were early parents, so their energies were subsumed by survival.

"And I had energy; you can't believe the energy I poured into these mini-revolutions against just about any big business out there. At the end of my sophomore year, I was censured by the university when I was listed as involved with the destruction of all the preserved food in the university's kitchens. Since two of my friends were among the seven who were caught, they knew I was involved in the planning. One of them told the university. A hearing was held. I did not attend the hearing. I did not, at that time, nor today, have the ability to lie blatantly. As a result, I was removed for one year from school.

"Looking back, I realize now the Authorities had no evidence against me and that I could have represented myself successfully. I never went back. I lived with my anarchist boyfriend for another year or so before I finally recognized he was a user and totally immoral.

"I also felt such deep remorse knowing I facilitated actions based on lies and planted evidence to hurt corporations. In some cases, managers lost their jobs. I don't talk about this easily, Captain, but this history is the sole horror of my life. I'm thirty-nine years old. I was twenty when I truly wised up to my part in the many actions perpetrated; and that as the planner, I was more culpable.

"I was the major facilitator. My boyfriend was the public relations front guy, but he never got his hands dirty then. About three years ago, when at the time he was a CEO of a financial investment group located in Boston, he was held responsible for multiple major thefts from clients of the firm. He ran before the indictments were handed down and is somewhere living on his ill-gotten gains. Maybe you remember the Brett Blanken Group investigation. Three of his managers are now in federal prison for theft of an estimated three hundred million dollars."

The Captain asked, "Your activism all happened in Boston or Cambridge?"

Martina said some of the corporations were along route 128, the north and south shores, but mostly metropolitan Boston. She said that

Brett, however, was originally from Pittsfield, Massachusetts.

Beauregard then asked whether Brett held it against her when she left him and whether she had seen him since. Martina answered with some hesitancy.

"You have to understand, Captain, that Brett was a different kind of man. In retrospect, he wasn't handsome, but tall; and presented himself in a way that everyone in the room noticed him. He moved fluently. His use of language was brilliant, and I'm talking about his use within the Harvard University standard. Faculty respected him. I'm telling you that you had to be with him for a while before you saw he was a fraud, a liar, a cheat; and he showed no mercy for his victims.

"When I first tried to leave him, he threatened me saying, 'You leave, Sweetie-pie, and you watch your back. I or someone will always be there waiting for your weak moment. Go ahead and leave.' And he laughed.

"I finally left and came home to West Side. I had a nervous breakdown. My parents treated me like a baby. With the help of some drugs and therapy and my music, within a year I was functional; but I was still filled with constant anxiety, for which much later, Candido Rodriguez helped me. I finished college locally, gained a Master's in music, and ended up as music director for the West Side school system. I love my work. You may have seen me in some of my more public events. I write and arrange for musical productions at the theater in town, and I work with musicians from all the local colleges and the university on productions and events. That work has given me a great deal of publicity; more so lately, when I was featured on the cover of the area business magazine for an article on music education."

The Captain asked: "I understood you were majoring in history at Harvard; why the switch to music?" Her answer floored the two detectives.

"History is too dangerous, Captain. It makes you think you can make changes with revolution. You can't. Real change occurs slowly; unless there is violence. I'm so afraid of violence. I'm afraid I'm that serial killer's next victim. You see, I knew two of the other victims. I know I'm next."

Detective Aylewood gave Martina a stern and questioning look, to which Martina responded immediately with tears and said, "What's wrong, Detective? What are you trying to say?"

The Captain was perplexed. He had no clue as to what was going on in front of him; except he was certain there was something. Was he looking at the next dead woman? Before he could figure out the extent of the drama he was viewing, Petra pointedly said directly to Martina.

"You've left something important out, Martina. Tell us. To protect you, we need the rest of the story, do you understand?"

Martina's reaction, more tears, and sniffling, confirmed Petra's hunch. Haltingly and resentfully she finished her story.

"I didn't tell you that the spark that gave me the fire to leave Brett was my pregnancy with my daughter Elisa. Brett never knew I was pregnant. If he had, it would have been impossible to keep him out of my little girl's life. Imagine what he could have done to her; a fragile little one trying to grow up in the presence of a manipulative, demeaning, and immoral father. No, she was safer with me and my parents. But Elisa is a little older now and well, Captain, if you have children, you know we can't stop them. Elisa bought access to two of those look-up-your-ancestry sites on the internet. One came back with DNA matches to two half-brothers. She was so excited she had siblings. She had given her name to both of them. To date, they have not contacted her.

"I'm a wreck. If they have any contact with their father, then he, just for spite, will try to get Elisa in his clutches. Believe me, she's an innocent and no match for him."

The Captain, rather impatiently said, "Martina, it sounds as if you think that Brett has had something to do with following you. If that were to be true, then why are you afraid you might be the serial killer's next target? Brett would not have the same relationship with those other women as he has had with you. Are you just using the police to help you face your history?"

Shaking her head from side to side, Martina said, "No, believe me, I wouldn't do that. I am so confused. You see I have a good reason to suspect the serial murderer may be my stalker. It's probably farfetched for me to think that Brett could be the stalker.

"See, Captain, that's why I called Candi. He was my therapist throughout my resolving my guilt issues, as I continued to live with the guilt after returning home to live with my parents and have my baby.

"It was at Candi's office that I met two of the serial murderer's victims. I talked with them in the waiting room. We got on; we were part of an even bigger group. I never met some of the others because I had Elisa to think about. I even had drinks and dinner with the two from the group a couple of times years ago. They understood me, and their company was good for me at that time.

"Candi helped us all to go on and that's why I called him for help. I think I'm the next one. Did the other two women get calls like me? If they did, then I'm in trouble. You know I knew Lisa Moliano a little. She wasn't called Moliano then."

The two MCU detectives sat straighter after hearing this information. Captain Beauregard excused himself stating he needed to finish some business but would be back shortly. Before he left, he asked Martina for a written statement, after which Detective Aylewood would have it typed for signing.

"I'm happy to do all that, but do you promise to protect me? Martina asked. "I know when I'm in trouble. I used to case companies to prepare for our political actions. I know the feeling of watching and being watched. Tell me that you will help me."

The Captain said, "We will come up with a plan that I hope will make you comfortable. It may involve some changes in your lifestyle, but we'll talk about it when I come back, okay?"

4

Four Ladies and Common Ground

The Captain entered the conference room and addressed Norbie Cull's client.

"Tell me about Martina McKay. Can you think of any connection between the victims and Martina McKay?"

Before Norbie could stop him, Candi said, "She was a patient in therapy with me, but that was quite a while ago. What does Martina have to do with this? Don't tell me she's dead too. I haven't seen her in years. Please don't say she's dead."

"Candi, don't say another word," Norbie said. He then turned to Rudy and asked, "You've been fair to him so far, but what is going on? Why is this Martina McKay important? I brought my client in here to make a statement. Not another word from my client until you give up what's going on."

The Captain scowled and said, "Jim Locke brought Martina McKay in to give a witness statement."

He looked at Candi and said, "Do you know that Martina McKay tried to contact you today? She was in such a state that your wife called Jim Locke. Why would this Martina call you? Has she tried to reach you before today? What relationship does she have with the other three victims?"

Norbie asked for some time with his client but was stopped by a visibly emotional Candi. "No, Norbie, I knew all these women. They're good people, or I guess I should say were for three of them. I want to do what I can to help. I counseled them all. I helped them all. They were some of my success stories, and I can't think how their cases are related. They have a couple of things in common. They were very good looking, intelligent, and kind; but they all were victims of life. That's all I know."

The Captain questioned whether the four women had been referred to Candi by another therapist; the answer included the process whereby either a crisis center or a friend or family member gave his name as a recommendation. Candi didn't think there was anything remarkable from the referrals in these cases. Candi was questioned about any transference issues he may have had with the women while they were in therapy. He reassured the Captain he was particularly careful in that context and explained the complexity of transference in therapy.

"Captain, there are many schools of thought about dual relationships between the therapist and the client. I certainly don't think a therapist should, at any time during therapy, or after therapy, have sexual relationships or any financial relationships with a client.

"However, whether there is a bonding that is legitimate and in what circumstances a bonding is legitimate is entirely situational. There are publications questioning the appropriateness of relationships as related to their frequency; for example, is it appropriate to attend a former client's wedding? I've done that. I considered it appropriate.

"Should the therapist develop a close, not sexual, friendship with the client after therapy? That gets into some hairy problems. Sometimes a patient may become a bit obsessed with the therapist. There could continue to be a power differential between the two parties that could not be erased or the patient's reliance on the therapist as a father or mother figure could continue long after treatment. So, the therapist must be very careful in continuing a relationship after therapy. The therapist should be certain the former patient has a strong and lasting recovery. The short answer is that I did not have a continuing friendship with these women and generally would not."

"So, tell me, Mr. Rodriguez, if you did not have a continuing relationship with any of these four women after they finished therapy other than attending one or more of their weddings, why would all of them telephone you when they each felt they were in trouble? Your reports to the three police departments state you were contacted by each woman sometime before their murder. Seems unusual, don't you think?"

The Captain continued. "I can't remember the name of a doctor who did surgery on me two years after the fact. These women haven't seen you in years, but they run to you."

Norbie cut in. "Captain, I won't allow this conversation to continue. You're being disingenuous with us. You well know that a therapeutic relationship involves the patient sharing their most intimate secrets; normally that doesn't happen with a surgeon. They're not comparable. If you think there is enough to charge my client, then I want to know that now. If not, we're leaving. My client will be happy to help in the investigation, but there must be a structure to his further help. As far as this Martina McKay, I hope if she is marked by this serial murderer, that you will be able to protect her. I will, however, advise my client not to speak with her and I ask that you tell Martina McKay not to call Candi again."

Captain Beauregard regarded Norbie thinking, *I've gone a little too far here. I know better, but how else could I judge whether Candi is being truthful; and I think he is, maybe? How do I get the connection between these four women? Are there more women out there connected in the same way? Do I have enough to get a warrant for women's files who used Rodriguez as a therapist? And even if I am somehow able, who else had access to these women? Maybe, they met other people in the waiting room -- possibly the serial murderer? No, I need Candi and Norbie; they're sitting on something. I just don't know quite what it is yet. And I don't believe they know either.*

And so, Captain Beauregard, with a humility that was rarely seen, apologized... sort of. "I have a duty to ferret the truth from all witnesses. I was much firmer with Martina McKay than I have been with you, Mr. Rodriguez. Perhaps I pushed a little. You must be aware your situation is rare. You are the nexus in the cases of three women who have been murdered. I doubt if any other person, place, or anything will connect them as well as their experience with you. Add to that, Martina McKay.

"You may be the greatest therapist in the world, but I don't think your excellence as a therapist is a good enough reason to explain your position in these cases, do you? Don't answer that now. Your position, in this case, is very important for a reason that is not therapy. Your value is so important that I need your help. I know I can't get that help without your attorney's acquiescence. Perhaps we're at a place where we all have to reconsider what we think we know or what our normal roles are in an investigation. Cull, would you be willing to bring your client in tomorrow afternoon? You and I could talk earlier wherein you could lay out your ground rules. I may have an inkling about what I am looking for by tomorrow."

Norbie Cull glanced at Candi with a scowl, but then agreed to Captain Beauregard's offer.

Norbie was silent for the first few minutes of the drive to Candi's home. *Candi's wiped,* he thought. *He can't take anymore. Christ, just another flaky client. None of these social workers, teachers, and nurses, none in the helping professions are good clients. God save me from these brave souls. They always want to help the police; especially if they are innocents, and Candi, though no angel, is an innocent. I need to get him out of here. Goddamnit, you ninja, your attitude is dangerous; it's got to stop for your own safety. You can assist the police tomorrow; my way.*

I'll give him the silent treatment. A little silence is a good thing with Candi who apparently doesn't know enough to keep his mouth shut. You would think a therapist would be used to listening to the patient and wouldn't be talking all the time. Well, not therapist Candi who couldn't wait to tell the police about every thought he's ever had. Let him squirm in his seat a little. He needs to feel some guilt about talking too much. He'll blame it on his culture, but fuck, it's his own inability to shut up; always had that problem.

"I know you're ticked off, Norbie," Candi said, finally, "but I had to tell the Captain the truth. He needs to know what I'm all about. You're my friend, but they aren't. You're a lawyer so you think I shouldn't say anything and let myself get arrested. And then what? My life turns to shit. I've been digging myself out of the hood since I was a kid. I won't be blamed for killing women I only helped bring back to the living. Hell, Norbie, why the hell would I do that?"

"Cut the feeling sorry for yourself stuff, Candi. You're smart enough to know that telling the police all about how good you are, won't get you anything. You know better. Stop the emotional stuff. You know what we learned at the Boys' Club, remember?"

Candi recited with resignation, "You mean, 'The story doesn't end when you give it all up; then the punishment begins?' That was fine then, Norbie, but this is my fucking life."

Norbie grimaced but only said, "All the more reason not to give up. It's not the end of the story. And if you let me do my job, we'd have gotten more out of Captain Beauregard. If you just had shut up and let him ask you for each new detail, then we would have discovered more, but I discovered enough to know you won't be arrested now."

"How are you so sure? He acted like he was giving me a big break letting me leave with you. He thinks I'm guilty."

Sighing heavily, Norbie said, "What the hell kind of a therapist are you anyway? Do you believe everything someone tells you? Take my word for it, everybody lies and sometimes even the persons you trust the most. Politicians lie, your wife lies, your kids lie, and even your mother lies. But what kind of lie, well that's the big question. Beauregard would not have let you go if in his heart he believed you were guilty unless he's setting you up with this Martina McKay lady."

Now totally collapsing into a third of his size in his seat, Candi asked, "What do you mean? How could I be set up with Martina, or do you mean by Martina? Is her call a ruse? Can't be."

Perturbed at what he believed was feigned denseness in his client, Norbie responded, "No, idiot! I've already told you that you are to have nothing to do with Martina McKay. You are not to talk with her, see her, email her, message her, etc. I hope you get my point. The police will be watching both you and her, first to see if you try to contact her and secondly to protect her. I want you to be with someone else in your presence twenty-four-seven until this is resolved. No sleeping alone without your wife, mother or kids in the house. Drive to work with someone. No disappearing for a while. Can you do that? Remember, Candi, this is not a game. As you pointed out it's your life. So, don't take what I'm saying lightly."

The two men had just rolled into the driveway of Norbie's house as Norbie's kids were being dropped off. All three came over and were introduced to Candi, and all three loved his name saying, "Cool, are you the Candyman?" to great guffaws and laughter. Norbie sent the kids inside and told Candi to take his Mercedes right home.

"I'll call you in ten minutes, and you had better be home. I want to talk to your wife about your needing company for a few weeks on all your activities. Put her on the phone when I call. Also, be at my house tomorrow around ten in the morning. We will talk then. I'll have my assistant Sheila run over with some papers for you to sign. Bring your checkbook. Then, I'll call Rudy and schedule another interview, and I'm telling you right now; do what I tell you or I'm off the case."

5
Questions and Questions

L avender James was in a tizzy, and no matter how Jimmy tried, he could not get her to calm down; he'd tried a drink and a smoke, but nothing worked.

Fuck it, he thought, *she's crazier than usual, and I get stuck taking care of the kid -- not that Lulu baby isn't a great kid -but she's only three! She has needs, and I've got to be careful around little girls. You can't trust their mothers. Mothers bring shit charges against you when they're pissed. No sirree, I'm not taking her to the bathroom or cleaning her up. I don't mind cooking for the kid, she is damn cute, but she's been throwing fits for the last two hours because her mother's so engrossed in her self-made drama. The kid needs some attention too. Christ, Lulu baby's not even my kid, and I worry about her.*

"Lavender, so you know the three murdered ladies, and you all saw the same shrink. Tell me something, were they in your business? I didn't see that they danced naked, nothing like that in the papers. Did they do private parties with you I don't know about? You can tell me, Baby, I won't get mad.

"There always has to be a connection if there's a serial murderer, and I guess there's one around now. I saw a whole documentary on one of them, and there's mostly a reason why they choose a victim. But seeing a shrink as a connection sounds like a made-up plot. Besides, this Rodriguez guy is a therapist; he doesn't give out drugs. If he were a doctor and gave out drugs or maybe hypnotized ladies into doing stuff, well, then, maybe there'd be a reason for you to worry he'd come after you."

Lavender wasn't having any of this garbage stuffed down her throat.

"Jimmy, did I say I was worried about Candido Rodriguez; no, no, no? Do you get it? Just listen for once. Candido wouldn't hurt a fly, but he had some weird patients in there at different times. And you know; I know weird from just different. I'm a dancer in a strip club. I'm not turned off by different; most of my clients are different, but I watch out when I smell the other type. You may think I'm ditzy, Jimmy, but I've lasted in this business. I see trouble before it hits me. I think one of Candi's patients could have known all those dead girls and acted out. Maybe he will include me next. I don't want to die, and the papers don't say what he did to the girls. That could be worse than dying. I'm no S&M artist, I'm a dancer, and I don't like pain. I think the police should be told about this connection. Maybe they'll protect me."

Lavender started to pound her fist into the couch pillows hitting all ten of them, over and over and over. She only stopped when Lulu baby said, "Mommy, are the pillows being bad? What did they do to get a beating?"

Lavender, Jimmy, and Lulu babysat on the pillows and hugged each other laughing and crying until Jimmy said, "Okay let's call the police. I don't want you hurt, Lavender. I'd have to kill the guy and end up in jail. Why should we be frightened and not know anything? Better yet, let's call the guy who comes into the club all the time. He'll connect us. He'd do anything to get a smile out of you, Baby." And Jimmy did not mean Lulu.

Joe Stellato was doing paperwork at his desk in Springfield Major Crimes Unit, bitching out loud about the new directive from the chief's office requiring timely weekly reports when he received a call from Lavender James. *Shit,* he thought, *it's a good thing I'm at my desk. All I*

43

need is another cop getting the call. She probably already told the operator I'm her friend and with the name Lavender, well, that alone would start the ribbing, 'Joey, Lavender's on the phone; wants you to tape her G-string on her!' No living with those assholes once they get hold of a tidbit to razz. Probably got a parking ticket. Hell, can't do anything about those anymore." Joe took the call.

"Hi, Lavender, what can I do for you. I'm kind of busy here at work. We're working on a major case here, the phone lines are taped, as we're hoping for new info from the public."

All the while Joe Stellato was thinking, *Take the hint, Lavender. I hope the hell she's as shrewd as I think she is.*

"Joe, that's what I'm calling about, that serial murderer. I'm afraid he might be after me. I know all those girls who were killed, and I know what you believe, but you're wrong. None of them were in the business. I know them because we used the same shrink and I think someone knows us all from his office because that's where I met the murdered girls. I don't believe that's a coincidence and Jimmy my boyfriend doesn't believe it either. I want protection from this pervert. I work late, and I'm afraid. Jimmy goes to work at two in the morning to get all the trucks out; he can't be at the club to take me home. What'll I do?"

Now Joe's antenna had moved from self-protection to solving crimes, and he said, "Lavender, who the hell is this doctor?"

"He's not a doctor, doctor, he's a Ph.D., Joe. His name is Candido Rodriguez, and he's a psychotherapist, and he is wonderful. He's not the problem. I think the killer knows about all of us from his office. He sure had some weird patients.

"You have to help me, Joe, I'm scared. I called the club and told them I need two weeks off for personal reasons. Rat Face gave me a really hard time, and then he gave in. He knows what I bring in and that I'm reliable; hell, I don't do drugs or drink, and I show up always on time. I've had offers from a lot of area clubs. But he's only given me a break for two weeks and tonight is the last night I have to go in for two weeks. Can someone follow me home tonight? Please, Joe."

"Listen, Lavender, I'll have a car there tonight. Can you come in tomorrow? We need a statement, okay?"

Lavender was accommodating and said, "Sure, Joe, I want this on the record. Is noon okay? That's the earliest I can make it. I don't get to bed until close to five after work."

Stellato told Lavender that it was fine and to ask for him when she showed up at Pearl Street, and tell the officer at the window that he was expecting her. She was thankful and clicked off.

When Stellato informed his Captain at his home in the middle of the game, there was no kidding about Lavender's calling him first. This was a serious turn of events and called for the detectives on the case to review Candido Rodriguez' call records again and prepare for the next day.

———

Rudy was surprised to get a call from Springfield's MCU Captain questioning him about Candi. Surprising since he had already spoken with the Springfield Captain after Lisa Moliano's body was found in West Side. He was further surprised to learn that this new lady dancer Lavender James also knew Candi from his therapy practice and she was concerned.

Lots to wonder about here. This is the fifth lady who is maybe connected. Has she received threatening phone calls, too? All I was told is she's being interviewed tomorrow. He didn't ask me to join his interview with Lavender, and I don't have to invite him to my interview with Martina McKay. The interview with Lavender, well I bet that interview will be interesting!

Rudy *informed* the other detectives about this new lady Lavender.

"I know Miss Lavender, Captain," Mason said to Rudy's surprise. "My cousin Latoya used to dance at the big club in Springfield, you know the one with the restaurant, and she was always bringing some dancer home to my mama's spreads. Those girls can eat, I tell you. Although, if I remember correctly, Lavender was a lot slimmer than Latoya. She was a nice girl.

"Hell, that was ten years ago. Is she still dancing? They don't normally last that long in the business. They move around in the area or get married, or get in trouble. She must be good if she's still in the same club."

"I know Miss Lavender," Ash piped up. "Hell, I understood that was her stage name. She's a platinum blonde who sometimes dyes her hair lavender. She's pretty hot, but not a player. She did private parties that I played. She never went upstairs with the guys. You know she can sing.

"She was going through a divorce when I first met her maybe a couple of years ago. She's not flighty, so I'm surprised she'd scare so easily, just because she saw the same therapist. That's the guy who was in here a while ago, right? Surprising -- Lavender must feel something. She told us once at a party that she can feel trouble in people."

Well, that's enough of that. I had to deal with a psychic in the kid serial murderer case; now I have a psychic stripper. Rudy had had enough.

"Okay, if Lavender and Martina have come out of the woodwork, how many more do you think there are? Where the hell is Petra today?"

"Captain, did you forget this is Sunday? You know the day of the play-off that you ruined with the potential but not actual, arrest of Rodriguez," said Ash. "And, it's nine o'clock at night. Petra came in to help and then left to go home to her new husband, leaving us truckin' here."

"I'm certain you are all happy to be here to assist in solving a case where women are being murdered. Get the info on the murder board and get out of here. Just go home to your parties."

Rudy was left thinking about motive, opportunity, and evidence.

Just another screwed up serial murder case. Problem with this case is that so far there are three police departments involved. Looks like with McKay that we could lead but Springfield's got Lavender, and they're bigger. I already have the District Attorney and State Police investigator involved in my murder case, and they are also involved in the Wales case. Springfield is normally left alone to investigate their murders, as is Boston and a couple of other cities. I'll have a conference with the District Attorney and have Norbie Cull to deal with as well.

Well, there goes the rest of this month, March; and April, and May. Mona will kill me. She had this great idea of leasing a condo in Singer Island in Florida for all of us for vacation. The kids are so excited even though we're going to drive both ways, meaning an overnight in the car both ways. Not my idea of restful. I am so screwed. Mona thinks traveling this way for the vacation is special but within the budget. Ach, I might love you Mona, but you drive me crazy.

The next morning found the detectives finishing up the list of questions for Candi Rodriquez, all of which were previewed for an okay from his attorney, Norbie Cull.

Ash remarked, "Captain, what makes you think Cull will give us any of this stuff. Rodriguez is going to claim patient confidentiality? I mean we're asking to look at files during the time periods he was treating these three women. It is a three-year time period, he must have had a lot of patients during that time. And if we only look at beautiful women around that age and we don't think it's Candi as the perp, well, who else was there when they came?"

"Yeah, Captain," Petra said, "the perp is more likely a man. So, who other than Candi would see them all, maybe a male patient or the maintenance man or security guy? We'd have better luck if the perp is not a patient." Before Rudy could stop, what he thought of as "splatter talk," Mason inserted his opinion. "Why couldn't it be a woman, a patient who was a psychotic bitch? Let's look at the evidence around where the women were found and the ME's report, see if we can rule out a woman before the District Attorney calls the FBI and brings in a profiler. It feels good to be a step ahead."

The Captain had had enough. "Why does our murder board only have our murder up there? You have only a few items relative to Tonya and Janice. We have more data than what's up there. Update for what we know about the other two murders. The ME reports are important, and after we meet with Candi and Cull, we'll go over them."

At that moment Millie, the MCU administrative assistant, advised them their visitors had arrived. The Captain and Petra would meet with them. Rudy wanted Petra's picture of what could make Candi the go-to guy for killing these former patients.

It didn't take Norbie Cull long to review the proposed questions before he started moving his head like a two-year-old from side to side while he mouthed the words, "No, Non, Nada, Nein!

"Captain, you know the rules on client confidentiality, even after death, the rule holds. You can go to court for these records and probably even then the judge will want to do an 'in camera' before it would ever be released. Further, the judge might decide there's nothing there, and you'd never see them anyway. And then the dead women's files aren't enough for you to pursue. You also want all patients within ten years of the ladies' ages who were patients around the same time. Hell, you know better, Rudy."

Petra redirected the conversation. "Mr. Cull, help us here; let's get away from the records for a minute. You raise a valid point.

"Let's look at what is obvious. You now know there are four women who have called your client; four. That's more than coincidental in anyone's book. Try to explain what it could mean. Give me your best defense strategy. You know you really can't. Your client is in the midst of something; someone has put him in the midst of three serial murders and an impending fourth one. He gets the calls and then the woman is murdered. Surely you realize that his client base at that time is the murderer's source of victims. Mr. Rodriguez's patients may be the 'who is next.' There is an obligation here to help protect the safety of the next woman potential victim. Help us see another way around this, please."

Rudy was about to speak when Candi asked to speak to his lawyer alone. The detectives were about to leave them to conference, when Norbie said, "We'll talk tomorrow, Captain. My client and I need to go over some issues first."

At Norbie's office ten minutes later, Candi was vehement in discussing the confidentiality problem.

"Norbie, how much can I tell them? I don't want another of my patients murdered. All my good work to assist them in living more productive lives for nada. All the hard work they did making changes for nada. How can I help?"

Norbie was slow in his response. "One of the outs you have under Massachusetts Law is that the psychologist may only disclose information which is essential in order to protect the rights and safety of others. That would include your safety as well. You also don't have to take any action that would endanger yourself or increase the danger to a potential victim. But even with that understanding, confidentiality stands as a general abiding requirement. You've also acknowledged that the three murder victims and this Martina McKay were your patients, and you've told me there may be more. I think you're okay here. Certainly, Martina McKay is in the best position to tell the police a lot about other patients based on what she knew or saw. She has no duty of confidentiality. But you simply cannot give out or discuss patients' files. The police can use the courts for that."

"Tell me what I can say if I have reservations about some of my patients."

"What do you mean by reservations, Candi? Think carefully. Did you ever feel unsafe with any of your patients? Do you feel one of them is trying to hurt you by killing these women? I mean that's a stretch, more likely in that case to be a sick competitive colleague. How the hell successful have you been as a therapist to be thinking like that?"

"I can't be sure," Candi said. "I have to look at my records for that time period. I think I was in a solo practice and to answer your question, I had built the practice to a level that was noticeable resulting in an offer of some big money to run external programs for the state. It caused quite a stir in the community at that time. I mean the money I received."

Sheila entered the room and called Norbie out for a moment to tell him that a woman named Lavender was calling for Candi.

"She said she had tried his home and his wife told her to call you for contact. She said it is about the three women who were murdered and that she was one of Candi's patients. I told her I would forward the message to Candi but that he was in a conference right now. Norbie, she's one nervous woman and a talker. She said she has to talk with him before her meeting with the Springfield Police at noon tomorrow."

Norbie sat down at his desk. "Candi, do you know a woman named Lavender? Unusual name, don't you think?"

"Yeah, nice girl. She was one of my patients. Oh God, don't tell me, she's not dead too. I never got a call from her, Norbie."

"Relax, Candi, but she was directed to call here by your wife which I think is unusual. Maybe your wife is ticked off you're in trouble. Maybe just having a woman called Lavender calling you did the job. Either way, what's up with Lavender?"

All Candi could tell him was that Lavender was a patient around the time that Tonya, Janice, Lisa, and Martina McKay were and he should talk to her immediately. He worried she had maybe received some of those calls like the others. Norbie decided Candi should do a conference call.

Candi said, "Lavender won't talk to me unless I'm alone. She's smart enough to know about confidentiality."

Norbie explained that Lavender is a potential witness. After all, if the Springfield police are going to talk with her at noon tomorrow, it would be better to get the scoop on the information she had to share before they told her not to talk to anyone, which is certainly what they would do.

"Candi, you make the call, tell her I'm your lawyer and she can trust me. Tell her we are only talking about her and other women's safety, not anything having to do with her therapy."

Candi made the call, and Norbie could almost hear the faith Lavender had for her therapist. *What a soft voice does our lady Lavender have,* he noted, *with a touch of Southern charm. And she's crying. I wonder what she looks like.*

Lavender agreed to a conference. She said she would rather meet them in person, but she didn't have time given her appointment with that nice Sergeant Stellato who is a good friend whom she often sees at work where she dances.

"Candi, I'm so scared. All those ladies who died, they were all your patients. We all just loved you. I'm afraid I'll be next. Can you see me now; I'm just so stressed. I can be there in ten minutes."

"Lavender James, is it?" Interrupting, Norbie asked. She confirmed, and he introduced himself saying, "Ms. James, I'm sorry you are under this stress. It's understandable that you may be frightened. How can we help you? And don't worry, I am available for you. Please come to my office immediately."

"Oh, thank you so much. Nobody understands me, Mr. Cull; not even my boyfriend, Jimmy. See you soon," Lavender said.

Lavender arrived looking stunning in skin-tight jeans and a low-neck white silk blouse. Smelling wonderfully of an expensive perfume, she wore no jewelry and did not need any.

"Oh Candi, give me a hug," she started right in. "Oh, never mind this is not a time for hugging. How do you do, Mr. Cull? To continue my conversation, well maybe Jimmy my boyfriend will understand my situation, now that the Springfield police are interested in me.

"I knew all those ladies, all three of them. We became friends you know. I met Janice first. I was the next appointment. Most of the time I would walk out after a session and didn't speak to any other patient waiting. It's not like at the dentist or regular doctor's office where I would chat with someone in the waiting room for a half hour before my doctor would see me. No, that's not how it was.

"I was leaving one day, and Candi took a phone call as I was leaving. Most often, Candi, you would walk me out. That day you didn't, and I stopped for water from the cooler. Remember you'd have those little triangular paper cups. Well when I finished, I tried throwing it in the basket and missed. Janice was sitting near the basket, and she said, 'Not a hoop player, huh?' Well we just started talking, and then you came out for her, and I left. Her appointments were right after mine for a while, and finally, we had coffee, and we got along.

"We connected and would talk. I met Tonya the same way and brought her to one of our coffee breaks. I met another patient Martina McKay, and she joined us. She was very conservative but really nice. She brought Lisa Flaherty in. She's that Moliano woman who was murdered. I recognized them all from their pictures, not their last names. They were nice ladies, friends I normally wouldn't meet in my profession unless they were neighbors or something. Tonya much later actually babysat for me when my Lulu Baby, that's my little girl, was a baby."

Does she ever stop talking to breathe? Norbie thought. *But she's a wealth of information. I wonder what else she knows about Candi's practice. It's what the police will want to know.*

"Lavender, did you ever see some other really nice-looking women waiting for Candi, in addition to the four you mentioned; you know around your age?"

Lavender paused and gave what Norbie and Candi considered was a brilliant smile saying, "Thank you all very much for that compliment. I need that kind of what my boss calls affirmation. He says all we dancers are looking for affirmation. I honestly was surprised he could use a high-class word like that. He's normally doesn't; you know the kind of guy who only gives orders.

"To answer your question, there were two more that I saw, but only one who joined our group. Her name was Calia Georgas. She was fun, but I only had coffee with her once. The other woman was that good-looking redhead and a show stopper, but she was always with some boyfriend who would wait for her. Candi, you must remember her name; you couldn't forget her."

"Lavender, did this group of women get together when you were not there?"

"Sure, we all had busy lives. You grab every opportunity if you're smart. It didn't matter if there were only two of us to meet, we would meet. And, Mr. Cull, all these ladies were smart as well as good looking. We enjoyed each other. At least I did. It's too bad we didn't hang on to this gabfest. I think it was good for me. And now, three of my women friends are dead."

Norbie tried to prevent the next crying jag while Candi leaned over and touched her head as if he could comfort her, but pulled back when he saw Norbie frown. Norbie in attempting to sway her attention away from tears, asked, "Just who, Lavender, sent you to Candi as a counselor? Was it through a crisis center or a friend or another therapist?"

"Mr. Cull, I was never in crisis. I just needed to talk. In my business, I meet men and women who are kind of off the mark if you know what I mean. After a while, you just don't know what makes sense anymore, what's normal.

"I was talking to a friend and probably unloading too much on him because he said I should talk to a therapist and did I have insurance. Well, of course, I did and do. I mean I'm a businesswoman. I mean until recently we dancers would pay for the privilege of dancing in a club. Sounds bad! Nope, better than now when some of us are employees. Some dancer sued for employee status. I guess that's what it's called and she won. Well, my accountant, one of the dancers I used to work with, did a Schedule C on my return. It was great. I could deduct all my expenses: dance classes, make-up, little cosmetic changes, everything including my computer and cell phone. Now I can't do as well."

Norbie trying not to show any impatience asked again, "Who was the friend, Lavender, and is he still a friend of yours? And how did you know him?"

"My friend is Jack Ladd. Candi, you know him. I think he's an old friend of yours. At least that's what he told me. He said you were kids together. In fact, he said he saw you as his therapist. He did, didn't he?"

Norbie, to prevent Candi from answering repeated, "And how did you know him, Lavender?" She laughed.

"I don't want to speak out of turn, but Jack comes to the club with all his buddies and some time alone every week and has for years until a couple of years ago. I haven't seen him since then. He's a good guy. He likes pretty girls, and he's kind of like your boy next door from high school, as no threat, you know what I mean."

"Lavender, why did Jack suddenly stop coming to the club, do you think?"

"It's strange. Jack took one of the dancers out. She was a graduate student; nice girl. In it just for the money! Actually, she was from Albany originally, kind of homespun appeal in a drop-dead body. That went on for many months. When she got her degree, she took a job in Boston in some kind of biology lab or something at Mass General Hospital, I think. Things didn't work out well for her. After all that hard work, she was murdered. They found her body out near the projects, you know near where the JFK Library is in Dorchester. Sad! After she was so diligent in getting her education heading for a great job and future, she's dead! I think it was about two years ago when she died. I never thought about it before, but maybe Jack went into mourning. He never mentioned it."

"Lavender, do you remember her name; I mean the name of the dancer who was murdered?"

"Of course, I remember her name," Lavender said. "It was Loretta Loren; you always remember the nice ones. And that was her real name, sounds like a stage name, but it was real. It's the name the papers had on the obituary notice and the articles on her murder."

Norbie noticed that Candi's face was ashen gray. *What's going on here?* he thought *Candi's got a sick look. I know that sick look.*

Suddenly, Lavender jumped up announcing, "Oh my God, I'm gonna be late for work and then I'm seeing Detective Stellato at the Springfield Police tomorrow. I really need to see him. He promised to follow me home nights after work for the next two weeks. Thank you, Candi and Mr. Cull. Somehow, I feel better now after talking to you. Can I call you, Candi, if I get nervous again?"

Norbie suggested if she needed Candi's help that it would be better not to use him as a therapist right now, instead she could call the police or himself. Lavender was pleased with that idea "You represented one of my friends, and he said you were tough,' she said, "but really a good guy for a lawyer. Thank you. Bye-bye for now, you two!"

Lavender was barely out of the office when Candi said, "She was my patient too! Loretta Loren. I never heard she was murdered. Do you think it's connected? Shit, what am I, therapist to murdered women?

"What the hell is going on here, Norbie? I'm scared shitless. If the police find out about Loretta; well, they'll arrest me for sure."

Norbie told Candi to wait there for a minute while he spoke with Sheila about canceling his next appointment. Instead, he asked Sheila to research the Boston papers and find the date of death for Loretta Loren. Sheila was instructed to just bring it in on a slip of paper for him, not to discuss it in front of Candi.

Norbie, in an effort to calm Candi, brought in two coffees on a tray with just sugar. He remembered from way back that Candi never drank milk. Said he was allergic to it. In those days lactose intolerance was not a term used, at least that he could remember.

Norbie asked Candi if he could remember back when Loretta Loren was his patient. He was not pleased with the answer. Candi thought it may have been during the time he was treating the other women. He said she wasn't in therapy for long.

"Did you take any vacations two years ago or change jobs, or travel for business or lectures?" Norbie asked. "Do you keep a diary? I'm interested in establishing a timeline for two years ago and what was going on in your life then. Also, do you have any of your therapy sessions records for these women? I'm not asking you to breach client confidentiality, but I am asking you if you still have access to those records? If you do, it's time you review them. Look for common people connected to each woman such as previous therapists or boyfriends. There has to be more than you as a common denominator."

Candi said, "There is, Norbie, and you won't like it one bit. Jack Ladd sent me all those cases, even Tonya who came from the crisis center. Jack knew her through the counselor, and he suggested me as a therapist. Jack is a good guy. He's always sent me clients. He wouldn't hurt me. He's from the club. My brother from another mother, you know that about him."

Sheila knocked and upon entering the room gave Norbie a sheet of paper and left. Norbie looked at the paper and after reading noted, *Found Sunday morning November 1, 2015; about two years before Tonya's death. Smells bad! My radar doesn't like this at all.* Norbie put the paper in his folder.

"What were you doing around late October through late November in 2015, Candi?"

"Why are you asking that, Norbie? Never mind, that I can answer. In fact, I could never forget it; it was stressful, a very stressful time. Heather's mother had a heart attack while vacationing in late October that year in the Poconos. We went and stayed in a resort in Pennsylvania nearby until she was released from the hospital. We stayed a couple of extra days with her in the resort until she could travel home. I remember because we went to Mass on All Saints Day to pray with her before we traveled home. She died four months later. She was a nice lady. Why is that important, Norbie?"

"I'm just checking how good your memory is," Norbie replied. "If you can remember events from 2015, then maybe we can pin you down on some of these other dates. I know you were alone on the nights the three women were murdered, but where were you when they called your home? Do you or Heather remember the details? Did you save the calls on your home phone? We can get the telephone company to release the times before the police do and hopefully you were busy at those times for at least one of the calls. Not to worry, Candi, I don't think you did these crimes, and we will somehow prove that. It's time to call it a day. We have to go to the police station now."

6

Nexus and Nexus

C hief Coyne and two of the five members of the Board of Police Commissioners interviewed Petra for the open lieutenant's position. Petra had aced the civil service exam a year ago beating all the other testers by six points, but a position was not available at that time. Petra met the service requirement leaving Rudy fairly confident she would eventually be appointed; after all, she had a great good record with no negatives. *Making lieutenant is a political process. And I have a deep distrust for political processes. She's a good cop. I want cops like her on the force. Hell, I want the best for her but MCU needs her. Petra is chief material. I better not say that to anyone; they'll throw her under the bus or kiss up to her.*

If she gets the promotion, I have to fight to keep her. The Chief needs leadership, especially a lieutenant, in other areas and will probably want her on another shift. Promotions always screw up the department's budget. This murder investigation should work to stall and give me some time. I'll have to think of something. I think Vice kept a new lieutenant on in that unit based on need a few years ago. I'll check that out. Sometimes precedent doesn't kick you in the ass; sometimes it saves your ass.

Ash interrupted Rudy's thoughts. "I just got a call from the McKay woman. She says her parents aren't there and there is a strange car across the street. She wants me to come over. Did Millie put in the order for regular drive-bys? I know we developed a plan for drive-bys for when Martina is home alone, and she was to stay home today."

After the call from the Captain, a frustrated Millie entered the room. She was peppered with questions by Beauregard on the protection plan he thought had been implemented.

"Captain Beauregard", she said with emphasis, "I cannot direct the uniforms. I can only send in a request to the uniform Captain for a watch. The Captain insisted he could not immediately meet the request as he did not have the manpower until later tonight. I wrote his response on a report to you and put it on your desk. That is all I am able to do."

The Captain appeared, to the knowing eye to be livid. In fact, his full cheeks were red not a blushing pink. "Go on, Millie, but next time when I say urgent, come in and tell me – no, yell at me – that it wasn't done. Thank you. Ash, get over there and stay with her 'til someone's there with her. Was it a black SUV?"

Ash responded that it was a large SUV.

Walking into Mason's office, the Captain said, "Sorry, Mason, we have an interview to do. Get in here. I'll tell you more about it. It's with the lawyer Cull and his client the social worker/psychotherapist Candido Rodriguez."

Mason slowly and reluctantly got up from his chair thinking, *I hate fucking interviews; he knows I hate fucking interviews. This squad is too small. Petra's interviewing for Lieutenant. Ash just escaped; must have a good excuse. I'm a pattern person, an IT person. Now I have to listen to lawyer and client probably testa-lying as good as any cop. Well, I've got lie radar, and I'll play their game.*

Rudy meanwhile said, "Mason, you're as good as any of my detectives in listening and analyzing a witness and his or her statements. Why do you hate what you do well? You're creating a personnel issues, and you know that personnel issues kill me!"

Millie entered the conference room, announcing Attorney Cull and Mr. Rodriguez in a cold voice and, dripping with ice, voice. Millie did not like that women were being murdered and cut up, and she was apparently indicting anyone possibly involved; culprit and attorney. Rudy glared at her, and she left the room.

The visitors were requested to sit, and Rudy introduced Detective Mason Smith. Norbie acknowledged Mason's family history by going back to Mason's older sister's school days at Classical High School. She was in his class. Norbie asked that Mason give Dahlia his regards while Rudy thought, This lawyer knows too many people and gets too much information too easily.

Candido said, "Mason, I didn't know Dahlia was your sister. I was in class with her at Brookings School. She went there for a couple of grades, didn't she?"

"I'm not sure. She's older than me by quite a few years. I think maybe. We lived in that area, but my mom sent me to Lady of Hope Catholic School. I'm the only boy, and she wasn't taking any chances. I would have killed to go to public school then."

Norbie, quietly and happily reflecting on this old -time connection, asked the Captain just what did he want from his client that had not been resolved the day before.

Just about to answer Norbie, the Captain received a call on his cell from Stellato at Springfield MCU. He excused himself leaving the other three reviewing the history of Springfield.

Stellato said, "My Captain wants to know why you didn't tell him about Lavender James."

Rudy responded with, "We talked about her yesterday, and if your Captain wants to know, why didn't he call me?"

"Captain, you mean you really don't know that Rodriguez and his lawyer interviewed her yesterday before she came here. I don't think we got anything more out of her than they got." And Stellato summarized

61

Lavender's interview with them. The most important fact Rudy garnered was that Lavender had not received threatening phone calls yet. Rudy ended the call requesting Stellato to schedule a call later that day after four and that he had a new witness whose info should be shared. He would not answer any further questions but said that perhaps it would be a conference call to include the chief from Wales.

An annoyed Rudy returned to the conference room. His demeanor was obvious; there was no escaping that the Captain was ticked off. "So, Mr. Cull, you're withholding a witness in an active investigation. Since when was that not out of ethical bounds?"

Norbie responded, "Captain, we are here today and will happily tell you about a visit of one of my client's former patients who spoke to us both just yesterday. Her name is Lavender James, and she is frightened; thinks she is a potential victim. She was to visit the Springfield Police today. In fact, she called them yesterday. I believe she spoke with Lieutenant Stellato over there and told him her complete story. I really thought you would know all about it by last night. The one piece of positive information we received from her is that she has not received any threatening phone calls."

"Mr. Rodriguez," Captain Beauregard said, "don't you think it's getting stranger and stranger; now we have five women, your clients, three dead, one already having received threatening phone calls and the last one in fear. All call you. All believe in you. I don't want you talking with Lavender or as I made clear yesterday, with Martina. Do you get me?"

Norbie was thinking.

He hasn't spoken with Springfield yet. I'm certain when he does that Lavender will tell him about her dancer friend who was murdered in Boston. Now is the time to throw that little fact in. Candi has an alibi, a firm alibi, for that murder. If I can connect them all, create a little mud, maybe it will hold them off from arresting Candi. I need more time.

And so, Norbie relayed the history of the Boston murder of the former dancer, and friend of some of the other girls, Loretta Loren. Mason's eyes lit up, but he kept his mouth shut. The relationship the various girls had with each other was also shared. Norbie concluded with Candi's firm alibi at the time of Loretta's murder knowing that if Rudy connected the dots, then at this time he would see that arresting Candi was not the prudent thing to do. Norbie believed Rudy was surely prudent in his actions and not one to deliberately do an injustice.

The Captain spoke in a serious tone but in the familiar which from the look on his face surprised Mason. Rudy, despite his reddened face, to Mason's surprise, was alright with that. "Norbie, do you really think they're connected; and she was also Candi's patient? Do you have anything on that crime scene? When did that happen?"

Mason asked if the Captain could see him outside. "I have an important issue, Captain. I need to share it with you. It can't wait."

Rudy was put off a little, thinking, *What the hell, Mason, now? It's not like you. This had better be good.*

Outside the room, Mason said, "I know this Loretta Loren through my cousin Latoya. I read everything on her death because my cousin was so beat up about the girl being murdered. Latoya said she and Loretta were best buddies. While they were dancing, they both were also in college taking different programs. They would sometimes meet to study together. I'll get you the file on her death, save some time. Captain, might be the same MO. Hell, that changes the picture a little bit."

"I've got to believe you have more to say on this matter, Norbie," Captain Beauregard said when the detectives reentered the room, Captain Beauregard repeated, "I've got to believe you have more to say on this matter, Norbie. "You don't add, like you just did, a possible murder to the ones we are investigating, and the murder takes place ninety miles away with what looks like the same MO without a reason. And it appears you hope I will think that Mr. Rodriguez' perfect alibi for that murder absolves him of the other murders. Save time, and give it up. That is what you are hoping I will believe, right?"

Norbie's answer was brief. "Yup, it is a reasonable conclusion."

Candi tried to speak, but Norbie stepped on his toes, and he did not continue.

Rudy continued, "So, tell us about Loretta Loren, Mr. Rodriguez."

But Norbie spoke instead of his client.

"Look, Rudy, stop fishing. Do your homework on this Loretta. Get us some specific questions, and I'll figure out how helpful Candi can be. I think for now it is better we leave. I promise I will make Candi available at a later date."

Rudy, to Mason's surprise, was alright with that and the interview ended. Alone with Rudy outside the conference room, Mason asked, "Why didn't we push harder? Loretta was his patient. He must know a lot. I mean it's clear she was a patient around the same time as the others. She was really good looking. In fact, Latoya said she was special and had a big following.

"Like the others, she had a life after Springfield and Dr. Rodriguez. Captain, if it's connected, that makes it weird, like maybe the killer had a personal motivation for this kill, got a taste for killing and then is killing in an unending fashion. That's the only pattern I can see if this killing is connected and by the same perp.

"If I remember the facts, the Boston Police never did anything more than a background check. At the time she died, she was engaged to a doctor at Mass General Hospital. They brought him in for questioning but got nowhere. I don't think they questioned anyone up here except perhaps her family. So why didn't we grill Candi and press for info? This would be the first kill in the serial murders if it's connected."

Rudy thought *I'm not one to explain how I know Candi is not guilty in my mind. I do believe that Candi is sitting on lots of stuff that will help solve these murders. If I were him, I'd try to figure some commonalities related to his patients. He needs a bit longer to stew.*

Norbie will not be able to completely corral the therapist. Therapists have a need to explore and explain. Loretta was engaged to another man, and that went nowhere. If the murder is connected to ours, then the Boston boyfriend doctor would not be the perp. We need to investigate that, more so because Norbie didn't bring it up and that surprises me. He wants us to connect the dots. But he probably has more info than he shared. Well okay for now. We'll talk to his client later. We'll give Norbie some time, and we'll use it to ensure that Candi's stories make sense.

Candi was not happy.

"What the hell just happened in there? They wanted me to answer questions. I come here to answer their questions. What questions? Really; it took just ten minutes. What did Detective Smith say outside the room? The Captain seemed to want to get rid of us after that. Norbie, I feel a set-up. I want to talk with them. Make them understand I had nothing to do with any of this."

"You either listen to my advice, or you get another attorney. I won't say it again, Candi, you don't talk to the police about anything unless I am present and tell you, okay! Do you understand? If not, I'll give you a couple of referrals. Good attorneys who have more patience than I have with clients who won't listen."

A confused "But I don't know where I'm going with this, Norbie," Candi said, "You're supposed to be the best, Norbie, but you haven't made me feel better. You haven't given me one bit of reassurance things will work out, that I won't be arrested."

"I'm not a shrink. I'm not a priest. I'm a defense attorney trying very hard to keep you from being charged. That's the current mission. Once you are charged with murder, the fallout will forever change your life. I don't for a minute believe you are a murderer and I don't think the Captain thinks you are a murderer. But if you put too much out there now, the Captain will not be able to control events. Every interview is recorded. The District Attorney will be able to listen to every word. He's an elected official. Do you understand elected officials often respond to public opinion? If there is no perp in sight, you might look good just on your own words. So, shut up."

A chastened Candido agreed and also agreed to return home and spend his day looking at all his cases from that time period in which he saw the murdered victims.

"Look at all facts and circumstances," Norbie said. "Look for people connected to them. Look for motives in each case. I want you to view if they had common problems. I mean in a type of therapy, in friends, drug connections, anything. Call me tomorrow. I have to be in my office tomorrow. I'll have time to speak on the phone."

———

Heather was not at home when Candi returned, and he was pissed. He looked in the family room and found all his boxes moved into her new cabinets. When he opened the doors and saw neatly stacked boxes with no labels, he was overwhelmed. *Now she has to be Martha Stewart. Why doesn't she clean out her make-up table; now that would be a constructive effort!*

He took down one box at a time and went through it, finding it slow going at first until he realized she had filed by the organization he worked with and by date within that organization. After some consideration Candi thought, *During those years I overlapped with my own firm, Mental Health Consultations and Multiple Cognitive and Behavioral Therapies. Fuck it, I'll have to pull those years for each agency. I don't even remember if, when I stored a client after the case was closed, I consolidated the case for each patient. I fuckin' can't remember.*

Candi worked for two hours. He had some very thin files of the women listed, almost just an intake and exit sheet on each. It meant all the work was done in his own therapy firm, and he couldn't find any of those files there, and in fact, there were a few other patients he remembered that were not there also. He thought *they should be there. Why wouldn't they be there? I'm normally fairly organized. What the hell; and finally, I'll kill Heather.*

Candi unsuccessfully tried her cell phone. He called her sister and the assistant living facility thinking maybe something happened to her grandmother. He called one or two of her friends. And he waited.

Heather rushed in breathlessly at six o'clock and asked, "Did you start the oven? I left a note on the counter for you to start supper."

Candi stared at Heather for what seemed like a very long time. Finally, he said, "Heather, where are my files?"

Her response of, "What files?" didn't cut it for him. Her eyes glanced to the left to her T. J. MAXX bag for an instant, enough for him to move over and get the bag, while Heather said in a halting manner, "I'm such a lousy liar. You always see through me. What can I say, Candi, I have to know?"

There were more than just four files in there, and a steno pad with notes written on totaling about forty pages. Candido skimmed the notes. He was amazed. Heather had done all his investigative work for him. He was thinking, *What the hell am I going to do? I'm supposed to report unauthorized access to patients' files?*

Heather was now on a roll. "What did you think I was going to do, Candi? Accept all that privacy nonsense. No way, Candi, it's both our lives on the line. And after I went through those records, I found lots of connections to those ladies besides you. I was just trying to help. I can send bits of info here and there to the three police departments involved. All of it is true, and it would never be connected to you. I'm not going to sit here and let our lives be ruined for professional discretion illusions you may have."

Candi responded with, "Heather, that's four police departments. Four of them involved including Boston. You can't play those games, Heather. This isn't television. Let me look at what you think you found, but you're not to do anything, understand?" All the while he was thinking, *Hell, Norbie, now I understand what you mean.*

7

Duty

Detective Ashton Lent pulled over in front of Martina McKay's condo and caught sight of a dark SUV over on the side of the main road to the country club. The parked car started to move out just as Ash pulled right to access the condo buildings toward his destination. Ash thought, *Coincidence, maybe; but I better check it out.*

He tried to move back onto the road but was stalled by two cars on the road just as he entered. By the time he could break into the road, the SUV had sped away at a much faster clip than the traffic he was embedded in. *Damn, lost an opportunity.*

Martina McKay answered the door before Ash could ring the bell. She was in a state of obvious anxiety and thanked him for coming, as tears began to stream down her cheeks. Ash thought as he attempted to reassure her, *The lady has pretty cheeks. She is one good looking woman, with class and style. Perhaps this is a good day for me. I look forward to this interview.*

Martina made coffee for them, all the while talking a blue streak. "Did you see that car. It's been there for two hours that I know. I went through the backyards up to one house before the place it was parked. I couldn't go further because that house has a fenced in yard. I could see a man in the driver's seat."

Ash heard Martina's every word because the condo was set up as an open space with kitchen, dining area, great room and study, all one space with partial dividers to let you know what area was what. The entire area was painted in shades of ivory and white and all the furniture in earth shades. He thought, *I've never seen a palette of color with only beige to brown with a touch of ivory or orange. I think it's nice, kind of restful. Maybe she needs this subdued look. She is one uptight lady.*

They talked. She wanted him to know that she wasn't crazy. She played the calls she got on the phone. The voice was definitely a computerized voice, and it was eerie. Ash spent a half hour chatting about the character of the voice. As a musician, he explained, "Sound, voices and general noise play in my brain a little differently than in many folks. Do you detect anything familiar about this voice? I believe it is a real person using software like Voxal, Voice Changing, or Morph Vox; but I think I hear a cadence that is real."

So, they replayed it over and over. Martina was a quick study and said, "It sounds local, and it was on my cell. I think it's local because the voice says 'Yaah can't run away." I don't hear that 'yaah' everywhere. It's more of a slurred jargon than spoken in ignorance. You know, Detective, like the local expression, 'You guys.' That's how it sounds to me."

And Ash thought she may be right. He asked if he could take her phone and she agreed. Ash was surprised the Captain didn't take the phone the day before. Martina asked when the uniformed cop was coming over. Ash explained that he was to stay with her until her parents came home and the uniform division would take over maybe tonight but probably tomorrow. He then asked, "Where's your daughter?"

Martina said apologetically that she was with her parents; they all wouldn't be home until nine in the evening saying, "I hope this doesn't put you out too much, Detective Lent. I'll make some supper so you won't starve."

He told her, not too strongly 'no,' but she was not having it.

Ash helped Martina in the kitchen thinking, *I've been on a lot of protective details but never wanted to help cook dinner before. I've played ball with kids and sat with grandparents, but this is a lot nicer.*

He asked her about her history, and she repeated her story from the day before. His internal lie detector told him she was truthful. Then again, if she was a crazy or a sociopath, you couldn't rely on anyone's personal lie detector, could you? Didn't matter, he knew he wanted to believe every word she said. Ash thought, *I've played bars and concert halls. I've met a lot of women; took a few home with me! Never before did I want to play house. In an hour she's got me sautéing onions and peppers, and I'm singing. Well, I better find out everything about her. I may be the one at risk here, and a relationship with a witness is not allowed in the police playbook.*

Martina had joined in singing in tune with Ash, and she clearly had a beautiful voice. They talked about music, his violin, and her career. There was much about their work each understood. Martina said, "I'm surprised to have an intelligent conversation with a man who doesn't work with me. Any dates I've had, the conversations have focused on bars, restaurants, concerts and I don't mean classical music concerts, but partying, drugs, and booze. This is nice. May I call you Ash?"

And Ash was happy to let her. At 9:30 her parents and daughter returned. Ash now had a glimpse of the lady and her background, and he thought it okay.

———

After leaving the station for the day, Rudy headed for the nearest supermarket with a list of necessities given him by his wife, Mona. Much as he hated grocery shopping, he could not say no to her. Mona was really ill this morning which was a rarity for her. On his few occasions of shopping, Rudy would always enter the store on the produce side, deliberately staying away from the bakery side. He thought, *I'll never overeat apples; but bagels, I could eat two or more at a sitting.*

Inspecting the bananas for brown spots, he caught sight of Mariska Rozovsky and, rare in his life, Rudy was uncertain about what to do, in this case, how to be sociable to someone he knew well.

He thought, *She is at least out shopping. It's not really that long since we charged her for a murder I knew she didn't commit. We eventually finagled the situation, so the real serial murderer was charged. What do I say to her to make up for that manipulation? Why does it bother me so much? I tried to stop charging her and I worked to correct the error. I can't ignore her just because I'm responsible for helping to put her in the middle. Hell, she put herself in the middle. She is like all of us normal people; when we're hit with a horror, we don't want to deal with. Well, she hunkered down and hoped it would all go away. It didn't, and we go on, and I will face her.*

So, Rudy didn't ignore her. Instead, he asked how she was doing. And he felt better when she looked directly into his eyes and said, "Well, Captain, very well! You wouldn't think I would be doing well, but now, at least I have hope my daughter is getting the help she needs. We couldn't give it to her. I was always in denial. My problem is I must live with the damage done to innocents, that if I had opened my eyes completely, I might have prevented. Thank you for stopping me from allowing further damage. Even Sergei thinks you are a good man. Now I must go before I start to cry."

Rudy could not help but think, *What a brave woman. She is facing head on her horrors. What about me? Have I searched yet for my brother? My memories of my early childhood where I was left tied to a chair next to Billy haunt me; Billy who may be my brother or half-brother or step-brother. Well, didn't I send my spit into one of the DNA companies to satisfy Mona? Can I help it if there was no sibling match? Who am I kidding? I have not done an investigation locally which I could easily do. Christ, they found us in a motel type apartment in Holyoke. All right! Tomorrow I'll start. I'll take a lesson from Mariska about facing your demons.*

On his way home Rudy's mind shifted to business, always a safer bet for him than revisiting his history. *He debated the characters in these multiple murders. The equation, as he had been taught in algebra, right now had too many variables to solve. He needed more lines of information. Candido was the therapist common to the three dead women, and also to Martina and Lavender. Who sent the women to Candi? Who is Jack Ladd? The chief in Wales and the Springfield MCU Captain both said that Jack Ladd recommended Candido Rodriguez as a therapist in two cases that they knew. And Lavender James told the Springfield police Jack Ladd had a crush on the murdered Boston lady, Loretta Loren.*

He thought, *Mason's going through the three murders, and now maybe, four, looking for common denominators. That will be tomorrow's work.*

Ash greeted Petra with a cup of java saying, "So, Bolt, do you think you have it? Did you get treated well yesterday by the Chief? What's next? Does the Mayor stick his nose in this for the 'Good Ole Boys Club'?"

Petra could not believe her answer. "Slow down friend. It was pretty friendly. I was told my file was exemplary and that my service was stellar. I don't know the difference between the two, but they apparently do. Doesn't my file just record my service, Ash?"

Ash responded, "Nope. You could have great service and have remarks in the file from your supervisor at some level complaining about your appearance, your attitude, etc. There is some difference. What about the Mayor?"

"Well, he walked in at the end of the interview and said he was proud to have me on the force. I hope that's positive. I'll find out by

Friday. Ash, I want this promotion, but I love Major Crimes. I hope that the Captain will fight to keep me here. Chief Coyne asked me how, as a lieutenant, I would like to run the Vice Unit. I told him I would serve where I was needed, but I thought that I had a gift for major crimes."

Ash reassured Petra saying, "The Captain will do what he can. This serial murderer may help your case. We need you now!"

The Captain walked in with Mason and motioned them to the conference room. And the analysis began. Mason loved this stuff.

"Well," he said, "there is a great deal of consistency in murder methodology: One, Victims are beautiful women who have Candido Rodriguez as a therapist; two, two of the victims were directed by Jack Ladd to Candido as a therapist.

"Three, all the women were hit on the head multiple times with apparently great rage with some sort of heavy metal object, weapon not found at the scene. Seems the perp may have brought it with him. Looks like a male perp.

"Four, all the women had post-mortem cuts to their breasts and vaginal areas. The weapon used to cut appears to be a sharp knife; for example, one may be used for hunting. And the perp apparently has some skill with the knife because there are no hesitation marks.

"Five, The women were not raped but were left with a piece of rough pine stock two by four-inch stock in their damaged vaginas. However, the stock was just inserted; not twisted or rotated. The damage was from the knife. Medical Examiner thinks the wood insert was maybe a statement of something else. The knife cuts were post-mortem after the bashing of the head.

"Six, all the women had troubled pasts, some with multiple men in their lives. This Martina McKay, Candi's patient who reports being surveilled and followed, well she's only had one man in her life that

I've found so far. That's based mainly on her testimony. I've looked at their backgrounds, and all of them have lived, at one time or another, in Springfield, mainly in the Hungry Hill, Six Corners, and North End or Mason Square areas. That includes Martina McKay whose family moved to West Side fifteen years ago. Also includes Loretta Loren and Lavender James.

"Seven, a black SUV, once described as a Nissan was seen near two of the crime scenes and outside Martina McKay's home. Ash can attest to that.

"Eight, there was mud on the scene at the river where Lisa Moliano was found. No car could be there at the scene without evidence of mud. Ash said that Candi's Mercedes, he saw at Cull's when they pulled Candi in for questioning, showed no evidence of mud. It was pretty darn clean. That would have been only about fifteen hours after the murder, so he'd have to have had the car washed.

"There were plenty of footprints at all the murder scenes, but get this, they were made by big feet covered in some kind of cloth. Forensics hypothesized that the perp may have hit the victim once hard enough to knock her out and while the victim was alive brought her to the dumping grounds and then hit her many times and inflicted the knife wounds after she was dead. All the blood work was done at the scene, but there was no evidence the victim fought off her attacker. Further, there was no evidence of drugging in the blood tests.

"Nine, there have been no reports of the dumping being witnessed other than the report of a black SUV near the dumping in two cases.

"Several men have been common, in each case, to two of the women. I can't find a connection to the others; doesn't mean there isn't one. Lavender and Tonya both lived in the same condo complex down near South Main Street, and State Street in Springfield and a guy named

Myron Hicks lived next door to them. The Springfield Police interviewed him on the Tonya case and just today called him again after Lavender told them she and Tonya both knew him. Lavender also thought he knew Loretta through Latoya, who worked with her. Latoya is my cousin, and she's married to Myron. Not that it counts, but he's really an ordinary guy who couldn't get a parking ticket if he tried."

Mason continued with info about a guy named Gerry Valle who dated Janice, the second local victim, and Lisa, the third local victim when they were both drinking up a storm. Both women met him in the Celtic Belles Bar in Springfield.

"Haven't turned up anything on him other than he had known them both! Jack Ladd who referred some of these women to Candi was mentioned in three of the five files. Another guy, Janice Shaunessy's uncle's friend, Devon O'Brien, was a friend of this Jack Ladd. We learned from his interview after Janice was found murdered. He told the Springfield Police that Jack Ladd, who is the owner of the Celtic Belles along with a bunch of bars and restaurants, helped connect him with Stellato at the Springfield MCU. Ladd and O'Brien are old friends, and I was surprised to find out they were also friends with Gerry Valle. O'Brien said Valle's relationship with Janice was short lived because O'Brien told Gerry that Janice was his friend's niece and he was too old for her. I looked at the age difference, and it's only nine years. Hell, Myron is ten years older than my cousin Latoya. All were graduates of the Springfield Boys and Girls Club.

"I don't have a lot on Vic Cramer, another friend of the others, other than what you read in the newspaper or see on television. He's a real estate developer, supporter of politicians, has a wife but no kids and is one of the Boys Club boys. He frequents every club in town buying drinks for all the free-loaders; sometimes with his wife and sometimes not. His wife is a dermatologist in the city and quite well thought of. Her name is not Cramer; it's Connell."

Mason finished his report with, "Boston, Springfield, and Wales police as well as this unit - I see too many similarities; it's a serial murder case. The Behavioral Analysis Unit from the FBI will be working on our pattern analysis this week. They already have all our reports. The District Attorney is waiting for you, Captain, to sum it up for him. Do you want to take it from here?"

Rudy asked for feedback, and he got it, but in such a barrage of ideas he thought he had ten detectives in the room.

"Slow down. This is not helpful. There is a lot here. The methodology of the kills hypothesized by the ME and forensics must be followed through with a careful synthesis of all the details. We need to determine if there are inconsistencies among the four murders. All that footprint detail; well just what kind of shoe covering was used. I can think of homemade covers, hospital gear booties, booties our techs use for crime scenes, and hunting foot covers, but the depth of the footprint may indicate the weight of the perp. Get info on that. Ash, you take care of that.

"Also, I was thinking we can't easily get the therapy files from Candi, but maybe Lavender and Martina will release their files. Try to get them to do that, Ash, while you're out meandering. No, scrap that, Ash. I'll have Petra get them. She may be able to make better arguments."

"Meanwhile, Mason, can you get Latoya in here along with her husband? She could be sitting on a wealth of information. She knew Loretta. Get her in here, Mason. Loretta's death as a possible connection is our excuse, and Boston Police won't care.

"Now Petra, we have to tread a little more carefully on interviewing this Devon O'Brien. He's the friend of Janice Shaunessy's uncle. The

Springfield Police will want to do any re-interviewing of him, and we can't argue with that since they have notes on their first interview with him. Jack Ladd is different; and so are Gerry Valle and Vic Cramer. We've pulled the connection to our victim from the records. They haven't noticed it yet.

"So, Petra, try to get Ladd and Valle in here. Use Lisa Moliano's murder and new information needing clarification from witnesses as your ruse. No sense in questioning Vic Cramer until we find a connection to the ladies. He's in and out of all the bars, but so far, no mention of ladies in his life other than his wife. Mason, when you have time, pull up everything you can find on his early and current life."

"Look, Captain, I know Devon and Jack," said Ash. "I've played all the Irish celebrations all over this part of the state; many played in Jack Ladd's bars. Devon is often there. They're old friends from childhood. If you want, I'll chat them up informally at the bar, see what I can get. They don't think of me as police. I don't know if that would be okay or not?"

, "Go ahead, Ash," Rudy's answered. "Petra, nix my request. Ash, if you feel anything is up, cut it short."

8

Look-back

Rudy called his personal connection in the Holyoke Police Department, Sergeant Luis Vargas. The first words out of Vargas were, "What the hell, Rudy, it's been three years. You don't even show for the 'Manuary.' What's up? Is it that new murder in West Side? I heard you caught the latest big one. It's another serial killer, right, making West Side a serial murder capital."

"Not funny, -- Lu, not at all funny! Yeah, that's part of why I didn't come this year. Also, I wouldn't know you all with all the facial hair. 'Manly January,' who the hell thought of that name anyway? I like the cause, veterans' suicide prevention, but let's face it, I wouldn't know one face from another with all the mustaches and beards. That's not why I'm calling, Lu. I'm calling on a personal matter. You know I'm adopted, right?"

"Of course, I know, don't you remember I'm adopted too? Well, not quite the same; my grandmother adopted me because her daughter, my birth mother, was a no-good addict. Good thing she got me out when I was nine months old. My mother didn't die until I was ten. If I'd stayed with her until then, I'd have been running drugs. Please don't ever talk to me about no-good parents having rights over kids. My abuela knew right from wrong and would fight for it. She fought for me. So, forget about my preaching. You ready to look back, Rudy? Don't you remember our talks in junior high; you didn't want to know. Now you're ready, right?"

"Don't you ever stop talking, Lu," Rudy answered. "How do you interview witnesses if they have no time to answer? And yes, I'm ready. My birth mother was Mavis Eaton. I maybe even have a brother called Billy Locario who is around three years older than me, and my name, and don't you fucking laugh, was Rudolfo Eaton."

Luis Vargas could not keep from laughing. It was not insensitivity, more the welcoming of a brother. "Amigo, ha, ha, we finally have it, Rudolfo! Spanish! Italian! And matched with Eaton. No wonder you're a screwed-up Frenchman. Maybe you spoke Spanish baby talk. You were pretty good in Spanish class as I recall.

"So, you want the file. I'll get it if you can send me any paperwork you have. I know one guy who worked the courts then. How old were you when Lizette and Roland got you? 'Cause, I think you were probably adopted just before there was a separate Juvenile Court; I think that came in the late sixties. Probably be easier to access if the records are all in the Juvenile section of District Court."

Rudy explained he was just about three and had only a couple of memories.

To which Lu responded, "That's what you think. Your body and your sub-conscious remember even if your brain appears to repress the memory. That's what I know. For you, Rudy, remembering and renewing will be a rocky road, you've been repressing something for a long time. Maybe it's some kind of guilt; those are the memories that are the most troublesome. But I'm not worried about you. You've got Mona and Lizette. They're both rocks.

"See, if you have a balanced partner, you can live through any mess. That's what makes you the greatest detective in western Mass. All the cops say you're good, and there is no greater compliment than that. They normally find only the flaws in other cops. Unless the cop is charged with something, then they pull the old blue line."

Rudy asked how long it would take to get the file. He was told the court documents would take longer. That the file his parents received from the court and their attorney was minimal. Meanwhile, once he received info on Mavis and Billy, Luis would do a search.

"I have a friend, a computer geek, not controlled by ethics. He says he can find anyone. Might cost two hundred, if that's okay?"

Rudy agreed. When he was alone with his thoughts, he was surprised.

I feel ten pounds lighter. I'll even stay on my diet for lunch. I've made a start and whatever will be, will be. Now if I get another email from the DNA people, I don't think I'll be afraid. There is something good about starting the action; not running away.

The first email from them took me two days to open, and it was not surprising. I'm equal parts French, British Isles, Greek, Italian, Irish, and Spanish. I kind of like being a mutt; I have never identified with a pedigree. I have always thought I look more like French, Italian, and maybe Spanish, with Irish and English lighter skin. The kids think it's cool. Maybe Mavis has a story; a larger-than-life story why she disappeared and left Billy and me. Christmas!

Now it is Billy and me -- after so many years of my denying Billy! I guess I am ready. Must be all these murders; seeing all these families suffer and I running away from a memory. I've been shamed. Think I'll find a novena over at Sacred Heart Church in Springfield, there's normally one coming up at this time.

———

Candi had been tasked by Norbie to find connections and names in the files that were common to some of the women. His work was easy. Heather had done it all for him, and he was deeply concerned.

What the hell was I thinking? I can't believe I agreed to counsel five of my old friends. I can't believe I was so stupid, so non-professional. It's just that their problems seemed so superficial to me at the time. It wasn't even a stretch. Come in for a few sessions, I listen, I comfort, they feel better, they go on with their lives. None of what they said is even relevant to these cases … I hope. Thank God, I wouldn't let Heather work with me on this. She already noted she thought they were friends and jotted question marks next to their names saying 'Why friends for patients???'

Candi went through each file of the women Heather picked and was impressed she chose the extra files of women whom she did not know but saw their file as being within the profile. *Hell, maybe she's not intuitive, just jealous. They're all exceptionally good looking.*

On further study, Heather had constructed a timeline; although not perfect there was an eighteen-month period of crossover amongst all the files she had pulled, including the five men. He tried to remember that period of time but was having trouble. He had been through a bad period with his own divorce from the crazy lady, and then he met Heather. His focus at that time was protecting his daughters from their mother. He thought about that for a minute. *I really had no focus. I was grasping at straws. Let me read each file. There have to be some things in there I overlooked.*

He started with Loretta Loren's file. It was quite slim. She was studious, and though a dancer in a strip club, you'd never know it from her demeanor or her use of the English language. *I always notice how folks speak,* Candi thought. *I was diligent in eliminating traces of my ghetto Latino language use except when I want to use it. Loretta could have been a student at Harvard, like Martina McKay. They both looked so refined to me.* She didn't talk much about her love interests in therapy, just how to keep the hordes at bay at work. She complained about one guy who came in and watched her all the time and said he was no different than Jack

Ladd, who was always at the bar. But she said she never felt threatened by Jack. In fact, she dated him a couple of times while she was in therapy, which he noted on his list. *I'm not worried about Jack. He loves to be a lover.*

Next, Candi looked at Janice O'Brien's file, and there was a lot going on in her life. She'd have multiple relationships all centered on party time. The file documented her many, 'what she called her dark periods,' and dark they were; she could not remember where or with whom she had been. Her daughter, Marti, was a product of one of those periods. It was a case of a family supporting the fallen away little lamb until she became scared enough to help herself. His job, which he believed he had done well, was to help her realize what she was doing to herself and her daughter.

When she decided to change, she did it with a vengeance. Recovery came quickly, and she met a nice guy. It looked great. He found no one else connected to her. He remembered Lavender said that she *"Met Janice in your waiting room when you were too busy to walk me out." Maybe it's connected to my waiting room?*

Candi grabbed his old calendars and looked at the timing of the appointments. He wrote them down for the eighteen months and found multiple intersections of appointment dates amongst all his patients. *Doesn't mean they all talked to each other*, he thought, *but they could have, that's all I have is they could have.*

The next file he looked at was Tonya Brown's. Tonya was, in his mind, already on the way to recovery when she came to him. Alcohol abuse was the root cause of problems with her mother and her, along with a childhood without structure and an unknown father. Tonya had dug herself out of most of her former outrageous and flamboyant habits. She had a decent marriage to which some of her behaviors were impediments.

Life sometimes seems to jump up with knock-out punches for some people. She worked on her marriage with me and then the husband gets killed in an accident. Tonya had guts. She worked through her problems for her boys, I give her that. And now she's a victim of a serial killer. I wonder about the new husband she had married. Maybe she went back to her need for attention, and he got jealous. Nah, that's stupid. What would he have to do with the others?

He reviewed her background over again. She had been a barfly during that time. She frequented them all. Although she identified as black, she looked white, dressed white, and frequented a lot of the local white bars, not the Black or Latino bars. In fact, Tonya met her husband Danny at the Corner House, a local pub; Candi didn't know if it was still there.

He thought, *My early notes show she has an associate's degree in business from a community college. It doesn't say in here from where. These notes also say her casual time was spent on dance classes all through her childhood, for a total of twelve years. Here's a quote from her: "I've danced professionally." I remember now. I pushed her to find out where and she wouldn't tell me. I never got back to that. Stupid, I never followed up; not like me.*

He said aloud, "There's nothing here; she was careful about saying names, and I never asked."

Candi pulled Lisa Moliano's file and found his brain almost recoiling from reading this one. Her wedding to the doctor gave her what he thought was a stable and maybe a high-class future, and now she's just another murder victim, leaving a grieving husband and two children. In reviewing the data, he thought, *Lisa spoke the Irish. She would go to all the Irish bars with her first husband. She never appeared to have a drinking problem, but if she was out at bars, she was with drinkers. Tonya was always at bars, and so was Janice. Tonya may have thought she was black, but she was drinking at the Irish bars. Could that be a connection?*

Candi was excited. His energy renewed, he was able to scan Lavender and Martina's files quickly. He could fit Lavender and Loretta into a potential bar scene because they were both dancers. The question he thought was, *Do dancers from strip clubs go to Irish bars? I don't know. I only went to Irish bars on Saint Patty's Day celebrations, and that was after I met Heather; I don't look at pretty girls now. But Martina McKay doesn't easily fit in this scenario, although she is Irish.*

Candi perused the other files Heather had in the seven bricks, the large red folders that hold multiple files, in which she had stored these patients' files. Only seven bricks for seven women and six men's files. There were approximately two files for each brick; not heavy cases. Lavender's file was straightforward. As to the other two women, *I can't find a pattern of drinking in either file, and both were beautiful. Calia Georgas was trying to find some purpose as a stay-at-home mom.*

Out loud he said, "The gorgeous redhead mentioned by Lavender is Valencia Longtin, really an all-American beauty, Maria Elena's friend." He read further and thought, *Says here they met at some cooking class in Nonton. Funny I don't remember that. Valencia was not crazy, not at all like Maria Elena. Probably, I'm a therapist because Maria Elena was so screwed up I needed help to find a way out of that marriage. But her friend was normal. Valencia had gone to Smith College. She got all wrapped up as she said, "Candi, I need to find a mission in life. Every woman I know is involved in some cause bigger than her or is an artist or a performer. They make me feel worthless. I'm great in sales, but nobody respects that. I want to find meaning in life, I need therapy."*

There was nothing wrong with Valencia except the sales lady got confused by her friends' sales pitches. Nope, I think I have all the files."

As to the guys, Candi thought back to his history with Devon,

Gerry, Myron, Vic, and Jack.

Well, they all liked to party at one time, but their therapy wasn't related to booze. Funny how they all remembered the Boys Club Camp on Winthrop Lake in New Hampshire, and for different reasons; when six of us were so unhappy, and one of us was ecstatic. Six of us were sore losers, and the other was an obnoxious winner. I just don't see a connection to this mess. Norbie can help me with that, we'll go back in time. These other two guys were both gay and trying to come out at the time of therapy. I saw one recently with his partner. Nope, I rule him out, and the other one lives in New York City now.

With that task concluded, Candi called Norbie and set up an appointment.

———

Ash decided it was late enough in the afternoon to head over to the Celtic Belles, but before going there, he would do a drive-by Martina's condo. He blushed when he realized he called her Martina in his head, not witness or subject or Ms. McKay. Still, he did not change direction. As he approached the turn-off to the right from Country Club Road, he noticed parked cars on the left side all the way down. He thought, *Must be a big event. Maybe some political party or Chamber of Commerce annual. Late enough at four-thirty in the afternoon, with all high-priced vehicles.*

As he turned, he caught sight of a black SUV pulling out of the line of cars. *Fuck it, I got caught again. I can't turn around and get to him fast enough. Where the hell are the police?*

He pulled in front of Martina's condo and found her chatting with a uniform. A good-looking uniform. He felt a pang of jealousy. *Couldn't be jealousy! I'm not the jealous type.*

He did make short shrift of the cop. He pulled him over and asked how long the black SUV had been parked on the main road in sight of the condo. The cop apologized for not seeing him.

"Detective, now you're here, I'll do some rounds. I promise when I come back, I won't miss that car again. Ms. McKay's family will be home in half an hour."

Ash was pleased. Half an hour seemed like a good chance to say hello again. He was not disappointed. Martina seemed pleased to see him and asked if he had time for coffee. *I have time for coffee. The bar will be a lot busier in an hour or two. She doesn't seem unhappy I'm here.*

They chatted about life, about music, about West Side. He asked where she lived before she moved to West Side. Martina said she had gone to Cathedral High School in Springfield before she entered Harvard; at that time her family lived in East Springfield.

"We had a good life there, but I thought it was too limiting when I was young. I was somewhat of an egghead who also didn't want to miss a party. I had good friends. I know now I didn't want to get too close to any of the guys because I wanted Harvard and a really big future. Everyone wanted it for me. Hell, now, what am I? Basically, I'm a music teacher; not what the plan was. Yet, I'm very happy. I can't believe how happy I was until I started getting those calls and felt I was being stalked. Then all that craziness with Elisa's father erupted again in my brain. I was a basket case when I came to the station last Sunday night."

"Well, why wouldn't you be, Martina? He answered carefully, "You have had quite an experience in your past, and that experience makes you afraid, for your daughter and yourself. I think you've acted prudently. Tell me though, why didn't you call us first? I mean you haven't seen Mr. Rodriguez in many years. Why did you call him before calling us? He certainly could give you therapy, but he couldn't help with your safety, could he?"

Martina smiled almost with a twinkle. Ash realized she had a small dimple on one side of her cheeks and a larger one on the other cheek.

Her answer made him blush.

"Detective, I thought maybe you came to see me, 'Martina.' Instead, you're re-interviewing me for more information. I'm telling you now, I am disappointed."

Ash, normally a good performer, stammered, "I… I'm on the clock, so I have to ask you questions. It doesn't mean I don't enjoy seeing you." He thought, *What kind of a fucking wimpy answer is that? You jerk! I do like that she wanted to see me. I wonder if she means it. God, she is really pretty when she smiles.*

And he again asked her to answer his questions when she stopped him.

"I'm happy to tell you anything you want to know, Detective."

Without thinking, he said, "I told you last night to call me Ash. It's short for Ashton, that's Ashton Lent, and you won't find anything I'm embarrassed about on Facebook about me."

Laughing with him, Martina said, "I called Candi because he always said the right thing when I thought I could not live with some of the things I had done, when I thought I didn't deserve my daughter, that I couldn't protect her, and that I didn't deserve the kindness and love of my family. I needed him at that moment, but I do think Jim Locke's insistence that I go to the station was very important. You know, Ash, I believe someone up there knows that I'm a decent person and has always worked to give me protection from myself. And you make me feel safe, Ash, you do."

Ash tried to control his demeanor, but it was not easy. Nevertheless, he continued with his questions, all the while drinking a great cup of coffee she prepared and greedily eating what she called her homemade raisin and brown sugar cookies.

Martina's work now took her in many directions. She had made a name for herself in music education in the Western Mass area. He already knew that. What he didn't know was that she managed about five entertainment groups as well. She would get them bookings in bars and restaurants, halls, education format events, theatres, weddings, and parties. She got expenses plus ten percent off the top, and she loved doing it. When she listed some of the groups she represented, he was surprised. He knew three of them well, having played with them.

"Martina, did you go to all the venues, you know, to check them out before you would book them?"

"Of course, I did, Ash. Two of the groups have members who were very young, in their teens, when they first went out. I couldn't have them anywhere they shouldn't be. You know the Springfield School of Music students often play in restaurants, and I know their teachers know exactly which venues not to place their students in. I'm an educator first. I'm really good at what I do."

Ash said, "I know, and I love your singing voice. Do you ever sing as well as write, arrange music and direct? It seems a bit of a waste to me, not to use that lovely voice."

"Thank you, Ash. I do sing, mostly in choirs but occasionally in small venues. I used to sing with Lisa at some Irish functions. She did all the fighting, and happy songs and I would sing more melodic ones, while she'd do the Irish portion. But that was a long time ago."

Ash asked her why she didn't tell the Captain she sang with Lisa and she replied, "I told you all at the station that I knew Lisa a little, and that's the truth. It was only a couple of times."

"Where did the two of you sing together, Martina?"

When she said the Celtic Belles, Ash tried to keep his face from showing a reaction. They talked about other things after that. Ash spent over an hour at Martina's house overlapping the time her parents and daughter returned. Finally, he left.

Walking into the Celtic Belles, Ash ordered a draft of the special dark and was greeted by the bartender who asked if he was playing on Irish Week in March. Ash said he had two gigs in Holyoke but nothing in Springfield. They talked sports for about forty-five minutes before Jack Ladd came in with a couple of guys. Ash thought they may be regulars.

He didn't see Devon O'Brien. At least he didn't think he was one of the guys with Jack. He'd last met Devon a while ago, and although he couldn't remember his face, he could remember his size. These two were well under six feet in height; couldn't be Devon. Jack walked over to him to talk.

"Dirk says you have no gigs in Springfield in March. Would you do something here, like the week before Irish Week? The sixteenth is a Friday, we can draw a crowd on a Friday. You know that group you had up on Boston Road would be good. I kind of like the songbird. She looked good and drummed up the crowd. What do you think?"

Ash told Jack he would see what he could do and call him. Jack gave him his card and wrote down his cell number. They talked sports and about the bar and music business when Ash asked him about Lisa Moliano.

Jack said, "She was a good singer when she was available."

"I know," Ash replied. "She sang with a friend of mine sometimes. Maybe you know her, Martina McKay. She's pretty broken up about Janice's death."

Jack's eyes, normally opaque to showing emotion, flickered. "I suppose you know Martina because she's in the music business," he said. "I haven't heard of her singing solo for a long time."

"Jack, she does small stuff; and I've been there for some of it," Ash replied. "She's not too keen on publicity. I think she was quite put out to be on the front page of the Business magazine. Martina said she thought it was going to be an article about the kids. My concern is her sadness over this Lisa's death. How come I never heard of Lisa Moliano singing before? I thought I knew all of the Irish singers."

Jack Ladd put his hand on Ash's shoulder saying, "You apparently don't know shit. Lisa was a regular all over the area before she married this guy from Worcester; a neurologist or something. She used the name, Lisa Talbot. She was good, had this nice Irish lilting voice, but could rev up with passion for a fighting song. She was married to a bum; a regular Romeo. Everyone knew it but Lisa.

"Too bad about her being murdered; don't know why she was in West Side, a married woman living in Worcester. Seems strange to me, don't you think? Listen I got to run. I bring payroll on Fridays to my bars, got four more to go.

"Nice seeing you, Ash. Call me about the sixteenth."

Ash was furious with himself.

Idiot. I went too fast. I exposed Martina; but what else could I do? There was no other way to get to the core of things. I think he already knows I'm a cop or, if he didn't, he does for sure now. Dirk knows I'm a cop. He was a bartender at a cop's daughter's wedding and all of us, who played that night, were cops, all for gratis. Hell, Dirk probably was the bartender for tips. Some cops are cheap. Like firemen, they like to exchange services and keep Uncle Sam out of the equation.

So, for all of that, what the hell did I learn? I learned Lisa was an Irish singer who sang with Martina and probably at Irish bars. So, what's the connection: bars, Irish, Irish bars, someone who likes entertainers, a watcher? Hell, Lavender and Loretta were both dancers. Janice had a serious alcohol problem, and Tonya was a player. It's too late to get to the ME. I'll go tomorrow. And Ash went home alone, reviewing images of a good cup of coffee and raisin cookies and one really nice lady.

9

Family Business

Latoya Hicks could not understand why her cousin would want to interview her at the West Side Police Station. First of all, he knew she did not like police stations. It didn't matter that he was police. That was his choice. She didn't have to like it. Why drag her into being a witness?

I know you, Mason, I know you up to somethin'! How come that Captain he likes so much didn't call me; 'cause he knew I would not come in and that I'd make him come' round here. And just why is Myron commanded to be in this justice parade? Stupid man, he thought it was all okay to accompany her; "I'll go with you, Honey." Idiot that he is, he thinks I'm worried about today. It's later when they have a record of everything you say and try to entrap you. Doesn't he know he's a black man, and black men and police stations, if you're not a cop, do not sync, no, they do not! Mason knows better. The family won't like this. And he asked me, as if it were the most normal thing. Well, smartass, you're not getting much out of me. The less said, the better. Now, what have I already told Mason about Loretta?

Mason greeted Latoya and Myron in the station's lobby. Just looking at Latoya set Mason's family tuned nerves ajar. He thought, *Captain, you ask too much. You don't understand. Latoya will enlist all the ladies in the family to go after my scalp, and not one of the men will defend me. Looks like Myron was told to shut up. He barely acknowledged me.*

Sometimes this is a shitty job. I never went on the Springfield force, deliberately trying to avoid family and friends while on the job. Now a murder in West Side brings family across the river. Hell, I normally don't do interviews. The Captain knew Latoya would tell him nothing; what makes him think she'll be straight with me?

The three settled themselves in the conference room. Mason brought in coffee and some nice and icky sweet pastries he knew Myron would love. Latoya would never eat a sweet -- always watching her figure. He thought, *She may be a cousin, but she's still lookin' good.*

"Latoya and Myron, I know you think that bringing you in to make a statement is inconvenient and, in your minds, unnecessary."

"You got that right, Mason," Latoya broke in. "I'll make one statement. Myron has nothing of relevance to say. So, understand, it is going to be singular, just one statement."

Mason responded, "As I was saying, a statement relative to a murder victim found in Boston. You may think that's Boston's business, but I know for a fact someone from the FBI Behavioral Analysis Unit will be sending their profile on the perp in her case here soon, and the District Attorney and the state police will also be involved. Your name has come up, and therefore there is every reason to believe you will be of interest to them. Let's get a statement down that gives your facts, will satisfy them so they won't bother you again, and work to solve the murder of your friend Loretta.

"Not yet, Latoya, don't interrupt me. I'm interested in the other women who were murdered and also in Lavender James and Martina McKay, who may be at risk. Now, I need to know about the people these women knew and maybe were involved with. I need to know any commonalities among them. I don't have to repeat everything to you, Latoya. You probably have your own murder board on these deaths posted in your bedroom. So, please help me out here. Don't hold back, Latoya, women's lives are at risk."

Latoya looked at Myron before she spoke. Myron nodded to her appearing to give her permission to speak. Mason was astonished.

Never for a minute did I think Myron was ever in charge; looks like I'm wrong. Although, this is a good strategy for her to use. Myron's smart but Latoya has a mouth that can shape most conversations to go her way; way better skilled verbally than Myron.

"You may as well know that Myron and I, between the two of us, knew, at one time, all these women; not particularly well in most cases. Myron hits all the bars with his buddies, not Black bars but White bars. I don't understand his connection to them, they look like boring white dudes to me; only saw one or two of them ever dancing. But it all goes back to his childhood. Myron, you can tell a little about that. I could never make it sound believable. It wasn't my experience, I can tell you that."

And Myron told a story Mason had never heard. He did remember Latoya's wedding and the bunch of white couples that filled two tables, but Myron was in business and doing well. He thought it was just workmates and spouses.

"Mason, as a kid I lived in the Six Corners area of Springfield. It was a racially mixed area, although we didn't use that term then. My older brother wasn't much of a student, and my mama made up her mind that I wasn't to follow in his footsteps. Mama worked as a nurse, and she wouldn't get home until an hour after I got home from school.

"She said that's where she made a mistake with Calvin. She let him come home to an empty house, and he'd promised to stay home and study until she came home. He didn't. He'd run the streets, and when she'd get him home, he'd do a half-assed job on his homework. It was a struggle for Mama. And his Daddy didn't help; probably didn't want to pay for college. He did all right in the end, but probably not as good as he could have.

"Anyway, Mama's solution for me was the Springfield Boys Club after-school program. It cost maybe a quarter a day. If you could find your way there, you were welcome, and color had no meaning. It became the center of my life from fourth to eighth grade and thereafter. Later, I played with all the guys in the Springfield Touch football League; we were the most aggressive of all the players, even more than some of the former professional players.

"We were good. Lots of the guys were from the Irish section of the city called Hungry Hill or East Springfield and had gone to Lady of Hope School. I know as much about the counties in Ireland as I do about the sections of my city. Lisa Moliano's first husband, Shaunessy was one of our best players. Hell, he was a great player, and if he paid attention in school when he was young, he could have been a pro. I used to watch his school games. He could have been like they say, 'a contender.' But he was a player with the ladies, always was. Too bad Lisa got wrapped up with him. Like all of us, we don't see the truth when we don't want to see it."

Latoya couldn't help herself. "Like you chasing that no good gal for five years and not knowing she was dating your friend at the same time. That was damn obvious to all the brothers, but not to you, not you!"

"Don't go there, Latoya. You're out of line. But to answer your questions, Mason, I knew all the ladies that were murdered. I know Lavender and her boyfriend Jimmy, and he's a bit rough, but he's goin' be okay for her. He looks out for her."

And with a warning look at Latoya, he said, "Don't give a damn about all this feminist stuff; women need men that'll look out for them. In fairness, so do men. Trouble is, everyone now just looks out for themselves. That's why I agreed to come here. Going to tell you what I know, but know that not one of my friends from the Boys Club would hurt a lady."

Mason thanked him, saying, "Tell me which ladies interacted with each other or with any of your friends and you? Whoever drank together is an example; you know, was socially connected in any way?"

"Jack Ladd, for sure, knew them all, not only the three killed but my wife, Lavender, and Martina. As a bar owner, and he owns many bars and restaurants, he always goes out of his way to meet any pretty lady. He would tell you it's to make sure that the lady isn't a working girl using his bar, but that's bullshit. Especially today when you can't tell a working girl from a co-ed. Jack has always loved the ladies, and it's cost him two marriages. The last lady took him for two of his bars in divorce court plus the house. He was pissed.

"Devon is with Jack pretty often; so, I'm guessin' he knows all the ladies too. You should ask him. He's a good guy and will tell you anything you want to know. Even as a kid, he couldn't shut up. Wouldn't want to rob a bank with him, I'm telling you that.

"Gerry Valle is more of a quiet guy. He's always been a handsome dude: tall, well built, but quiet. You know he wears horned rimmed glasses and looks like a college professor. Gerry is smart, in a bookish way, but not street smart. Somewhat surprising, as he was with us at the Boys Club. We all hung out together. I think he tries to use logic to solve all situations. He gets frustrated, really frustrated when logic doesn't do the job at hand. He is pretty successful, I know, but he doesn't show it. Drives a Honda, wears no jewelry, no rings, just a Piaget watch. Someone told me it was worth over a hundred grand. Couldn't prove it by me! I know where he lives, and the house is mega, you know what I mean. It's out here in this town.

"As far as Vic Cramer is concerned, he was making business deals when we were seven, and he was the go-to guy for illegal licenses when we were fourteen years old. They were good fakes, I'll tell you that. He liked the girls, but he's a guy's guy. He shows up with a buddy or sometimes his wife. She's a dermatologist, and he sends all his golfing buddies to her for sun-damaged skin treatment. They all like her. He's okay, but there's not a lot of emotion there. His parents were never home; always traveling or arguing. I think his single aunt brought him up.

"We also hung out with Candi Rodriguez at the Boys Club; now there is a cool dude. Talk about a lady's man who has willingly been corralled by his wife Heather. I understand Norbie is representing him. Norbie was one of our Boys Club gang. He was the rich kid in the Club. Funny thing is the rich kid had cookies and baloney sandwiches for lunch, while the rest of us had big cold cut grinders with chips and homemade cakes and pies. Norbie would always talk us into musical sandwiches, and one of us would end up with his lunch. Don't know how he always got away with it. He was a cool kid. I could bend over to touch the floor, and I'd be his height, but I could never take that guy. First of all, Norbie could bob and weave and tire me out. He certainly could run like a gazelle."

"Why would you think that Candi needed a lawyer?" Mason was annoyed.

"What the hell, Mason, everyone knows that. I've heard it from so many sources. You cops think you can keep everything under wraps. And why you think Candi would or could hurt a lady shows you up. Candi is a soft guy. He couldn't hurt anyone of us. We all took care of Candi."

Mason started to answer when Millie called his phone relaying a call from Lavender James who insisted on speaking to a detective.

"She said she tried Detective Stellato in Springfield, but that was two hours ago, and he hasn't called back. She's gotten calls. She's hysterical.

She can't find her boyfriend, and she goes on and on. Better take this on the line out here. I can keep your witnesses entertained, no one else is in the office right now."

Mason was left with a situation he was not happy about, a hysterical woman crying.

Norbie Cull and his wife had a busy day for Palm Beach tourists. Instead of sitting by the awesome (and Norbie used that term sparingly unlike his sons) Breakers Hotel pool, drinking Tito's vodka Collins and sunning, Sheri had dragged him to a lecture by Susan Eisenhower and Clifton Truman Daniel, two grandchildren of former presidents, about Russia. The big problem was he thought it was worth it. He even enjoyed the infamous story about Putin's dog, where supposedly Vladimir Putin staged his Labrador Konnie to sit in the room during a visit with German Prime Minister Angela Merkel who is reputedly fearful of all dogs.

Norbie thought, *Using a sweet Labrador as a prop to instill fear in the other side in political negotiations. That is Putin, I believe the story.*

Now he had just been informed by Sheri that they could lunch, and go to the pool, and then, rest. Later she had tickets to see the international singer and percussionist NOA, who though born in Israel, was raised in Riverside, New York, and then returned to Israel at age seventeen, only to stay there.

He'd heard about NOA when he was in Italy and read she had been honored by the Italian Government and furthermore sang the Ave Maria for the Pope. Sheri was impressed he even knew about NOA and they were to see the show at a temple in Palm Beach. He didn't know you could have entertainment in the main part of the temple, the Bimi. Well, there is always a first in everything.

His phone rang while they were at lunch and he excused himself noticing Sheri touching her watch and motioning she would order for him. *How the hell long does she think this call is going to take?* The call was from Candi.

"Norbie, I just got a message from Lavender James; she's getting calls. She said in the message she tried to reach you, and Stellato, and Captain Beauregard, and Jimmy, her boyfriend, and probably every cop in the world. Can I call her back? You told me never to call her, so I'm calling you. You have to call her back. When she's like this, she needs a calming person."

Norbie tried to explain that he and Sheri were away for four days in Palm Beach. He had a case down here and would be returning by the weekend. But Candi was insistent that Norbie call or he would call. Norbie agreed thinking, *with any other client I wouldn't even have listened to this. But Candi is a pro; if he's worried about her state of mind, a telephone call won't kill me. Sheri might kill me because this Lavender is long-winded.* He called Lavender, and she immediately answered.

"Oh, thank you, Mr. Cull. He's going to kill me next. He called and left a horrible message; over and over and over again. I was feeling pretty safe until now. I'm telling you I'm not leaving this house until Jimmy comes home. I told my mother, and she's all in an uproar. She'll keep Lulu Baby, but thinks I should come there to live for a time. I'm so nuts, but living with my mother makes me really crazy. She has all these ceramic statues all over her damn house. Lulu Baby loves them and handles them all carefully. I want to bust them in pieces and clean the joint out."

Norbie had had enough. "Lavender, did the caller use your cell phone?"

"Well, yes he did. Why didn't I think of that? Who has my cell number? Mr. Cull? That won't help, everyone at the bar has my cell number. I actually am one of the names used by the security company for break-ins at the bar. That's because I'm local and also responsible. I can get a texting tree done in seconds."

"Lavender, just what did the caller sound like and what did he say? You know voices, Lavender, even if he disguised his voice, see if you can figure out age and accent or unusual cadence."

"I love that you've used the word 'cadence,' Mr. Cull; I just used it in my crossword puzzle this morning. I do them to keep my brain active. Dancing only helps with my body."

Norbie groaned, but Miss Lavender was not to be rushed. "He sounds like a man. Of course, it could only be a man. What woman would want to kill us? I've always stayed away from married men. At least I did when they were up front, and you know, told me about being married. The voice is weird like talking through a bunch of cloth or something like a computer monster. I don't know about accent, but the words were slow in coming: 'You kept me away all these years. No more, Lavender, no more!' He said the same thing three times, and that's all."

It took ten minutes before Norbie could get Lavender to slow down and calm herself. Norbie promised he would get someone from the Springfield Police there as quickly as possible. He would also try to get someone to sit with her until Jimmy came home.

Next, Norbie called his go-to detective firm to get someone to sit with Lavender. Jim Locke, a former detective with the West Side Police department, was his choice. He hoped there would be a Chinese wall between Jim and the West Side police. Private detectives are not supposed to interfere with police investigations. He told Jim to make Lavender understand he was a friend and for him to disappear when the Springfield cops came by if they did. The arrangements took another fifteen minutes. By the time he joined Sheri, he had to negotiate good humor, all the while thinking, *a lot of work, trying to have a nice lunch when I'm on a quasi-vacation. Some vacation!*

―――――――

Meanwhile, Mona was planning for the Beauregard family trip to Singer Island. They were flying out on Friday with or without Rudy. Enough is enough. He can take four days and fly back on Tuesday; serial murders or no serial murders. And she told him reminding him that only one of the murders was in his domain and maybe one potential. He gave her that look of disappointment which she found so difficult to accept and found her thinking, *couldn't you give in for once? Four days, Rudy, just four days! You look so tired. It really would be good for you. I don't want to go without you. You're the guy I want to experience the world with. This condo is nice, on a beautiful beach, not far from some places for food and a supermarket. It's been too darn cold this winter. Please smile at me and say you'll come.*

In the hall, Rudy was sorting some mail and checked his home computer when he heard an email ding from the DNA people. To his surprise, he was eager to open it. The report showed new connections, and one showed a close relationship or sibling. His heart raced, and his judgment was slow. *Should I acknowledge him? I have his email. He might be a bum. Mason could probably trace the email address. He took a chance, why shouldn't I be as brave?*

And that was the end of that. Rudy thought, *I could write an email and say, "I don't remember much, and the much was not good. Tell me about yourself. I hope you survived and found happiness, brother." When I sign off with my name Rudy, well he'll remember that name. I'll do it tomorrow; always best to think twice before jumping into a precipice!*

Rudy was a much happier man as he entered the kitchen to face Mona and the kids and the trip to Florida. He knew he was going to lose this one, and that he would be going to Florida.

10
Who's Up Next?

Detective Petra Aylewood was tired from all the running around connected to this latest murder. Right now, she wanted to go home to Jim.

God, she thought, *we're newly married, and we've just purchased a new home in a prestigious neighborhood. We've no complaints other than finding together time. When Jim and I were on the force together, we saw each other all day long. Now I'm lucky to get a couple of hours a day. I miss that closeness from before.*

Her cell rang, and she saw Jim's picture before she connected -- only to find he wouldn't be home until he was home.

"Honey, I have to babysit for a client. Call me if you need me?" *Babysit? He gets paid to babysit. Well, let him get some practice; maybe he'll need those skills soon.*

She heard her cell again; *late in the day to get a call from City Hall,* she thought. It was Mayor Fitshler's office calling. The aide put her through to the mayor.

"I'm here with Chief Coyne, and we congratulate you, Lieutenant Aylewood, on your promotion. We wanted you to know before we made a press release on all the promotions. Chief Coyne has written an order for assignment changes. There are three promotions that have been made: one for lieutenant, yours, and the other two for sergeants.

"Normally, your duties would be changed, but Chief Coyne has met with Captain Beauregard, who has suggested you be kept in your current position, at least for the near future. You are currently a part of the investigation into a murder, possibly one of several serial murders. A new detective who could be assigned would not have your investigative experience and certainly would not understand all the nuances and impressions you have gained from your interviews to date. Based on the seriousness of the crime under investigation and our desire the community be protected, we have been persuaded that your service is important to the MCU. It is unusual but not unprecedented, Lieutenant Aylewood. If you have reservations, express them now."

Petra happily shared she had no reservations with Chief Coyne and Mayor Fitshler. She was then informed that Mayor Fitshler would be hosting a ceremony for the three officers being promoted at City Hall the following Tuesday evening, as the event room was open that evening. Petra tried to be professional in her thank-yous to them both but feared she may have gushed a little.

Petra called Jim and told him. He was so excited for her, he practically gushed, and Jim never gushed. Could life be any better? She did not think so!

The next thing she heard was, "Jimmy, do you like cream in your coffee?"

"Who is that talking to you, Jimmy? You're Jimmy now? Some babysitting job you have. What's going on, and, where are you?"

Jim asked if he could call her back to explain, that he could not talk right now. It was business, and she shouldn't jump to conclusions. She hung up and sat down in desolation while Jim was thinking, *Don't go there, Bolt. Don't jump the gun. I can only explain some of it. It's related to her case. I can't tell her everything. Maybe part of the truth will satisfy for now. She has to trust me.*

It was early, and Petra could think of nothing she could do to calm herself. She looked at her notepad and realized she should try to get a release of Martina and Lavender's therapy files. Chasing them down would keep her occupied. It would keep her from creating jealous havoc in her marriage. She jumped in her car and decided to go to Springfield first thinking, *Maybe I can be back in West Side to get to Martina's before dark.*

Fifteen minutes later, Petra parked illegally, but used her police placard. A flummoxed Petra was invited into Lavender James' home by her husband Jim, who put his finger over his pursed lips and whispered, "SHHHH." Petra walked in and Jim introduced her to Lavender as Detective Aylewood.

Lavender hugged her and said, "Captain Beauregard promised he would be helpful if he could and look, you're here before Detective Stellato. Mr. Locke, you can go home now. I have a real detective here now, and I will feel so much better if I can have a little 'girl talk' to calm me. Thank you so much."

Jim Locke escaped, as quickly as his long legs could take him. As he drove away, he prayed, *Thank you, Lord, for saving my marriage and maybe protecting me for the future from Petra's inclination to distrust. God, Petra did look beautiful, confused but beautiful. Well, now she'll get really confused by Lavender, who never stops talking. Jim contentedly drove home to his empty house a happy man.*

Detective Aylewood, trying to put aside the look of surprise on Jim's face, attempted to keep a professional demeanor in her dealings with Lavender ... but that attempt was lost within five minutes. Lavender wanted to know all about her, about why she became a police detective. Did she ever work vice, and was chasing a murderer frightening for her?

"You could never be more fearful than I am. I'm the little chick the dreary fox is chasing. He called me. I'm getting the calls. I heard all about the calls. When you get the calls, it means you're next."

And she went on and on, finally offering Petra coffee. Petra insisted upon helping Lavender, hoping she would open up with real information or give Petra an opening for requesting a medical release signature from her.

Looking around, Petra found herself amazed at her surroundings. On the outside, the home looked like a normal, though large, two family home in a decent city neighborhood. But inside, she thought *is beautiful, gorgeous, fashionable and quite quietly decorated, not including the more than twenty pillows on and around the couch.*

This is not what I expected. A woman named Lavender should live in a pastel room. This room is done in shades of taupe and brown and some lavender. All around, I see lots of ivory and touches of healthy-looking green plants. The kitchen is a Swiss designer's dream, minimalist and stainless with ivory and lavender and mellow yellow strip tiling for a backsplash. And the whole thing is as large as the first floor of my new home. There is a dining section, and the table is handmade cherry. It looks similar to the one I saw in the Nonton Art Show last year, and that one went for $5,400. I guess dancing pays, and she's no ordinary dancer unless her boyfriend is an interior designer.

Petra complimented Lavender on her good taste. Lavender answered, "Thank you, Detective, I've taken some design classes, and if dancing didn't pay so well, I think that would be my career. Now I just help my friends with their homes. You know a home is a sanctuary. I told Jimmy, that's my boyfriend, my sanctuary has been invaded with those calls. Now I'm the bait."

Petra was certain that with the volume of words Lavender could spew out per minute, that now might be her only opportunity to ask.

"Lavender, I don't know if I can fathom the depth of your fears; I know I would be upset if I were in your position and this is my trade. There is information you have, or your therapy file has that may lead us to this perp. But the police can't access that info unless you allow us.

"I have a medical release form with me. If you sign it, then Dr. Rodriguez will let us view the file. He is a therapist and is not looking for what we will look for. He won't see what we will see, he is not professional law enforcement, and he is not at liberty to give us the file unless you sign this release. Now eventually, we could get the court to release the file, but that would take time, and we simply don't have the time. Will you sign this form?"

To Petra's immense release, Lavender happily signed the form saying, "Well why didn't anyone tell me they needed a release before? There is nothing in my history that can't be put in **The Springfield Republican.** Hell, my file with Candi is probably boring as hell, but probably a large file; I talk a lot."

Petra listened to Lavender's discussions on childrearing, the joys, and pitfalls of erotic dancing, interior design, and many other publicly discussed topics. Petra thought, My *ears are going to fall off; where in hell are the Springfield Police?*

The bell rang. Petra told Lavender to go in her bedroom while she answered it. Petra approached the door and looked through the peephole. Upon seeing Lieutenant Stellato, she let him enter.

"Hell of a long way from West Side, Petra. I sincerely hope you aren't on the job here without first having your Captain notifying my Captain."

"And hello to you too, Lieutenant. Not to worry, you know me, I'm an official rule-follower, a cop from West Side."

Petra's brain was tracking an earlier conversation with Lavender. *Remember Lavender, I'm happy to cover for Jim Locke, but you must* understand I'm here as a friend. I can't be here in my police capacity without notifying Springfield Police. As a friend of yours, I will always be available. I loved her response. 'Petra, I just knew we would be friends the minute I met you. I'm going to tell the police that I'm helping you decorate your new home, okay?'"

Stellato said, "So, again why are you here with a potential murder victim in my city?"

"Look around, Lieutenant," Petra replied. "Lavender's got great taste, and she's agreed to do some interior design on my new home. We were trying to fit her schedule in with mine so she can go do a look-see at my new place. Now that you're here, I guess I'll just disappear. Let me tell Lavender I'm leaving."

Petra went into the bedroom leaving the door halfway closed just enough so a whisper could not be heard. She filled Lavender in on her conversation and realized that Lavender could add acting to her many skills as Lavender quickly left the room and hugged the lieutenant while happily stating, "Oh, Lieutenant, you're here now. I feel so safe knowing nobody will bother me. Thank you so much."

Petra left to return home groaning at the remembrance of Stellato's look. She had explained to Lavender it was important for Candido that West Side Police look at her file first, that her department had more time to focus on things. Her Captain would then share with the other police.

I flagrantly lied to Lavender, Petra thought. *Well not really a big lie. I actually was truthful when I explained bureaucracy in the other police departments like it didn't exist in my department. She's smart. She knew I was fibbing a bit, but she bet on us. I'll make sure I do what I can for her.*

Jim was making a snack when Petra walked in. Somehow his presence filled the house and made her welcome.

"Hi, Jim, what's cooking besides babysitting?" She laughed until she looked in his eyes.

In a most serious look and tone of voice, Jim answered, "Trust is cooking, Petra. Trust is needed. Trust is an underlying concept in this marriage. Never let me see you don't trust me again. I won't stay here without your trust, and only you can assure you will trust. I will never do anything that would undermine that trust, regardless of how it may seem at first. Like tonight, Petra.

"Now I'm making wicked good grilled cheese, bacon, and tomato sandwiches. You don't get one until you agree that you trust me."

Petra cried and laughed at the same time. "I have to agree that I trust you. I really need one of those sandwiches." She hugged Jim tightly and knew she was home.

Rudy noticed that his three kids had found Riviera Beach near the shops as their destination. In other words, the location to head to, when they wanted to slip their parents' watchful eyes during their stay near Palm Beach. While Mona was happy to lie in the chaise on their beautiful stretch of beach sipping a long, long iced tea with vodka, and chatting with her new friends, Rudy was antsy. He could do an hour, or two at the most, sunning, after which he found himself walking the half mile and meeting up with his kids at the shops. The boys had found a low-price store with every type of beach clothing one could wear and every type of apparatus for the water.

His youngest son insisted Rudy buy him an iced cappuccino, which Rudy was certain he had never had a sip of before this visit. The boy had just met two girls from New York City the day before. He thought, *That's the problem. He's a suburban kid looking with big eyes at the big city; got to watch that one now. I'm just like all cops trying to keep my kids in a bubble.*

I know it doesn't work. I'll just keep the talk going, keep our relationship up and try to be subtle. What a laugh, I'm more of a sledgehammer. No one thinks I'm subtle.

Rudy was reading a T-shirt logo stating that 'Misogyny Sucks' and a few more he turned his head away from when he ran into a good-looking guy with blonde hair. It took them both five seconds before they knew each other.

"What the hell, Norbie Cull, in shorts and sandals; not dressed for court, I guess. Is Palm Beach one of your forty a year vacations?"

Norbie laughed thinking, *Rudy in Palm Beach, couldn't have predicted that one. Must be with the kids; it's school vacation time.*

He said, "Rudy, you look nice and rather harmless in this setting. Normally you're putting fear in the hearts of my clients. On vacation, I guess, 'cause you're tanned. The color looks good on you."

"Well, Norbie, if Mona has her way I'd be sitting on the beach for hours. Just can't do it. I get antsy, so I'm over here. What are you doing here, on vacation too?"

"Quasi! I've a client down here, so I took Sheri with me for a few days. She's at the pool, and like you, I can only take a little of that. So, the guy at the hotel told me this outlet was great for getting weird stuff. I'm searching for outrageous Palm Beach T-shirts for my kids, all teenagers. I think that the directions were on point.

"How's this one: 'Never Trust an Atom, they Make up Everything;' or for my daughter who hates math, "Dear Math, I'm not a therapist, solve your own Problems' or for my lazy son, "Please Don't Make me do Stuff.' Better not get these, Sheri hates my sense of humor. Look, there must be a thousand of them. The kids would love them."

Beauregard couldn't help himself. "Norbie, I thought you were smart. I'd let Sheri choose. That way if the kids think the saying isn't cool, they won't think you're the old fart. Wives can get away with a lot of stuff that's not allowed for us."

Norbie laughed. They both agreed to go next door to the Drunken Goat and get a beverage. Rudy said, "Neither of us needs a clear head now, do we?"

Mid-afternoon found the Drunken Goat Bar filled with a diversity of beachcombers, parents grabbing food, and folks just enjoying the feel of the place. Rudy and Norbie sat at a hi-top table near the bar.

"Probably this is as good as life gets, Rudy," Norbie said.

They enjoyed some light conversation before two of Rudy's boys entered to tell him they were going back to the condo. Introductions were made, but the kids were not interested in talking to adults. *Fine with me*, Rudy thought. *I just want to listen to this bluesy music and imbibe.*

Beauregard remembered his updates from Mason and Petra and decided maybe now was the time to get to know Norbie's history.

"Norbie, what's this Springfield Boys and Girls Club bit? Stellato at MCU in Springfield says a whole bunch of guys connected to Candi were really tight including you. He says one of them said and I quote, 'They're brothers from another mother.' Don't know what the hell that means." Rudy thought, *not really the whole truth but could have been, and he'll never know.*

"Nothing to get uptight about, Rudy! We were tight. It was a great time for kids. No parents hovering over us. Doing things, I know I wasn't allowed to do at home. Going places with a group of kids and acting out like kids. Meeting kids, I never would have met any other way. Not like today. Practically all the schools have race, ethnic, and religion diversity now. Not then. I went to Our Lady of Hope with one of the guys. It was a Catholic school, not there anymore. Some went to public school. At least one of the group went to the French Catholic school. My parents were better situated economically than the others, but the other kids had more toys. I questioned my mom about that, in not a very nice way. Her answer was, 'Keep talking, and you'll not have any toys.'"

"So, you were a jealous punk, Norbie."

"Not really, I was just trying to understand the economics of it. My dad did well. We had a really nice house, but I didn't have a color television until I was in high school. My friends, some of who were on welfare, had a color television. Didn't compute for me then! Doesn't compute for me now!

"Hell, we learned from each other. I'd go to their house for chips and television. They'd come to my house for help with their homework. We had some great counselors at the Boys Club who would catch us at our shenanigans. The nice thing about them was they never made a big thing about our behavior. They'd just put us in time out with no big lectures. I've learned from that not to over-indulge in lectures to my kids."

"How bad could you have been? You were what, about seven to thirteen?"

"Yup, we were, and I'm telling you we were pretty creative. This experience alone probably laid the foundation for my desire to represent those disenfranchised and accused. Candi and Gerry Valle were the first to discover the value of the girls on the girls' side of the club. You see we were kept separated, except for cooking classes occasionally and the twice-a-year fashion shows that we were allowed to attend. The girls would model the outfits they made in sewing class. My sister was always modeling something. Also, we would see the girls when we would go to Mountain Park, remember it used to be in Holyoke, your hometown.

"We went to all kinds of events including a big Christmas party that was held at the Mountain Laurel in Connecticut. Well, Candi and Gerry figured out how to snoop on the girls during their swim time.

The rest of us would join them, then we'd get caught, and all would be in trouble. You see, not one of us would squeal on the other. Never, ever, ever did any of us break the trust! So, I guess it was all for each other or 'Brothers from another mother.' I loved the loyalty and camaraderie. I think I had the best childhood and I feel a great understanding of all those guys."

"Is that why you're representing Candi so vigorously, Norbie?"

"Sorry, Rudy, you're barking up the wrong tree. I represent all my clients vigorously. You know that."

"I do know that, but finding Candi at your home on the day we came to bring him to the station, well, that's more vigorous than usual, don't you think?"

"I told you, 'Brothers from another mother' or what about 'I've known him for a hundred years.' Of course, you found him at my house. He's a good friend."

"Norbie, cut it. Candi told us he hadn't seen you in a long time."

"That may be true, Rudy, but he is still one of my closest friends. I could go to him if I had problems. Clearly, he thought the same about me. But, you aren't still looking at Candi. I can and have told you that Candi would never hurt anyone and especially a woman. So, get off that one, Rudy."

"Well, who doesn't like Candi? That is a more pertinent question. There is a bunch of your 'Brothers from another mother.' So, how's the brotherly feeling between Candi and Jack Ladd, Myron Hicks or Vic Cramer or Devon O'Brien or Gerry Valle? Maybe there are more brothers in the group I haven't mentioned yet. But listen carefully, Norbie, all those guys I mentioned know all the ladies murdered and the two ladies who have received phone calls."

Rudy had lied thinking, *I still haven't seen a connection with the ladies and Vic Cramer.*

Norbie did not react quickly to Rudy's words letting Rudy know that somehow Norbie knew Lavender had also received phone calls from the perp. He thought, *Lavender must have let Candi know about them.*

"Norbie, tell me about your group of guys from before and their interaction with girls when you were kids. Who was popular? Who did the girls like? Which ones treated the girls badly?"

Norbie laughed and drummed his fingers on the table; perhaps signally Rudy to be more careful before asking these kinds of questions.

"Now you know, Rudy, that more than once I've been willing to help you find alternative motives for crimes committed, especially if the alternative helped my client. Now you want me to go through my group of old friends and find a potential culprit for you. You know better."

"Not to worry, Norbie, I'll listen to any theory you have. If not one of your 'Brothers from another mother,' then who else could it be? Maybe Candi knows something about the women that is common to them all. You know, where they hang out: strip clubs, Irish bars, or whatever. Now we know that Lavender and Loretta were both dancers, but Martina, Tonya, Lisa, and Janice were not, but they all hung out in bars. Well, maybe not Martina, but Martina did sing with groups in bars. So, help me out here. Got any ideas?"

"Has the FBI brought in a profiler yet? While I'm asking questions, do serial killers normally kill people they know unless it's like killing a series of husbands or wives? Look, Rudy, at most, some guy had a relationship with these women or a wish-for a relationship. The ladies have only one thing in common; they're all good looking. You have three murders and maybe two more potentials. You have the numbers. All the women are from western Massachusetts.

"I don't know how these facts fit in with the known concepts for serial murderers. I do think however if you and I look at our two recent common experiences with what we called serial murders, we can develop some thoughts. For instance, in the twelve-year-old Anya's case, she just wanted her own way, and her ego could not accept being bested by anyone. In the case of Leana Lonergan, well she had a horrific early childhood, without which she may never have killed anyone, and when she did kill, it was because she felt threatened. Those were motives, Rudy. We need motives. This is your business, not mine."

The men drank their beers and listened to a great but crunchy version of "Alleluia" from a local blues band.

"I guess anything's possible, to answer your question," Rudy said. "I never heard this kind of version of this song before. Mona likes KD Lang's version, but this one is quite satisfying.

"So, I think serial murderers, like this song, have many varied personalities. They are like all of us, ninety percent the same. It's the ten percent that's different. Within the serial murderers' grouping, well weirdness and evil have great diversity. That's the best answer I can give. What kind of background does this perp have? That's the question making me want to know about these friends of yours as young kids. Maybe something's there that is important."

"It is difficult right now for me to think that any of them could be capable of that kind of violence. I'll think about it, but I make no promises, Rudy."

The two men finished their beers and left, one for the extravagant Breakers Hotel, the other for a very decent but more modest condo. Both were deep in thought as they walked away.

11

Before

I t took several calls before Petra caught up with Gerry Valle. He was apparently a busy man. He suggested she come to his office saying, "Sergeant, or is it Lieutenant, I'm busy today and won't have the time to come to the station. Please come here. I'll have a half hour in a half hour if that's convenient."

"It's Lieutenant, Mr. Valle; thank you for asking."

Petra found the meeting time and place agreeable and set off for the ten-minute ride to his offices located in a swanky new building near Holyoke. She parked in front in the visitors' section and was waiting for him in the foyer, ten minutes early. He came right out and greeted her. She thought, *This guy looks really, really good, and he's not married yet? He has all this money, a big house, and he's not married yet?"*

"Lieutenant Aylewood, thank you for coming out to visit. Please join me on a tour of the facilities."

Petra thought, *I do like the ring of that word, 'lieutenant.'*

The two walked down corridors with many beautifully arranged offices off to each side. They finally settled into comfortable chairs around an ultra-modern glass and wood table in the Café Middle Man. Gerry got them two espressos with lemon peels and a couple of croissants with jam. She noticed he didn't ask her if she wanted coffee, but just brought the beverages. "I figured if I asked if you wanted coffee, you might think I was trying to compromise you," he said. "Instead, I'm just compromising you."

They laughed, and Petra questioned, "Café Middle Man? I take it, is named for your business' function and the business, right?"

"It is, and that is our function. I personally love the name. My middle managers love the name also. I'm a distributor of every type of construction-related small equipment for many government contracts in the New England/New York area. These digs here are for offices only. I have warehouses in four satellite areas servicing the various geographical sections of my market.

I started small in the Western Massachusetts area, and quickly realized that service was the name of the game, long before my competitors understood its extreme importance. I recognized the future of inventory control, developed close relationships with manufacturers, never stiffed anyone and then, earlier than most in the industry, bought into computer software. I was always ahead of the curve. I think developing this business has taken a piece out of my life – my social life, I mean. I've never married, but then I've never been divorced. I have no regrets."

Petra tried several times unsuccessfully to talk to Gerry about his early childhood. He seemed to desire instead to regale her with stories to impress her. And she was impressed. He name-dropped about exotic places visited and important people he had met.

Finally, she said, "Mr. Valle, I'm here to talk about three murder victims; I understand you knew all the victims. It's very important that we learn more about them, hopefully using any information we can garner from their friends and associates."

Petra felt Gerry's stare at her for a second before responding. "Lieutenant, I knew those ladies quite a few years ago. In fact, I did not know their married names. If the papers hadn't put in old photos of them, I wouldn't have been aware I knew them at all. I don't see what I could possibly say about them that would interest you today."

"It really isn't your job, Mr. Valle, to figure out what's important. It's our job. We find people are often sitting on important information about a victim without realizing that they have any information at all. Perhaps we can start with the first victim, Loretta Loren. Tell me about your relationship with Loretta."

"I really didn't have a relationship with Loretta. I saw her dance. She was talented, but I can't say I knew her. She was the studious type. The minute she stopped dancing she'd don these wire-rimmed spectacles. I always thought it was a way to keep the guys at bay. My friend Jack Ladd dated her, but that didn't last. I think she liked to show her body off but deep down was a prude. She didn't act like the other women."

"Mr. Valle, was Jack Ladd disappointed when she moved to Boston? Did he take it hard when she stopped dating him?"

"Please call me Gerry. Nobody calls me Mr. Valle. I don't even like my name. It was originally 'Valliere,' but one of my stellar ancestors thought that 'Valle' was more American sounding. What makes you think Jack Ladd would be disappointed if a woman stopped dating him? I never heard that concept before about Jack. He's a ladies' man; don't think he ever worries if one gives him up. He's got the bars giving him a new source of new ladies all the time."

"So, you think Jack chases ladies all the time. Is that what he's always done? I know you were friends with a bunch of guys at the Boys Club, and these guys all know the four victims, as you also do. What was Jack like when you were kids? Was he always a ladies' man, and what about you as a kid? Did you two like the girls way back?"

Smiling that winning smile, Gerry moved slightly in his chair. *He looks uncomfortable,* Petra thought. *Maybe his history as a kid is problematic.*

Without waiting for an answer, she asked, "Gerry, how did you get to the Boys Club after school? I mean did your mom drive you or was there a bus?

"I heard the Boys Club was pretty diverse and at that time some parents didn't want their kids there. They were worried about their kids learning too much from the underprivileged kids. Would you consider yourself underprivileged by those standards then?"

Gerry practically sputtered in his answer.

"Underprivileged, hell no! My mother didn't want me to go there. Thank God, my father insisted. He thought my mother, who spoke very little English, was overprotective. My experience with those guys gave me a life where my mother couldn't control how I thought. Talk about a helicopter parent. My mother invented the term. She even tried to change the rules at the Boys Club. When I'd go on a Saturday, she wanted them to heat my lunch for me. It was downright embarrassing. Devon O'Brien took care of that. One of his grandmothers was French, and she spoke enough French to convince my mother the kids would laugh at me if she made that happen.

"Devon was a cool talker, almost as good as Norbie. Maybe my family didn't have quite the same amount of money that Norbie's did, but I had a lot more stuff than he had. I liked gimmicks then and I like techie stuff now."

Petra renewed her questioning. "What about girls at the club? I heard you always liked the girls, at an earlier age than the other boys in the group. Is that true?"

"Hell, no; well maybe before Norbie and Devon or Myron. They took a little longer to figure out that girls could be a whole lot of fun. Of course, I liked the girls, pretty ones especially. My mom was a beauty, and I guess I appreciated good looks from hanging around her."

"I hope you still have your mom," Petra said. "She sounds special."

"No, Lieutenant, my mom died just over two years ago in a freak car accident. She was burned on over three-quarters of her body. I don't think about it often. It is a horror for me, what some careless driver did to her. She was so beautiful and to be disfigured just before death -- forget it, let's get on another subject."

"I'm sorry. Gerry. Again, what was the bond for you guys as kids, and have you maintained that bond?"

"Lieutenant, we're all in different careers. We don't see each other on a regular basis, but if we did, it would be like old times. Hell, all we need is a pool table, and the competition gets rough.

"Norbie, Myron and I are pool sharks. I'm not bad. Jack owns all the bars, but he can't play the game at all. He just counts his cash, books venues, and flirts with pretty ladies. Candi never had the time to play pool because he's always psychoanalyzing someone. You'd be surprised what a good hook-up being a therapist is.

"We know each other really well and try not to get in each other's way. That way we ensure good will. Our comradeship has history. A good enough history, a history that makes me never want to injure any of those guys! Now, is that a good enough explanation for you?"

"It is. Is the closeness so great that you would cover up for any of your friends, or would any of them cover up any of your misdeeds?"

"Lieutenant, we are all making a good living and are well regarded. Why would you think any of us would do something so wrong that it would need covering up?"

"Gerry, I think that at least some of you have been closely involved with the murder victims and all of you have known them. I was informed that you did date Janice until her uncle's friend and your good friend, Devon told you to 'butt out,' that you were too old. I heard that you really liked Janice and you were pissed to be told to stop the relationship."

"Whoever told you that is a liar. I wasn't really that interested in Janice, but who the hell was he to tell me I was too old for her. What a joke."

Petra moved right along. "Gerry, you also dated Lisa Moliano," she said. "She also was younger than you; do you have a thing for younger women?"

"Yeah, what of it? Not one of these women was more than ten years younger than me. Well, maybe it would be more like twelve years younger at the outside."

"Gerry, I think you dated them all. Maybe just for coffee, but you dated them all."

Gerry got up abruptly and said, "Don't come back, Lieutenant, to talk with me. Talk to my lawyer." And he walked away.

I've hit a nerve here, Petra left, thinking. *Didn't get all I wanted from him, but I think I know the guy better. I wonder if he is as stable as he looks.*

She left for her second interview for the day.

Devon O'Brien agreed to meet Petra at Russ's little breakfast and lunch restaurant at Springfield's Glenwood Circle, near the Chicopee line. Petra had been there before, for breakfast with a couple of Springfield cops. The food was decent, and the service was fast; the place exuded hometown feel. The waitresses and cook staff knew most everyone by first name.

Petra knew Devon immediately. He matched the description given her to a tee: *a handsome Irishman, tall and solid; always smiling.*

He was smiling as he greeted her. "Today must be my lucky day. Normally, police lieutenants don't look like you. Let's sit in this last booth by the door. It's got the most privacy allowed here. Besides, I've been here for ten minutes, saving it for us. Practically had to kick out the previous occupants who were just dawdling. Now, call me Devon, and how can I help you, Lieutenant?"

"Well, Devon, as you have probably guessed, I'm looking for information about four women who have been murdered. There is enough evidence to point to a connection among the women. We've been informed that perhaps you knew all the murder victims and further, that you and a group of your close friends from the Boys Club were all acquainted with each victim. We're interested in what your associations were and any information you have that would further our investigation. We believe it is imperative we understand all connections; that perhaps there may be potential victims out there."

All the while Petra was thinking, *Devon, don't play dumb with me. You know all this from your friends. I'm certain Gerry Valle called all of you right after I left him. Probably, Lavender has talked with the whole world about her phone calls.*

"Lieutenant, I know about the murders of course. Janice was my friend's niece, and I am heartbroken. I've known her since she was a baby, cutest damn kid you ever saw. You're right, I knew all the women killed. All three. Who's the fourth one? Also, I don't understand why you can't get my interview with the Springfield Police from them. Why are we talking now?"

Petra started to rethink Devon. *Open and friendly, but then questions why I'm talking to him. He's not as comfortable as he'd like me to believe.*

"The fourth victim was killed first. It's just that we didn't know about her until we received some recent information. "She was murdered in Boston. Her name was Loretta Loren. Did you know her, Devon?"

"Of course, I knew her. She dated one of my friends. I'd see her a lot. I heard she died, but we all thought her doctor boyfriend killed her. There was no local investigation, other than a little on her history. At least that's what I heard from Jack, who's in the know about what's going on with police. He gets all the info. She was a dancer, so they thought maybe her killer was a stalker. Loretta didn't invite that kind of attention. She was an egghead who just danced for money to get her through her graduate program. She was a good dancer, just never put that extra zing into it. I think because she never felt the desire to show her sexuality. She was strange that way, not like the other dancers. I know one dancer who's the best at letting you think she's all about you; you know, like she was dancing just for you. That wasn't Loretta."

"That other dancer you just referred to, is that Lavender James?"

Devon stared into space for a minute, perhaps to collect his thoughts. Finally, he said, "Yes, but how did you know? Are you talking with Lavender? No one's after her, I hope. She's a veteran at the business and a nice person. Again, Detective, Lavender lives in Springfield, and Loretta and two of the others also are not from your city. Why are you investigating their deaths?"

Petra was startled at this deviation in the interview. *I'm the one asking questions, and he tries to change the power dynamics. Might be a sign of discomfort!*

"Devon, again there are multiple murders. Bodies were found in different jurisdictions, but the cases appear to be connected. That means all the affected departments will be investigating, working in concert. Everything we discover will be turned over to every department for deep analysis."

Wouldn't that be lovely if it were true, Petra thought. *There are always holdbacks. Each department wants its edge.*

Devon said, "I know all the ladies who died, and I know Lavender. I also know Martina who I understand from my sources may be on the list. I know her. Look, Lieutenant, I'm in all the Irish bars. I love the

Irish Pub culture. Did you know I've often sung at some of the Irish events? I also play the uillean bagpipes, not so much lately. I've been with all the ladies when they sang. Martina too. She has a lovely voice, as did Janice. Lisa was a great Irish singer. I liked them all."

Devon blinked his eyes, looked down at his coffee and, with a bit of the Irish lilt in his voice, said, "Aye, all were lovelies and put in the ground before their time. Tis a great loss, yes, it is."

"Devon, it's not poetry we're talking about. It's murder."

They sipped their coffees, ordered a sandwich each from the waitress, and were momentarily silent in deference to his homily on the murdered ladies.

Petra asked about Jack Ladd's relationship with Loretta, whether he was upset when she got engaged to a doctor from Boston.

"Detective, Jack Ladd has been through many relationships. The only break-up that caused him concern was the last one, and that's because she took some of his pubs as a settlement. He had to buy them back a year later, after she almost ran them into the ground. A bar or restaurant, or I guess any kind of business, has to have daily oversight to be successful. The ex-wife surely didn't understand that. She thought they ran themselves. So, to answer you, much as he liked Loretta, Jack doesn't like any woman that much."

"Tell me about all your friends from the Boys Club. What were they like as young boys? Did they get along with all the boys and girls? What about their families?"

"Detective, I'm telling you this upfront. My friends are good guys. I'd go to the wall for them and vice-versa. Don't be thinking I'll tell you secrets. We were all different, that was the magic. We taught each other ways of thinking that were not taught in our homes. Norbie Cull was the thinker and by God, the very best planner of trouble amongst us. Yet for all that, Norbie had an honor code he wouldn't break for anyone. We all knew he was headed for success if he wasn't arrested first for some peccadillo or juvenile scheme. The rest of us have all done well, which is a surprise to us all. I can't think of anything to help you here. Now I have to be off soon."

Petra asked, "Before you go, Devon, what career path did you take? I don't think I know."

Devon laughed. "I'm into many things including ownership of a small construction company. I have a separate roofing company along with a large in-home care agency. I have a license in nursing home management. I also have a Massachusetts License as a Construction Supervisor. I guess I'm all things to all."

"What about marriage, Devon, are you or have you ever been married?" His reply surprised her.

"I don't know if you would call it a marriage. I was married for five days when I found out my beautiful bride was a thief, liar, and bigamist, thanks to her fourth ex-husband who read about our marriage in the newspaper. She was only twenty-eight when I married her. She was sharp. She fooled Jack and Gerry and Candi. She didn't fool Myron who said she was trouble. I never introduced her to Norbie. He only saw her at our wedding. He probably saw through her, but wouldn't say anything on my wedding day.

"I was smitten, but that wore off quickly when the police arrested her at our new home, and I found out she had withdrawn all my money from our joint savings account. I had to get a loan from Jack for a couple of months to meet business expenses. No, Detective, I'm not married. Everyone had a good laugh on me."

Petra responded, "Perhaps I'm not being sensitive enough, but does that experience make you hate pretty women?"

"No, Detective, it just ensures I won't marry them."

"Devon, I thank you for your honesty. You will most likely hear from me or some other detective on new questions we may develop. I appreciate your assistance today."

How much of what he says is true? Petra left, thinking. *He is charming but clearly damaged. Could he hate good looking women enough to murder them, and why take so long? I remember the Feds saying that most serial murderers hide in plain sight. This guy could hide. He is attractive. Many women must have come on to him by now. He's got to be really scarred. Look how long it took me to get over a very young marriage. Finally, I found Jim.*

Devon left the encounter with Petra thinking, *She thinks I'd hurt a beautiful woman because I married a crazy lady. What must everybody else think if a detective could so easily show her discomfort with me? That must be what Valencia saw. That's why she wouldn't agree to marriage. She thought I had to change. Change what, history? You can't change history.*

12

Another Brother

Rudy told Millie he had to run home for a few minutes. He said there was a maintenance emergency. When he arrived at the house, knowing Mona would be out all day, he immediately went to his personal computer and brought up the connection. *I don't understand. I have second cousins and various amounts of matching and then a brother, but I don't understand the matching. What the hell!*

Rudy walked into the kitchen and grabbed a slice of cake; normally forbidden for him. "I'm a stress eater," he said aloud. "Today is cake day for me. Mona will think the kids ate it. Now I'm energized to face the music."

Rudy wrote an email. It took a couple of tries because he typed some letters twice on his first attempt. He wrote: "Dear Billy, At least that's the name I remember for you when we were both tied up sitting in our chairs when the men broke into our room. I hope you have not suffered too much. Please tell me about yourself. Rudy"

He thought *it sounds so cold, but I don't have anything else to say. He could be and maybe has an excuse to be, a sociopath. I have a family to protect and I can't expose them to a bad deal. Still, human nature is so resilient. I feel hopeful, fool that I am.*

I've known I'm not a sociopath because I have so much guilt. Lizette says it's because she raised me in the French way, but I know that sociopaths are in every group. Billy had eight years of our hell. Were they all like the little bit I remember? I hope the hell not. Sometimes I wonder why, with all the drug-

addicted parents giving horrible conditions to their children, why we don't have even more sociopaths?

Rudy took a detour up to the Holyoke Police Department to visit Sergeant Luis Vargas. He thought, *It's been a while; long enough for him to have some information. I'm freakin' anxious. Now I want to know everything. I guess now I'm ready. All these years of avoidance and now I'm in a hurry.*

Luis greeted Rudy with an attempt at a bear hug. It was not successful. Rudy said, "Enough of that Luis. You can't even get your arms around me. So, do you have anything for me?"

"I have a lot, Rudy. I have a lot. Not everything, but enough to answer some questions. Mavis Eaton, your mother, was found murdered in Vermont three years after you kids were found. They figure she had been dead about three years. She had been strangled and sexually assaulted. Also, the perp cut her somewhat.

"She couldn't have come back for you and Billy. Rudy, she was dead. You two were not abandoned. The police up there found no evidence that would help solve the crime. She was dumped near a lake. There were tire tracks, but too old to be the perp's tires. Who the hell would drive up there and not report the body or the skeleton? They have crime scene pictures but didn't do any tread sculptures, and the pictures are not like today."

"Luis, where was Mavis from? Was her name Mavis Locario, and then she married an Eaton, or was she an Eaton who took her name back once she divorced Locario or was she never married but Billy's father gave him a name?"

"Mavis was born Mavis Pappas in Quincy, Massachusetts on July 12, 1945. She had three siblings, and all three are dead. The family reported her missing about a month after you two were found. Apparently, she would always call home monthly. When that didn't happen, they reported it to the police who of course did nothing. The family knew she had one son from a marriage to William Locario. They said he was a bum and they felt it took her too long to get rid of him. The family didn't know about you or about any guy named Eaton. Remember there are reports of them going to the police for several years before Mavis was found. In the reports, they say they hadn't seen Billy since her divorce which they said occurred when Billy was about five years old."

"Well did you find out about this Eaton? Is he my father?"

"Maybe, maybe not. Mavis only came home once during the last three years before she died and she came home alone. They could tell she didn't have very much in the way of money. She came by bus and got a ride later in the day to Ashmont Station in Dorchester where she said she would make her connections home. She led them to believe that she lived in Framingham."

"Did she ever live in Framingham? Did she have a work history?"

"We caught a few connections in and around Framingham for short jobs. She didn't have a driver's license. The family said William Locario was very controlling. He wouldn't let her drive. We found out she worked in two different nursing homes as a caregiver in Framingham for nine months when you were a year old. There are a couple of other employers in the Boston area for restaurant work. They were in the file from her friends' interviews from the nursing homes.

"In those days there wasn't as much employer control on personnel in nursing homes. We figure later around the time she disappeared that she probably worked in a nursing home in the Holyoke area. We checked for domestic violence complaints in Framingham and found several at an address for a Locario in nineteen sixty-five through nineteen sixty-nine. Mavis never followed through on the complaints, which was normal in those days. Her divorce took place in Boston. Just before you were born, she married John Eaton. He was her attorney; a young attorney. He died four months later. I don't think he's your father, because you said that the DNA put you and Billy at a high connection, therefore you and he must be brothers. Your father could not have been Eaton; he was helping her get away from an abusive situation.

"Your mother was nice looking from the photos the family had given the police. John Eaton had no other children, but I have an address for his younger sister who is still living in Framingham. She never married. Her name is Estelle Eaton. You may want to contact her. She may know more about the relationship.

"It looks to me, Rudy, that Billy is your brother, that your mother did everything she could to protect you guys, and that you don't have to run away anymore."

"Luis, what about Billy? Have you located him? What is his history? Is he trouble? I need to know."

"It seems to me he's family, the only blood family you have outside of your children. Lizette tried to adopt him. She wasn't afraid of him. If he's a bad dude, you'll know. When you meet him, try to think like a cop, and you'll be able to separate yourself from your emotions. Sometimes avoiding risk is avoiding the wonders of life. Think like a Latino, Rudy. We're all family until we prove we shouldn't be family.

"I'll keep working on this. I did learn that Billy was at some forerunner agency of Brightside over by Providence Hospital for a period of time. He was adopted, that's what some old timers from Brightside told my friends. Just where he went after that, I'm trying to find out. I don't have his new name yet, but I'll get it."

Rudy thanked Luis and left the Holyoke station.

———

When Rudy entered the West Side station and was greeted by the officer in charge, a man who was in the waiting room approached him.

"Hi, Rudy. It's been a long time. You're looking good."

"I'm sorry, but I can't quite place you." The man did look vaguely familiar.

"Well, it's been a hell of a long time. Let's see I was eight and you were three. It seems likely that I'll remember you more than you could remember me."

Billy Locario gave him a brilliant grin, what Mona would call infectious, and hugged Rudy. Rudy was not used to this broad display of affection from what seemed like a stranger but found he could not hold back. He gave into the hug thinking, *This feels normal. In fact, this feels really good.*

Rudy took a look at his brother. *He is handsome and burly and smart looking.* He welcomed him to join him in his office telling Millie along the way that he was not to be disturbed. Her left eyebrow raised, a signal telling him she knew something was up.

From his office, Rudy called Millie and asked if she could bring in two coffees and whatever unhealthy snack they had today.

"Yes, sir," she answered. "He must be important. You don't always get coffee for the Chief."

Once established in their seats the two men inspected each other and they both appeared to comfortably settle in to discuss their history together, what little bit there was.

Rudy said, "So tell me about what you remember, and after that tell me about your life. I want to and need to know. Then I'll tell you about myself."

"Well to start with," Billy said, "I insisted my adoptive parents keep my first name. I was eleven before the agency considered me suitable for adoption. No question, I was a fighter and out of control when they found us. I wanted Mama. I knew she would come back. At least I thought I knew that. I used to fight with her, but I knew she wanted what was best for me. Although if there had ever been a fire in our apartment, we would have been toast, all tied up like that.

"She didn't trust me. She tied us because I would run, and she didn't want you alone. She thought it was at night and we would sleep. She was right about one thing, I couldn't be trusted. I would have been out on the streets playing. I would have left you alone. I was and still am the type of person who tries anything, not always thinking things through enough. However, in business, it's paid off for me.

"Mama was murdered, and our father William Locario killed her; of that, I'm certain, Rudy. I believe he is still alive and has never been punished. The police started an investigation into Mama's murder when she was found. That was three years after she died. He was nowhere to be found. I don't know where he is, but I would like to know."

"Why do you say 'our father'? I had a different last name. How do you know I'm not Eaton's son? And why would you want to know where he is?"

"I visited John Eaton's sister Estelle. She is a nice lady who was devoted to John. She told a story that makes sense to me, Rudy. In addition, the DNA test showed too strong a connection for us to be half-brothers. You know I was adopted by a couple of social workers who wore rose-colored glasses and still do. They see good everywhere. I don't know how many couples looked at me and decided not to adopt me; I was not considered an easy kid.

"My parents looked at me and saw the resurrection of Jesus. Talk about validation. I couldn't disappoint them. I needed that kind of love. Estelle is one of those kinds of ladies, and so was John. I remember him.

He wasn't a big guy, but I saw him frighten the hell out of our father and throw him out of our home. He helped Mavis get her divorce, and I heard him tell her not to worry, that he would give William money and adopt me. I read the court report. I was adopted, but the agreement stated my name could not be changed.

"William Locario didn't know about you. John married Mama, and Estelle said he told everyone you were his son and he was adopting Billy. But she said that John couldn't have been your father because the numbers don't work. Mama was pregnant when she hired John as her attorney. Estelle said John was a born savior and was crazy over Mama. She said Mavis was the sweetest lady. When John died, and he died suddenly, Mavis disappeared. She left a note stating it would be safer for all if no one knew where she had gone."

"So, Billy, it is Billy, isn't it or is it Bill by now?"

"My wife calls me Liam. That's Liam O'Callahan. She says it's more Irish and really goes with my last name; she's from County Roscommon. I go by any name that's not a swear word.

"I'm married, have two daughters and two grandsons. My wife thinks I'm great, a bit difficult at times but a good husband. I'm an institutional financial investor and make good money. I'm lucky.

"You know, Rudy, I've known about you for a while. When I saw your picture during the investigation into the six children who were murdered by their twelve-year-old friend, I recognized you. You have that same look. You're always watching. You're guarded. But you show you care. I knew you, and maybe the name Rudy helped, but I told my wife Delia that I knew you. She didn't think it was possible to remember a three-year-old all these years later, but she was wrong. I didn't call because I was afraid you wouldn't want to know about us then, about the past. When I got your note, I came right over here."

"Wait a minute, Billy, how could you possibly be sure that Rudy was me? I didn't identify myself."

"C'mon, Rudy, there are apps that let me search for email origins. You police have professionals do it. We civilians do it ourselves and a lot faster because there's no protocol. When I got my message, I told Delia, I've got a brother. He reached out to me. Her answer was, 'Let's hope he's as happy to know about you as you are to know about him.' Wives are very protective, don't you think?"

"Sometimes," Rudy answered, "but other times they'll throw you to the wolves unless you shape up. My wife's name is Mona, and we have three sons, one of whom is going to college next year.

"I don't like that Mavis' murder was never solved. I don't like it at all. I believe murderers need to be brought to justice. I thought that long before I became a police officer. My mother, oops, adoptive mother always said we were loved by our mother because we were in such good health when we were found. My mom's name is Lizette, and she says all the time, 'Your brother was eight, and you were over three when you were both found in good condition. Your mother had eight years of child care and didn't give up on the kids. She kept them as best she could. You had a good mother. Of that I'm sure.' Again, it looks like Lizette is right.

"What was William Locario's last known address? What did he do for a living? I will follow any trail to find him. He may be an old man, but he needs to face us for killing our mother.

"We were lucky to find adoptive parents who did so much for us. Not every abandoned kid is so lucky."

Liam said, "Not abandoned, Rudy. Victims of loss and maybe trauma, but Mavis never abandoned us. Our birth father was a real estate salesman at that time. Even then it required licensing. He worked in Quincy and later in Framingham. So, let me know when we can have a family reunion."

Rudy stood up as Liam was rising and he hugged his brother. Liam sniffled and made an attempt at a smile. Looking down on the slightly shorter man, he said, "Brother, I feel like I've come home. Try to find William Locario. If you're successful, we'll talk. Remember we need a family reunion. Cousins should know each other."

Liam walked out of Rudy's office, leaving Rudy in tears – tears of relief and happiness.

Who do I call first, he thought, *Lizette and Roland or Mona? Hell, Mona's helping out at the High School today. Lizette it is.* Then the dark thoughts returned. *Can his story be true? Maybe he's a danger. I don't want to expose him to my family until I know it's safe. I know he suffered. No, I'll go forward with this and hope I'm right.*

Millie marched into his office before Rudy could call Lizette, "Okay, out with it," she said. "Is that man Liam your long-lost brother or something? You look a lot alike. He's just bigger and friendlier, and politer than you, and lighter haired, but has the same kind eyes. He must be related to you."

Ticked off at her acute observation, Rudy asked, "Whoever told you I had a brother?"

"Well Captain, Mona did. Lizette told me once when we were at one of the high school games. Let's see, somebody else told me. Yeah, I remember Sergeant Vargas told me two years ago when he was trying to get you involved in the Manuary event in Holyoke. So, I'm right, aren't I"?

Rudy couldn't help but laugh thinking that, *There are no secrets in a police station,* but said, "Yeah, Liam O'Callahan is my brother. What did you think of him, Millie, not like me really?"

Millie answered, "More than you think, Captain, more than you think."

13

Stupid Moments

Norbie Cull woke up from a restless sleep with severe pain on the left side of his neck. His first thought was: *What the hell is wrong now?* Trying not to wake Sheri, Norbie slid out of bed, only to trip on his dog, WinWin. He fell on his right shoulder while trying to break the fall with his left arm. He heard the snap.

"Owww! I've broken my hand." he yelled, "or my fingers." *Hell,* he thought, *I'll have to collect from my homeowner's insurance.* WinWin made the first response by trying to lick his master's face and then directing his attention to Norbie's hand. *Damnit, WinWin, why are you always under my feet? Who's going to believe this one? Why put my hand there? My shoulder is meant to take some trauma. There's a lot of muscle in the shoulder.* "Alright, I'm sorry, WinWin, it doesn't hurt too much."

Sheri, a light sleeper, jumped up and said, with what he thought was a lack of wifely devotion, "Norbie, you probably just have a sprain. Don't be so dramatic. You're worse than the kids."

Then, she looked at his hand and gasped. "Oh, I'm so sorry, Norbie. You're really hurt. Get dressed, and we'll go to the emergency room. I'll leave a note for the kids. They'll be able to get out by themselves. What time is it? Ooh, it's only three o'clock."

Sheri drove, and he told her to head out to the hospital in Ware.

"Are you nuts? Why would I go twenty miles when I can go six miles to Springfield?"

Norbie replied, "Wing Hospital in Ware will take me within ten minutes of arrival. Either hospital in Springfield will have a five-hour wait unless you're dying. I'm not dying. I just fucking hurt and have to be in court at nine."

Fifteen minutes later, Norbie was admitted to the emergency room. He could not believe the sight before his eyes. The charge nurse was Claire Breen, Devon O'Brien's ex-wife, just as good looking twelve years later. Norbie groaned inwardly. Sheri did not seem to recognize her.

"Hi, Claire," Norbie said, "who's on duty who's good with hands?"

"Norbie, I was always good with my hands. Why do you think I had four, no, now it's five husbands?" Her wise guy response brought back his first impression of her he'd had on her wedding day.

Playing the straight man, Norbie said, "I meant a hand surgeon, Claire."

Claire took a look at his hand and said, "You've just got fractures of your baby and ring fingers." And she pulled them a bit, while he turned ghostly white.

Claire then said, "You won't need a reset. Not to worry, you'll be out of here in twenty. I'll get the surgeon on call, but he'll have me splint them."

Her prediction turned out to be accurate. As Norbie and Sheri were walking out of the ER, Claire followed them.

"What happened with those women, Norbie? I heard the police were looking at Candi and I can tell you that's a waste of time. Candi is a one-woman-at-a-time kind of guy. You know that. I heard the murderer is trying to set Candi up. You'd have to hate him to do that, and Candi doesn't inspire hate, except from that dipshit first wife of his. So, it's some guy, probably a patient of his. That's what the talk is."

Norbie laughed and said, "What do you know about Candi's first wife, Claire?"

"I know Candi and one of his daughters were brought in here with broken noses which were explained as 'walking into a door.'"

Norbie suppressed his surprise. "When was that, Claire? I never heard about it."

"I thought everyone heard about that. It was right after he announced he was engaged to Heather. He went to get the girls, and she was ready for him with a tennis racket. One of the daughters tried to stop her, and she received a nice hit in the face. Candi went to pick up his daughter from the floor, and she took a fireplace iron to him, over and over. Good thing he's so strong. He survived."

Norbie couldn't believe he had not heard this news before.

"Were the police called to the house?"

"No, Candi didn't want that. One of the kids was still in high school. He surely didn't want social services inspecting, and also maybe having to defend his license. After his ex-wife Maria Elena quieted down, she realized she was in legal jeopardy. As a result, she was more amenable to normal conversation and negotiations about the last daughter. She's a nut case, I can assure you.

"Don't think, Norbie, that I'm crazy. My third marriage included me as the wife who was psychologically and physically abused. I couldn't have divorced him. I ran from him. I thought I had successfully gotten away. I couldn't tell Devon the truth. He was so against multiple marriages because of Jack Ladd's history. I'm not the bad woman you think I am. In some ways, I have to thank the horrors of Devon finding out about me.

"My ex brought me up on bigamy charges, but they were later dropped. I used our money for that. I later tried to repay Devon, but he wouldn't take the money. I did my best, Norbie, for what I was faced with. Please don't judge me."

Norbie thanked her for her help with his hand, thinking, *She marries five times, once bigamously, steals her new fourth husband's money, and thinks someone else is crazy.*

He shared some of his new info with Sheri, who was delighted to be let in on some gossip and immediately suggested maybe Maria Elena was murdering all Candi's ex-clients to shame him.

"Help me, God," Norbie said, "My wife thinks like Claire Breen. Too easy, Honey, it's just too easy a solution. Maria Elena would be more likely capable of burning Candi's house down in a fit of anger. Killing three women requires thoughtful and careful planning."

Four hours later, after a shower including covering his hand with plastic kitchen wrap to protect it from the water, Norbie was in court, inventing a more plausible story for being slightly late than WinWin's tripping him. In the hallway, he ran into John Diggle, a cop from Nonton. John was a buddy from high school who now was living the good life among all the college students and great eats in liberal Nonton. He pulled Norbie aside and asked about Candi and the murdered ladies.

"How did you hear about Candi, John? He was just a therapist for some of the ladies."

"Norbie, don't kid me. It's all over the area. You know we police love knowing about murders in the area. But I have a real reason for asking you some questions. We picked up a local lady in Nonton after an apparent mugging.

"It was about two a.m. last Sunday morning. She's in a coma, but it looked like someone was trying to put her in a car over by the lowlands near Peter's Brook. Some guy was sleeping in his car nearby waiting for a friend to go fishing. He got suspicious when he saw two cars and what looked like someone dragging a body from one car over to the other. He started to yell, and the guy took off. It was a dark SUV. The witness couldn't see anything else. I just wondered if your perp was expanding his work into Nonton."

Norbie's face flushed red; one of the few tells he would give off when he was knocked off balance by information affecting his clients. He said, "Do you have a name for this woman? Was she a working girl, and is there a shot she'll regain consciousness?"

"Yeah, her name is Valencia Longtin. She's pretty wealthy, certainly not a working girl, some sort of sales rep. She's in a long-term relationship with a married congressman from a nearby state. She's a good-looking woman. We don't know how she's going to do. She got a hell of a whack on the head. We also don't know why she was way over in that area. It's not near the hot spots."

"Didn't you notify other police in the area?" Norbie asked. "I mean I've heard nothing about this at all. Although to be truthful, I just came back from Palm Beach and am not in the swing of things yet. Have you called Springfield, Ware, and West Side to see if there are any similarities?"

"I don't know what the brass did. It was an assault, not unheard of, and she wasn't maimed or killed. Maybe they saw no connection. I'll let them know to call. So, you heard nothing, huh? Strange, that you've heard nothing!"

Norbie had no time to churn the wheels of his brain on this subject until lunchtime when the ache in his hand required a couple of ibuprofen. He grabbed a chili at Luxe's and fortunately was left alone to think.

He needed confirmation for his memory and called Candi, who answered his call in one ring. Yes, it was confirmed. Valencia Longtin was his patient, and yes, he had a firm alibi. He was with a big crowd at his house until one-thirty, or maybe two a.m. At any rate, there was not enough time for him to drive to Nonton to hit Valencia over the head.

Candi was distraught.

"Who's doing this? Who has my files? This is too much of a coincidence." Norbie reminded Candi that he said Heather was with him at the house, so he was not to worry.

"But you'll hear from MCU, of that I'm certain. Stay cool. Remember, Candi, no talkie without me being there." Norbie left the restaurant shortly and drove to the police station at West Side.

Time to talk to Beauregard. Rudy's a better bet than the cops in Springfield and Ware because he has better judgment and he can handle the others. Better to bring him into my confidence now. I like action better than reaction; mostly we on the defense have to work hard not to be in reactive mode.

Millie met Norbie with a broad smile saying, "Y'all are not expected. But I'm certain the Captain will see you. I'll just let him know I'm bringing you in."

Norbie knew this was not the normal course of action here at MCU. *Either something's up, or I stand in good stead with one tough police Captain,* he thought.

He was greeted with, "Well, Mr. Cull, what brings you over to enemy camp on a good legal billing day and after that sumptuous vacation in Palm Beach? I thought you would be triple billing to pay for such luxury."

"I would be, but crime just gets in the way, Rudy. Picked up some cop chatter in court today from Nonton! I thought maybe we should have a conversation about it."

Beauregard looked puzzled, enough to let Norbie know that, *Rudy had not connected the dots yet. And if he hadn't, then it was certain Springfield and Ware cops also did not know.*

"A woman named Valencia Longtin was assaulted in Nonton early Sunday morning," Norbie said. "Do you have a bulletin on it because I think we should talk about it. I think it's connected to the other women."

Rudy looked at his computer and then called Millie saying, "Get me that bulletin. It came in from Nonton on an assault by Peter's Brook."

Millie brought it, and Rudy studied the fact sheet, finally stating, "Yes, it's a bad assault, and by water, stopped in time, maybe. Why do you think it's connected, Norbie? Who's this Valencia and because you're here, how is she connected to Candi?"

Norbie noted that what he expected Rudy would say was exactly what he said, that Rudy would catch on immediately, and so, he said with a bit of drama, "Valencia Longtin, the victim, is a former patient of Candido Rodriguez. Before you ask, both Candi and his wife were entertaining a crowd at their home until almost two in the morning and could not possibly be implicated.

"But this is a problem. First, Candi did not get any calls from Valencia. In fact, he has not seen her since she left therapy, almost nine years ago. As far as Candi knows, she was never a dancer or a singer, but was a friend of his crazy first wife."

"Norbie, do you think his first wife had anything to do with any of these murders?"

"No, I don't. I knew her. She's just an explosive and selfish lady and not capable of paying attention to a long sequence of events. She's only in the moment of passion. These murders do take passion, but passion by itself is not enough to explain the facts. Anyway, according to my source, there was a guy in the SUV in Nonton, not a woman, and Candi's ex-wife would never be mistaken for a guy."

"Norbie, it is not in our procedures for a defense attorney and me to be deciding who the murderer is. However, as long as we're here together, let's have a theoretical discussion. How 'bout we talk about your friends at the Boys Club, or maybe again I'll ask you to think about old times.

"Mason has done some analysis and says the perp is inside the group. He doesn't talk out of his ear. You know that. I'll let all this go now because pushing you has never been fruitful for anyone. But get back to me."

"Rudy, I don't want to tell you your job, but get her cell and/or her home phone and see if there are messages on it and what they say. Probably can't trace the throwaway phone sending the message, but maybe the location of service to all of these phones may help cluster the whereabouts of the perp. Perps are often lazy. I have to get back to paid work.

"Candi is willing to talk to you, but only with me there."

That said, the two men said their goodbyes.

Driving back to his office in Springfield, Norbie was again remembering the club, as it seemed to him as a kid. It was a wonderful haven for him, not because he didn't have the best of homes, but because it offered him an island of other kids who gave him a glimpse of the world and how other kids lived. His mother told stories about his escaping from the family room and running out the door when he was only two years old. She insisted he was by nature a wanderer; always looking for something else.

He thought, *You have it wrong, Mom, I just want to know what's around the corner. I don't do sci-fi or otherworldly, no, just worldly. I love to travel. I love to see what other people do and why they do it. Perhaps that's why I love the law. It gives me a view into other worlds, and mostly my clients tell me the truth about their worlds.*

The Boys Club offered me a plethora of experiences I would not have gotten in school, on the playground, or taking trips with my relatives. Not that those activities weren't important to me, but I was in control with minimum behavior rules at the club. We swam, played basketball, learned to cook, and took trips to Sturbridge Village, Mount Tom, and area lakes.

We went bowling, to baseball games, to Christmas parties, and dressed for Halloween parties and Valentine's Day parties. It was a blast. And best of all, I learned about other kids and their families and how they cooked, managed money and discipline, and what were their soft spots; the ones that would make moms and dads' tempers flare.

There were different soft spots I learned, different from those of my parents. I learned the elements of marketing myself. Now, Rudy wants me to remember the negatives about my friends. I knew, when Candi married the first time, that it was a mistake, but I didn't tell him because I may have been wrong and I didn't want to make him unhappy.

Maybe I am overlooking something important, something that I've buried. Maybe it is really time to think.

Norbie stopped to fill his tank at the station on Columbus Ave. in Springfield. In the next car, he saw Jack Ladd giving hell to a woman passenger in his car. The conversation was at the yelling level, so high in volume that a driver of another car went over and asked if there was a problem. Norbie walked over then.

"Jack, maybe I can help out here." Norbie then leaned over to the lady, and she looked like a lady, and said, "Hi, I'm Mr. Cull. You two are raising a ruckus. Perhaps a coffee is in order. Join me at Starbucks, okay?"

The other driver nodded at Norbie, mouthing a thank you and Norbie drove over to Starbucks, hoping his guests would join him in a cool down period thinking, *Some kind of fortune or divine guidance wanted me in this spot today.*

As he waited in line, Jack and the lady entered, grabbing the last table in the crowded café.

Over the three cappuccinos, Norbie met Noreen Sanavista and discovered the loud discussion that, to the naked ear sounded menacing, was, in fact, an argument over running two of his restaurants.

Noreen was vehement in explaining that Jack did not understand the youth of today and their desires. This was important for these two restaurants because the patrons were mostly under thirty. They wanted their music, their food, and a really high-end espresso machine. Jack insisted Noreen didn't understand finance and further, he didn't want to buy two high-end espresso machines.

"Jack," Noreen explained slightly raising her voice, "you never looked at the spreadsheet that shows you your bottom line. You can't mouth off if you haven't looked at the full proposal, and you know I have a Master's degree in finance.

So, get off with the 'you don't know finance.' You're too young to act like an old man who wants things the way they were in 1990."

This topic was discussed, and the two tried to bring Norbie into the conversation. He refused, saying, "I'm just a legal scholar. You'll have to talk to my wife Sheri about the importance of a cappuccino machine in a restaurant. I'll learn about its importance when you retain me to look into it. That's how I learn about the world. It's when I'm on retainer."

Norbie realized these two loved an audience because, when he wouldn't play the game, they changed the subject. Taking the space between two sentences, Norbie asked Jack how much contact he had with the old gang.

Jack responded, "You sound like a cop now. Ash Lent was in the Celtic Belles fishing for info about our crew. It took me a minute to realize he was from West Side Major Crimes. I knew him as a musician. Hell, now the cops are violinists and play freakin' chamber music. It's impossible to know who's what now. I know we knew all those women, but to think that any of us would have anything to do with that kind of violence is a joke. Noreen, have you ever seen me be violent?"

Noreen laughed. "You're an angel. You only get upset when the cash in the register doesn't balance. No, Norbie, he's nuts but not violent. He's a bulldog with no bite. I bet you already knew that. Who else do you want to know about? If I know them, I'll give you an unbiased opinion. Just tell me what you're looking for."

"Noreen," Norbie said, "I'm just interested in relationships the guys had with the murdered women and some other women. Why do the women seem to have all frequented Irish bars? Do you remember ever meeting a Valencia Longtin?"

Both Jack and Noreen looked startled. Finally, Jack said, "How do you know Val, Norbie? Until recently, she hadn't been around. She was in the Celtic Belles recently and was distraught. She said someone was following her. I haven't seen her in years, and she shows up like that. She's dating a congressman. You know him, and you know he's married. She wanted to know if I thought it was just political, that maybe someone was trying to get some stuff on her boyfriend. Val's really smart and has made a lot of money. Is she in trouble?"

Norbie told them he heard from a Nonton cop that she had been assaulted and was now in a coma. They didn't need a road map to figure out that this might be the latest for the serial murderer.

"I am surprised she would be a victim of this murderer," Noreen said. "Everyone says he murders dancers or music people, and serial murderers have a certain type of victim in mind. At least that's what I've heard on TV. She is a handsome woman, but I don't think she was musical, was she, Jack?"

"What are you asking me for, Noreen? I haven't seen her in years."

"Oh, come on, Jack, you probably used to date her along with every other gal who walked through your bars, and you married quite a few of them too."

"Hell, you won't go out with me, so it's not every girl I go out with.

If I married you, you and I would kill each other."

Noreen told Jack, "I wouldn't kill you if we marry, Jack. You'd die of exhaustion in bed first." Both men tried to suppress their smiles, but Jack couldn't and responded, "If you mean it, I'm willing.

"Val is musical but in a different way," Jack went on. "She writes and arranges music for quite a few local artists. She also has a collection of ethnic musical instruments. She does also sing. I picked up what looked like a weird banjo to me. She said it was an antique oud and was very valuable. She then tried to tell me about its eleven strings, peg hole, and sound holes until I told her it didn't mean anything to me. She has old lutes and some old Irish instruments. That's how I met her years ago. She was looking for some weird Irish fiddle and thought some of our players from Ireland would help her source it. That's what she said, 'source it.' At that time, I never heard of anyone sourcing stuff. And that's probably your answer about her frequenting the Irish bars, Norbie."

Norbie excused himself thinking, *It can't be Jack. He doesn't kill them, he marries them.*

14

Incident Sharing

Beauregard spoke with Nonton Chief of Police Pete Provast, who was eager to share info on the incident. He was resistant to any connection between the assault in his city to the murders, explaining that first, Valencia was still alive and second, he hoped this was more of a sexual assault gone awry, rather than an attempt at another murder in a series. "You have to understand, Rudy, this is a city filled with young women. We're keeping a lid on this, and I don't want it out until we know what happened."

Rudy explained it was one of the Chief's own who told a defense attorney from Springfield, who then gave the information to him, thus clearing any suspicions on who it was. "So, it's out there. Don't think it's not going to go all over," Rudy cautioned.

"Get in front of it as an assault, and any other charge by the public can be pooh-poohed away. I'd like to know about Valencia and get into her apartment. If available, I need all calls to and from her for the month preceding the assault, and of course what she did the night of the assault. Can I get your help here?"

Two hours later, Beauregard was at Valencia's home accompanied by Provast and, with one quick review of the house's contents, realized that, if not a musician, she was a lover of music and instruments. The Victorian home had been restored with skill and style. Carefully arranged in her large living room and connected office were two sofas, one chair, a fireplace, and at least one hundred musical instruments. She also had some modern computerized keyboards and piles of handwritten as well as printed music sheets. All were carefully organized but densely packed.

The kitchen and dining areas along with the sunroom were bright and cheery, and he believed they were the location of her everyday life and where she entertained her visitors. The other space was for her passion.

Looking around, he prayed for her recovery, thinking, *This is a woman who has passion and probably musical gifts and certainly goals for her leisure. I want you to live, Valencia, please live.*

Beauregard moved into her bedroom and found a tiny notepad by her bed with three pages filled, each page dated. The contents on each page were the same: "You can't slip away from what you've done. The hurt you've done, Valencia."

"Sorry, Pete," Beauregard said, "but it's connected to the others. Where's her phone? Was it in her handbag or car?"

The two men discussed why the notes were important. Rudy was informed her phone was missing, but the department's IT officer was getting her call log from the carrier.

Rudy said, "First, Pete, you need a protection detail at the hospital. This perp has made his first mistake in not killing her. He doesn't know if she'll live and whether or not she'll have any memory of the night. Chances are if he can get at her easily, he will. Secondly, see at what location the cell phone activity stops. Our department has a great dog who can sniff out anything. Unless that phone's in the water, he'll find it. Let me help you."

Pete said he would call him when he had some info on the phone and would get a security detail to the hospital immediately. He told Rudy there was a briefcase in her car, and it had a handwritten log for her sales calls appointments, with other appointments also noted.

The Chief had brought it with him, and they sat at the kitchen table to review the lists. Provast was the first to say, "She has a regular appointment on Thursdays at six p.m. in Springfield, but she doesn't say who or give an address."

Rudy looked at the book and then on the front page found a list of names. He pointed out Celtic Belles, Thursdays at six p.m., rep.

"This is it. This is a regular appointment. What the hell, she's still going to a bar; and this bar is the center of activity for most of the women who have died. Jack Ladd owns it. You must know him. He owns the 'Irish Crystal' in Nonton."

"I know him. A little arrogant but he's not a bad dude; likes the ladies, but tends to marry too often. Funny thing, one of my cops says he gets taken by the wives. He said that Jack's faithful when he marries but marries some of the worst types of women. The last wife took him to the cleaners. Has to be a fool, because even I know that one wife is a lot to handle."

Rudy inferred he thought his wife would say that about him. The men wound up their search, noting that Valencia made no references to her boyfriend except by the single letter for his first name.

She was careful, but it caused Rudy to say, "What was she doing -- there -- way down by the brook? What could tempt her to go down there early on a Sunday morning, actually middle of the night? Her car was there. She may have followed someone, but would only follow someone so far if she had a good reason and trusted him. Have you traced her travels for that whole night? If she hit the bars up here, maybe there's a witness to identify with whom she may have had conversations."

"Rudy, until now it was just an assault. I don't have a lot of gossip on her. Here, let me photograph a couple of these pictures. I'll send a clean copy to you, and we can both use them to see where she might have been in the last few weeks. You check all of Jack Ladd's bars, and I'll check the whole scene here. This Valencia is a woman of many interests."

Rudy left the Chief there to lock up and headed back to West Side. *I'll have Ash check the local bars, especially the Celtic Belles. A gorgeous redhead like this would not go unnoticed.*

While driving home, he decided to take a detour to pay a visit to his good friend Sergeant Vargas in Holyoke. Rudy was in luck, Vargas was in his cubbyhole and pleased to have a diverting chat with an old friend. It took Rudy a few minutes before he asked the favor. Vargas' reaction was annoying.

"You find your brother, who is well employed and has a great family and you want me to search him out. I just got his name yesterday, haven't told you his name, but you've already met him. Meeting him should be enough. Rudy. You do nothing but look for trouble. You've been a detective much too long.

"I'll do it, but you stay out of it. He'll expect you to trust him and he won't appreciate the new brother investigating him. What makes you think he's lying to you? Can you tell me that much?"

"Luis, simply stated, he's looks and acts too good to be true. I'm afraid that he's not what he seems to be. He wants our families to get together. Before that happens, before I let him in my home, I need confirmation."

"Hell, Rudy, sociopathic friends of our children are in and out of our homes all day. You can't control this stuff. But I will do some research, right away. I don't want you to hold up this relationship. Now get out of here. You're making me see Satan everywhere I turn. Didn't Lizette teach you trust, baby?"

"Yeah, she did and what did it get me? I'm surrounded by serial murderers!"

As Rudy was leaving, he turned and said, "I have an even more important quest. William Locario, Sr., my birth father, may have murdered my mother. He was a real estate agent in maybe Quincy and or Framingham. Liam does not think he's dead, but if he's not dead, he's been hiding for almost fifty years. Can your special friend look for him? I don't want the police involved because it's an open investigation. I'll pay your computer geek."

Lu said, "Go away, Rudy. I'll take care of it all. I'd like to find the bastard who took your mom away."

When Rudy left, Luis called his investigator friend and asked him to research the brother and the criminal father, who commented, "He doesn't know anything about this guy. I'll check him out. Rudy's a police Captain. I agree with him. I'll call you when I get his background. As to the father, I'll find him. The police have jurisdictional limits case rules; I have none of those constraints."

Luis could not help thinking, *What the hell, am I the only guy left with faith in his fellow brothers of the world? Well, maybe not much faith in mothers on drugs.*

The beautiful redhead lying in intensive care brought cluck-clucks from the staff. "How could he do this to her. She's like a sleeping beauty. Look, she's not a kid, but has the most wonderful skin," said one nurse to an attendant. "She never went in the sun, I can tell you."

The nurse went to answer the buzzer for a visitor for Valencia. She told him to wait while some procedures were finished. She would let him visit but informed him of the ten-minute limit on his visit. She saw two more visitors waving to her, and both wanted to visit Valencia.

"You will have to choose who goes first. We allow only one visitor an hour, so go have some coffee. We're very busy now, and I can't have this be Grand Central Station."

When the nurse went to get the first visitor, she was greeted by a police officer who told her that Ms. Valencia Longtin was to have no visitors other than family. She questioned him about the three men who had just tried to see her, and he asked if she got their names. "No, Officer, I'm a nurse, not a social secretary."

The officer asked to be let into the IC unit promising he would stay outside the glass cage. "Are we in any danger, Officer? I mean, she didn't commit a crime. I thought she was a victim of a random assault or an assault by a boyfriend. Is she being targeted? Shall I instruct the staff?"

The officer had no additional facts he could share with her. *This is serious*, the nurse thought. *They think someone's going to get in here to kill her.*

She did a reconnaissance around the unit and saw four new faces. *Well, I am able to check things out that this cop won't be able to. He doesn't know who should be here.*

And she did check them all out, taking the names of everyone in the unit, thinking, *Nothing's going to happen on my watch. June will be on the next shift, and she'll go along with me. Good till tomorrow. After that, I don't know if I will be able to keep these controls in place. This is what happens with evil people, they wait until your guard is down. This Valencia is in too good a shape to have lived a risky life. She met the wrong kind of man. It often happens to the beautiful ones.*

Pete pushed the buzzer on the intensive care unit while speaking to Rudy. "The phone is hiding somewhere over near the assault site. My guys will meet your detectives and the dog in an hour. They go off shift in two and a half. Don't want overtime. Okay? Also, they're sending you the log for her calls. I gotta install some rules here at the hospital. I don't want anything to happen to her. Oops, got to go."

The nurse, whose nametag said Rita Worthy, looked him up and down and asked who he wanted to visit. She had a clipboard and said she wanted some ID. Pete was impressed thinking, *She'd make a great cop; looks downright suspicious of you. Maybe has seen as much as I've seen.*

He explained he was the Chief of Police, saying, "Ms. Worthy, I'm here to put some rules in place relative to visitors for patient Valencia Longtin. I hope you will help with this process. I know you're very busy, but I came to help you understand the seriousness of this request. We believe that Valencia may be in jeopardy."

Rita showed him her clipboard with every name listed with those who came in or out of the emergency room except for known regular staff. She explained she checked IDs.

Pete did a double take and looked at Rita again. He thought, *Even in those duds, she looks good, but more than that, she takes charge. Maybe that's why they call them charge nurses.*

"Ms. Worthy, is that why they call you guys charge nurses because you're so good at taking charge? I'm impressed. Have you explained to Officer Dieter the whats and whys of what you're doing?"

Rita laughed. "I think our name comes from the fact that we'll charge you right out of here if we don't like what you're up to. And as to Officer Dieter, I've explained everything I'm doing. I notice now he's paying close attention to everyone. He even scrutinizes the doctors. I'm taking this very seriously, Chief."

She then told him there were three visitors for Valencia earlier and that when she went to get the first to visit, they all disappeared. She thought it was because Officer Dieter came in. She had asked Officer Dieter if he had seen the three in the waiting room, but he said he hadn't looked in that direction. She described the three men in detail and said she had to get back to the unit. "I have my work to do now, Chief. Drop back someday when you have time. I'm here Mondays, Tuesdays, and Thursdays for twelve-hour shifts. I take lunch downstairs at eleven-thirty."

Pete watched Rita walk, and he thought, *She's got a nice walk. Pushy! But maybe, in this case, I like pushy. Am I coming back to the world of the living? Paulina's been gone three years. God, I'm lonely, and I'm not ready for computer dating. Maybe lunch at the hospital will let me know if I really like her. What the heck, I'm not dead and I am so very lonely.* With that decision made, Pete left for the station.

———————

Petra left for the Brook assault site to meet Weasel and Willi. Weasel was West Side's K-9 officer and strong enough to handle the dog, Willi, who had the reputation of being the best sniffer dog in the western counties.

Upon arriving, Petra realized why the perp would choose this site. There was not much going on in the area. It had a narrow road access which would normally prevent heavy thru or by-pass traffic, and there were lots of evergreens to shade from the road both next to the road and several hundred feet above. Basically, it was an access road, and if it wasn't for the energy of a fisherman, Valencia would be dead. She thought, *This one's different from the others. The victim's car was not on the scene in the other murders. This victim was dragged from her car with the bystanders thinking the perp was trying to put her in his car. Probably was just moving her away to kill her there or perhaps move her to another site away from her car. Why change his style unless he couldn't find a way to get her into his car to bring her out here. What would bring her out here at that time in the morning?*

Petra greeted the Nonton police and said hello to Weasel and Willi. Willi greeted her with the most enthusiasm. She restrained herself from frolicking with Willi thinking, *I just love Willi, but no hugging until we find what we're looking for! Sorry, Willi.*

Willi took eight minutes after sniffing Valencia's scarf before Willi began barking repeatedly. He was at the edge of the brook and stuck near the water was the phone, but it was not in the water.

They all agreed the perp had probably thrown it but missed his mark by about five inches. The brook was quiet with no real movement, and fortunately, there had been no rain or snow or heavy winds.

Petra took another quick view of the site and saw a flash of white half buried in the bushes. She had to dig it out from behind a rock and some weed trees. The effort was rewarded when she read a calling card for The Celtic Belles Bar with this assault location printed on the back of the card, along with a two-a.m. time.

The card was generic, with no owner or manager name, just phone, address, and email. She put it in a separate evidence bag, handed it to an officer, and saw it bagged by the Nonton officers. She thanked them for their assistance and as much as she would have liked to, she knew enough not to give Willi a treat. Weasel would never allow any contact with his canine without authorization.

Not quite happy that she was not in charge of the evidence retrieved, Petra called the Captain who said, "Not to worry. I'll get right up there to push their forensics on the cell phone. As to the card, just knowing the connection to the Celtic Belles is helpful. Don't know if they'll get prints, but we'll work with what we know now. Good work and fast, Bolt. Thanks. I'm really interested that we have such a strong connection with the Irish bars. Candido Rodriguez is not the only common theme in these cases."

15

The Bars

Rudy told Mona he would not be home until late. He asked Ash to join him for a little bar hopping in Springfield and maybe Chicopee, Nonton, and Wilbraham.

"Jack Ladd's bars and restaurants, right?" Ash asked. "Which one will we dine in? There's a great little one in Wilbraham."

Rudy's answer was disappointing. "Remember we are visiting the bars, not as police and not armed. Despite that, we're not in this for the culinary experience, Ash, although from your long, skinny build, I can see you need more food than I do. No, we'll eat some cocktail stuff. I'll drink seltzer, and you drink what you want, with two to three waters between every beer. I need someone sober enough to witness what we hear."

Rudy had informed Ash and Mason about the Celtic Belles Bar card found at the assault site in Nonton. "Petra had observed and relayed the info, that both the victim's car and the perp's were seen at the site; a new development. She wanted to know everything about why Valencia was different from the other victims. She got phone calls, and we believe she was marked. Petra believes the note on the back of the card with the address of the assault location was enough to lure Valencia.

'So, the question is who had access to and could use the Celtic Belles Bar generic card? I thought we'd visit a few of the restaurants and ask questions. Once we do a couple, Jack Ladd will be looking for us. We'll go to the Celtic Belles Bar last. Don't mention the Celtic Belles Bar cards to anyone before we get there, but we'll see if the other bars have cards out for the public. Once we have Valencia's itinerary for that night, maybe the person who left the card out for her also left an image in a bartender or waiter's mind. That's all we expect tonight."

Ash was comfortable in all the bars they visited, much more at home than the Captain. Rudy told him that marriage takes the experience of visiting pubs regularly right out of the everyday for him. They were enjoying themselves and made sure the bartenders knew they were West Side police and were interested in the victims' patronage of the bars. They also found no calling cards for the bars each time that Ash requested one for the address to give to a friend. At the first two bars, the bartenders said they had no cards. In fact, one explained the bar never had calling cards, saying it wasn't that kind of 'joint.'

The bartender in the third bar they visited had some, he thought. He looked for ten minutes and came back with an unopened box of cards for Celtic Belles Bar. Ash asked why the cards were for the Celtic Belles. The bartender, whom Ash thought was a real cutie, said, "Well, Jack's main center of activity for all his pubs and restaurants is the Celtic Belles. So, he's the only one most customers are interested in. This card gives his email and address for the Celtic Belles. His office is above that bar. Anyone interested in this restaurant will always find a bartender available for complaints or sales requests to be forwarded to Jack. Jack is controlling and runs a tight ship."

The detectives left the bar ready to visit the Celtic Belles. Rudy said, "I don't think we have to visit every pub to be sure, but if you're out drinking, it wouldn't hurt to ask for a card from all of them. But only if you don't mind."

"Captain, I'll be happy to visit all of them in the next two nights. I feel it's my civic duty to drink at all Jack Ladd's restaurants to assist the

MCU."

The Celtic Belles was hopping by the time they got there, and there was an Irish singer belting out a good fighting song. Rudy thought, *A call to arms to fight for your country in song is central to this old chieftain culture, along with some of the most sentimental and romantic ballads. No wonder the Irish survived.*

Rudy and Ash ordered at the bar, where Ash started a conversation with the glamorous redhead named Kelli. He spent some time explaining he was a violinist and played Irish music as well as blues, rock, and classical.

She said, "I thought you were a cop. Jack called and said you two would be coming in, and to tell you he would be here in half an hour."

"Kelli, I didn't say we were cops. You either have a picture of us, or you have cop radar. Were you a juvenile delinquent?" Ash grinned broadly.

"You're right, I do have cop radar. My dad was a cop, and let me tell you it's not easy having your dad double checking everything when you're a teen. Although in retrospect, I think it made me think twice about a few risky things. My dad was a sweetheart, despite his cop side. But to answer your question more directly, your friend or I think your boss next to you, is the essence of a cop. He could also be an ex-con. He has great peripheral vision without turning his head. That's what triggered my cop radar if you want to know."

"Well, Kelli, what I want to know is do you have any business cards for the Celtic Belles. I'll give some out to my music friends from Nonton; they don't know where to relax in Springfield."

"Sure, we have business cards for this place. The other bars and restaurants want them, but Jack is a control freak. All cards used have only his contact information and are imprinted with this bar name. The other managers thought he should at least list the other bars, but he pointed out that the less out there for the public to know the better. I quote, 'Someone trips on one of the premises and realizes I own twenty pubs and restaurants and his lawyer's first number in the suit against me will be twelve times the norm.' Jack's a thoughtful man."

Kelli gave him a generic card, identical to the one found by the brook. All this while, Rudy was listening with one ear to Kelli and Ash and to other conversations attempting to assess if there were other activities going on in the bar.

I don't see working girls here, although it is not always easy to tell, he thought. *I don't see drugs being sold, however, that guy over there is smoking a joint. I can't see any real action, and the music appears to be the draw. Maybe on another night, there could be other activities. It is a comfortable bar, and I think I understand why it draws such a crowd. Funny, the age range in here is broader than I thought it would be. Must be the music venue. Probably the norm would be twenty-five to fifty-five-year-olds.*

He scanned the room and saw Jack Ladd and Devon O'Brien enter the room. A wave of people moved out of the way to let the two men move through. Rudy could not help thinking, *Bloody royalty, that's what these guys are.*

Jack Ladd and Devon O'Brien joined them at the bar introducing themselves to the two West Side detectives with Jack saying, "Hi Ash, you are going to introduce me to your Captain, Rudy Beauregard, right?"

The introductions made, the jostling began with Jack Ladd. "Captain Beauregard, you are famous in the annals of Springfield, where every cop watched while the feds and the state police chased a child serial murderer. I guess it took a suburban cop to figure out the kid was the murderer. You guys have all that touchy-feely ability, you know, creating an instinct. You don't always just look at facts. You use your gut."

Rudy decided then and there, *This guy's a jerk.* Instead of reacting, Rudy said, "Jack, we're just two detectives looking for information about what women were in this bar last Saturday night, anytime during the night. I'm specifically interested in a good looking redhead. I've been told you were here much of that evening."

Rudy said what he didn't know, thinking, *I suspect he was here on the busiest night of the week. This is his most active pub. If he wasn't, he'll know I'm just fishing, but he's not a naturally helpful kind of guy anyway. So, nothing's lost in this lie, except my ego if I'm wrong.*

Jack glanced at Ash quizzically as if to get assurance the Captain might be fibbing, but Detective Ash Lent displayed his musician's straight face, the one that says that the twelve-year-old Elvis impersonator should be given a country music award for his performance.

Realizing the detectives were not to be dismissed easily, Jack was wary in his answer. "Look I was here, as you know, all Saturday evening, leaving late, but you can't expect me to remember every woman who comes in here, even if she is a good-looking redhead. Hell, how long was she in? I could have just missed her. Do you have a picture of her? And, you don't mind me asking, since when does a Captain go out looking for a missing person? It's the second time Ash has been here asking about someone. Martina McKay was the one you were interested in then. Everything okay with her, Ash?"

Fortunately for Ash, the Captain played poker well and never flicked an eyelash. "I'm interested in any redheads you know," Beauregard said.

Jack did not give in easily, guessing he was suckered by the first statement that had him saying he was in the bar all night.

"Devon, do you remember any redheads in last Saturday night?'

Devon had been speaking with a young lady at one of the high-top tables and had not heard all the conversation. He did hear this question and turned and answered Jack.

"Don't you remember, Valencia was in here on Saturday and looking good. She was after an open bodhran Celtic drum that the Irish group performing supposedly had for sale. Trouble is that Brian, who owns the drum, was out sick. One of the other guys was going to get it at break, but he didn't have time. She stayed here until about midnight hoping he would be able to fit in a few moments to get the instrument, but the crowd was wild, and he couldn't leave."

"Do you mean Valencia Longtin?" Ash asked. Both Devon and Jack nodded their heads.

Jack asked, "Why, is she contacting Candi too? What the hell is going on? She never mentioned anything to me, but she did say she was going to call Candi and talk with him. She didn't say about what."

Ash noticed Devon's face, normally a ruddy color, turn white. Ash questioned whether Valencia left the bar alone.

"She spent the whole evening sitting at the tabletop next to Devon," Jack said. "She's always liked that table; it's an exclusive table, saved for friends. Valencia's a friend. Nobody would bother her here. Everyone knows the table's for my friends."

Beauregard butted in. "You're saying she sat for three or four hours and no one talked to her?"

Devon answered before Jack, saying, "No, she's good-looking. Lots of guys chatted her up and tried to buy her a drink, but Valencia is able to handle herself. She can get rid of a leach with finesse. Why don't you ask her? Or are you telling us she's missing?"

Beauregard noticed Devon was trembling.

"No, she's not missing," Beauregard said, "but somebody bothered her that night, and we think that someone was from here. Who could it be?"

Jack was now in "prevent litigation mode."

"Wait a minute; you're not saying some guy from here tried to rape her. I don't want the Celtic Belles in the papers. Our patrons are working men and women. We're not that kind of bar. She was perfectly fine when she left here."

While Jack was talking, Beauregard noted further changes in Devon. He appeared almost deflated. "Just tell me she's okay," Devon said. "Please, tell me that."

Ash said, "She was accosted, but is alive. That's all I can tell you. We're leaving now, but we'll be back, or maybe you'll have to come down and sign a witness statement. We'll have Springfield police get hold of you to make it more convenient. But we have evidence someone was from this bar who accosted Ms. Longtin."

When the two detectives were back in their car, Ash said, "I hope I didn't give too much away with the card evidence. And Jack didn't seem too upset about Valencia, more concerned with potential litigation."

"Doesn't matter, Ash," Beauregard said, "Bar owners do nothing but worry about being sued. You know that. Jack has wires into every police department in the area. He'll know within a couple of hours about the business card from the Celtic Belles being found at the assault site. Did you notice Devon's face turned white when he realized that Valencia was in trouble? Wonder what that's all about."

Ash and the Captain spent the rest of the drive back to the station discussing their evening. "We've established Valencia was at the bar that night, but who gave her the bar's business card? If Nonton police don't find prints on it, where are we?"

"Don't worry, Ash, we're getting closer. What we didn't find out, and I don't trust those two to be truthful, are the answers to two questions. Who of their Boys Club crew were in and out that night, and who may have informed the crew Valencia was in the bar that night? Funny thing that I can't quite get is, why so many of the Boys Club crew still hang out at an Irish bar. They're not all Irish. Jack is and Devon partly; Cull is but doesn't go there often; Rodriguez who's Spanish used to go there before he married; Valle goes there and he's not Irish at all; Myron is not Irish and never dated white ladies; and Victor's not Irish. Probably from their connection at the Club. Probably is not important."

16

Almost

Ash was heading home, having been dropped off at the station by the Captain. It was early in the weekday evening. *What the hell, I'll drive by Martina's home*, he thought. *Maybe she'll ask me in for a late coffee. Not compromising at all, since her daughter lives with her and her parents are almost always there. Who am I kidding? I want to see her, to make sure she's safe. And to see her again!*

He pulled up Country Club Road in time to see Martina running down the road from her home toward him. He pulled up as "Let me in, Ash," she yelled. "I saw someone outside my back door. Nobody else is home."

Ash drove Martina back to her part of two attached condo units and did not see anyone. Martina's condo was well lit, but the attached one was dark. To reassure her, he said, "Probably some kids, Martina. Let's go in and talk about it," all the while, thinking, *If it's the perp, he's getting desperate and changing his MO. Why the hell did her family leave her alone?*

Ash calmed Martina down, questioning why she was alone.

"The man who is after all of us has never gone into a home to get the woman. My dad had some errands, and my mom and daughter had an event that was planned long before I ever got any notes.

"Ash," Martina said, "we have to live our lives." Her answer was reasonable, and he felt he couldn't fault her logic.

"We don't know how the perp got the women to the site. He perhaps goes into their homes, despite the fact we have not found any evidence

165

of that. I want you safe. By the way, why were you running toward the country club road? Why didn't you run to one of the other condos?"

"Ash, my neighbors all have pretty set schedules, and tonight, if they are not out at some event, they are at the club. Tonight is the favorite night for dinner at the club. I go sometimes, but thought I would be safer here rather than walking up the road which could be dark later on. I would not want to stay as late as the others and didn't think it was prudent to come home in the dark alone."

Ash investigated outside the back of Martina's condo and saw footprints in the dirt that revealed the person walked out back through the woods. He asked Martina what was on the other side of the woods, and she said there was an access road that went around some of the holes on that side.

"I'm not a golfer, Ash, but I do know the access road breaks off way down low from the country club road and goes around part of the course."

Ash called the event in as a potential "B-and-E with assault intent." He asked the Captain on shift to bring kits to make forms of the shoeprint before the expected morning raid by police.

"It's important, Captain, and may be connected to the Moliano case. Keep it under your hat, but I'll be here to make sure the uniforms don't mess up the site." Ash knew the watch Captain would send his best officers knowing the attempted break-in may have important implications in serial murders.

After his call to the department, Ash went into the kitchen to find coffee and sandwiches on the table, and Martina bringing cake over as well. "That's pretty darn fast," Ash said, "Thank you. I'm really hungry, and those sandwiches look awfully good to me." He noticed that Martina actually blushed.

The two had about fifteen minutes alone before the police arrived with lights and tape. Ash initially directed how he wanted the work done, followed some uniforms with lights into the woods, and saw evidence on the other side of the woods of truck tires impressed in the soft shoulder. He requested casts of those tires.

He spent the rest of the time keeping Martina from going outside to explain to her neighbors what had happened thinking, *Hell, she really wants to tell them why they are being inconvenienced. I'm going to have to explain to her that we say as little as possible, especially since she's in jeopardy. Let the neighbors think there is a serious criminal trying to break into their homes. They'll all become good sentries.*

Ash stayed about two hours longer than was required. He waited until her dad came home and then stayed until her mom and daughter came home and then stayed until it was quite late. He couldn't think of a reason to stay longer. Staying there with Martina was a big perk that made his heart sing. It hadn't been singing for a long time. Martina said, when he was about to leave, "Ash, please come by again for a longer visit the next time."

Ash nodded affirmatively. *How much longer the next time? It's one-thirty in the morning now. Yup, I'll try to figure out how to make our visit last longer the next time.*

On his way home Ash texted Rudy to call him the minute he got over his ZZZs.

———————

Candi and Heather were attempting to calm themselves after discussing the news that Valencia Longtin had been assaulted. Heather pointed out several times Valencia was a friend of Maria Elena's. "Do you think she's involved in this?" she asked. "I mean, Valencia has never been in the bars like the other ladies. Maybe this is another kind of assault. Thank God we had a party Saturday night so you have an alibi from more than just me, and vice versa. Those cops will be starting to look at me next."

Candi gave her what Heather thought was a disgusted look. "You get emotional, Heather. You have alibis for lots of the nights. I, at least, have an alibi for this last one, if it's connected. As to Maria Elena, she's just an ISIS type fighter; nothing secretive. She'd just blow you up with a hand grenade. She is not implicated in this, but I do agree that having every woman attacked by one of my former patients makes me wonder if someone is trying to punish me."

"Candi, can you think of someone you've hurt before? Was there something going on in your office at that time? Did any of your patients commit suicide? Maybe you gave these patients the same advice that caused some common person a problem. Did you ever think of that?

"Maybe all these women have a guy out there who was trying to date or marry them, and all of them turned him down. He could then blame you thinking you knew about him and told them to stay away, all inadvertently, of course!"

Candi was now exasperated with his wife. "Heather, this is real life, not a mystery novel with absurd motives."

Her reply stopped him. "No, it is a serial murder mystery novel with an unknown motive but with a very weird plot."

Heather walked out of the room to make some lunch, equally exasperated with her husband.

———

The Captain, Petra, Ash, and Mason were writing their thoughts under the heading of 'Almost.' Beauregard had been to a touchy-feely police management seminar with a Ph.D. from Columbia in either Philosophy or Sociology. He could not remember which, but the professor said she thought that taking a word out of context and making it a heading could shake the sub-conscious into looking at actions or data or events differently. Since Rudy traditionally loved looking at evidence from different lenses, his colleagues must again join him in suffering this new alternate reality of his. Mason was the first to break out of the mold with, "'Almost' what, Captain?"

The look the Captain gave was chilling and, in an effort to relieve the tension, Ash said, "Well, the 'Almost' label calls for an examination of how or why did Valencia almost get murdered? Why or how did Martina 'Almost' get broken into? Did the 'Almost' for Valencia have a meaning that implies it belongs to another perp? Valencia's phone calls and stalking sites 'Almost' fit the pattern of the others. The attack on Martina is 'Almost' timely for an assault. We have 'Almost' profiles on all the men from the Boys Club group except for Norbie Cull, and his life appears to be an open book and mostly in the newspapers winning cases or at some gala with his wife or at a sporting event with his children."

Petra, not to be outdone by Ash said, "The perp 'Almost' sent phone messages to Lavender James on a timely basis, but not quite. They were delayed until after she notified the police. Valencia 'Almost' got murdered, but fate in the form of an aggressive fisherman was thwarted. Candi "Almost' didn't have an alibi. Maybe the perp thought he would be in bed by ten o'clock like always, but his party ran late giving him the alibi. Consider Devon O'Brien married a thief and the marriage was over in five days leaving him quite poor, "Almost' bankrupt. Or what about Mason's cousin-in-law, Myron Hicks, who 'Almost' got suckered into marriage according to his lovely spouse. Then again, we have Gerry Valle, who 'Almost' got bullied by the kids at the Boys Club if not for Devon O'Brien's Irish charm used on Gerry's mom. Then, Captain, from your report, there's Jack Ladd, who's 'Almost' getting into another marriage. What about the 'Almost' permanent girlfriend who threw him over for a doctor in Boston, Loretta Loren? And finally, are we 'Almost' solving this case?"

Mason now jumped in to redeem himself saying, "Nah! We have 'Almost' most information on the victims for the night they were murdered or assaulted, but not enough. What do we know about the whereabouts of Loretta Loren, Lisa Moliano, Tonya Brown, Janice Shaunessy, and Valencia Longtin? What about the 'Almost' boyfriend of Loretta Loren, Jack Ladd, who may have gone into grieving after her death. Maybe he's an 'Almost' perp. We have 'Almost' their total itinerary for that night but not all."

Beauregard gave a great and loud sigh, saying, "Alright I give in, but notice you've focused in on what we don't know. Let's fill in the blanks. Give me some ideas and get to it. Mason, I've not received a report from you on Cramer. What gives?"

Mason's answer implied there were only so many hours in a day, but that he would have something ASAP. The Captain said, "Meanwhile, I want Martina McKay's ex-boyfriend Brett Blanken looked at. Ash, go after him! He might be a guy who's also looking at her and make sure Martina and Lavender are being protected. Petra, take her to your house for a decorating party and see what else she has to say, especially about this Valencia Longtin." The 'Almost' party was not over.

Rudy took a call from Nonton Chief Pete Provast, raising his blood pressure. At three o'clock that morning a fire alarm was set off by a small paper fire near the intensive care unit. The officer on duty was smart enough not to leave Valencia Longtin. A guy dressed as a doctor tried to move Valencia to protect her, but the officer wouldn't let him. The doctor shrugged his shoulders and went back out of the unit. Unfortunately, the description was only of a man with darkish hair and a good build.

"My guy has white coat syndrome. He sees a white coat, and he can't see anything but that damn white coat. We're lucky he didn't let the doctor move her because I called the IC nurse Rita Worthy, nice woman, at home this morning. She checked all the doctors on call and not one of them admitted to trying to move Valencia. The guy was going to finish the job. My officer said he wouldn't leave her because the staff said Rita would be furious if something happens to this patient. She's coming out of the coma but thrashes a lot. I heard the doctors will put her into a drug-induced coma to watch her while they slowly let her come out of it. It looks like she will come out of it, but how helpful she can be, I don't know. I'll call you the minute she is awake. It may take one to three days, but I think we should both be there for the questioning, Rudy. This was not a sexual assault. This is your serial murderer at work. By the way, I'll have to talk with the DA now there's confirmation that someone wants her dead. Maybe later we can do a conference call together on this?"

"Pete, the guy almost got her today. It's too close. Almost means he's not going to give up. Let's do the conference call now. The DA can authorize the Staties to help out here. You need enough staff to protect Valencia, who is our only witness to date."

17

Last Brother

Petra entered Vic Cramer's corporate private office, led by a handsome older woman who said she was Mr. Cramer's administrative assistant. Vic Cramer rose from his oversized leather executive chair, came around his desk, and welcomed her with a very strong handshake. Petra thought, *You don't need to impress me, and thank God I work out. That handshake was overkill for most folks.*

Petra thanked Vic for agreeing to meet with her. "Let me save you some time Detective," Vic said before she could go further in the conversation. "I know you're here about the murdered women. Gerry told me you were out to see him. He said you tried to get him to roll over on our brotherhood. I laughed at that. I told him that not one of us could ever kill a woman. Maybe we could get into a bar fight that was out of hand; but murder a woman, no. So, ask me what you like about any of us, and I will tell you what I know."

"Tell me about yourself, Vic. I'm interested in your life with your 'Brothers from another mother' at the Boys Club. How often, and under what circumstances, have you seen them since the Boys Club, and that includes recently?"

"Come on, Detective, we were kids, happy kids, given an environment away from family controls. Don't get me wrong, the Boys Club had strict rules for behavior, and you could get into big trouble if you tried breaking the rules repeatedly. The worst punishment was, for any of us, to be thrown out of the Club for a week. The second worst punishment was to be forced to sit under the telephone booth not far from the front door for all the kids to see you were in trouble. We made sure that wouldn't happen.

"Some of the kids' mothers worked during the week, and they'd go home to an empty house or to a strict grandmother. Others of us found home to be stifling. My parents were both heavy drinkers and would get into fights. My dad worked night shift, so he was there all day with my mom, and then there were the fights over gambling.

"It was different for everyone. Gerry Valle had an overprotective mom, whom he truly loved but tried to get away from as much as he could. Norbie had perfect parents but, as he'll explain to you if you ask, he was not a perfect kid. Plus, Norbie just has to know everything. If he were Adam in the Garden of Eden, he would have eaten the apple to find out what it tasted like, long before Satan could tempt Eve. No, Norbie is a 'Curious George' if ever there was one.

"Devon was the typical kid with a stay at home mom who cooked for everyone and a dad who was a mechanic. You know, work all week, watch football, have a few beers, never read a book. He was that kind of guy. Devon's got a couple of brothers and sisters and had his Aunt Lilly. He's in the middle. The father put up with no shit, excuse my language. That's all I know about their early background.

"As to Candi, let's just say he's a lady's man who has been put out to pasture now he's married to Heather."

Petra tried to get Vic to open up about how often he saw the brotherhood now they were adults. Vic was vague, mentioning some drunken parties when they were in their twenties, some weddings, and a couple of christenings.

"You know, Detective, the normal kind of thing. We all went on to live our lives but were happy when our lives intersected. I saw them all at different times because I'm out and about a lot with political events I have to support, real estate parties and conferences, and medical conferences and hospital parties with my wife. I see everyone. I probably see Norbie and Gerry more than the others. When I go to one of Jack's bars or restaurants, I might see Myron, Jack, Devon, Gerry, but I never see Candi much, if at all, anymore."

"Vic, how well did you know all the ladies? We are aware one way or another all the ladies frequented the Celtic Belles Bar and you are and have been in and out of there on a regular basis. You also have been known to visit the club where several of the ladies danced." Petra was thinking, *I'll let you think we know more than we know.*

Vic responded with, "Detective, I'm everywhere in this city and all of Western Massachusetts. My social habits don't necessarily make me a killer or a witness to a killing. I'm normally focused on where I'm able to make my next investment. So, don't think the fact that I know these ladies means anything at all relevant to what you are investigating."

"Yes, your experiences are relevant, Vic, which means you should be able to be as open about these ladies and any relationship you have or had with them as you are open about your friends. I need your insight, *capisce?*"

"*Capisce,* Detective. So, what do you want to know? Remember, I've been married for the last few years, so I've not been dating; you see, married men who date get into trouble." Vic smiled at his little joke.

"A lot of them get into trouble eventually," Petra answered, "because a lot of married men don't understand that rule of marriage. I'm glad you do." They were both quiet for a long moment and then Petra started with her questions.

"Tell me about the four murdered women; Loretta Loren, Tonya Brown, Janice Shaunessy, and Lisa Talbot Flaherty Moliano."

"What's to tell, Detective, all four were drop-dead gorgeous ladies? I knew them all. I tried to get personal with Tonya, Loretta, and Lisa, but I just knew Janice. I didn't date her because Devon made it known she was under his protection. He censured Gerry about the age difference between Gerry and Janice.

"Who wanted to face Devon's fury other than Gerry Valle? And I don't think at that time he even knew Devon was so close to Janice. Dating Tonya was not a lot of fun. She was just looking for a friend.

"I say I dated Loretta, but it was more like going out with your sister, all business and discussion about the world. Although she was intelligent and I really don't know why some pervert would kill her. She was hot looking but not hot acting if you know what I mean.

"Lisa, on the other hand, at that time was exuding sex in every movement. I picked up really quickly that her attitude was about being rejected by her husband. But it was clear after a few dates I was not her type. I tried but with no success there."

"So, none of them bought into you? Didn't that make you angry? I mean no for three?"

Vic laughed. "You mean no for about twenty, Detective? A friend of mine who is using one of those computer matching services says she had to 'have coffee with a lot of frogs before she found her prince.' Same experience here when you meet someone at a bar!"

"Did you meet these women at the Celtic Belles or at the strip club where they danced?"

Vic laughed but showed no discomfort, "I can't remember," he said. "Probably saw them all at both places and other places. I just don't ask a woman out the first time I meet her just because she's good looking. There'd be no possibility for success then unless she was after a psychological one-night stand or drunk; and I don't take advantage of inebriated women, although I certainly wouldn't mind if one would take advantage of me in that state."

Petra was not happy with that remark but ignored it remembering a conversation between Beauregard and Mason instead, *"Serial killers have trouble with animals sometimes. Do we have history on these guys? I mean, did they have dogs in their childhood?"* Mason had asked. *"Some don't because their parents don't let them, but some have them and don't treat them well. I suppose only their old neighbors would know about dead and missing animals in their neighborhoods. Remember Anya, the twelve-year-old serial murderer, whose neighbor's dog was found dead; poisoned it was thought."* This led to her next question,

"Vic, do you own a dog or a cat?"

"No, I don't have a dog or a cat. So, if you have forensic evidence of an animal, you can't accuse me. My wife thinks animals are dirty. In fact, she's a nut about cleanliness. She'd never allow one in our home. I always had a dog when I was a kid. I miss having one, but truly I'm out too much to give a dog the attention needed to have a good one."

"Did any of your friends have dogs or cats when they were young, or maybe have an animal now?"

"Then or now, Detective, what are you looking for? Norbie has always had a dog. He's crazy over them. Myron had a little French poodle when he was a kid. I don't know about now. Gerry's mother wouldn't allow a dog. Devon had a mutt. I've been to his apartment, and now he has a cat. I know because I'm allergic to them. I won't go there again I can tell you that. His cat is a Maine Coon cat. It's pretty friendly, and he likes it because that breed of cat can survive if it gets left out in the cold sometimes, which it does. That breed handles cold weather pretty well. It's a nice cat, all different colors. Jack Ladd has a German shepherd at home. He's always had one, even when he was a kid. Have I missed anyone?"

"No, Vic, and thank you." After a few more niceties, Petra left to return to the station.

———————

Petra was driving back to West Side and pulled over as a thought occurred to her: *Maybe I should do a drive-by of all their homes*

Two and a half hours later she returned to MCU, typed her notes, and tried to look at the big picture. The more she studied the details, the more she thought she was missing something. She asked Ash, who looked like he was daydreaming at his desk, "Want to help me review some details? I need some feedback. You know, another set of eyes."

Ash and Petra attempted to put all the Boys Club members' interviews together with background information into a coherent form. Ash said, "Petra, we can decide what we look for in a typical sociopath and see if any of them fit a few of the characteristics, but these crimes appear to not quite fit the idea of the general pattern of a sociopath. First, if one of these guys did the murders, and it sure as hell looks that way, then he knows all the victims and has been forthcoming about it. So, what can we conclude from that?"

Petra was quick to answer. "The son of a bitch is arrogant and doesn't think he'll get caught, or he's stupid. I'll tell you right now, Ash, none of these guys are stupid."

"Do you think his motive is sexual? There are knife slices on all the bodies, "Ash continued, "post-mortem, mind you."

"It's either sexual frustration, or he's destroying their beauty, which could be interpreted as a sexual hold on him." She continued, "There has to be some hatred against gorgeous women exhibited in the perp's life before, or some event triggering the desire to destroy beauty. Who knows? Every individual has a pressure point with a button when pressed allows movement in a direction that may be extraordinary. At least that's what I think. In most cases extraordinary is well within the constraints of society. Hell, I think I've been married to Jim too long."

"I notice from your report, Petra, that when you went by Gerry, Norbie, Candi, Vic, Devon, Myron, and Jack's properties, you described three of their homes as being 'grand' with perfectly manicured lawns, three as normal and nice, and one was a condo which was well done but not a help in this analysis. What about the economic differences among the group? Maybe the perp feels he has not done as well as his boyhood friends and is taking it out on the women by showing his power over them, even when he can't win in his power over the brothers. For instance, Gerry has a really extravagant home, with, as you report, three vintage autos in perfect shape sitting in the open garage doors. Maybe one of the others couldn't take it."

Petra could not see this as a line on a motive, especially considering none of them were hard up financially, and told him so."

"There may be an obsessive-compulsive behavior presented here," she wondered aloud. "Maybe Gerry, who is clearly dressed to perfection and has an architectural design awarded home, must have order in his life without which he would dissolve into depression or become a monster. The same could be said of Vic, who has a doctor who won't allow animals. Living with a control freak's view of perfection may not be easy.

"Devon and Jack are both currently single, but it doesn't look as if Jack worries about that. He may be getting a new wife real soon from my conclusions on the Captain's conversation. Devon could possibly be one capable of hating good looking women. After all, his only wife of five days not only took him for all his current cash, but she left him a public laughing stock. That experience could fuel a lot of anger. It was a long time ago, though."

Ash shuffled the lists, holding them out at arm's length and laughed.

"I'm trying to take the Captain's advice and look at this list through a different lens. It always works for him. Me -- not so much, except maybe we need to sum up the data on each guy. You know, pretend you're him and figure out what motivates him, annoys him, and turns him on."

The two detectives decided that effort was worth their energy when Millie called. "Captain Beauregard wants you both over to Nonton Hospital. Valencia Longtin is awake."

18

Reunion and Recovery

Jack called Devon, who called Myron and Gerry, who then called Candi and Vic. They left Norbie out of the group for the meeting for good reason. Jack said Norbie would color everything said in the effort to give legal protection for his client, Candi, and, maybe through his professional efforts, pick up something negative about one of them.

"After all," he said, "nobody is able to trust a defense lawyer when the subject is related to his current case."

Candi was the most difficult to convince but agreed when they said he did not have to talk at all, just listen.

"It doesn't matter," Jack jokingly told Devon, "Candi can't shut up, no matter what he may plan to do."

Devon thought, *It only took four murders to get everyone together again. Here we all are, congregated in the Celtic Belles Bar's private dining room with beers and munchies in front of us. God, it feels good, almost safe, to be with the brothers again. Funny I should feel safe when the police are looking at us for their perp.*

Myron started with toasts to fellowship or rather a review of old antics "My cousin-in-law, Detective Mason Smith from West Side would love to be here," he said, "so he could gather dirt on us all. I told him there isn't one of you guys who could hurt a broad, particularly if she was good looking. But they are still looking. Have you all been interviewed? If so, by which detective?"

Vic was the first to answer. "Detective Petra Aylewood, and let me tell you she is one little hottie, and smart too. She wanted to know everything about us, as kids and now. I told her everything I know."

Devon said, "Don't worry, guys, per usual, Vic is claiming knowledge again he doesn't have. Telling her everything he knows took ten minutes is my bet. Vic, how'd you get the dermatologist to marry you? Must just have talked real estate and finance to her and impressed her with your brilliance?"

Gerry was not pleased with the discussion. He demanded they take these interviews seriously. "Look, who else could be the murderer? They are right; it has to be someone who knew all the women. Let's face the fact that it's someone who knew Candi when the women were his patients, and that was seven to ten or more years ago. None of us are off the hook except Norbie. These murders were on Saturday nights, and Norbie has a standing date with his wife when he's not traveling. He's got perfect alibis.

"I think they really wanted Candi for these murders, but Norbie took care of that. I, for one, don't have an alibi. I looked at my calendar, and as far as I have documentation, I was home alone most of the nights of the murders. I'm worried."

"You can't say that!" Myron shouted. "Keep it to yourself. Being home alone does not make you a suspect. There has to be a reason to kill those women. We all knew them and pretty well. I had coffee with Tonya a few times but didn't with any of the others. I haven't looked at the dates to alibi myself, but I'm sure my wife has checked it out and knows where I've been on those nights. I wouldn't and couldn't murder anyone; my wife's leash is too short. Please, stop running wild with your imagination, Gerry!"

An undercurrent of mumbling took over the room, much to Jack Ladd's disgust. He attempted to quell the chaos, only to hear Candi take charge.

"Look, guys, this is a serious problem for me. I've been on the hot seat with the police putting me in the center of these murders, just because I was their therapist. You all know, if that knowledge went public, my living would be destroyed. Fortunately, I have a good alibi for the latest related assault. Not murder, but assault." As Candi spoke, he noticed some eyebrows raised. He then realized he had said too much.

"What assault?" asked Vic. "Who else was hurt? Who? How many are there to be killed? Is there a pool of future victims? This isn't good. I can't have anyone looking at me. Candi, who else was assaulted?"

Jack quickly stood and with his usual panache said, "Look, they have us acting nuts now. Slow down, brothers. None of us would do this. So, let's figure out how we can help the cops and at the same time protect ourselves."

"I want to know who the latest victim is, and why didn't the detective tell me about it. When did it happen?" Gerry said quietly. "Who is she, Candi?" Candi did not answer the question. That fact was not lost on Jack

"Valencia Longtin is the latest victim, but she's not dead," he said. "She's in a coma." Vic, Gerry, and Myron's faces showed shock.

Myron said, "She really didn't go out with any of our crew I can recall. She was a knock-out redhead with class and education and a good job. I haven't seen her in a long time. I don't understand this at all."

Vic couldn't hold himself back, saying, "Looks like the police are right, Candi. You must be sitting on the motive. What's in your files on the ladies? One of them had to have confessed to you about someone stalking them. Did anyone give you a name? We need to know."

Before Candi could answer, Gerry said, "Don't you fuckers know anything about the law? You, Vic, have a wife who's a doctor and should know about confidentiality. Even if Candi knew, he couldn't tell us. Am I right, Candi? You'd get in trouble; could get your license pulled."

"I don't give a rat's ass about protocol," Myron said. "If there is something you know that would help, don't tell us, but find a way to tell your lawyer or the police. I can see from your face that you're what my wife calls 'conflicted.' Do something about it. I'm not staying here. I need to know if one of my closest all-time buddies is not -- do you hear me -- is not a sociopath who kills women. I'm leaving."

Then, Candi received a call that clearly upset him. They heard him say, "We're just trying to figure out why they could think it was us. They're our friends, Norbie. All right, I'll get home."

Norbie clicked off his cell and pulled his car over to a supermarket parking lot to think, actually to face his frustration. *I'm pissed. Defense attorneys should be able to control their clients. My client is supposedly intelligent and understanding of the precariousness of human nature. He's seen some really crazy folks, and despite that experience, he thinks he knows all the vagaries of the human mind and of his friends just because the guys grew up with him. He married a nut case, yet he thinks he can't be fooled. Who knows what the hell he told those guys and, if Beauregard's correct in his thinking, he just told the killer more than he should have. I'll bet on that. If Heather hadn't found his note, Candi would be with them until the cows come home. Why is it I always get the nutty client management problems?*

Norbie's assistant Sheila called him with the news. "Nonton Hospital called. The patient you were interested in is waking up."

Norbie made a call to his connection at the hospital, a doctor whose license he had salvaged after charges made by a young woman who had decided he should marry her. The charges did not hit the courts, but the hospital was ready to dump him just based on the charges until, despite all the privacy laws in place, he found three other men she had tried to compromise. All three had paid her off and then found she broke the contracts by spreading all kinds of dirt about them. She was crazy and fortunately left an ex-husband who had no limitations on sharing her antics against him and others. The doctor was waiting for his call.

"Norbie, she's waking, and the police will be here in an hour. I can't do anything more for you, and I hope this info will help. I don't know if she remembers or not." Norbie thanked him and sat for a minute deciding what to do.

Fifteen minutes later, Norbie walked into Beauregard's office with a big smile on his face. "Let me drive you to the hospital" were the first words out of his mouth.

"How the hell did you find out?" Rudy replied. "I just got the call twenty-five minutes ago. No, you can't come with me. We're police, and you're a defense lawyer and, although I like you, you can't be on this side of the table. So, get out of here."

Norbie's answer was: "Captain, this is your chance. I know a lot about these guys. You have to be careful about pointing the direction of your investigation toward seven well-regarded men. Notice I include myself in that group, despite the fact that I didn't know any of the victims until recently.

"I know I can't be in the room and, when it goes to trial, that a defense attorney helping you would create havoc with your case. But I need to hear what she says about each of them. I think I would know from her descriptions of her interactions with my old friends if there was animosity on their part. I know how they each react, and I'm not protecting my client because we know where he was the evening of the assault.

"Think of me as a behavioral expert who can help you. I suggest you bring both Detectives Aylewood and Lent. They'll throw her off guard enough. This lady wouldn't want to hurt anyone, and she's a saleswoman, so she'll think she's a good judge of character.

"People in sales are not necessarily good in analyzing personal relationships. They're not selling then. They don't have a focus, so they often get sold on a story themselves. Keep a conversation going with me, Captain. I promise you it will have rewards. Don't think I'm interested in covering for my friends. If one is a murderer, I want him stopped."

"I'll take good notes, Counselor, and I'll take both of my detectives. As to the rest, I promise you nothing, but I appreciate your offer."

———

There was a buzz in the Intensive Care Unit at Nonton Hospital. The staff knew the victim had been brought out of her coma and could move all her parts, which was surprising. She knew her name. They knew nothing else because no one was to question her until the police came.

The staff had become quite acquainted with Chief Provast, who had been visiting, sometimes twice a day. This led the staff to think this case was more important than the normal if you could ever say any assault is a "normal" assault case.

Rita, the day charge nurse appeared to take orders from the Chief, which surprised all the staff and doctors. Rita Worthy rarely took orders other than written medical orders. Some on staff thought there was a spark between the Chief and Nurse Worthy and had a wager on it.

One intern said, "Rita's a law and order fanatic. Stands to reason she'd be attracted to him. He's good looking, and he's not coming here twice a day to check on the uniform watching Valencia."

An onslaught of detectives walked in, and they were greeted by the charge nurse. She explained to them only one person should speak to the patient at a time, that she could be overwhelmed and could lose her focus with too much attention. Chief Provast said Detective Aylewood would do the interview, while he, Captain Beauregard, and Detective Lent would observe and take notes.

"Rita, how fragile is she?" he asked. "I mean, we certainly don't want to set her back, but we have a killer at large looking for more victims. Do you think she's logical, and does she show any awareness of how and why she is in the hospital?"

"Chief Provast," Rita answered, "she knows she was assaulted, and that's why she's here, and that she was at Peter's Brook. She said, 'I should never have agreed to go there.' She cried, and we thought it would compromise your case if we asked anything more."

Chief Pete Provast thanked her and told her that she and her staff had done the right thing in not pursuing a story from her. They entered Valencia's glassed-in room. The three men stayed by the door but within hearing distance and Petra introduced herself as the detective looking at her case.

She started by saying, "Valencia, I am very interested in what you were doing the night of your assault. Perhaps you could answer some quick questions for me before we go into detail. They will be simple questions. Is that okay with you?"

Valencia nodded. Petra's first question was, "Do you remember what day of the week you were at Peter's Brook?"

Valencia said it was early Sunday morning. "I looked in my diary, and it was two days after my conference with Bougel Sales, which will be in there. I don't know today's date or how long I've been here, but that should tell you the day I was there. I was there very early in the morning, you know? Really, from the night before."

"Do you remember where you were on Saturday night and why you left where you were to go to Peter's Brook?" Petra asked.

"I was at the Celtic Belles Pub in Springfield," Valencia answered, "enjoying a band there and seeing some old friends. I heard one of the guys in the band had an old Irish fiddle I was looking for, but he wasn't there. So, I stayed. Around midnight one of the waitresses passed me a bar card, saying I could see the fiddle at the location on the back of the card. She said the musician called in and told her he was playing at another bar in Nonton, and to tell me he was going out of town for a month the next day. This would be the only opportunity for him to show me the instrument. I asked if she knew his name. She said he told her a name, but she couldn't get it with all the noise from the band. At the time, I was being approached by a couple of guys trying to talk to me. Somehow at the time, it seemed reasonable to me to go; it was an opportunity. Musicians don't have salespersons hours, and I really wanted that fiddle. How stupid of me to fall for that. I should know better."

Petra tried to comfort her and then asked, "Valencia, just who would know about your love of old ethnic musical instruments? Who could guess you would be willing to go to Peter's Brood in Nonton at two in the morning on a Sunday?"

"I'm afraid there are many who know about my obsession. Certainly, many Irish musicians and singers, Jack Ladd, Devon O'Brien, Vic Cramer, Myron Hicks, Gerry Valle to name a few and my girlfriends and family."

Petra asked if Valencia had ever sought psychotherapy for help with life's issues and was told, "Yes, quite a while ago." Valencia said in a surprised voice, "for quite a few sessions. I saw Candido Rodriguez, who was wonderfully helpful. He's such a lovely man, and he helped me see I shouldn't look at what everyone else was doing in order to measure the value of my own choices in life.

"I'll probably go see him after I get out of the hospital to help me deal with this. I feel very afraid, Detective Aylewood, very afraid. Just who would do this to me?"

"That's what we're trying to discover," Petra said. "Do you remember what happened after you pulled your car up next to the brook?"

"I remember I got there a little early and there was already a dark SUV parked there. I waited until the right time, the time written on the card, before I got out of my car. When I first arrived, I thought there may be lovers in the other car, but I saw no movement and assumed it was just a parked car. When the time arrived, I turned on my inside and outside lights so if someone was there, he could be certain it was me.

"I got out of my car and started to approach the other car, and I felt an awful pain in my head, and that's all I remember. I do remember seeing just before I got to the SUV, a truck parked further up with no lights on and wondered if that truck held the person I was to meet, but it was kind of tucked into the bushes."

Petra asked if Valencia smelled any odors or heard any unusual sounds before she was hit and was told she may have smelled a men's aftershave or cologne but could not be certain.

"Maybe I heard something because I remember looking away from the SUV while moving toward it. I looked toward the other parked car trying to see the occupants. That's all I remember."

Petra asked many more questions, but there was no additional information. Finally, she asked Valencia, "Did you ever have a dating or even a romantic relationship with any of the guys from the Celtic Belles?" The reply surprised Petra.

"Well, I dated a lot of the guys, but there was nothing there for me. They were a little older and speaking quite plainly, their attitude towards women was a bit Edwardian; you know, the idea that women have a certain place in life. Although I think Devon and I could have had a chance if he hadn't married that thieving wife of his. It colors his attitude towards women. I wasn't about to put up with a distrusting boyfriend suffering from the sins of his ex-wife. I told him to get help from Candido. I don't know if he ever did."

This response triggered Petra's next question.

"How many of those men in addition to Devon, Vic, Jack, Gerry, Myron, got counseling from Mr. Rodriguez?" Valencia smiled.

"I saw them all at Candi's office with the exception of Devon. We used to kid about the fact that Candi should give us a group rate. I knew lots of women there from the pub and some dancers from a joint in downtown Springfield."

They were interrupted with word from the nurse it was time to leave. Rita Worthy said her patient was getting worn out, adding, "Tomorrow is another day."

19

Hanging Threads

Captain Beauregard was guiding the MCU detectives through a review of the unit's cases for the week, working as quickly as possible to allow time for an analysis of the serial murder cases. Most of the other work related to an armed robbery of a convenience store, two burglaries, and a home invasion and serious assault in a suspected drug house. Much of this work involved other units such as Crime Prevention and the Drug Task Force. After an hour of tedious details in working each case, the detectives were ready to focus on the murder of Lisa Talbot Flaherty Moliano and the related murders.

The Captain asked each detective to list new information garnered from their reports that was not on but should be on the murder board, particularly with reference to the Boys Club.

"We'll use that name to identify what appears to be the only direct connection to all the victims. I think we can rule Norbie Cull out, simply because he has an alibi for all four murders. He was in another part of the country. Now there is the outside chance these murders are a conspiracy and he could be involved, but I'm not investigating something so farfetched. That leaves six possibles. We have not tied their alibis down, with the exception of Candido Rodriguez. He has an airtight alibi for the assault on Valencia Longtin, so, for now, he's not on my radar unless you have discovered something. Let's start with you, Mason. What about your cousin's husband, Myron Hicks?"

"I reviewed most of that with you but to summarize, he lived near

Lavender and Tonya at one time, is a pool shark, liked to go to the bars with the Boys Club guys, did not date any of the ladies, knew all the victims including Lavender, Martina and Valencia, played football with Lisa Moliano's first husband, said that Vic Cramer is a 'guy's guy, not a womanizer.' He also said that none of the Boys Club members could hurt a woman, that Candido Rodriguez is a prince among ladies men, that Norbie is smart and for a little guy, can handle himself, and that Gerry Valle wasn't street smart. Also, he appeared to want to be helpful and to be happily married. We all have learned that Jack sent some and maybe all of the ladies to Candido Rodriguez for counseling."

Ash was the next to summarize what he had garnered.

"Look, from my perspective, Jack Ladd may have been really in love with Loretta Loren. He was always a regular at the strip club until she died, and he dated her. His second of maybe three marriages cost him a good portion of his assets. I don't know why the third wife divorced him. I don't know the timing of that marriage and divorce but will get it. It's in the court records. Jack knew all the women and saw them all frequently. He and Devon are together often. Devon has some reticence about marriage which caused him to lose out on Valencia."

Before Ash could go any further, the Captain said, "Enough. We're going over the same territory. There is nothing new. What did we discover from Lavender and Martina's therapy files? We should also get Valencia to sign out her therapy files. Petra, give us the scoop."

"These files are not juicy like you hear about on television. Valencia dated Devon O'Brien, but basically inferred his failed marriage burned him, preventing her from continuing in their relationship. I got the impression she stopped it, that it was not him. Captain, I read in your report you once met his ex-wife. Her take on Devon was he was against multiple marriages. Don't know if that means anything.

"Valencia has never been married but is known to be having a long-term affair with a married congressman. Maybe Devon has a motive. Maybe Devon and Jack, who are together more frequently than most friends, are a killing pair. Jack mourned the break-up with Loretta and Devon was smarting that Valencia replaced him with a married congressman. I don't see a big connection to the others, although Jack certainly dated or tried to date them all."

"Petra, tell us about Vic Cramer and Gerry Valle."

"Vic Cramer is a let-me-tell-you-everything kind of guy, which of course makes me particularly suspicious. He's like all politicians who, in my mind, pretend truth and empathy while they look around the room to see if there's someone more important to speak with. We were alone together with all his charm. He gave a version of his friends' history at the Boys Club, but I don't for a minute believe it was inclusive of any negative experience. He is absolutely certain not one of his friends would ever hurt a woman."

Ash noted, "I'd like to know more about his marriage to the doctor. Have we got a report yet from forensics about the foot coverings used at the hospital? If we could connect the type used to the ones used at the murder scenes, it could be helpful. Vic would have easy access to the coverings."

Beauregard questioned, "Ash, that job was yours. Remember, we wanted to know how much the perp weighed and if it was consistent over all the crimes."

"Well, Captain, I can't control the speed of forensics work, but I'll go call on it now. I do have an approximate weight on the perp at 180-195 pounds, and the weight is consistent even with the perp at Valencia's assault. I'm waiting on the make of the shoes or boots from the tread at the scene of the assault. I think they're boots. I still think it's funny no foot coverings were used in the assault. Our perp is getting careless."

"Petra, what about Gerry Valle. Tell us about your interview with him."

"Captain, the guy is handsome in a debonair fashion. He's perfectly groomed, and I think he's OCD if I've ever met one. He straightened his placemat three times over our espressos. He's noted for being quiet, but he isn't quiet when he's talking about himself and appearances are really important to him. He's quite successful. He's a distributor of construction supplies and equipment and from the outside looking in he's really made good.

"I drove by his house, and it is an *Architectural Digest* centerfold, with multiple roofs, stone facing, porches, and landscape to die for. He was very sensitive when I questioned him about dating younger women. Gerry's noted for being all logic. He has everything to turn a woman on, so why is he still unmarried? I'll tell you the answer; because it's apparent he's only about the superficial. Finally, he's the only one I questioned who told me he would not talk to me again without his lawyer."

Beauregard asked, "How tall is he, Petra?"

"He fits the bill, Captain. As do Jack Ladd, Devon O'Brien, Candido Rodriguez, Myron Hicks, and Vic Cramer. Only Norbie is left out. By the way, Gerry says Devon O'Brien has the verbal charm equal to Norbie Cull. Do you think it's true, Captain? He certainly tried to charm me.

"I can tell you he is a kind of portrait of the slightly gray, but well-built man seen on television advertising high-end wines. He is easy to talk with, but I think he's a lot deeper than one would think. I don't buy his easy openness. I believe he is a lot more philosophical about life but also deeply distrusting of women. He may have liked Valencia, but she, at the time of his interest in her, was no older than Janice was when he prevented Gerry from seeing her. So, something's up there.

"Maybe, Petra, he thought of Janice as a daughter; if you know someone when she's very young, some of us are socialized never to think of them in a sexual way. Or for maybe a good reason, he didn't trust Gerry. We need more information about those two and about Vic."

"It's time to rule some folks out," Mason spoke out. "I'm starting with Myron Hicks, my cousin's husband. Now, I know what you're thinking, that it's a black thing. Nope, you know me. Unlike my family, I'd put away a murderous dude if he were my father. Let me tell you why he should be excluded and, Ash, don't give me that suspicious look."

"I didn't look funny. I'll wait for you to clear him," Ash said. "Not to worry, Mason, I don't think you're a racist at all." They all laughed.

"Well, I've talked to everyone in the community and no one, I mean, no one, has ever seen Myron date a woman who wasn't black. Believe me, he couldn't keep quiet in a city the size of Springfield, but he's noted for frequenting white Irish bars, mostly with the Boys Club brotherhood. He has quite a flooring installation business, lives well, and with my cousin watching him, is home every night or else. Top it off, just about anybody who has ever known him thinks he's totally lacking in having a violent streak except in self-defense. He is tall enough, and he does have a navy-blue SUV as one of his company cars, but regularly drives a Volvo wagon; not even a brother's car. What do you think?"

Beauregard said, "We'll put him aside, Mason, but not away. We don't know everything about anyone, even those closest and dearest to us. You can put him aside for now."

Mason went on. "I'd dump Norbie because he has an alibi for every murder and he's too short, and he doesn't have an SUV and without prevarication, you like that word, I'd bet my life he's innocent."

They all agreed, with Petra saying, "Hell, can you imagine trying a case with him as the perp?" Heads shook like a two-year-old saying "No, no, no."

Mason concluded his exclusion from suspicion with Candido Rodriguez. "Has an alibi for the assault on Valencia and unless it turns out she was attacked by a different perp, it rules him out. Also, he's noted for running away from confrontation. His soft talking is his defense weapon. His vicious first wife, who created hell for him, never riled him enough to break furniture or hit her. Naw, I just don't see him as the perp."

Ash couldn't keep silent. "So, the two minority potentials get a pass. Not racist, Mason, just maybe you think only white men can murder. Tut!"

Petra laughed and said, "Good thing we're not looking at women as perps, Ash. You know women couldn't possibly murder! If you accused them, I could call you a misogynist."

Beauregard stopped the conversation with a hand movement and said, "In this politically correct environment, you, as detectives, know we don't kid about this stuff. The next thing I know is we'll all be brought in for a harassment suit. Knock it off. I know you think it's funny, but we have to careful about our language. As to you, Mason, I'll give your guys a pass for now, but we don't have all the evidence in yet. Your arguments are logically based on what we know now, but logic doesn't always cut it in a serial murder case."

Millie walked in with a report for Ash. He scanned the report and summarizing it said, "The shoe coverings are of polypropylene breathable, fluid-repellent, and of a spun bond material. They are non-skid and probably a size large, commonly produced for medical and other use by companies like Medline. The boots at the assault scene are between a ten and a half and an eleven and a half. Forensics couldn't tie it down closer because all the prints that were usable were incomplete.

They're estimating based on the heels and a partial front last. The boot has a round toe, shaft measurement of maybe six inches, a heel of one and a half inches, and a synthetic sole. Several makes of boot meet the criteria; one being Red Wing Heritage which is priced on the high side. One Red Wing model has the look of a Doc Marten's."

Before Ash could continue, Mason said, "I'm right again. Myron Hicks has a size thirteen shoe, and Candi has this skinny foot, probably size eight and a half, and would never be caught dead in a work boot. So much for my racism! You may kiss my ring as you apologize for your insults." Ash ignored Mason.

"If it's a Red Wing Heritage, it is not exactly a normal work boot. This is a higher priced work boot. The kind some businessmen wear to show they're real men without giving in to the 'are you wearing Doc Martens' concept."

The Captain was antsy. "Cut the conversation," he said. "Maybe we can put your guys on permanent hold now. So, let's look further at what we have. I have a report from the detectives attached to the DA's office on Tonya Brown. It seems the owner of a cottage two cottages away from the murder site in Wales is a snowbird. He just returned from Florida and while drinking in one of the local bars was told about Tonya's murder. He knew Tonya way back when she was drinking and running around and used to let her use his house when he wasn't around for what he thought were romantic trysts.

"He said in the report and I quote, 'She had a body that would make you want to sin, but she wasn't interested in an old guy like me.' He's a retired fireman. He said his neighbor said that she would come with a man, but it didn't look to her like a romantic tryst. They would just sit and talk. He was handsome looking from a distance, so the neighbor tried to meet him. She brought over a cake supposedly for me, and knocked on the door, Tonya answered but wouldn't let her in. She just took the cake and said thank you and shut the door. My neighbor Lolly was furious. She baked a cake for nothing." The investigator talked with Lolly who still lives there, and she only remembers the man being tall and well built.

"Just why would Tonya go to Lake George in the non-season early on a Sunday morning?" Petra asked, "Did she trust the guy? He must have been what she thought was an old friend."

"Not necessarily, Petra, she maybe went there to de-stress. The report says she had a key. Further, if I am able to finish relaying the report, it says her phone was never found, but the police got her record of calls. She called her mother about three hours before the estimated time of death, telling her she should hear from her in a couple of hours, and her mother never initially told that to the police when she called to say her daughter was missing. The cell calls record show calls received from several throwaway phones; one of those at ten o'clock on the Saturday night before the murder."

Mason said, "So, she got a call from some guy she trusted, went to a place with no lights or people, and got murdered?"

Petra said, "Yeah, it is kind of strange. If she trusted him, why did she call her mother to tell her she would call in the early hours on a Sunday morning? The mother knows something and is keeping secret about it. Could be the two women didn't want her husband to know. Something's there."

The Captain said he would notify the chief in Wales to follow through with a second interview with Tonya's mother. "Good point, Petra, it's possible the mom knows more. "Beauregard then initiated a conversation about the foot coverings, saying, "I don't think every person would think to use medical foot coverings, and I don't for a moment think we will be able to trace the foot coverings to a vendor. Chances are they're sold to a hospital, construction or cleaning company in bulk. What I think we are able to do is look into the work life of our five possible suspects to discover if foot coverings are ever used. This has to be done quietly. Petra, you've been to Gerry Valle's offices, and you said they are in pristine condition. Maybe the cleaning people at his offices use them. You know, after vacuuming so you don't leave shoe prints on those broadloom rugs."

Laughing, Petra responded, "Could be a requirement at that place. Gerry's compulsively neat and would require his maintenance people to be just as careful."

Beauregard wondered aloud, "Do we know how the perp got the ladies' cell phone numbers?"

"Well," Petra answered, "Lavender said when I questioned her that everyone has her cell number. I didn't ask about the other women. Honestly, I don't think Martina would ever give her number out, because of her problems with her ex-boyfriend."

"Captain," said Ash, "the therapy files we reviewed were pretty boring on those two. Lavender's had the most content in length, but that's because she never stops talking. They were the most discreet ladies and didn't mention names of people other than their current boyfriends if they had one. Martina did not have one. There isn't anything much there other than they all mentioned going out to bars during their time in therapy. I think that avenue's a bust, but maybe the other therapy files have something.

"You have a close relationship with Mr. Cull. He could tell you if there's something of interest in the other files. Don't tell me he doesn't know, Captain. I'll bet Candido went back through those therapy files and even if he wouldn't let Cull see them, he may infer from them something of value. Remember he thought he was on the hot seat for a while. That can be pretty motivating to push him to reread his files carefully."

"Not sure Candido would tell Mr. Cull, but even if he did, I'm not certain Cull would tell me. They take that confidentiality stuff seriously. It's time to get back out there investigating the shoe coverings, Tonya's mother's story, cell phone numbers availability, and our five persons of interest alibis. Mason, you go after the alibis."

20
Family

Rudy hurried to a meeting with Luis Vargas at the food court at the Ingleside Mall in Holyoke. He had asked Lu, why there? Luis explained his investigator would be with him and, in Holyoke, if you meet at the mall no one would think anything surreptitious was happening. Not one to question the wisdom of a street cop, Rudy agreed but was uncertain his meeting the investigator was a requirement. After all, he was sure the investigator's search methods may not all be by the rule of law.

The mall was not very busy today, and Rudy spotted Luis on a table under the escalator not far from MacDonald's. It was a good choice he thought. *"Wormy looking little guy, unshaven, but hell everyone under thirty was unshaven today, even Prince Harry on his wedding day. After all, this guy is a computer nerd. Probably hasn't seen the sun in a year.*

After introductions around, Luis said, "Rudy, Maurice has some information for you which will require you to make some decisions. He has found William Locario, your birth father."

"Well, it does not sound good, Lu, just from your introduction. Maurice, just tell me!"

Maurice opened his folder and skimmed the contents. "Captain, William Locario is at the Holyoke Soldiers Home. He's a veteran and was living with some lady who had some connections and got him in there. He was lucky to find a spot. Apparently, according to their staff, William has memory problems, liver problems, maybe fits of crying, and some self-harm practices, as well as fits of uncontrollable rage and acting out. He's on some heavy medication to prevent him from harming himself or others.

"Let me tell you, Captain, he was fortunate he was admitted in the facility, given that the police in Quincy and Framingham have old warrants out for him. The FBI's National Crime Information Center didn't exist at that time, allowing William to escape. I think maybe you have to settle on his being punished at the Soldiers Home by his own body and guilt. What do you think, Captain?"

Rudy looked particularly stressed. "Wouldn't you fucking know it! He killed my mother, and now I'm supposed to feel sorry for him. He doesn't have my name so he could be tried in Framingham without too many problems, public relations-wise for me, but there's not enough evidence to convict him. All the evidence is old. My mother and her second husband are dead. Only Liam is alive as a witness, and his testimony would not be taken seriously. He was too young. Even a lousy lawyer would crucify him on the stand, despite the fact that he looks pretty tough and could probably handle himself quite well. It would not be a triable case. If the state won, what would be the punishment? No, the bastard is not chargeable. I don't want to see him. I don't want to remember his face. What if he looks like me, or Liam, or my kids? Why should I open up that possibility?"

"You're doing it again, Rudy," Lu responded, "running away again. You've finally faced your background. Finish the job! Interview him. He has good memory moments according to the file. Might take you two or three visits, but you should get the truth out of him. Make him know you've survived and think highly of Mavis. Do it for your own sake. It is important for you to put all the ghosts away."

"Captain, there's more," Maurice said. "I investigated your brother

Liam. He is both feared and loved; feared mostly because of his business acumen and loved because he is what he appears to be, a good ole boy. As a boy, he got into some trouble such as fighting, stealing an English exam and giving it to the football team, stealing the cheerleading team's clothes, and giving a pro-pot speech in front of the class assembly while a junior in high school. Altogether appears to be typical hijinks for the time.

"There is a note in his school file about his adopted parents. I'll read it to you. It quotes his mother, 'Liam is just a normal red-blooded American boy fighting the constraints of a system set up for those who just want to go along. Not once have you spoken about his standing up to the class bullies, or his tutoring his friends in math or his service for the veterans. I will not have you just look at a few peccadillos when he's clearly a superior student with a high moral interest in our society.' Looks like his adoptive mama was not overwhelmed by the school administration's perspective on her son!

"He is well thought of and as far as I could find out is a faithful husband and does a lot of work for the community. He's also quite wealthy, Rudy. Mavis' kids took after her, I think. Rest easy, Captain."

"I guess, Maurice, that you have found a potential felon, presented him to me and told me that I can have faith in my newly identified brother. That's quite a day's work. How much do I owe you?"

"Nada, this is on Luis, whom I owe. Relax, Captain, go have a party with your brother and his family and your family. Share it with your wife and kids. Family's everything, that's something I discovered the hard way."

Maurice left Luis and Rudy alone to talk. Lu started a discussion.

"Let's say your father says all kinds of shit, you know like, 'I'm sorry. I really loved your mother. It was that bastard lawyer she married.' Don't believe a thing he says. That's not going to bother you, because you know it's fucking bullshit. Let's say he's all apologies saying, 'I didn't mean to kill her. It was an accident. I loved her and William and you.' Now you know that's bullshit because it looks like he didn't even know about you, and it's what all those guys say.

"Go see him. Let him think you're from the police, not too much, just a little pressure. He doesn't know who you are and if you're questioned later, well you just say you're his son. Get the truth out of him although I really don't think he'll ever tell the truth. Read this file as we travel. You'll find holes in it to set him up. See him as he is. It will set you free. Go now. I'll go with you. We'll get it done, Rudy; get it done!"

Luis Vargas was well thought of at the Soldiers Home, and with very little fanfare the two officers were directed to William Locario's room. The nurse said William could be the most charming man and then in a quick turn-around be the most disgusting man. She explained to Sergeant Vargas because Rudy did not identify himself, that William's lady friend was devoted to him. She brought him food and clean clothes regularly, but she appeared to also be afraid of him.

The man sitting in the chair by the window looked up with a bit of confusion and said, "Billy, is that you, finally?"

Rudy thought, *You son of a bitch, you look like me. Only one of my kids looks a little like me, but you, you bastard, I have to resemble you.*

Rudy introduced himself as Captain of the Major Crimes Unit and let him believe he was from Holyoke. He flipped his badge, not leaving it open long enough for William to see the city on it.

"William, let's talk about Mavis Eaton and her death, which we have evidence you caused. Thankfully,"

Rudy continued, "There was enough forensic evidence saved all these years later to finally pull you in. You've run long enough. I want your story."

If either of the two policemen thought for a moment William was not all there, they saw all the clouding leave his eyes replaced with a wary intelligence.

"What evidence are you talking about? Mavis wasn't found until three years after she was killed and she was found in the woods. There'd be no forensics left. Who do you think I am, some rube from the sticks?"

"No, William, I think you murdered her, partially buried her in the woods, and disappeared so you wouldn't be discovered. But forensics was not a honed investigative tool at that time. It is now. The funny thing is that even in the woods, there was a little bit of protection under two rocks and some wood. We found and matched your DNA. You're in a federal facility, William, we have your DNA."

Lu thought, *Talk about bullshit, Rudy is really laying it on. How could we get his DNA without a warrant?*

William Locario's face drained of what little color he had. Rudy thought, *He must have been good looking and never that dark. In fact, my skin is more olive, maybe from Mavis' Greek side. He's slimmer than I've ever been, but he's an old man, and maybe that's the reason. My dad Roland is older, but he's still a solid man despite being in his eighties. He's thinking maybe he can con me. Well, I'll put on my dopey look and let him think I'm falling for his poor old man routine.*

"You have to understand my wife Mavis was cheating on me. She had a baby by that divorce attorney. Nobody cheats on me. It was a crime of passion. She tried to hit me, and I reacted, the same as any man who'd been cheated on would. She was seeing him before our divorce; she was a bitch. Worked in all these bars and told me she was working in nursing homes. She was always looking for a man, just because she was a looker and could get them. Her family wanted nothing to do with her.

"She's lucky I married her and saved her from disgrace. But did she appreciate anything I did for her? No, she was a lost cause. Why do you think she didn't go home after our divorce? I'm sorry, but in a way, I'm not sorry. She and her asshole husband cheating on me. She hooked me into marriage by getting pregnant with Billy and then gets pregnant while she was cheating on me. He was such a sissy, all brains, no brawn, and he has all that power to make me give Billy up. I thought you were Billy, but I guess you don't look like me. You're not tall enough."

"William, tell me about what Mavis did to make you so upset. I mean it's important It will help us to wind things up. I can't make my recommendations to my chief about leaving you here and not going forward with an arrest unless I can tell him the whole story. He's a stickler for details. You know, he's got to cover his ass. I need all the details. We know many of them from forensics, but where was she killed because she didn't die where she was found. Help me out here, William."

"I don't believe you. Forensics can't find anything after three years in the snow and storms and with animals going after the body. There'd be nothing left."

"So, William, you're now an expert in forensics. How do you think we found you? We even have DNA from the scene. We didn't just find you by chasing you as the husband. The science has gotten ahead of us. There is some pilot program out of Boston University examining all open murder cases, and they finally got to yours, tested the DNA that was on the body that wasn't Mavis', and lo and behold, whose DNA shows up – yours. I told you before; the stuff can be hidden in strange places. We know the body was moved because of how the blood settled in the body. You just can't fool them, William. You should have eliminated the body by burning it or something. You left the trail for us."

Lu tried to keep his face from showing his thoughts. *What a serious piece of fiction he's telling. Why the hell is this guy still talking to us? It must be old age, or he really believes that Rudy will leave him here. Christ, maybe he will. It's a perfect solution for him.*

Rudy whispered, "Don't fuck with me, William. Give me the whole story, or I'll call for a cruiser, and you'll sit in a local cell and wait for your arraignment. The press will love this. You'll be famous. Your lady friend will write a book about living with a domestic abuser and murderer. It'll be like a retirement plan for her. I'll even give her the name of a ghostwriter. You choose."

"Fuck her and fuck you. How do I know what you're saying is the truth?"

"No problem, William, you'll know when I place this call."

"Captain whatever your name, just because you have some lousy DNA evidence doesn't mean you'll get a conviction. The jury will feel sorry for me. I'm an old man who's sick. Besides, a trial will be interesting, more interesting than sitting here."

We have definitely lost in this sideshow of lies, Lu thought. *The guy's been stoking the system for a lifetime.*

"Ah, William, just how naïve do you think a jury would be? They hate domestic abusers and remember what you did to Mavis. You cut her – a lot. You killed her, and you cut her, and you run away and never saw your kid. So, you want a trial. Good for me! I can watch you suffer getting to court, sitting in a cell, waiting to be called up. Won't matter if you don't feel good that day! If you can't go, no problem, they'll hold the trial without you. I get the story, or you get the trial. Doesn't matter to me! When I first saw you, I felt just a few qualms about addressing this injustice, but I don't feel that way now. So, give me the story or you get a trial. I want an answer now, not tomorrow or the next day; now. This is D-Day."

William did not answer. Rudy motioned to Lu and said, "Sergeant, you watch him while I go in the other room to make the call."

Lu walked away for a moment and told Rudy, "I think the son of a bitch is trying to figure out just how uncomfortable a trial will be. If he says no, just what will you do next? I hope he doesn't lose it."

Before Lu could return to his watch, William yelled, "I want a deal! I want to see my son and explain his mother was a bitch. She took my son away and her big-time lawyer husband forced me to sign the documents. It's not right. I want to see him. I want to know that I've left something behind me."

Rudy's reaction was immediate, and his voice in a hoarse whisper said, "Your son is dead. He was not well taken care of by the system. You're responsible for that because you killed his mother. Your son had no children. So, I can't make a deal unless we pretend I'm your son, and if I were, I'd kill you myself."

Lu was about to put his laptop away thinking, *I hope Rudy doesn't mean it.*

"How'd he die? I'll sue Social Services if they were responsible."

"William, you're a piece of shit. Your son died of a drug overdose. You didn't care enough about him when he was alive, so now you won't care enough to mourn him. Your answer now!!"

As Rudy moved to leave, William stopped him. "I killed her, and I'm happy she's dead. No woman ever left me and what good was she anyway? She only thought about the kid. She said she was ashamed of me. She wouldn't visit her family with me. They had this great cottage in Hull with boats and deep-sea fishing equipment. Do you think she'd take me there for a weekend in the summer with all her relatives there? No, she said I was coarse. Did she think her fuckin Greek relatives were angels? I knew what some of them were into with their restaurants and amusement stands.

"What a joke. They'd sneak gifts in the mail for her and Billy. When I found out, I'd burn them right in front of her. I told that bitch, 'If his daddy isn't good enough for them, then their presents are shit to me.' She called me a monster. I moved her away. Sometimes she'd sneak to visit them, but after a few beatings when I discovered her deceit, she finally got the message.

"Ashamed of me. What a joke. She gets pregnant by her lawyer, that's the same way as before. She gets pregnant again before the ring. She was nothing but a little hottie putting out for anyone. She thought he was better than me. Then she gets her just desserts, he dies. You think I was going to take care of a kid who wasn't mine?"

"Look, William, I don't want to hear about your disappointment in Mavis. How did you find her to kill her? She ran away. Why didn't you find where Billy was? You could have just taken him away without the other kid? That would have been a better punishment for Mavis, just taking her kid."

"I never found her apartment. I only found out where she worked. It was in a nursing home. She had the night shift and was on her way home from work, stopped at a Seven-Eleven, and I was at the same spot pumping gas. I'm telling you God put her there for the taking. I had heard she was in the Holyoke area and was driving around. I don't sleep good at night, never have been able to sleep normal hours. I go to bed from ten a.m. to five p.m. She never saw me.

"Funny, I remember watching and wondering what the gal in the nursing clothes, whose back was to me, would look like. She had a great shape. I was going to approach her and shoot the breeze. I pulled my car in next to her junk and when she turned around to leave the store, there she was looking better than she had in a long time. She opened the front passenger side of her car and put in her bag and groceries. I came behind her. She never knew what happened to her."

Rudy took almost two hours grilling William while Lu took notes. William seemed pleased to share his story and remembered most details, but could not remember how far in from the road in Vermont he had partially buried the body.

"Do you know how fuckin' difficult it is to bury a body and how heavy one hundred and twenty pounds of dead weight is? By the time I finished burying her I needed sleep." he said.

"I got sloshed in this little hole in the wall bar in Brattleboro. By this time, it was noon. I slept in my car. It took me about two days before I straightened out. I found myself in this trailer with some godawful broad who was ugly as hell. She was the barmaid at some hole in the wall. I'll say this for her though, she made great pancakes. I stayed for a few more days, and while she was at work, I skipped."

"William, why didn't you check her bag for her address so you could get Billy?"

"The bitch didn't have any identifying information in her handbag. Her car was registered to an old address in Framingham. I didn't find her license or credit cards. She had about fifty dollars in cash in her wallet and pictures of the kids. She also had a paycheck she must have just gotten. I was afraid to cash it, so I ripped it up and dumped it with the other make-up and stuff in her bag."

"William," Rudy whispered, "you didn't want the kids, did you? If you did, you would have followed Mavis and found out where she lived. You could have grabbed Billy when she went to sleep or to work the next night."

"What would I do with a kid? Besides, if they found one kid, the cops would go crazy looking for the kidnapped kid. They would know it was me if I didn't take the other kid too, and I wasn't going to take him. He wasn't mine. It's what they say today, I made an executive decision. It was a good one. Billy died anyway, so what have I lost? You've just found me now, and I'm dying."

Rudy asked Lu, "Did you get it all?"

"Yeah, all, Rudy."

"Go get it printed out for signing. Put in a date and a line for a witness. I don't want to be back here again."

William thought Rudy appeared to be annoyed with having to wait around. He asked him, "So what happens now? You know I have pancreatic cancer, or so they say. I think they just want me not to drink. All I do is sleep here. My lady brings me in vodka, and I sip it a little bit here, a little bit there, kinda regular like so it doesn't get noticed."

Rudy watched him with disgust wondering, *How the hell can he be Liam and my father? He's a menace. Mavis tried her best for us. I had a wonderful birth mother and Satan for a father. I'll bet Mavis is in heaven and directed both Liam and me to the best adoptive parents.*

Lu returned with two copies of the documents and a nurse who was to witness the signature. She had agreed William was certainly in his right mind, but thought she was witnessing his signing a robbery confession to close a case. William signed the confession quickly.

"I guess this means I'm here for the rest of my short life," he quipped. "Do I get a copy of this, Captain?"

"Absolutely not, William. That's the deal. I don't want some newspaper reporter in here wondering why we let a murderer go. You beat the system again, William, that should make you happy."

21

A Brother Looks Back

Norbie thought, *I remember them, 'my brothers,' often: of the hijinks, celebrations, mischief, sports, and day trips we took at the Boys Club; sometimes with the accompanying other side, the Girls Club. I remember the Christmas party thrown for us at a restaurant in Connecticut owned by one of the directors.*

Looking back now, the club had one hell of an active board of directors. We kids knew when there was a directors' luncheon. Not like today, at that time the directors were dressed mostly in suits and sports jackets. Some had come out of the old club. To us, the staff would report they were important men of business and politics, and they were men. My father was an attorney, so he knew many of them and told me I should be respectful. Hell, what my dad didn't know is that we were all respectful, even more so than we were at school. At the Club Christmas party, I told the owner who I was, and he laughingly said, 'I have to pay for you. You don't need a lunch. Your dad can afford to pay for you.'

I replied, 'Yeah, but he wouldn't take me to this fancy place.' Apparently, it was the right thing to say because he chose me to hand out the gifts. At the time I was afraid one of the other kids would hear what he said, but no one was paying attention.

Sometimes it's difficult for me to recall the time when I wanted to be like everyone else. When did that change? Now, I just want to be me. It must be true of most kids, at least Sheri tells me so. She says it's something all kids go through, but for some, they never get over it. She's pointed out some of our friends who are like teens. They wear what everyone's wearing and call each other to see what the fashion dress is for the evening.

I do know my aggressiveness was honed at the club. Built a little like and with the will of Napoleon, I was a scrapper. Perhaps I had to be to get noticed, but also not just I, but my whole family hates bullies. We'd all die fighting a bully to protect someone from being bullied. However, as I remember we all liked a fair fight. We all, except for Candido. He simply could not be cajoled into fighting even if one of the guys called his mother a 'puta.' The kids could have called my mother 'puta' because at first, I didn't know what it meant, and later I realized they were really saying 'whore,' which, at the time, didn't seem like that big a deal or using it instead of 'fuck'.

Three of the guys were all about money, maybe I could be added there. I do have an entrepreneurial side outside of defense law. In criminal defense, I use my sheer and sometimes fearless, streetwise and endurance skills whereas, in my entrepreneurial development, I use my experience as the best salesman for school and club activities. Mostly I worked diligently for recognition, prizes and, to be honest, to prove I could accomplish the most sales. Money itself was just a bonus.

The other three guys didn't think that way. They would just make money and hoard it. In fact, Gerry is infamous for only spending on his own lifestyle. At least that's what I've heard, whereas Jack Ladd counted his money carefully, worked his bars well, but was generous to causes and to people in trouble. He was always the go-to guy for short loans when we were kids. He sometimes charged extra if a kid was jerking him off, but I always thought he was fair.

As to Vic Cramer, he loved the easy life, and he'd found it. His face was on every other real estate sign in the valley. If his revenues match his signage, then he is sitting pretty, particularly if you consider his wife's very large practice. No, these guys are doing well.

Myron never dabbled outside his homegirls. Don't know why he'd have a *motive to kill these women. Maybe Tonya, but Myron's just a really neat guy, keeps track of his business and home life and old friends.*

When it comes to Devon O'Brien, I have always really liked him. He was a great kid, but he lacked the home life he wanted as a kid. His Aunt Lily was special, the kind of fairy tale aunt you read about who takes over the unfinished job of rearing her sister's kids. She was good to him, but Devon wanted his mother. Devon's mother would cook for every kid in the neighborhood, but didn't have a lot of time for him. She finally died, and for a while he was inconsolable. Still, his Auntie Lily was there for him again. She died a few years ago. He still won't talk about it.

Sheri came into the room, suggesting they go outside and catch some rays and quiet time, saying, "Norberto Cull, get out of this sanctuary of yours. You look so serious. What's bothering my honey?"

"Sit down please, Sheri, I want your input. You see your girlhood friends frequently. Now I personally think I don't understand why you were so close to them as a kid since I think some of them are quite silly now. But that aside, do you personally see traits in them today that were there when you were young? I mean traits that have grown into something you don't like or will get them in trouble."

"Give it up, Norbie. Give me the specifics. You know I don't particularly enjoy esoteric questions. I'm an application kind of person. I have the patience to learn theory only when I can visualize an application. It's who I am, you know that, and you're fortunate I process things that way. You and the kids would be behind the eight-ball if I thought like you; you know, exploring what could be and forgetting to cook dinner. So, baby, I want the facts, just the facts, and I'll answer your question."

"You can never make it easy, can you, Sheri?"

"Nor can you. I have to keep up with your supposedly logical mind which, may I say, I question. You often jump from point A to point

D completely missing two points and expect me to know what you're talking about. So, tell me what's bothering you."

Norbie told her about each of his friends as he remembered them as kids, about the scrapes they got into, the funny quirks they each had, their family backgrounds, some idiosyncrasies of each he could remember, and not too much about their dating years. He didn't relay some of that because today was not a day for him to get into a discussion of his old girlfriends. Sheri would want to know every detail.

"So, let me state what I think you want for my input. You are wondering what issue you missed in the character of your old friends that may have festered over time to make one or two or more a serial murderer. If that's all you have to go on, then you're in trouble. But... but, I will still try to answer your first question. There is not a doubt in my mind that what's important to a kid at ten normally continues to be important unless there is a strong motivation to change, implemented by parental involvement, psychiatric treatment, or some life crisis.

"Not to be too theoretical for you, Norbie, I believe you may, by analyzing your friends, which you have already done, find some inklings about their characters today. That's all, just some inklings! Then, get off your duff and find out about their current lives, particularly recent traumas. After all, these deaths started just two years ago.

"You remember Susan, my girlfriend, who went off the deep end and was put in the psychiatric ward for a while," Sheri went on. "Well, she needed to have all the guys want her when she was in high school. Nobody's boyfriend was safe from her then. When she married, right from the get-go, she still flirted as if she were single. It took ten years and two children before Doug, her husband, wanted a divorce. Sue went off the deep end and ended in a psychiatric unit when she threatened to kill her children and her husband. That was ten years ago, Norbie; don't you remember?"

"I do. In fact, I handled the commitment for her husband and her parents. How is she doing now?"

"God damn it, you never told me you handled committing her to a psychiatric ward. That's what I'm talking about, Norbie. You leave me out in the cold. I grew up with Sue."

"Sheri, when I represent a client, whether it be family or friend, I am dealing in sensitive legal matters. Would you want your mother to know about your financial issues? The answer I already know. The answer is 'no,' a resounding 'no.' Sue's affairs were not for your ears. You may be a friend, but you are also a lawyer's spouse. If Sue shares her info with you, it's her business, but I will not share. You know that, why the questions?"

"Well, anyway, you have your answer. I never saw any of this potential in her. I just thought she was narcissistic as hell, almost like the kids today. Looking back, I see she could never be alone because she needed an audience. Her husband was busting his chops to make a go of his IT business. She hated the long hours he put in. She hated taking care of children. I know she had an affair with some guy she met online, but he soon tired of her. I guess it was all too much and she flipped, but of course, I can't ask you about any of that, but you can ask me."

"That's a pretty radical change in behavior for a gal brought up in a nice upper-middle-class home, don't you think, Sher darling. I think you've helped."

"Well, lucky me, I've helped. But I warn you, Norbie, a lot of people are narcissistic, but they don't try to kill their kids and spouses. You need more. I'm going to give the legal guru, some advice. Talk with Captain Beauregard, and be honest with him about your friends. Look for what was most important to each of your friends when they were little. The good and the bad traits are always there. I see them in our three boys, and your mom saw them in you."

"What bad traits did I have? Mom told me I was perfect."

Devon was having a relaxing hour in front of his television switching between CNN and Fox, using his own interpolation of the information to find answers to the world's problems. He liked Trump's direct agenda but thought he needed a filter for his tweets. He reviewed his concepts of this president, questioning as if Trump were with him on his couch,

Were you always like this, I mean as a kid? Did you always decide ahead of time what you wanted and just pushed forward with it? They say your mother was distant and your dad expected great things from you. It looks like you always expected great things from yourself. You've made some really big mistakes but continued on, and I believe you have some good values, unless, like the New Yorkers and Californians say, you're a sociopath. One guy on one of the channels said Obama was a sociopath and certainly Clinton was and that you'd have to be a sociopath to want to be president.

What would happen if you lost it all, I mean everything: your money, your family and your prestige? I think you'd be okay, probably huckstering a film about your life the next day. I think you have something my blessed auntie called grit, which my mom did not have.

A call interrupted Devon's daydreams. It was from Candi.

"Hey, guy, I've been thinking about us, the boys from the club. I've been reflecting on some stuff. What say, you come over. Heather's gone for the day. You and I have some memories to explore, especially with these murders. We've had some issues in the past and given that I'm being questioned, it'd be best if we put our minds together. Not to worry, Bro, I won't talk to the cops until you and I go over what should be said."

"What the fuck are you talking about? There's no issue I care if the cops hear, but if you need me, I'll come right over." Candi clicked off but was annoyed at Devon's answer.

Ten minutes later, Candi called while Devon was en route and canceled the meeting with a cockamamie excuse that Heather had returned home unexpectedly.

Something's up. He'd normally just tell Heather to go in the other room. Someone else showed up. If he thinks he's fooling me, he's nuts. Christ, as long as I'm out I'll drive by, see whose car is there.

A few minutes later, Devon saw not just one car but two. One was an unmarked police vehicle, and the other was Norbie Cull's new Porsche Cayenne. Devon did not go in.

———

Norbie Cull and Rudy Beauregard pulled into Candi's driveway. Always observant, Norbie, who was driving, caught a glimpse of Devon O'Brien's car as he drove by Candi's house. *Not an accident,* Norbie thought after entering the front door, *Devon's driving by. Not an accident. Suspicious, Candi seems out of sorts as he opened the door.*

Candi then left to make a phone call. When he returned Norbie explained why the Captain and he were visiting. *Contrary to Candi's culture and sense of hospitality,* Norbie noticed *he never even asked if we wanted coffee. What was he seeing Devon about when I told him to stay away from the guys? He can't shut his mouth with them, yet he's a smart cookie and should know better. I wonder if Beauregard and I will be able to get him to tell us what's going on.*

Norbie initiated the interview with, "Candi, Captain Beauregard and I are here to ask a few questions.

"Captain, you were interested in personality disorders that may indicate a person going off the track. In this case, you mean going way off the track. Now I have advised Candi that he is unable to disclose patient information. However, as a professional in this area, I think he could give us some professional opinions, naturally only from his general experience. Candi, do you understand a theoretical discussion would be okay and helpful? I know you want to help prevent more of your patients from dying."

"You know I do, Norbie, but I've made some mistakes here. I've had patients who were friends, maybe shouldn't have signed them on, but their stated problems didn't involve a conflict for me."

"Candi, I don't want to know who your patients were. I want you to look at this case and tell me what kind of issues the perp may have, given that the perp is probably originally from Springfield, is around fifty years old, is a male, and flies under the radar. What I mean is he doesn't normally look or act crazy."

"You really believe it's one of us, don't you, Norbie? Why can't it be you? You're one of us."

"It could be, Candi, if I didn't have a foolproof alibi on at least two of the occasions. But include me in your structural concepts about a potential perp. I'm not sensitive."

Beauregard was shifting in his seat, which was a sign to Norbie that he was sick of this level of discussion. He wanted to go right at Candi.

"Look, Candi, normally I would try to shake you up about what you may be think you know, because I am absolutely certain you know more than what you're saying," the Captain said.

"Let's start with an analysis from you that answers these basic questions. First, why these particular women? Second, what about the order of their deaths and later for the assault and phone calls? Third, what does the cutting of the women after death mean to you? Fourth, why were the women not raped? Fifth, what kind of issue could take a normal acting fifty-year-old man to embark on such a horrific trail of death at this stage in his life? Think analytically, not emotionally.

Answer these questions without referring to your files, and you'll make your lawyer and me accept that you're doing your best for the women not yet murdered."

"What do you think I am? I would help in any way. I'm trying to sort this mess out. I'll try to answer your questions, one through five, but it's not quite that easy.

"Why these women were chosen? Well, I have come to the realization it's because I was their therapist. That is the only common denominator I am able to see. But I don't think it's related to me. I think it's because the killer is someone who didn't want a secret out that all these women have, that I don't know, but the killer thinks they know. I'm trying to put together bits and pieces, but I'll be damned if I can connect the dots here. And if I know the secret why doesn't he kill me. Is it because he's a 'Brother?

"There may be something in the order of the deaths. Maybe Loretta, who was the first woman murdered, had the most knowledge about the killer, and if that works, then we go down the line to the next one to receive a phone call who hasn't yet been killed. That woman would be Martina McKay. She may have some information about this murderer if this logic bears out. But it might be something else.

"Postmortem cutting of the women on their breasts and vaginal areas certainly implies as the FBI spouts, a signature. I saw in the papers the ME thinks the cutting was done with a large hunting knife; an old one."

"Candi," Beauregard broke in, "just what do you know about signatures? Did you know a signature is often developed as a fantasy in a killer's mind long before a first murder is committed? Cutting women's bodies after death, with no preceding rape may be a signature."

"I haven't answered your questions fully yet, Captain Beauregard. But before I proceed, let me be clear, I don't know who the killer is. I'm working on it. Answering why the women were not raped is a problem. You know the obvious answer, that the killer is impotent. Also, the killer's relationship to women in his past can't be overlooked.

"Does he hate beautiful women, because he is only killing beautiful women? Does he hate them because of their lifestyle and he won't soil himself to rape them? Did a woman he admired disappoint him, and he's unable to take his repressed rage out on her, so these other women get it instead? Is he looking for the perfect woman and these women have disappointed him, so he doesn't want them, but marks them to put them down?

"He is organized with what I believe are long repressed fantasies. If one of my friends did these killings, considering they are all around fiftyish, then I think an important event has opened an old trauma or wound in his life, and that event would have happened before the first murder unless the first relationship and murder was the trigger event. That's all I can help you with."

Norbie said, "That's it, Captain. Knowing his files, Candi can't even lead you to a specific theory for the perp's motive. You'll have to figure it out."

As the police Captain was leaving, Norbie held back to say a few words to Candi.

"What were you doing scheduling a meeting with Devon O'Brien. I told you to stay away from the Boys Club. Are you ever going to listen to good legal advice?"

"How'd you know, Norbie? I was just going to go down memory lane to see what was important in all our lives. I thought if I treated it like old-time storytelling, I'd recall the emotion prevailing at the time because with my therapeutic skills, I could identify traumatic events."

"Stay away from them. Call me if you think of something, but stay away, Candi. I'll walk away from you if you don't."

Devon had called all four of the boys and casually asked them what they were doing while thinking, *If they ask me about Candi and a meeting, I'll just deny it.*

Only Jack and Myron and Gerry asked him if Candi had called him for a meeting. Not wanting to lie, he said, "What meeting? When did he call you? Did you go?"

He thought, *I haven't lied; I don't want to lie to my friends. But I'm more than surprised they all said they were to meet Candi this afternoon and the meeting was canceled. What's on Candi's mind that he wanted to talk to all three of us is the question.*

22

Beauregard, Ash, and, Petra

Beauregard called Ash into his office the moment he returned to the station.

"Tell me about this McKay woman," Rudy said once settled comfortably. "You've been watching out for her, and I think you've developed a nice connection with her. What do you think makes her different from the other victims or potential victims? I have a reason for asking, but I will explain later. Right now, I don't want to influence your answer."

"Different in what way, Captain? She's a very nice woman who's living with a guilty conscience over her actions taken when she was twenty years old. She has repressed guilt, but I don't know the psychological make-up of the other women; maybe they also had repressed guilt. She has a closely-knit family, and there is mutual respect. She's a recognized professional and musician. What else can I tell you?"

"You're a good musician, Ash, and my wife tells me that musicians see patterns. Someone raised the possibility the perp may have a pattern in the direction of who he has priority for killing. I, for one, had not considered the concept that the timing of the victims being murdered is based on their knowledge about him or his past, or the strength of their interactions with him. I'm using the order of the phone calls that were made, not the order of the attacks. For instance, Loretta Loren was first, Tonya Brown was second, Janice Shaunessy was third, Lisa Moliano was fourth, but I'm not sure whether Martina McKay or Lavender James was next. We do know, that the next assault victim Valencia's calls, came after McKay's and James' calls. What do you think?"

"Can't see a directional pattern here yet, Captain. Lavender James is only in the running for potential victim number five. Lavender will tell you her panty size within the first five minutes of meeting with her. She doesn't keep secrets; doesn't have to because her life is really an open book. I'll think on it for a bit and let you know."

"Detective, think carefully; maybe talk to Martina. Perhaps she'll see a connection in the order of victims. Maybe she'll know about some trauma that occurred in the lives of the five guys from the Boys Club. I'm most interested in a traumatic event occurring before the first murder.

"Candido Rodriguez mentioned a serious trauma in a person with repressed anger or rage could open an old wound. I believe there is always a reason or motivation for an action, even in such insanity as murder. Get over and see Martina as early as she's able to meet you. I'm going to interview Valencia again. She's ready to leave the hospital. I'll ask Petra to talk with Lavender again. I don't have the patience for another interview with Lavender. I do miss Jim Locke; he could always work someone like Lavender better than the rest of us."

Martina happily took Detective Ash Lent's call telling him she could cut her day short and meet him at the Storrowton Tavern for lunch. She said she had a gift certificate she was trying to use and couldn't think of anyone she'd rather have lunch with and treat, saying, "I can have lunch and feel safe. I haven't been out since I first received the phone calls, Ash. I'm looking forward to it."

Ash thought, *Neither can I, Martina, think of anyone else I'd rather have lunch with. Hell, I've lost all objectivity. I want to be with her. I don't want to be questioning her. She is not a suspect, only a potential witness to something she doesn't even know she knows. I can't tell her too much, but I'm sure as hell not burning any bridges with her.*

Bing! It finally occurred to him. He finally got it. *Ashton Lent, you dumb-ass. I'm stuck on this lady. How fucking stupid of me. I don't just want to be with her. When was the last time I ever felt like this? In fact, have I ever felt like this before? I'm mooning over Martina. Hell, I'm crazy over her. Why not? She's beautiful and intelligent and kind, and she likes me. Thank you, God. I just hope she's game.*

Sitting across from Martina made Ash a little jumpy. He was surprised to hear Martina say, "I'm nervous, Ash, sitting across from you, you know like two real adults enjoying lunch together. Most of my lunches before the calls were with two of my colleagues, Hal and George. They are such great fun and are always trying to find a heterosexual male for me to date. Unfortunately, as they say, 'Not our specialty, Martina.' They have so many interesting stories to tell and are wonderful musicians and really good friends, but having lunch with them is not quite the same as having lunch with you, Ash."

"I hope not, Martina. I believe I might have a different view of you than, perhaps, Hal and George have. This is a nice traditional New England restaurant. I really dig the service here at lunch includes cottage cheese with chives, crackers, whole cranberry sauce and corn salad, just to wet your whistle before ordering. I like a few of the choices best myself. New England pot roast versus chicken pie, versus meatloaf, versus baked stuffed shrimp, and then mashed potatoes tasting like my grandmother's, and they always have winter squash. It's like going home, Martina."

The two slowly and willingly gorged themselves, not for a minute considering calories. The cop and the witness, as they laughingly called themselves, enjoyed the moment for at least an hour before they talked seriously. Ash finally reminded Martina he had work to do.

"Martina, can you think about the women who were murdered and yourself and tell me what you all have in common. For instance, did you ever date the same guy or was there one guy who tried to date you all? Or maybe you all witnessed an event involving some guy you all knew, and the event bothered you somehow? That's what I'm interested in, anything that strikes a chord in your psyche. You're a sharp lady, whose experience is out of the norm for most folks. Give it your best shot, please. Your life and other women's lives are at risk."

Martina's response was unexpected.

"Ash, I'll think about it, but not now. Now, I want to enjoy you and to be candid, I can't think with you across the table from me. I could play some music with you around, could cook with you around, but not think.

"I'll make a deal. We'll finish lunch. I'll go home and give it serious thought. My mom and dad are at home now, but they're leaving at six for a play, so I'll need protection then. If you're available, come by. I'll have every odd thing I ever experienced written down. After you digest it, well, Ash, I'll play some really good music for you. How does that sound?"

Ash's eyes lit up as he assured Martina, he was available for protective detail at six that evening. He thought, *The rest of this day is going to be slow, just as slow as filling in reports for Millie. Yet all I can hear is music and Roy Orbison singing "In Dreams I Walk with You." Well, at least I'm not singing "Only the Lonely."*

———

Captain Beauregard entered the Nonton Hospital area outside of Valencia Longtin's room and saw Chief Provast, Nurse Worthy, and Devon O'Brien. He was not surprised to see Provast and Worthy there, for he'd been told the Chief was there every day supposedly looking over the safety procedures used for protection of Valencia. It seemed reasonable. In fact, Rudy had asked for strict protection after the second stab at Valencia's life and the Chief was more than happy to comply with Rudy's wishes.

No one, either in the Nonton Police Department or at the medical center, was unaware of the sparks flying between Chief Provast and Nurse Worthy. What was most interesting was the betting pool, the stakes of which were more exciting than at the Belmont for Justify. Rudy thought, *Everyone, even me, the cynic, would like to see these two make it. Something good may come out of the attack on Valencia. Although that's a high price to pay for someone else's romance, but what the hell is Devon doing here, and why are they letting him visit her, and why is he visiting her?*

Beauregard greeted them all, asked about Valencia's recovery and pulled the Chief aside for a little talk.

"So, Pete, what is Devon O'Brien doing here? I thought we agreed on no visitors."

"You mean our Devon O'Brien, Rudy; hell, he was Parade Marshal on the Saint Patrick's Day Parade, wouldn't hurt a fly, and besides, he's my cousin. I'll vouch for him."

Beauregard groaned. "Hell, be a professional, Pete. I don't care if he's your brother or mine, we just don't know who's after her. Regardless of that, visitors say too much to the outside world, and that is dangerous. You know we're looking at a group of five guys who grew up together in Springfield and he's one of those guys. Aside from that, what's your security going to be when she goes home tomorrow?"

"Rita, I mean nurse Worthy is taking her home. She has two neighbors who will babysit her while Rita's working and we'll have a round-the-clock detail driving by especially in the evening. Naturally,

I'll be checking in with the two ladies on a regular basis."

I bet you will, thought Rudy, who then asked Devon O'Brien to join him in the waiting room nearby, immediately addressing him with, "You were told before to stay away from her. What part of that don't you understand?"

"First of all, Captain, with all due respect, there is no reason why I am not to see her. I don't think you ever gave me that direction. I have known Valencia for many years and intend to see her through this horrific attack on her life. For your information, Valencia called and asked me to come. I didn't meet her standards before because I was so self-obsessed with my marriage experience I found myself distrusting every word said to me. Take my word, I have a chance with Valencia now. I'm not going to blow it for you or for anyone. I don't apologize."

"If you've had a thing for Valencia for many years, tell me everything you know about her, such as her dating any of the other 'brothers' or her seeing something going on with one of the other 'brothers' and one or more of the victims."

"Do you think I wouldn't do anything to help you solve this case? Valencia was approached by all the other guys, but she was not into a quick jump in the hay or looking for marriage. She told me a solid friendship with trust on both sides and common interests was what she wanted; and if that worked out, she maybe would want marriage. I lost out on the trust issue. I would never cheat on her, but I found it difficult to trust her. She's in sales. She travels. I was certain I wasn't enough for her. She accused me of being insecure, and I am. She told me, 'Dev, grow up, or there's nothing here for either of us.'

I was pissed, and I didn't call her for a couple of weeks. When I finally broke down, she wouldn't take my calls and sent me a note to 'bug off.' The night of her assault was the first night she has spoken to me in a long time, and I had hopes it might mean something.

"As to any of the other guys, they knew I was crazy about her. I don't think any of them would have moved on her particularly since she didn't, you know, dress or act sexy. If someone wanted to punish me, well that might be a rationale for hurting her because it certainly has damaged me, but I don't bring on those kinds of vibes from people."

"Devon, I'll talk to her now. If she feels you're not a threat, then you can visit, but none of your friends, do you get me? The Chief says you're his cousin and he vouched for you. Something happens to her, you ruin a bunch of folks. Keep your mouth shut about this. Don't tell your 'brothers,' since there's a good reason to place suspicion on any one of them—and you too."

Beauregard entered Valencia's room and found the gorgeous redhead looking almost gorgeous again and acting as if the stark room was filled with roses. He spent a few minutes questioning her.

Valencia said, "I've been away for a while. Captain, I don't think any one of the 'brothers' outside of Devon is after me. Jack tried to date me, but that's who Jack is, and he takes 'no' quite gracefully. I think the other guys, excuse me for saying, like a more overt look in a woman. I wasn't ever a dancer so there was no real opportunity to see my assets, as my mother would say.

"I saw interaction amongst the guys. I know Devon told Gerry to stay away from Janice, that he was too old for her. Frankly, I think Janice was years more mature than Gerry. I told Devon that and said he should have butted out of their business. Besides, Gerry really doesn't want a long-term relationship. He wants a gal as a prop. I remember a tough break-up for Myron and his former girlfriend. He was moping for a while but got over it. My thought on that was he dodged a bullet. He's a good man, and I think his marriage is good.

"Jack is Jack. I recently met his bookkeeper and think that might be a go for the two of them. She's a legitimate and feisty gal. I don't know Vic as well, but he's a salesman, and I'm in sales. I guess we talk too much. We don't execute deeds easily, certainly not a planned murder. And he's happily married.

"Some of the spectacles I've witnessed are just related to what I have previously told you: some heated debates over sports, the aftermath of Devon's divorce which was decidedly a public spectacle, Gerry's soliloquies on being unhappily unmarried, Vic's sales talks on his importance in society, Myron's embarrassment at being had by a former girlfriend, Candi's bringing kindness to everyone, Jack's constant attempts to make every gal feel welcomed at his clubs, and multiple conversations about Norbie's bravado at the Boys Club, and later in defending the supposedly innocent. Although you must know by now I have never met Norbie Cull before? I have nothing more to tell you."

Beauregard gave Valencia his card, told her to be careful.

"Valencia, it's imperative you check your safety at every juncture. There have been two attempts on your life, which means whether you remember something or not, the perp wants you dead. You don't think it's because of some disappointing past romantic liaison, but there's something, some event you've witnessed that makes you at risk. I understand you have asked Devon to be with you. Are you certain that is a wise move?"

"Captain, are you insinuating Devon would ever hurt me? If so, you are oh, so wrong. Devon is an exceptional man. He's honest, often too honest. I didn't always appreciate his honesty, but this assault on my body made me reassess my life. I will marry Devon if he ever asks me again, and I will do everything in my power to make him ask me again. Does that answer your question?"

"It does, Valencia, and my bet is he'll ask you within a week. Good luck."

———

While the Captain and Ash were interviewing their witnesses, Petra was at Lavender's home going through swatches of material for drapes and curtains and paint colors for the walls of her new home. She'd already been there for an hour, and Lavender had been able to change her mind from blues to shades of greens for her home.

"Men think they like blue," Lavender said. "It's a leftover from their mothers decorating their bedrooms in blue. Happens all the time. Now, I'm not for a lot of crazy colors, despite my christened name of Lavender. All colors have a place in our lives, but some colors are better used as accent colors and not base colors. Well, except if you like bold contemporary décor. which I think is actually more difficult to effectively pull off."

Petra couldn't help but daydream during parts of the technical lesson on home décor with which she was presented. *How can an exotic dancer go on and on about décor like this? Am I ever going to be able to direct her to more serious questions? I have learned about the mistakes I should never make in design, all of which, if I'm to be honest with myself, I would have made. I would have painted the whole house in shades of blue, because when I asked him, Jim said he liked the color blue. What am I, a superficial idiot?*

Another quarter-hour later, Lavender brought them to Petra's reason for being there.

"Now, Petra, I know you must have some questions for me or you wouldn't bother with a visit during working hours. I am happy to give you design advice during your workday. I like to think the Captain doesn't have to know you need a little rest so newly married and all and with a new house. Let's get down to business."

Petra practically sighed with relief and explained her reason for the interview.

"Petra, I told you before I knew all the boys well with the exception of Norbie. Went out with some of them. They have their problems as do we all. My gut tells me Myron is A-OK and Devon, other than being hung up on Valencia, is as straightforward as he seems.

"Jack is Jack. There are times when I think he's a big jerk, but that's normally over money and the bar business details. He looks normal to me for a bar owner, although he was absolutely crazy over Loretta and she rejected him. She didn't like that life. You know the bar life. That leaves Vic and Gerry, who both seem to me to be harmless enough, although a little weird in different ways. Look at me calling anyone else weird!"

"Think, Lavender, your instincts are as subtle as your taste in design; you see things. What strikes a note in you as a problem? Women are dying, your friends are dying. Help me please."

"I have lasted years in a difficult job as a professional dancer. Regardless of what you may think, Petra, it is a profession. I do good work both in dancing and in helping people. I've directed patrons of the club and dancers and staff at the club to work toward a more balanced life. I've even helped some of them find God. I certainly sent them to Candido for help. I want to help you. I do remember some of the resentments I've heard about when the good old boys were young.

"Norbie was always a leader, but some of the guys resented his direct management 'tude.' One of them said, 'Hell he didn't look old enough to tie his shoelaces, but he led the charge on every venture.' The girls loved Norbie. I think because he was known to treat them with respect. Hell, Devon and Jack said he treated everyone with respect, unless they didn't deserve respect and, in that case, he was still more controlled than the other guys.

"Candi was the lead lover when they were young. I thought that was amusing at first until I realized that Candi, like Norbie, was always nice to the ladies. Neither of them pretended they were big shots. I could say that about Myron too, although never underestimate him. He didn't build his business by being a pushover.

"Jack had some resentment about his childhood. He had trouble in school with dyslexia. In those days, the teachers had no patience with active boys who also had learning problems. Jimmy, my boyfriend, will tell you about his experiences and he's younger than Jack.

"Besides, Jack has accommodated his problem. He has two people read everything he signs. I think he still has a reading problem. He always says things like, 'I forgot my cheaters again.' He never forgets anything. He's pretty sensitive if someone makes a joke, like calling him a 'dummy' when he doesn't get the punch line. It's rather silly because we all know he is quite intelligent. His family wasn't that sensitive, and he plays and acts tough, but I think it's just a shell.

"Gerry is a loner, an only child, someone who's always hanging around because he's lonely. He's probably dated all of us at least for a coffee date. He's the perfect looking man like on a Marlboro commercial except I think he's a 'wus.' Maybe not that exactly, because I heard he's really tough on his employees. Makes sense, I suppose because he's OCD about his dress and everything else. A waitress dumped a vodka and tonic on him by accident once, and he went ballistic. Went home to change. There wasn't even a stain on him.

"Victor is the last one I'd ever want to talk about, Petra. He's a self-absorbed bloke. There are dozens like him. He was a wild man with the girls until he married. Now he's just a blowhard salesman with lots of money to spend. I don't know anything about his personal life or childhood. He's one of those folks who tells you anything and everything but nothing you really want to hear about, certainly nothing important."

The ladies enjoyed coffee, chit-chatting while Petra thought, *I have never done this in the middle of the afternoon, just shooting the breeze. There may be much Lavender can teach me.*

23

The Barbeque

C ontrary to Rudy's wishes, Mona invited the detectives and Millie from the MCU and some friends to the family barbeque get-together. Her rationale was, "It will be a lot less uncomfortable for you, Rudy, if you have to play nice to a bunch of friends. There will be less pressure on your brother and his family and you and the kids. The MCU knows all about the reason for this party. They said they were honored to join us. It's important you understand that there's no going back to before when you could pretend you had no other family than Lizette and Roland. In fact, this party is Lizette's idea."

Lizette had said Rudy would just have to stop keeping secrets, although not about work secrets. Mona also said that Lizette wanted to meet Liam his brother, the one they wouldn't let her adopt. She wants to know that you have lots of connections. "I want Rudy to be surrounded with family before Roland, and I leave this world," Lizette said.

"What did Roland have to say about this fiasco, Mona, or did he have anything at all to say?"

Mona repeated Rudy's father Roland's remarks verbatim: "Hell, the kid's finally faced up to the time before us. Good thing, it will make Lizette and my grandkids happy. As for me, the kid has always just tickled me. I don't need anything more. If this is good for Rudy, then it's good for me."

"Why is it good for the grandkids? What do they care about people they've never met before? I'm telling you, Mona, I'm really nervous about this public event."

"There you go again, Rudy, afraid of interaction with people you're unable to control. This is not only a great opportunity for our boys to meet some relatives, but it's important for you to continue to be more open with folks.

"By the way, before you find out from my friends, I was just hired for next year by the West Side School District. I took a position teaching science. It was the only position open, and I have a certification, although that's not the subject I taught before."

"Why didn't you tell me last night, and are you really ready to work full time after all these years? You don't have to, Mona? I will miss being able to talk to you whenever, well, whenever I need to talk."

"Rudy, do you know how you sound? You sound like a controlling husband when you are not. You rarely call me at home during the day, for one reason because I'm never at home. So, my working will not make any changes for either of us from that perspective. Enjoy today, Rudy. Don't be afraid of change." And Mona hugged her husband.

He sighed, thinking, *There she goes again, knows me better than I know myself. I'm so goddamn lucky to have found her.*

He then heard a booming voice. Liam O'Callahan entered the yard and gave Rudy a bear hug before he could react saying, "Say, Bro, try introducing me to my good-looking sister-in-law and I'll return the favor. My wife's a bit shy, but she's coming along with the girls and the babies."

The party had started.

Rudy's boys, Roland, Jeremiah, and Lucas relished playing with Liam and Delia's two grandchildren, Maurice and Michael who were Meghan's children. Meghan's husband would come later when he finished his golf tournament. Liam's other daughter, Sharon, was already busy socializing with a bunch of cops who had been invited.

Liam said, "You got to watch that one, Rudy, she's afraid of nothing. Apparently, I see she likes the boys in blue. You know she just finished a fellowship in neuroscience at Cleveland Clinic, and she says the Ohio boys were not for her. They wanted to live there, not come to New England. For her, that was the kiss of death."

Lizette and Roland were busy talking with Mona and Delia. Liam had moved over to cooking the burgers and dogs with Ash, the Chief, and Petra. Rudy thought, *This is family. This is what a real family feels like.* He turned to find his dad, Roland, next to him.

"Rudy, this is good. This is the day you stop worrying about your past. Live today, my Rudy, it's all we have. Learn it now. I didn't learn it until you came into our lives. Wasted some time, just like you have. Lizette, she never wasted a minute. She always knew that good would come about. She says it different, but means the same thing. Nice brother you have. He must have had parents who loved him too. You should have asked them to join us; maybe next time, huh?"

Rudy's eyes teared when his dad walked away. He realized everyone was eating, or getting their food, his sons were on their second helping, the toddlers were running around with their mother following them trying to force feed them, and his wife and mother were smugly chatting with Delia and some neighbors.

As Rudy was starting to ruminate about the potential future of his enlarged family, Liam said, "I just talked to Luis Vargas from Holyoke. His tale was quite a surprise' only surprise is that you didn't kill him. What a fucking son-of-a-bitch.

"You did good, Bro. I could not have done so good. Let him rot there. He doesn't suffer guilt or shame from what Lu said. He's a fucking psychopath, and you are smart not to let his psyche interfere with us and our families' lives. Delia says that in Ireland, they talk about relatives like William and say, 'May the cat eat him, and the devil eat the cat.' Says it all, I think, a double curse on William."

"Quite a turn of phrase, Delia has. Maybe if she returns to Ireland sometime, Mona and I could go with you?"

"As Delia would say, 'Aye, that would be good,' except the word good sounds like 'goot' to me. You have filled a hole in me, Rudy, in my heart, I think. This is the last time I'll mention it, but having a brother and his family is something I've longed for. I knew I had a brother, so I couldn't let it rest."

Rudy questioned Liam. "Did you ever have a close boyhood friend or friends, you know a relationship that felt like you two or more than two were brothers? Maybe you went to camp or something, and you got close to one or more boys. I'm asking you this from a professional perspective.

"I was too shy as a little kid to let anyone get close to me. I remember thinking if I got too close to a friend, then someone would take him away. Mona, well that was different. She wouldn't let me hide. She made me want her so much that I couldn't hide from her."

"That's called 'Breaking through the defenses.' She's one smart lady. I hung around with a crew of kids, all guys, and we got into all kinds of trouble. My parents always fought for me, even when I was wrong. I learned a lot about loyalty from them. What I didn't understand then and what has taken a long time for me to learn is that not everyone deserves loyalty.

"Let me explain that, Rudy. I was charged by my group of friends with getting a final exam to save two of my friends on the football team from flunking. I was certainly guilty, but that's when I knew my 'bros' were not my brothers when the heat was turned up. Here I was, an 'A' student and I'm helping them out.

"One of my friends confessed, and furthermore said it was my idea. All the guys agreed it was my idea, leaving me the only one facing the music. If my parents weren't convinced I was the second coming and fought the administration, I don't know where I'd be today. Face it, Rudy, you and I are truly connected, not just by blood, half of that pretty tainted, but by a common understanding of what it's like to be tossed around as little kids not knowing our future. Maybe then we thought we just wanted three square meals, but we wanted loyalty. I think we both got it in our marriages. Maybe we were lucky to have our problems when we were young and live out our comfortable lives now."

Rudy moved his head in a no-no and said, "Never think what is going on today will continue. The universe, I think, likes to toss us around for a good laugh."

"You are a fucking cynic, Rudy. It must be the cop in you. Is your interest in brotherhood loyalty related to that case you're working now?"

"Yeah, Liam, I can't tell you too much, but it looks like it's one of these five childhood friends who all met at the Springfield Boys Club when they were small, and so I think they feel strong loyalties to each other. It's a diverse group, all have done well in life, and they often see each other at one of the Irish bars. At least most of them do.

"But I think it's one of them. We're doing some research on their characters and events in their lives, but so far nothing big stands out. I have learned something about sociopaths and psychopaths, and that is they practice being normal and get so good at the act, they fool everyone, in some cases, for long periods of time. I have to solve this case soon; this perp is probably chomping at the bit to kill the next woman."

"I'm assuming you don't have much in the way of circumstantial evidence. That's what they call footprints and weapons, right?"

"Right."

"So, you're into the soft sciences. Bro, I probably can't help you too much. But I am a great judge of character. If I meet the bunch of guys, I can tell who, amongst them is the misfit. I've had great experience and good luck with that. I have spotted sociopaths in business on first meetings, but I guess you can't tell me who you're looking at, can you?"

Before Rudy could answer with a firm negative, Jeremiah, Rudy's middle son gave his dad a jab in the midsection.

"Good thing we found all these relatives, Dad. Cousin Sharon says Uncle Liam can help Rollie get a job when he gets out of college because he's big in finance; that's what Rollie wants. He wants to be rich. I'll need him to be wealthy. I'm going to be a lawyer and Congressman someday, and he'll handle my fundraising."

Rudy groaned and uttered, "Jay, can you never shut up. We don't know the future. We only know what may be. Hell, I suppose you know what Lucas wants too."

"Yep, and Mom's going to be mad. He wants to be a general or an admiral but hasn't decided which branch of the service to go in. He's really good in school and athletics but doesn't know if we have any pull for him to get into West Point or the Naval or Air Force Academy. Besides, he wears glasses, so he's betting on Virginia Military Institute, which he says is as good as West Point."

Rudy said, "Lucas is only thirteen years old, and this is probably just a fad. Recently, didn't he want to be an arson investigator?"

"Well, that was only because he saw you investigating the car fire for arson where the lady from West Side was killed. You know him, a new idea every minute.

"By the way, Mom wants you to help carry out the big 'Family' cake she made. You haven't seen it, but it's cool, with pictures of two brothers who look like you two, and it has big raindrops on it. They're supposed to be teardrops of happiness, but I tell you, Dad, it needs explaining. Get out of your chair, Dad.

"He's so slow getting out of a chair, Uncle Liam, the rest of us move fast. Drives us crazy. Mom says she's going back to work in September because Rollie's going to college. Did you know that?

"Well, I got to go; my friends have just shown up for a free hamburger. Better get moving, Mom wants you and Uncle Liam over there now."

Liam was laughing so loud he lost his balance and had to be supported by Rudy who said, "You think this family stuff is easy. That kid never shuts up, not from the day he was born. We try to keep secrets, but he hears everything."

"Rudy, I have two girls who talk incessantly. At least there's only one in your tribe like that. It's good, isn't it, Rudy? This is good."

———

A day later found Liam driving over to the Celtic Belles, a pub he had been to before with some buddies. *No reason I can't give a little help to Rudy. I'll respect his right not to tell me what is not supposed to be told outside the station, but I can be eyes and ears for him without him knowing.*

Within a half hour, Jack Ladd was buying Liam a beer on the house and discussing current events. Liam talked about the women being murdered.

"The papers said they were all somehow connected to the music industry as dancers and singers, inferring that they liked to frequent the Irish circuit. You must know them. I heard they were gorgeous. What a shame."

"You don't know the half of it. My friends and I knew them all, and they were not teasers or anything out of the ordinary, I mean in addition to their looks and talent. Hope it stops. They were friends."

Jack left Liam to take care of business. Liam noticed two guys at the bar who were drinking free. He thought, *Jack will give one drink to a new customer who clearly has spent some bucks, but he's not going to carry two guys unless they're his buddies or his vendors. Those guys are not vendors. Well, service is slow, giving me an excuse to mosey up to the bar. Maybe I can get to know these two.*

Twenty minutes later, Liam knew Myron Hicks' and Devon O'Brien's life stories. When he heard them talking about being kids at the Springfield Boys Club, he talked about growing up in the Holyoke Boys Club, which was not the country club these guys had then. They told stories about Norbie, their leader in trouble, who turned into a famous defense lawyer, which they thought was righteous.

"Given that Norbie started us on some of our worst escapades," Devon said, "he also kept us away from serious criminal stuff with some other guys. He was a shrewd kid."

Liam bought two more rounds before he got the names of the whole crew and what they were doing now. He decided that prudence should make him leave now. He could follow up again. He left.

A half hour later, Jack asked Devon about the big, good looking guy at the bar. Devon said, "He's a financial guy, been in here a few times with some clients, and said he'll try to frequent us more often."

"Did you talk about the murders with him?"

"Na, he never mentioned them to us. Why? I'm telling you he's not a cop. My cop radar did not go off, and you know Stellato from Springfield Police Department would have let us know if they were interested in us. You're getting neurotic. Besides, I could see his car out the window, and it was a Range Rover. Most cops only dream about owning one of those."

Liam O'Callahan had connections, not cop connections, but social and political connections he was willing to use and did. Getting an appointment with Candido Rodriguez was not that easy. He wasn't taking new patients and had only a few patients in total. He was making a living in mental health management, a fact Liam understood. But Liam had a good friend who had worked with Candi and, after a little song and dance, he got Candi to see him for what Candi could never ignore, "an almost crisis situation." His friend told Candi, Liam was a workaholic and was extremely stressed out.

"Just talk him down," he told Candi, "and I'll find a more permanent solution for him."

Liam spent the typical fifty minutes therapy session with a solicitous and kind Candi, long enough to convince the all-knowing Liam, at least how he would describe himself to his daughters, that Candi couldn't murder anyone. He found it tough to act stressed for the whole time, since he thought, *I know what real stress is and this is not it. I'm not a born actor. I really have to work at it. I am a born bullshitter, however, and I'm afraid this Candi may see through me.*

After returning to his office, Liam looked at the other names: Norberto Cull, Gerry Valle, and Vic Cramer. He'd heard of them all and maybe had met Vic Cramer's wife. He pulled up computer news articles on Cull and decided to let him wait until last.

Liam was familiar with Gerry Valle's company. It was on the watch list as fodder for going public. *I know a few venture-capitalists who are trying to talk Valle and his firm into accepting their backing an IPO, which would leave Valle sitting pretty. Trouble is that Valle is afraid of losing control. Not the first entrepreneur to think like that.*

I can get a meeting with him. I'll tell him I'm heading a new group that's interested in bringing his firm national before going public. He'll at least go for a conference because it doesn't rush him. That kind of guy needs to plan in advance for everything. He'll probably talk me into a partnership if the company's as good as the reports say.

Liam then went about setting up a golf match with Vic Cramer and a few of the guys from the West Side Country Club. Two of them were known political figures. Liam thought Cramer loved to be in the know with the important folks in town.

He'd do his own analysis and tell Rudy some kind of a story about accidentally meeting them -- except it wouldn't work for explaining a therapy session with Candido Rodriguez. Liam thought, *No one need ever to know anything about what I'm doing. What's a brother for, if I can't help?*

24

Wives Dig In

I'm sick of this life, Heather told herself, not for the first time. *Candi says we have to stay around together or have a witness for him if I leave for an errand alone. I can't even run out to the store without him tagging along, and that cuts out lunches with my friends.*

What the hell is wrong with the police? I hear there are now four police departments involved, if we include that hush-hush assault in Nonton. Candi says the state police, the district attorney, and the FBI all are working the case. The operative word in my mind is 'working,' not solving. Nobody's working that diligently.

Candi believes the police think it's one of his friends from the Boys Club. Well, I know it's not Candi and probably not Norbie, because he's working really hard to save Candi's ass. If he were the murderer, he would want to set Candi up. Candi won't release anything in the files, but he was the therapist for his five friends and all the women.

I'll bet there's something there, something I didn't see the first time when Candi caught me. He had to see a new patient in crisis today, which required my getting a driver for his patient trip. No problem, it gives me about two hours to review the files again. He doesn't lock anything because he trusts me. Still, it needs to be done.

Heather sat on the rug next to the files thinking she could just shove the files back if she heard Candi at the door. Knowing she had limited time, she decided to read the five men's files first. These files were much slimmer. She read all five files within an hour.

Candi, I never realized how boring it is to listen to patients rambling on and on about the most inconsequential things. These guys spent the first twenty-five minutes of each session going over their shared obnoxious behaviors together in their gang. Each one had a different story. If I were their mothers, I'd separate them. They could have grown up to be hoodlums; they certainly acted like sneaky little brats. Yet, they reveled in it.

Several common stories were found in three of the files, but one story was found in all their files.

This story may be important, I guess, she thought.

The story, memorable to them all, concerned an overnight camp experience the boys had at some lake in New Hampshire. One of the boys received a coveted present for perfect behavior, and the others didn't think he should have received it. The files did not say who got it and why he shouldn't have received it, but there did seem to be some rancor around the event. She closed the last of the men's files and thought, *Funny how no one claims to have received the coveted prize.*

Heather did not think she would have enough time to peruse the women's files but realized she could access them in the middle of the night.

Why didn't I think of this before? Candi's a sound sleeper. He'll never hear me come in here. I'll turn the television set on in the kitchen, and if he does wake up, he'll go there first and yell my name. That will leave me plenty of time to put the material in its place and say I was in the bathroom.

Smiling with pleasure at her plot, she started reading. After forty-five minutes of absorbing what she believed to be a lot of mindless junk, she paused.

Exotic dancers they may be, and yet I'm not hearing anything about paid sex or even fun sex. Hell, they could be me. All this stuff is about alcohol-abuse, or a cheating husband, or about the difficulties of relationships, or about not feeling she belongs or fits in.

Heather checked her watch and hurriedly placed the file box in the exact position that Candi had stored it, just as he opened the door from the garage and yelled her name.

Candi decided to cook this evening. He wanted some tacos, which Heather also liked. But he liked his version, and that was okay with her. She kept him company and made a batch of vodka with lime and seltzer. Heather was gluten-free and Tito's was supposed to be gluten-free making her feel quite healthy as she imbibed.

They sat at the kitchen counter, and Candi said he was confused by his patient today. He was supposed to be in crisis, but he didn't show any symptoms. "Maybe he's a businessman with some serious income statement problems because he just appeared to be a savvy corporate mover, just a little stressed. Not in crisis at all."

Heather listened and realized how difficult Candi's work was, and that she herself was not equipped to listen to most people's problems. She was sympathetic to their suffering, but that was her limit.

Candi's on his own in his therapy work. I don't think I'm any more interested in his work than I would have been if he manufactured widgets. At least, in that case, I could see the widgets produced and touch them, and know there was progress.

As he finished querying his latest patient's problems, Heather asked him why he was so loyal to his friends from the Boys Club. He stopped her cold.

"Why do you ask that now? Every time I've mentioned them in passing before, you weren't interested."

"Candi, we've had a scare with these women's deaths. In the past, I didn't want to know too much about your history, given your crazy ex-wife and dealing with her for the sake of your girls. I want to know what kind of support your friends gave you to cultivate the kind of loyalty you have. I mean, look at Norbie. Have we been with him much over the years? The answer is no, but when you went there in distress, he didn't turn you away. He immediately fought for you. Not like most lawyers would, but with a strategy before the arrest. That's unusual.

"So, tell me about some of your experiences with these guys. I've met them all, but I don't know them and really don't even have a line in my brain on them. You must have lots of stories, and if I know you, some will be outrageous. Sit here and entertain me."

Wallowing in her attention, Candi told stories, some of which, he had difficulty in recalling all the facts. And she laughed and told him he should write them down, that they were good enough to make others laugh. *Although the boys in the stories were often quite naughty, their escapades were generally annoying but harmless.*

Heather said, "Someday, we may have children, Candi, and anyway, even if we don't, your girls need to hear these stories. Such entertainment."

So, Candi told several stories, giggling as he reported the boys fooling the counselors, their parents, and some of the other older boys at the club. Adventures included sneaking into the kitchen on the girls' side of the club and stealing their just-baked cookies, locking doors with a special key one of the boys pilfered from his father who worked as a locksmith, which almost shut down the club for a day, pretending they were all sick from a luncheon served until they realized it meant the director was going to send them all home, and more and more. Heather was patient in listening thinking,

If we ever have kids, I'll have to really watch them. It's amazing Candi and those guys got through their childhood. My mother would have grounded me for months. And this is what he's willing to tell me. What about what he's not saying?

"Candi, did you ever go to overnight camp with the Club? You know, campfires, pine trees, lakes, and canoeing?"

"Yeah, we did and had a great time. Funny, I had put that memory away until you mentioned it. We went to New Hampshire one year; I can still smell those pine trees. We were having a great time. The counselors were going to give the boy who behaved the best a reward.

"You know, Heather, I can't for the life of me remember who got the award, but I do remember there was a brouhaha about the recipient. I know Norbie didn't get it because he had spent the three days we were there getting into nothing but trouble. I didn't get it. I wasn't too bad, not like Norbie, but I wasn't good either.

"I remember there was some incident at the girls' side, and the counselors tried to blame Norbie. It's easy to blame someone who is a kibitzer and is always fooling around. One of the counselors had it in for Norbie because he had loosened the salt shaker head on the Camp Director's breakfast table and ruined his breakfast. Everyone knew Norbie did it, but they couldn't place him in the dining hall.

"Norbie never did anything really bad. I remember that, even later when we were all adults, the guys wanted to know who and what happened. I wish I could remember who won the award because he probably did the dirty deed, and the counselors didn't finger him but rewarded him instead. As kids, we would have known the truth and wouldn't have liked that miscarriage of justice. Honestly, Heather, as a therapist, I think I have a brain block about that, which means it may be worth my trying to remember."

"Candi, you know these guys; you know who would do something out of control. Think about it. It may be important. Would it be Myron? Maybe he got the award because he was Afro-American."

"There wasn't a whole lot of that shit going on then. The counselors, like any group, had their favorites. For all the trouble Norbie created, he was probably a favorite, but would never get an award for best behavior. That being said, Heather, they wouldn't give Myron or me an award, just because we were minorities. Not then. Jack Ladd was a pain for the counselors because he had a big mouth and was always trying to run things his way. So, it must have been Gerry, Devon, or Vic who got the big award. I remember the award was something we all wanted, but what was it? I don't know."

Mona, hoping to reassure herself that Rudy was pleased with the party said, "It was really worth it, don't you think, Rudy?" she asked. "I mean the party. It was really worth the celebration. Every guest seemed to enjoy themselves. I got raves about the food, the beer is all gone, and the kids, your brother, and his wife were happy. So, did you enjoy yourself?"

"Hmm, what did you say?"

"Rudy, just what's so important you don't listen to me when I'm the only other person in the room? Work, work, work! I understand its importance to you, but listen to me, please, and tell me what you think about our party."

Blinking several times, Rudy appeared to Mona to come back into a conscious state, enough for him to discuss their big family party.

"It was great. Again, you were right and have made me aware of how lonely I would be without you in my life. I used to think it was the teacher in you; you know, always holding a lesson for me to learn, but I see now I'm often blind to what's in front of me. If I'd been more open, we all could have met Liam and his family ten years ago, but I was afraid. That's all it was, Mona, cowardice."

In language he had never heard from Mona, she said, "Bullshit. You had every reason to be in fear of the unknown about your family when you had only traumatic experiences to remember. And if you knew what your father did before you met Liam, you may never have taken this step for a family reunion."

"Mona, where did you hear that language you just used?"

"From your sons, who may have heard it from you or your dad."

"Tell me, Mona, Liam says he can assess character very well. He thinks that, if he met all of Candido and Norbie's Boys Club buddies, that he could easily eliminate one or two. I brushed him off because he's not a cop and I can't allow civilians to investigate. But I'm telling you, Mona, that I think he'll do it anyway, and it's making me nervous. Come to think of it, I haven't met all of them. I think I'm missing Cramer and Valle, but they're both in Springfield, and I have no excuse to meet with them. Any ideas, Mona?"

"Rudy, you're being narrow in your thinking, and it's not like you. Anyone can meet Vic Cramer. He's at every public event, political or non-profit or church. Do you have the weekend section of the paper? They're all listed, and we can go to one. He'll want to talk to you. He'll know you. As to the other guy you mentioned before, Gerry Valle, my brother knows all the businessmen from the country club. He'll set you up for a golf match. Wait, I think there's a private party at the club this Saturday for the Belmont race. Everyone's rooting for Justify. It's all businessmen going to it. And unlike most of those racing parties, no big hats are welcome."

"What do you mean, 'Big hats,' Mona?"

"Idiot, I think you're more Inspector Clouseau than the highly regarded MCU Captain I hear about. Be nice, or I'll tell the Chief how little you know. Ladies at the races wear gorgeous big hats. No women are invited at this celebration, at least according to my sister-in-law,

Sally. She was quite put out not to be allowed into the inner sanctum of men. That's how she described it."

"Why do you think Gerry Valle would be there?"

"Because Sally mentioned a bunch of big-time local businessmen were coming to the racing party. Valle was the first name on the list. He supposedly loves those men-only golf parties, card games, and the like. He'll be there, and I'll get you an invitation, but only if you take me out to dinner at a nice restaurant tomorrow night. We can celebrate closing your jaded family history saga. If you weren't such a curmudgeon, you'd write a book about it. What do you say?"

"I'll tell you one thing, Mona, there will never be a book."

On Saturday evening Rudy was seated at Gerry Valle's table with some other professional or business men. He was introduced as a cop from West Side, but not as a Captain or from MCU. Rudy spent his whole time talking to the other men at their table, which required him to converse outside his comfort zone; policing. Some of their conversations focused on family, and that helped.

"Rudy was seated opposite Valle at a large round table. Conversation with such a diverse group would normally have been difficult. But that was not his purpose. *I'm here to figure him out. What do I think I am, a friggin' psychiatrist? I can't question him without telling him why. I'm not undercover. I actually have to stay away from him. If later we go to court, there'll be all kinds of questions about my motives.*

Look at him. How could he be the perp? He'd never want to get his hands dirty, and although he's in good shape, I doubt he's ever done any real physical work. You can never really tell everything about a guy from his looks. He's in the de rigueur *dress, a golf shirt and he isn't muscular, though tall. That fits the bill. The guys like talking to him. He doesn't seem to brag, doesn't seem to have an inferiority complex, and isn't the biggest gambler on the race at this table.*

The race began, and Justify was a winner coming out of the gate. The crowd, thirty guys in all, went absolutely bonkers. Some because they won, some because they lost, some who loved being part of the action with no risk, and, then there was Rudy who was pretending to belong but had important work to do.

He watched Gerry Valle for over two hours making two distinct observations. Gerry felt entitled, belonging to this group and secondly Gerry drank less and ate less than any of the other men. Rudy believed Gerry Valle was a controlled man and thought, *He has his life in control. Petra says control is important to him. Even his company's name, 'Middle Men,' is either a play on the lack of control middle managers have in business, or it answers the complaint that employees have over middle managers not allowing them access to upper management where decisions are made. The question is what Petra asked about why he isn't married? Do we have a dating history on him? I think Devon O'Brien and Lavender James are the best two to pump for that kind of info on Gerry. He does not seem to be the type to do any dirty deed; his clothes and behavior are so perfect.*

Rudy left with his brother-in-law, JR, as soon as the race was over, with the others booing them and calling them names in reaction to JR's big win in the pool. He'd put up the biggest amount and had bet the trifecta, only to come out on top. Rudy tried to pretend he didn't know how much money flowed through the group in two hours, thinking, *Not my money. Never could do this. Mona would kill me.*

———

Just one day later, Captain Beauregard and Mona, and some West Side politicians and lawyers had been solicited to join the fundraising dinner for disabled veterans at the West Side Country Club organized by Vic Cramer and his wife, Dr. Ginnie Connell. Mona said Sally her sister-in-law had heard that Vic's wife was a doctor in the service before she came here and was supposed to be very involved in veterans' recovery.

"She's gone back to Iraq as late as last year. Vic doesn't go with her, says he doesn't need to see all the negativity at this time in his life, and insists that his role is to raise dollars to help, not look at the aftermath of war in person. Sally thinks Vic fools around on the wife when she's out of town. He looks like the type to her."

The cost of the event was fifty dollars a person which was not in Mona's budget, but if it helped Rudy in his work than she was game. *This is different. I normally go to fundraisers as a volunteer worker, moving food, or collecting tickets or arranging chairs. I could get used to this, dressed up and able to sit and listen to the heartfelt stories and not being interrupted by a problem.*

Dr. Ginnie Connell spoke on a panel including two other doctors from Boston who served with Ginnie, treating the horribly maimed survivors of the Iraqi conflict. She had a no-nonsense voice and appeared to repress her compassion for her patients, although not successfully. Dr. Connell did not cry, but she moved Mona to tears.

Mona realized Rudy's focus was not on Dr. Connell and her colleagues but on Vic Cramer, who also sat at the head table. She tried to envision Rudy's perspective about Cramer but couldn't get the vision into her head. *Maybe, men look at another man and see something a woman doesn't see. And vice versa! Maybe I can see something that Rudy could never see about this man, Vic.* Mona studied Vic Cramer, ignoring the speakers. Something she saw seemed "off." *He's a big man, takes up a bigger footprint than Rudy, but he almost looks collapsed there at the head table. The more applause Ginnie gets, the smaller he looks. What's that all about? He's made lots of money, has no worries, lives well, and yet he looks lost.*

Rudy, sitting right next to Mona saw something else. *The son of a bitch is making eyes at the blonde at table two, and she right back at him. When I stared at him, he changed his demeanor in an eye blink. The guy screws around. He's married to a working saint, and that's not enough for him. She's a serious woman but seems awfully nice. What does this relationship mean? Dr. Connell is quite attractive, in fact, better looking than the blonde at table two, but doesn't show as much of her body; then again, no one in the room shows as much of their body as the blonde at table number two.*

How does this fit in with the murders? Lots of men cheat. He, however, maybe has little control over his cheating if I'm made aware of it in a public event. Need to investigate. I wonder if anyone has access to the wife personally, who may know what's going on in that marriage.

Rudy got a call; trouble down Country Club Road at McKay's condo. He whispered to Mona who agreed to catch a ride from one of the Mayor's aides sitting next to her, and he left.

25

Second Attempt

Police cars were blocking the road, with several on the lawns on both sides of Country Club Road. The road to the condo units was occupied by vehicles from the fire department first responders and several police squad cars. The lights in every condo were on. Rudy saw there was a man in custody. He also saw Detective Ashton Lent and Martina McKay standing in the doorway to her unit, and she was crying.

Rudy was sorely disappointed as he heard the man in custody screaming obscenities, yelling that Martina kidnapped his daughter. Rudy thought, *Just walking into this chaos and I know the whole story. The ex-boyfriend just found out he's a daddy all these years later. Poor guy, probably not the serial murderer but still a sociopath in my mind. Maybe he's another one who wants to murder Martina, but not the one I'm looking for. If he were, he'd not have come around with a crowd on the street. Yet, maybe that would be the perfect time.*

There was a story, as bizarre as Martina's history. "He is off his rocker," Ash said. "I was keeping Martina company tonight and questioning her about her thoughts around the women who were murdered."

Rudy gave Ash a look, one that said, "Bullshit."

"No," Ash said, "really, Captain. We were talking earlier, and she told me she was to be alone tonight. She knows that's a no-no, so for security, I came home with her. The lights were not on yet, and just when they were to go on automatically, I heard a key turn in the back door. You know the door's by the wooded area. She hadn't locked the screen door, and the inside door lock is easy to open. She forgot to lock the deadbolt that was installed at the time of the last incident. She said if she were alone, she would have gone around the house and checked locks, but with me here she felt safe. As we were sitting talking, he came in behind us, hit me with something, but I moved in time not to be really hurt too badly. He must not have realized I was not completely down because he had a strip of leather and then used it to try choking Martina. He appeared shocked when I wrestled him down and cuffed him."

The Captain couldn't help but notice the two martini glasses on the coffee table and the afghan spread out along with some of Frank Sinatra's most romantic music still playing. Rudy couldn't believe Ash hadn't at least tidied up the scene before he called for help thinking, *Ash, for your own good, I had better keep everyone that I can out of here.*

One of the uniforms approached the Captain and said, "There's a lieutenant from Springfield who was at the fundraiser up the street, and he wants in. The name is Stellato, and he says you know him and will want him in."

Rudy thought, *Like hell. I'll move out there, not stay in here for him to enter and nosy around, and tell the world what is obviously going on with these two. Stellato talks, talks, and talks; not the worst guy and a good cop, but loquacious and I think lonely. Still, runs his mouth.*

Beauregard corralled the detective and the witness and said it would be better if all conversation could take place outside. Ash, blushing, quickly walked towards the door while Beauregard glanced over and saw Martina take the martini glasses and dump them in the trash. He noticed they were not disposable and thought, *You are smart Martina, very smart.* She then folded the afghan and placed it on a wooden chair and smiled at him as she walked out the door.

Stellato questioned Ash and Martina, which he had no business doing, at least that's what Ash thought. But, the Captain did not stop the questioning. Therefore he must have a motive.

Martina and Ash acquitted themselves well with their answers. Beauregard thought it was just a case of covering your ass in a conversation that was no one's business. Martina's ex-boyfriend, Brett Blanken had stopped ranting when he realized he was being questioned about murders. His rage had now disappeared.

"Look, Captain, what's your name again?" he asked. "Oh, that's right, Captain Beauregard. I just came to see my daughter who Martina has kept away from me. I meant no harm. She can do a 209 A on me. I won't fight it. I was wrong. Please don't ruin my reputation."

Beauregard did not like this man thinking, *How come this guy is so familiar with domestic violence court document names? The average guy doesn't know the name unless he's police or social worker or abuser. I choose abuser for him.*

His facial expression showed his disgust when he said, "Mr. Blanken, you just wait here while we do a search on you. If nothing comes back, then we'll bring you to the station, and there will be an arraignment tomorrow."

The Captain told Petra, who had finally arrived on the scene, to search for state and federal warrants on Mr. Blanken. When Brett Blanken overheard that instruction, he went crazy and tried to attack Martina.

"You bitch, you're lucky you're not in jail for what you did. Let them look you up. The kid is mine; her DNA is mine, and I'll tell her about you. You're nothing, what – just a music teacher with her name in a magazine. My money will sink you."

The word came back and as expected there were several warrants for Mr. Blanken, and he resisted arrest by unsuccessfully wrestling with the officer before he finally was handcuffed and put in the cruiser. Martina was shaking.

"Brett will never leave me alone now that he knows about Elisa. How will I tell her I was such a loser? What if he gets out on bail? He won't obey restraining orders. He thinks he's above the law and I know he has pull to get out on bail; I just know it."

Brett's blowing up served a purpose, one he did not anticipate. Ash, Petra, and the Captain became convinced they should personally ensure the safety of Martina McKay. Ash now felt the need to protect Martina for very personal reasons that surprised him, while Petra had just an instinctive reaction to bullying abusers, and Beauregard was motivated by his knowledge that Brett Blanken was capable of anything.

In fact, Beauregard was thinking, *he tried to choke her. He wanted her dead. He knew she would not have discussed her past with her daughter and probably thought no one else knew about their relationship. He could then move in and make nice with a little father and daughter scene.*

The Captain motioned Ash, and they retreated to an open space. Beauregard told his detective, "She's a witness and a potential victim. What the hell were you thinking? Don't fucking deny it. This could have ended very badly for both you and Martina. She doesn't want public scrutiny and probably couldn't handle microscopic attention. You would have to give up your shield. Is that what you want?"

The normally controlled Detective Ashton Lent actually stuttered.

"N-no, Captain, I love being a detective, but I think this lady has my heart, a virgin heart, never been given to anyone before. I know I'm wrong, but I still thank God I was here, or he would have killed her. He wants her dead, and I don't think he'll ever stop wanting her dead. You know the psychology of people like him. He'll work his whole life trying to end her life. He has the money whether he's in jail or not. This is a problem that's not going to go away. My life now is intertwined with her problem, which also mine now."

Beauregard thought of his biological father, *The son-of-a-bitch found Mavis and killed her to punish her, but couldn't make the effort to find us. He had no guilt about what he did. Ash will have a difficult time protecting Martina, but as a police officer, he'll have an edge. Nobody knows what's going on here.*

Ash waited, noticing Beauregard was doing some heavy-duty evaluation of the situation and hoping there may be a little sympathy for him in that evaluation.

Finally, the Captain said, "As far as I'm concerned, and I hope Martina understands the situation as I see it, you were on protective duty tonight, and maybe you're in for a commendation. However, until we catch this serial murderer, I don't want a hint of a personal relationship between you two. Capisce?"

"Capisce, and thank you, Captain."

It took another hour before all the police cars were gone, leaving Ash and Martina alone. Martina was having difficulty in realistically assessing her safety for the moment, overwhelmed as she was with the future she faced dealing with an insane man. "Ash," she asked, "are they charging him with assault with intent to kill?"

His head nod let her know there was no negotiating the charge. Martina cried.

"He'll get in court and say he was just rescuing his daughter from a felon. Elisa will think I'm horrid, prosecuting her father, and she'll know about my history. I'll lose her respect and maybe her love, and he will still be focused on killing me to pay me back for leaving him. And when he finds out someone else wants to murder me, he'll use that to make himself look good. Two men wanting me dead. Ash, it doesn't play well to an audience."

Martina saw Ash looking at her with no hint of a smile. Her heart dropped as she thought, *It's all over now. The first opportunity I've had in twenty years and Brett ruined it.*

Ash put his hands on her shoulders and said, "Martina, we have to get some things straight here before I leave, okay?"

Martina nodded she understood. *Here it comes*, she thought. *The end of something promising, but I don't blame him. Who would want me with such baggage?*

"Martina, you have to come clean with Elisa. She has the right to know her history, and you have the duty to tell her about her father. She'll then have a choice that you've denied her because you felt guilty. You have to do this because it's practical to do this, but it's also something you've been running away from. You're too smart not to know we are never able to really run away from our problems.

"You and I have a relationship that to me looks like what I've wanted my whole adult life. We didn't look for it. I think that's when this kind of stuff happens. You can call it anything you like, but for me, I'm too old to fumble around with words. I'm in love with you. You think on that tonight.

"However, my feelings will need to be controlled. Moving forward with this romance, if you want to, is not in the cards until we find the serial murderer. You are a witness at this time. I can't have a romance with a witness. I'm a patient man; I can wait. I hope you will too."

With that little smirk he liked so much, but also with tears in her eyes, Martina said, "What if, I mean, what if you never catch him? Does that mean this special romance doesn't ever evolve?"

"Don't you worry, we'll catch him. I have the greatest motivation in the world. Now, I have to get to the station to write my report. Don't worry. I'm not leaving, you're safe for now. Your parents just pulled in."

He greeted her parents telling them what had happened while they were gone. He reminded them how important it was for her to have company for a while longer. How long it would take depended on the success of the investigation.

Her dad voiced their fears. "He'll never leave her alone. All these years later and he thinks it's yesterday. What do we tell Elisa? She has a friend two condos down who will tell her what happened here while she was gone. And the serial murderer, how long will this take, Ash?"

Ash explained he had counseled Martina to tell the truth to Elisa. "She's old enough to understand."

He said. "Martina's been a good parent, and who better to tell the story than Martina. She has to do it." Ash tried his best to let them know their safety was of concern to the whole department and left for the station.

On his way to the station, Ash couldn't control his thoughts.

When I touched her breast, she quivered and turned to me and told me to touch her all over, that she'd been waiting her whole life for me. The most magical moment in my life and that asshole tries to kill us. I want that moment back. I want her. We'll catch the fuckin murderer, and I'll protect Martina. I'll do anything for that moment, to get that moment back.

With a questioning look and "Okay, I'm the last to know" was how Petra greeted him as Ashe walked to his desk. "Mason says he's known for a while. I'm certain the Captain knows. Millie says you've been checking in on Martina regularly, and that's how she knows. What am I, low man on the totem pole for gossip? Give it up, Ash. You – in love?"

A blushing Ash informed Petra that although she may be correct, she also had gone too far. He let her know by walking away.

The Captain called with an arm motion for all to join him. Conference Room A had been newly painted in what Petra described as a subtle vomit shade of puce. She did not say that in front of the Captain, knowing he probably chose the color. *What we need here is the finesse of Lavender James,* she thought. *She'd have done it for free, no money, just to be helpful to the 'nice police.'*

"Mass Live has just posted a story about the assault on Martina today and is trying to connect it to the serial murders," Rudy said when they had assembled. "The Chief just called me on it. Let's take a look."

Millie had set up a large screen on the computer. The story was sensational without saying anything but posed questions that required answers the public wanted and wanted immediately.

"This man arrested, is he the serial murderer? Who is next if he's not the serial murderer? How could this man attack a woman in the high-end condos when, a thousand yards away, some top echelons of the police were at a fundraiser? Who is safe anymore in West Side?"

Mason had reviewed the film before the others saw it, "We're under a magnifying glass, Captain," he said.

"The film shows the West Side Country Club fundraiser with its overcrowded parking area running down towards the condos," Ash said. "Our police cars with revolving red lights appear to be a Fourth of July celebration, except it isn't the fourth. The visuals are stunning. Have you heard from the chiefs in Wales and Springfield on this yet, Captain?"

"Our Chief has, and there's a conference call tomorrow morning. Reporters have been storming their offices for news about today. The chiefs don't want a meeting because the reporters would be able to find out about it and would be waiting with cameras as we would exit. No, we'll talk on the phone.

"Also, somebody dropped a dime, reporting I was at the fundraiser and just had to walk the thousand yards to get to the light show. I hate this kind of publicity. It doesn't serve the public well to excite them with deception, and it sure as hells interferes with our work.

"This Brett Blanken is a sociopath, probably a psychopath, but not the one we're looking to arrest. It's too bad he isn't, but he, as the murderer, just doesn't make sense. I've explained it to the Chief. At first, he tried to press me into charging Blanken for all the murders, until I hammered the facts home about who Brett is and was. I reminded him Blanken has resources to create havoc in this city, charging us with a bogus attempt at prosecution, which it would be.

"We have a real question in front of us, and that is the black SUV that you, Ash, saw up on the road to the club on another occasion. Was it the serial murderer's or Blanken's, Petra? You and Ash go in there and question him. His attorney has not arrived yet. See if he has an alibi for that date. We need to clear him in our own minds for the stalking of Martina.

"But, before you join Blanken, I have another problem to discuss. It's been a while since the second attempt on Valencia. Our perp must be chomping at the bit. I'm hoping we've identified all the potential victims that appeal to him.

"I have a problem with his attack on Valencia. It was out of order. Martina should have been first. If the order of the women is determined by phone calls and he goes out of order, what does that mean? It could mean he wants to kill and, if frustrated, will not obey his plan.

"He's an organized killer, a psychopath, so, going against his plan doesn't sit well with my idea of him. Maybe the women aren't the motive. If we've missed the motive, we've missed an opportunity. Think about it. Anyway, I don't want him, in his frustration, to just kill some other pretty woman who's similar in characteristics to these women. We need a watch on Valencia, Martina, and Lavender. I also wonder what he will do if he finishes killing them all. I believe once this type of person gets a taste of the kill then, he has a need, and that need requires continual action unless there is a specific motive we don't understand."

"What kind of motive, Captain. I mean other than being a nut case, what kind of motive are you thinking about?" asked Mason.

"I believe cut marks on the body post-death are important. The medical examiner hypothesizes the suspected weapon is maybe a hunting or fishing knife but hasn't been able to identify the exact knife model. The perp is driving around with a large knife or has it secreted in his home.

"Why inflict the slices post-mortem? The women weren't raped. The women were all beautiful. Why cut them up? He wanted to disfigure them, yet didn't want them to know it. Maybe he hated their beauty, but he didn't cut their faces, just their sexuality. Did he want to put them in the grave as beautiful asexual women?

"There's something there, I just know it, or it's not about the women."

———

Petra and Ash joined the prisoner, who had still not calmed down. Amidst some venomous verbal assaults on Martina, the police, and Ash, he stood up attempting to grow bigger than himself. Obvious to the two detectives, Brett Blanken wanted to assert control.

Ash walked back to the door, motioned to the uniform guarding the conference room and asked why the prisoner was not cuffed. The guard approached Blanken, who was infuriated by being cuffed but did acquiesce.

"You may have the power to subdue me now," Blanken said, "but I almost had you at the condo. You got something going besides protection with her. You're a fool. She can't be trusted. Does a disappearing act on me and doesn't tell me I have a daughter? You read about people like that.

Petra cut him off. "I don't give a hoot about your domestic problems, Brett. I'm looking at you for some bigger crimes. I'll read you your rights now. I know they were read when you were arrested at the assault and B & E scene, but I'm going to read them again, on the record." And she did.

"I don't fucking care what you read me. This doesn't count. Nothing in here counts. I'm waiting for one of the best criminal attorneys in the state. He'll be here in a couple of hours, and I'm not saying anything to you without him here."

"Brett, I really don't want to hear from you. I wouldn't believe a thing you said, anyway. I have a duty to explain to you just what charges you may be facing unless you tell me a good reason why you shouldn't be charged, like an alibi or something like that.

"There have been several murders of beautiful women like Martina, who have connections to her. The similarities in the crimes are notable! Here you walk in and attack Martina McKay who is under a watch detail. That's what you're facing, one hell of a coincidence that you attempt to kill her. You look good, not for one assault, but for several murders and another additional assault. Tell that to your lawyer when he gets here."

Petra motioned to Ash to leave with her, and they both moved towards the door, not looking back.

As Petra left the room with Ash behind her, Brett Blanken yelled, "Are you off your rocker. You can't charge me with murders. I wasn't even in the state, other than the last two weeks. You can't charge me. I have alibis. When did these murders happen? I don't even know about them."

"No, Brett, I'm not falling for that," Petra said. "You think I'll tell you the dates and times and then you and your lawyers will scheme with one of your employees that you were together discussing business. We're not doing it that way, Brett. You tell me where you've been for the last four months and how you couldn't possibly be in Western Massachusetts for the past four months, and maybe, just maybe, you have alibis for yourself."

Blanken got very excited, saying, "I've been in Vermont and New Hampshire for the last six months. There are people who saw me who will vouch for me. I didn't come near Massachusetts or New York. I've been avoiding people who know me. And the only fucking person, outside my pitiful family in Pittsfield, I know in Western Massachusetts is Martina. And all I do with my Pittsfield family is send them money for nothing. That's stopped."

"Brett, just where in New Hampshire and Vermont and what dates and who on a daily basis can vouch for you? Remember, Vermont is next door to Western Massachusetts, and New Hampshire isn't that far either. We're not talking Florida or California."

"I live with a woman who is with me all the time, except for this week. She had a fit when I left her. Thought I was out with another woman. My cell phone should show you where I am most times. But every night from eleven in the evening until two in the morning, I'm at local bars, wherever I am. I'll get you addresses when you give me my phone. I have trouble sleeping before three a.m. Always have. I'm a night owl."

Petra asked, and he agreed to her looking at his cell phone.

"I'll get the phone from his belongings and have Mason go through it before his lawyer gets in here," Ash said.

26

Chasing Details

R udy had just taken a bowl of cherries from the high-end refrigerator, after searching and not finding any cookies. *That's the trouble with having three teenage boys,* he thought, *zero junk food. They are like locusts sucking it all up in one swoop. At least I can get some sugar into my system with the cherries rather than the grapefruit, which is the only other alternative today.*

The fridge is an over-the-top appliance, the only one Mona ever insisted she had to have. I argued against it at first, but she was firm. Normally priced at two to three times other brands, I had a hard time swallowing the purchase, until I realized this was for the family, that it would last a long time, and that she found a friend who sold her one at forty percent off. One thing for sure, it looks good there. She had it built in, or I guess that's the way it's supposed to be done. God, it made her happy.

Now I'll eat these damn cherries and have a cup of hi-test, and maybe I'll get some inspiration. Hell, it's only two in the afternoon, nobody's home, and it's quiet. Isn't that the reason I'm here, to break the cycle and clear my brain of junky details?

He munched away and found he was sated after eating only ten cherries. *Surprising,* he thought and realized he would have eaten his usual six cookies which Mona had carefully explained were sixty calories each, while ten cherries were only forty-three calories in total. *If I could only remember that, three hundred and sixty calories in my cookies compared to forty-three calories in the cherries. I really don't even want more than ten cherries. If I could just remember that, I wouldn't be chunky and could beat this adult-onset diabetes shtick.*

He later wondered if his clear thinking on calories had something to do with his next decision. *I'll go visit Valencia Longtin in the nurse's home in Nonton. I'll give a call to Chief Provast. He'll probably be there to greet me; any excuse for him to see Rita Worthy, the nurse who is so supportive of Valencia and is giving her protection in her own home. Never met a nurse before who would do that, disrupt her own life, and maybe put herself at risk. Yup, on to Nonton and maybe Devon O'Brien will be there – no maybe about it. Time to listen patiently! Hard for me but I can do it today. The cherries and coffee have brought out the best in me, I think. At least, maybe for today?*

He was greeted by Devon and brought into a room that resembled a Floridian Lanai. He had seen such attachments in Palm Beach but not in Western Massachusetts. *Nonton*, he thought, *is home for lots of artists, including architects, and so it's not surprising to see something different here.*

It was a beautiful space, and the casualness of the sofas and chairs welcomed him.

I like this. I think Mona would like this. We could build it on the back of the house; maybe after the kids graduate from college, just another nine years or so if they do the normal four years. I'm told by all our friends that's not an absolute timeline today, although Mona says it is for our kids.

Valencia, Rita, Devon, and Rudy were joined by Chief Provast. The conversation was general and fun, the coffee hot and perfectly brewed, and Rudy did not eat the scrumptious looking raspberry-filled Linzer tart cookies. He was amazed at his self-discipline.

Rudy eventually found a moment to casually turn to a discussion on Devon's friend, Vic Cramer. He told the group about his listening to Vic's wife, and how impressed he and Mona were with Dr. Connell's support and work for those bodies left so damaged from the Middle

East conflicts.

"Captain, you're on target there," Devon responded. "Ginnie is, in everyone's opinion, a special lady. Vic lucked out marrying her, and she's nice looking too. He likes nice looking women."

Valencia looked thoughtfully at Devon and continued the thought with, "You can say that again. He always dated beautiful women. Remember the gal he dated for a number of years, was engaged to her, but never married her; she was a knockout. What happened there, Devon? The other long-term relationship he had with a friend of mine, Patty Sleward, also finished badly. I know she broke it off because he was taking too long to get to the altar."

"I don't know for sure what happened in the relationship with Judith Borrender," Devon said, "but I do know after they became engaged, she wanted to see more of him. She complained he wasn't around enough. You know, he's out everywhere all the time meeting people. Vic never wanted any controls on him even when he was a kid. Tell him he had to be someplace or else and he wouldn't ever be there. He's chosen the best lifestyle for himself. He is everywhere but nowhere by design. Judith broke it off about two months before the wedding. She never spoke to him again and moved to New York City. I heard she married a guy who was a CPA and owner of a big accounting and investment firm. Best for both of them, I think."

"Valencia," Beauregard said, "were there ever any guys who stand out in your mind at the clubs when you were there. You know the type, the hangers-on with apparently no place to go?"

"Just Jack and Vic and Devon and Gerry and Myron, that's all I can remember. I mean there are always the regular alcoholics, you know, the guys that come in for two hours a day, count their drinks, and laugh at others' jokes. There were a couple of cops that were regulars at the bars.

One often worked the strip club. The ladies who worked there who came into the club said he was a go-to guy on the force."

"What about Vic now, Valencia, I mean is he a womanizer? For a guy who got around before, what's he like now, marriage doesn't always stop the playing around."

"Captain, I live in Nonton and am not at the big affairs in the immediate Springfield area. My frequenting Springfield centered around music, especially Irish music. But one of my colleagues has said Vic is chummy with all pretty ladies, especially young ones who dress in a showy fashion. But she thought it was just for show. This may be an unfair charge since most of the young women today dress more provocatively than when I was younger."

Beauregard thought the souls in the room bordered on sins of unkindness as they ruminated on recollections and discussed the habits of the young women today and their normal work dress. They laughed at their mature perspective of the younger generation's movements sartorially way to the left of center.

Devon broke the glee with, "Vic is a philanderer, has always liked pretty women, and I don't think he'll ever stop, but Captain, I see him as maybe, and I am not certain, appearing to be a lecher, not a murderer. I've told you before it's not one of our 'Brothers.'"

Rudy answered, "Is the womanizing a result of his inability to get parental attention, specifically maybe his mother had problems?"

"Don't go there, Captain, you're not the type to play psychiatrist. His parents were not alcoholics, just regular drinkers. Are you happy to know that? He has a need to fill. I agree with you on that. But he fills that need by trying to be important, to not feel unimportant to his family because his parents are now both dead, to not have to be embarrassed anymore. Not unlike other adult children, but he's busy making sure he's important, more important than his family thought. He would do nothing to harm his image as a self-made man, nothing! Maybe he needs women's attention to improve his self-esteem, but Vic respects women, wants them to think he's relevant, and frankly I don't think he'd cheat on her. Ginny gets this, and she loves Vic."

To relieve some of the tension created by Devon's answer to Beauregard, Rita Worthy questioned Beauregard on the physical traits of the group of men he was looking to as potentials. "Maybe one of them I can identify from that first day when there were three men who tried to visit Valencia in the hospital. Maybe not, but I can try. You know he is tall. Are these guys tall? He moves with grace according to the officer who was present on the second attempt on Valencia. Get us pictures, Captain."

As Rudy left the room, he noticed the two couples engaged in handholding. Valencia and Devon were snuggled up together. He thought they looked ridiculous, with the big lug of Devon hovering over slim Valencia. Worse yet was the vision he got from seeing the Nonton Chief kiss the charge nurse. He shook his head and wondered why this glimpse of happiness looked silly to him. *Have I lost the ability to respect joy from delving into the negative?*

Rudy met Ash, who was cooling his heels with Springfield's Sergeant Stellato outside of Lavender's home. Protocol required that Springfield Police be notified that West Side Police were interviewing a Springfield witness in her home on an open Springfield and West Side murder case. They had some questions for Lavender that Petra thought were key, but unasked by her in her interview with Lavender. Rudy did not like returning to a talking scene with Lavender, but thought, *Gotta do what I have to do. I don't like interviewing Lavender with Stellato here. I need some insight from her, and she'll hold back with him present.*

Sometimes I just have to be there to hear the voice shadings, the subtle misconceptions where a lie is not a lie but not the truth either, and to watch the eyes, not always a good shade for hiding the sins of the soul.

Lavender was welcoming. It was obvious she and Stellato were old friends. She hugged him, and he beamed at the attention. Ash thought, *Why not? We guys don't get that kind of attention every day.*

Beauregard spent some extra time, for him, talking generally, so much so Ash realized this interview had a real direction or else the Captain would not be so chatty. Detail after detail was presented and Lavender was requested to comment. She was quite willing to do so.

Ash realized Beauregard had discovered a way to keep Lavender on track. He thought she must be a great student, because she was awesome at answering direct questions, as long as there wasn't an opportunity to tangent over to a subject dear to her heart. He noticed after twenty minutes that Stellato was getting bored and left to get a cup of coffee from the kitchen.

"Joe, there's fresh coffee," Lavender said. "I made a pot for you all, but you in your hurry didn't even give me a chance to be a good hostess."

"Joe, get one for me and Ash. I know he wants one too and is just too polite to ask. He wants two sugars and cream," Beauregard said. "I'll have mine black."

"Christ, does West Side think I'm their maid? You're lucky I don't throw it at you when I bring it."

"Ash, go help him out. He's not used to collegiality." Ash knew the tacit message was, *Keep the guy busy. I need him away from this scene. Keep him busy as long as you can.*

He did, but it required talking to Stellato about a recent drive-by shooting that was more like an assassination and talking about Lavender's beautiful kitchen. He gained a good ten minutes alone for the Captain with his bullshit. *I have this gift, may as well use it*, he thought.

It took the Captain about two minutes to transition to the salient question for today. "Lavender, of all the special duty cops working at the dance club, was there a regular one, one who took the assignment more often than the others?"

"Oh sure, Captain, some of the cops' wives would never let their husbands request that assignment, and if it was the only one assignment available for a night, they would turn it down, letting the next senior waiting to get it."

"Well, seems like you're more likely to get single or divorced guys on duty or maybe some of the older cops."

"Got it right there, Captain, but mainly two guys took the assignment, and one is gay, so his boyfriend isn't worried, and the other is just not interested in us.

"He's a good guy, Charlie Lomadis. He's in his early fifties and headed for retirement. He has a place in South Carolina that's calling to him, his word not mine. Joe Stellato used to take all the overtime shifts he could before he made detective in MCU. I don't know the ritual over there, but I think the big boys didn't want him at the club, in case something happened there, and he'd be a witness, and they'd be short a detective. I think something like that happened. But he never left us. He hangs out several nights a week to check up on us. He's lonely, a widower who is lonely, lonely like a lot of the guys who come in regularly."

"I know you go to the Irish clubs on your nights off. What cops do you see when you're there?"

"Hell, Captain, the Irish clubs are cops' heaven and haven. Doesn't matter if you're Irish, it's goombah week for them all, you know, like the Italians say, 'He's my goombah!' I see Joe there all the time. It's like a women's 'Stitch and Bitch Club,' my mother used to belong to keeping herself informed. He keeps me informed."

Rudy grinned and whispered, "So we can gossip, can we? Tell me about Joe Stellato and why he frequents the dance club when he no longer works there. Doesn't he have a home to visit, sometimes?"

"No, Captain, not now. He goes to an apartment. He has no kids. His wife died about two and a half years ago. I'd love to have him meet a woman, but she couldn't be from my place of work. He likes me because I have homespun values despite my not looking homespun. He likes normal. I know he acts like a cop punk, but he's not. I guarantee you he's not."

A chastened Beauregard just responded with, "Glad to hear that about a fellow blue. Thanks, Lavender." Shortly after, Joe and Ash joined them, the Captain wound up the conversation. As he got in his car, he questioned Ash.

"What do you think? Is he a perp or not? His wife died two and a half years ago, and he hangs around the dance club now."

"Captain, Stellato is a pain in the ass, the kind of cynic we see on the job. Don't know about the other. He only talks about the job and Lavender's nice home. Got no sociopathic beams on my radar with him, but you know when a sociopath is careful, you never get any beams. Plus, he's a cop and better at the hiding. Barely any evidence in this case with lots of possible perps pointed to, and he's in the know about police investigations! Could be! Worth a look at him! I'll get on it."

"Did you ever ask Martina whether she gave her cell phone number to any of the guys we have in our collective focus on this?"

"No, Captain, it slipped my mind. I'll ask her."

Beauregard thought, *I bet you will.*

"We'll have to have another interview with Gerry Valle. It seems he's under our radar for what: he's never married, his company owns a lot of dark SUVs giving him access, and he knows all the ladies. He was told not to bother Janice Shaunessy by Devon, maybe Devon had a bigger reason than what we have learned. Valle told Petra the next time we talk to him, call his lawyer. We'll do that, but do a search first, Ash."

Driving back to the station, Beauregard felt a compulsion that took him by surprise.

What the hell, I want to talk to Liam and see how he's doing. Why not? I call Lizette and Roland all the time. I call Mona and the boys. It's okay to want to call Liam, he's my brother. I can want to talk to him occasionally. He was almost to the station before he gave in and made the call.

Liam was happy to hear from him, and his first words demonstrated his glee.

"Hey. Bro, so glad you've broken out of the cop mode and want to talk to me. I did some reconnoitering on your people who may be perps. Didn't go out of my way, so you won't be embarrassed, but I noticed some stuff. Want to grab a beer, and we'll talk?"

Rudy wasn't sure he was happy about Liam inserting himself in his investigation, but he did want to grab a beer and see him. They agreed to the Happy Hour at Cal's, a family-style restaurant nearby

Settling in with craft beers in front of them, Liam could not be prevented from telling Rudy what he thought about his peek-a-boo of two of the potential perps and a paper review of the third.

"Norbie is not a murderer. He is too well balanced and has no time to murder, although he could probably do it well. The other two, Valle and Cramer, for sure are control freaks. It has been my experience that control and domination fuel anger and rage and sometimes worse behavior. Go look into their backgrounds. My gut says it's one of them because they are so caught up in themselves. Look for their reactions to insults. See if it sets them off more than the normal guy."

The two finished their coffees, one thinking he was giving the other direction in his investigation and the other thinking, *I'm way ahead of you, buddy.*

Rudy walked into the station only to fine Chief Coyne in his office waiting for him with another man who looked familiar. Chief Coyne welcomed him in Rudy's own office.

"Captain Beauregard, meet Detective Theodore Toddington, from Vice. You are lucky today, Rudy, I've approved his transfer to MCU as of today, an additional detective in reward for your department's success. In response to your work on these current serial murders, I'm leaving Lieutenant Aylewood at MCU. These plans were approved by the mayor. Now I have to run but wanted to personally introduce you to Theodore. I have to leave shortly for an appointment. The clock is always the master!"

Beauregard was suffused with anger, and his thoughts were running amuck. *Who the hell does he think he's kidding? I know Toddington's the mayor's brother-in-law. No unit wants him, probably reports every action to the mayor. I've heard of him. He's an engineer and watches everything. Talk about avoiding normal protocol. All my work in getting the right people in here who work as a team, as true colleagues, is down the drain. What happened in Vice? Couldn't he cut it?*

Instead of expressing his thoughts, he turned to Toddington and said, "Why do you want to leave Vice, Detective?" While waiting for an answer, he took stock of the man, who though tall and broad carried himself with a humble but intelligent looking air, he did not show a hint of the Mayor's brother-in-law attitude of 'you better take care of me.'

"Captain, I've applied for a transfer to several other departments, even to traffic and been refused, at the department level. Not unkindly but refused. If you look at my jacket, you will see my service is impeccable. I am not being arrogant, but I do what the job expects always. I've eight years as an engineer with Sikorsky, and they were good to me, but I've always wanted to be on the police force. My tests are at the top of the class. If you accept my transfer, you can count on my loyalty."

Beauregard reacted by saying, "Welcome to MCU, Detective Toddington. Chief, you will excuse us. The detective here has to get caught up on our current major murder case."

Chief Coyne happily escaped. Beauregard addressed the new member of MCU. "Detective, I hope you are able to find your fit here. You've been around long enough to know this appointment is a surprise to me, will be a surprise to the other MCU detectives, and the ball's in your court to make it work. I will not throw obstacles in your way, but I will expect performance.

"Start with reading the Lisa Moliano file which is our case, study the facts, then read the files we have on the other murders listed on the murder board. Any questions in finding materials, ask Millie. You met her on your arrival. When you're through with your reading and notetaking, talk to the other detectives, Aylewood-Locke, Ash, and Smith. Millie will introduce you in case you've never met them. Later, I'll meet with you all."

Beauregard walked out to take a ride to cool down; the need to drive had nothing to do with temperature on the outside, but much to do he thought with a seething anger inside. He fumed, thinking, *No freakin' other place for the Chief's relative to be put but in my unit. He wants the guy to have a heads up on advancement. Well, I have murders to solve and ten other B & Es, one major drug assault case, and two home invasions. Let's see if he has the constitution for this unit. He didn't like Vice; I should follow up on what happened there. Time to go home!*

27

Character Analysis

A sh was in his car, parked under a cool shade tree, talking on his cell phone to Martina. He used a throwaway, like the hoods on the television shows. Later, there could be no proof of a relationship with him if she was called as a witness in Brett Blanken's assault and home invasion case if there would ever be one. He said a few words before asking her the questions for which the Captain needed an answer.

"Martina, did you ever give Gerry Valle or Vic Cramer your cell phone?"

"I really didn't know either of them well. Vic did have a contact, who supported one of my student groups' trips to Boston to perform. We received accolades and actually scored tops in our division. As to Gerry, I see him whenever one of my student groups plays for free for various causes. He never supported them but was helpful in getting them free gigs. You know, playing the music for a charity fashion show. That kind of thing, so I guess he has my cell phone number. Generally, I never gave the number out except for business. Why, Ash, you don't really suspect either of them, do you?"

"Honey, we're covering all bases. We suspect everyone. You know I've got to get to the bottom of this so we can get together."

"Whatever you need, Ash, whatever you need!"

"Tell me what you learned about these two guys. I mean did you ever feel they had a thing for you?"

"Ash, if I saw either of them at the Celtic Belles, I got a big wreck from them. Sure, they would be willing if I were willing. I think Gerry maybe wanted something more, but Ash, he really has no personality. He's pretty into himself and likes perfection. I don't think there's a woman in the world that could please him, in the long run. I mean any one of the women victims was beautiful enough, but on a bad day, we can all look like something the cat dragged in. I don't think Gerry gets that."

"Well, I'd like to see you on a bad day. You know, to see what I'm getting into, whether I can tolerate the horrible you, or maybe get another gal who looks good on your bad days. What do you think about that arrangement?"

"I think you're dead, gone, not ever to be seen by another living soul if you believe I could live with that." She laughed. And he laughed.

He said, "Never will happen, you are the only one, even if you resemble what the cat dragged in. Did I tell you I love you, today?"

Now that Ash had his answers to the Captain's questions, he said his good-bye and headed to the station. Ash found Detective Mason Smith at the table in front of the murder boards, with another man, multiple files on the table. He thought for a minute before he recognized Detective Theodore Toddington from Vice.

What the hell is going on here? Why would Vice be looking at our murder files? Cripes, the Captain would never let a cop from another department in here. There's only one answer, and that's he's been transferred in.

Mason introduced Ash to Theodore before he could say the wrong thing.

"Ash, or Detective Lent, meet our new MCU detective just transferred in, Theodore Toddington. The transfer announcement has been slow from the Chief's office. Ted is reviewing the case files on the murders, and the Captain wants a meeting tomorrow morning to refocus."

"You play guitar, don't you, Ted? Ash asked. "I played with you at a wedding about ten years ago. Sorry I didn't place you right away. It was a big wedding at the Salem Cross Inn out there in West Brookfield."

"Sorry, Ash, I don't remember you, but I remember the wedding. I'm not that good remembering faces. What instrument do you play? I'll remember that."

"Mostly violin, but I play piano and bass as well."

"Ahh, you did a classical set for the wedding service. I remember you now; thought you should be playing with the Springfield Symphony."

"I sometimes do. Thanks for remembering. What takes you to MCU?"

"A burning desire on my part and help from my brother-in-law, the mayor, brought me here. Please don't hold it against me, Ash. I will pull my weight."

Back to work, Ash asked, "What do you see in the files? Captain Beauregard believes in fresh eyes on the details. Do you see stuff we've missed? Ask us. Mason and I will explain anything not on the boards or in the files."

"The knife is the same in each murder, which means the guy carries it around or stores it at home. The expected size of the blade from the M.E. is 8.75 inches long and 0.125 inches thickness. Sounds like a Bowie knife. With the handle, it'd be close to 15 inches long. Who among your guys is a hunter or fisher, or do all the 'Brothers from another mother' have Boy Scout history? I think we should pursue that point for evidence if you haven't already. Another thing that bothers me is all the cuts are superficial. What does that mean?"

"We figured the cuts were just meant to disfigure the body. The pieces of wood, which are consistent with two-by-two fence posts, being placed at the entrance to the vagina may mean he wants them to stop having sex or what else, But we haven't really gotten to the reason yet. Those wood posts, in most cases, lie at the edge of the bodies' vaginas, because they don't fit. Be our guest and go figure why. What else do you see?"

"I notice in Detective Aylewood's interview with Gerry Valley that his company has a fleet of cars including dark SUVs. Can we question the auto maintenance staff there? See what cars were washed on Monday mornings after each of the murders. Also, there's a record Vic Cramer's businesses have dark SUV's. Probably there is maintenance staff at several of his firms. We should check that."

"Be my guest, Detective," Ash said as Mason looked on, stifling a giggle.

"Do I have carte blanche to go ahead?" asked Theodore.

Mason said, "Just get your time sheets and authorization for a car from Millie. If you need a car, it will have to be a squad car for now. And yeah, you go do your job as you see it."

Detective Toddington thought, *If this is the way they work here and I can go ahead the way I see things, then I'll be an asset to them. That's what they want, performance; then that's what they'll get from me. I hope I can take Mason Smith at his word and that he's not setting me up – after all, he's not the Captain."*

―――――

On the following day, Captain Beauregard was dripping wet when he entered the station, cursing the forever surprises New England weather presented.

"Perfectly fine when I got out of my car, and then the cloud opens up and drenches me in my two hundred yards to the building."

Already drenched from the rain, he accidentally spilled his coffee on his new khakis. Still soaking in shades of wet he held the scheduled unit meeting, the first since the addition of the new detective. After the shortest introduction to the unit imaginable by any of them, they got right down to work. Assignments of some of the unit's other cases were reviewed quickly before he asked for each detective's summary of their work on the serial murder cases. Petra Aylewood reported first.

"I went after Gerry Valle again. I didn't interview him, but I checked around talking with people who know him. Turns out, his chief assistant Jay Saunders served with my husband Jim in the service. He says Gerry is a closed-up guy, more closed up since the death of his mother a couple of years ago, but he has no problems in working for him. Other than business and fine cars and wine, Gerry has no other interests. He loves pretty women, always did. His mother, even when she got older, was an absolute head turner and he wanted no less for himself.

"After Valle's father died, his mother dated many important men in the area, which did not sit well with Valle. He'd complained constantly about those old men dating his beautiful mother. Jay said, and I quote, 'He had a fixation about his mother. I told him once he should get therapy. He said he had, and there was nothing wrong. He was just looking out for her, knowing what men are like and that she was an innocent.

"His mom wasn't an innocent. She was running around when her husband was alive, but Gerry just pretended it wasn't going on. Sounds to me Gerry could be whacked out about women, over-loved his mom, and then she dies in an auto accident, and her beauty is ruined.

"None of the women he wanted desired him. Mother dies just before Loretta Loren gets murdered. His motive could be replicating his mother who he loved dying and being maimed, and maybe he loved these women, but couldn't have them, and wants them dead like his mother, and he maims them afterward. The piece of wood post near the vagina is a symbol of what he wanted for his mother; no male entry. How's that for a report, Captain? Includes character analysis and maybe motive."

"Now we have a replica of an old movie, killing women to make up for the loss of mama. We're getting a little over the top here, Petra. Although, it does raise some questions! He saw a therapist, and you can bet the one he talked about is Candido Rodriguez. They all saw Candi as a therapist, except for Norbie. We don't have access to those records, and Candi insists there's nothing in his records of value.

"Valle is tall enough, and his feet are big enough to match description and evidence. What about foot coverings? Do I remember right that his maintenance people used foot coverings that match what we know? One thing doesn't match. Valle doesn't like to get dirty, so cutting the ladies seems to be against his sense of avoiding messes."

Ash jumped in. "When somebody is OCD, Captain, the mess is not the focus and therefore a mess may be alright if it's part of the process to get to the conclusion. I think we ought to see what, if any, successful sexual relationships he's had in the past. If he has and it's just that women don't want him long-term because he's narcissistic and boring, then I wouldn't look at him for the murders."

Theodore said, "I know the head of maintenance at his plant. I had drinks with him at the Rumbleseat in Chicopee after getting burgers at Luxe Burger Bar in Springfield. He said he remembered one Sunday morning date that required a car wash on the following Monday. There was no access paperwork filled out. He brought the info to Valle, who had a fit that protocols in place weren't being obeyed. The murder in Boston was too long ago for him to remember. Again, not everything, but maybe some evidence there. The guy remembered the date for the second crime. Maybe, Valle smartened up and had the car cleaned before bringing it back to the garage after that."

The Captain pulled out a report from Valle's file.

"Looks like he was a normal adolescent, who along with Candi, was one of the first to go after the girls. At that age, a guy doesn't have to be interesting. If he was successful then with the ladies, then something happened later to change that. We need to look into his personal life. He has two homes. Talk with his neighbors. He's not married but probably occasionally brings some ladies home."

Mason made a report that surprised the detectives. He said his sister worked in the healthcare system and knew Dr. Ginnie Connell quite well.

"Dahlia says that Dr. C, that's what they call her, well, some of the staff thinks she's bi-sexual. Actually, she said if Dr. C had not married, then everyone would have thought she was a lesbian. She says before her marriage and when she's overseas, she was never seen in a dress or skirt. She elopes with Vic Cramer, and now she dresses like a Talbot's model.

"Everyone loves her but thinks her marriage is one of convenience. Dahlia says Dr. C is intellectually brilliant beyond the medical field. I think Cramer is smart but certainly not an intellectual. Being married to a lesbian and keeping it a secret would be stressful for anyone. I've read about those English authors who had that type of marriage that mostly didn't work out well. On top of that, Dr. C is becoming nationally famous, leaving Cramer out in the cold. What about that for a motive?"

Beauregard looked at his detectives.

"What the hell are we talking about here? He asked. "Is anybody afraid of coming out of the closet today? My boys have friends as young as thirteen who say they are gay. Dr. C is noted for her work. Nobody in their right mind would care she's a lesbian, if she is one. So, what's her motive in this marriage? Maybe she loves him. Maybe she's sick of intellectuals, and a salesman is witty and charming...."

At that moment Millie broke into the room.

"Captain, the Westfield police just called. Lavender James insisted they get you. Lavender's car was in an accident near or in Hampton Ponds State Park. There was a dark SUV parked not far from the boulder she hit. She's screaming it was an attempted murder and that you know all about it. Two kids were running from the rain squall and came across the scene. They saw a man in a ski-mask trying to take her out of her car to his car. Her little girl was screaming in the back seat. She's bleeding and fighting with everyone on the scene."

The Captain and Petra left in one car, while he sent Ash and Theodore to babysit Martina. Beauregard was adamant.

"This guy is going to be really frustrated now when his goal of getting rid of all these women has been thwarted. Today's event will just accelerate frustration. I'm calling Devon to make sure Valencia is not left alone. The perp is getting careless. Damn, it's broad daylight and what the hell is she doing in Hampton Ponds in broad daylight on a morning when it's heavily raining?"

The accident scene was chaos, much of it produced by Lavender and Lulu Baby. Petra sat with Lavender and the little girl while Beauregard spoke with the uniforms from Westfield. It was called in as an assault in progress by the kids, which brought in what looked like the whole Westfield force.

No footprints were available at this site, which had about three inches of water in the depressed section of the gravel road. Two large rocks had been rolled into an area of the road after the road turned a sharp ninety-degree turn. A car going over fifteen miles an hour would not see the boulders in time to stop.

How the hell did the perp know Lavender was headed this way? Beauregard thought. *He had to know in time to roll the stones. He had to be following her or knew where and why she would take this route. He knows her well.*

Petra was hugging Lulu Baby. The child was glowing in Petra's calming manner, while the two were singing, 'If you're happy and you know it, clap your hands…' a song Beauregard remembered hearing Mona sing with the boys. Lavender was watching the two with amazement while blood dried on the left side of her head and she held ice on the back of her head.

The ambulance had come earlier but had not been able to get by the line of cars and was required to circle around for the other entrance. Beauregard told the cops on the scene this attempted assault may be related to the serial murders that had been in all the papers. The Westfield lieutenant on the scene, named Burton, gave him the go-ahead to question Lavender before the ambulance took her, as long as he was there to take notes for his Captain.

"I think she's in good enough shape to talk," he said. "The ambulance can wait. You'd have to have seen her, Captain Beauregard, she screamed and hollered and cried and swore. Her head was killing her, but she's something else. She's got energy, I tell you. Good looking woman but, boy, I'd run from her. She's draining and, remember, Captain, she's hurt but still is going at it. She practically killed the lady who was trying to hold the little girl to quiet her down. She kept saying DSS wasn't taking her kid for a ride."

Captain Beauregard couldn't help but smile as he reviewed his history with Lavender. *I don't do really well with talkers, but in this case, I love this woman. She's probably alive because she has such a desire to live for that little girl. The perp should never have tried to attack her when Lulu*

Baby, what a silly name, was in the car. Why can't she just call her Lulu? That's different enough. Don't need that baby stuff attached to her name. She hears it, and she'll act like a baby.

Cripes, now I'm criticizing her name choices. Let's see if we can't get the facts from her without a tangent about home decorating or Lulu.

Beauregard found himself holding Lavender's hand. He wasn't sure how that came about. He thought maybe she reached for his and it just happened. "Lavender," he said, "you need to go to the hospital. The ambulance is here. Petra will take Lulu Baby and find Jimmy and your mother to take care of her. Okay with that?"

And she started with no additional question from Beauregard, while he thought, *She's always in control of all her conversations. Even with me, but that's the best way to get her to talk.*

"Captain Beauregard, Lulu Baby was crying all morning. She's had a bad cold and keeps coughing up stuff. The doctor says to keep her sitting up, when all she wanted to do was lie down. The only way to keep her sitting up is to put her in her car seat and drive. She loves to ride in the car. We often drive around this route in the park. It's daylight for God's sakes, Captain; you never said I couldn't go out in the daylight.

"It was him, the killer, I know it was him. He was tall. I didn't smell cologne or aftershave, but he was nervous. I can smell fear. He saw Lulu Baby in the back seat. He must have seen her, but that didn't stop him. He's one dangerous man who wants what he wants. He's a psychopath. He has a mission. He has to kill us for some reason. I hit those rocks, and my airbag blew up, and somehow, I hit my head on the side of the car. I thought it was just an accident. I was trying to see if Lulu Baby was hurt, 'cause she was crying really hard when he opened the door and hit me with a rock on the back of the head.

"I'm telling you, Captain, I saw stars. But he's stupid. Everyone knows that part of the head is hard and a hit will give you a concussion. He was probably trying to hit me on my temple, but I had turned to check on Lulu Baby. She saved me, Captain, my baby saved me. And then I heard those kids screaming, 'Hey, man, whatcha doin' to her!' I think I went out then for a minute or two. Next thing, these two kids, maybe twelve years old, a boy and a girl, all soaking wet had pulled me all the way out of the car and had put their backpack behind my head. God, I have such a headache."

"One more question, Lavender, please tell me, who has ever known you drive up here all the time. And who, if any, knew Lulu was sick and that you might go up here today?"

Lavender's eyes opened as wide as saucers.

"Oh my God," she said, "Captain, I called in sick last night because Lulu Baby didn't want me to go to work, and Jimmy and my mother were both going to be late. So, anyone who was at the club knew I wasn't dancing. The club would have put Rusty, the new girl, on the marquee at the entrance in place of me. You could drive by and know I wasn't there, but that was last night. Lots of people know I love this area. Maybe I was followed. You know it was the third time I went around this route today. There were no rocks the other two times. In fact, I was driving faster this time because I was ready to go home. Lulu Baby had fallen asleep."

Lavender was put on the stretcher and into the ambulance.

"Captain, my Captain will be calling you about this," Lieutenant Burton said. "We'll keep it as an accident until you give us the go ahead with a joint news story. Westfield doesn't need this kind of publicity."

Beauregard thanked him for all his work. Before leaving the park, Rudy looked to where the SUV had been parked. There was no evidence a car had been parked there, with the exception of a flip-top from a soda can. He told a uniform to get it collected for evidence.

The two witnesses were waiting in a squad car. The rain had not yet stopped but had narrowed to a drizzle. He got in the squad car with them and got their story. The two had been hiking in the park, and when the rain opened up, they ran to the road because it was the quickest way home. They lived nearby.

What they saw looked like a kidnapping to them, and they didn't hesitate to scream at the guy who they saw trying to drag a woman out of her car. She was kicking and screaming and wasn't going easily. He had a rock in his hand and was about to hit her again when he realized they were watching. He dropped her half in her car and ran about a hundred feet to his SUV. The license plates were covered with mud, and the kids thought the SUV was either a Toyota or a Honda and was either black or blue-black. The man was in black athletic pants and a hooded sweatshirt with a ski mask. He wore boots. The boy thought they were Doc Martens, but the girl said they weren't. They looked more expensive to her.

Rudy drove home. He stopped by Dick's sporting goods and checked on high-end athletic pants, what he would call sweats, and asked about current popular boots one would wear with sweats. He was told athletic shoes were mostly worn with stretch athletic pants and hoodies. He did wonder if the sweats were in the perp's car; convenient in this case to put over his everyday clothes. He called Toddington and requested that he get alibis from Cramer and Valle. He then made another call to Norbie Cull. It was time to go with his instincts.

28

Choosing One of the Boys

As Rudy settled into one of the soft chairs in Norbie's office, he was grateful the lawyer suggested the meeting place, and particularly for agreeing to meet after closing hours. Rudy did not want any witnesses to this conversation.

Norbie offered the opening gambit. "I'm thinking, Rudy, that I'm not a witness now or I'd be at the station. Knowing you, I think you're probably almost, but not quite, ready to close in on the perp."

"Right on both accounts, Norbie. You're right on both accounts. I need some help with analysis. Since I've personally ruled out Candido and you as perps, it leaves five up for grabs. I've practically ruled out three of those but would like confirmation. Nothing leaves this room, so I'd like to hire your professional services to ensure I have attorney-client privileges. Here is a ten-dollar bill, not your usual fee, but you can consider me almost indigent. Actually, everything we own is in Mona's name, so it's quasi-true."

"New low for me." Norbie took the bill, smiled, and wrote on his lined yellow pad. "You don't need this drama, Rudy, I'd keep your secrets. Lawyers keep lots of secrets; it's our job. I remind you I'm not willing to set up one of the bros. However, if you have good evidence one of them is the perp, well, I'll do whatever's needed to get him off the street."

Rudy explained the evidence for excluding Myron, Devon, and Jack.

"Your analysis is valid based on what you know," Norbie replied. "What I know also supports your conclusion. Not one of those three has a violent streak, even under pressure, and I've known them for a long time. What makes you think Gerry Valle and or Victor Cramer could be the perp? Why specifically must it be one of these guys? I've heard of clients who run the spectrum, from thinking they are Jesus Christ protecting some innocent, to their desire they must get rid of the riffraff of the underworld. I've seen it all. I think, Rudy, that I may be too close to see any danger in these two guys. Ask the right questions, and I'll give truthful answers. Maybe that's how we should do this."

"Is Vic Cramer gay?"

"No." Norbie looked surprised. "Well, I've never seen any evidence. He's had many girlfriends but never seemed to want to close the deal to marriage. Ginnie and Vic as a couple, well, it was a surprise to us all. It happened fast.

"I do know Ginnie is a friend of Bill W. and Vic's parents had some problems with alcohol. He had a lot to live down. His mother, like some women drinkers, was sometimes loose with her mouth and her body when she could get her husband out of the house. It was difficult on Vic.

"I personally found it interesting he would marry a recovering alcoholic, but Ginnie is exceptional. I think it's a good marriage and she understands him. She knows he's not really self-confident and that explains his over the top grand gestures. She gets it, and he knows he's a lucky guy to have found her. Sober, she'll never embarrass him. Drunk, he'll let her go because deep down he's a survivor."

"Norbie -- why didn't you tell me any of this before now?"

"Like everyone in the public say to the cops, 'Because you never asked me before.'"

"So, you think he couldn't murder these women?"

"I'd never say never, but not from what I know. He is really a good guy and a gentle guy. He was engaged once and then broke it off. Everyone thinks it's because he was afraid of marriage. Not so. The future bride was sleeping with a guy who worked for him. He covered for her. He always covers up. He's really a public relations guy at heart, making things look good to outsiders. He had his training covering up his parents' behaviors. He's probably not your guy, Rudy."

"What about the New Hampshire overnight trip you kids took with the Boys Club?"

"What about it?"

"Someone got a prize he didn't deserve. Who was it and what was the surprise?"

"Why are you asking about that? Do you know how long ago it was?"

"I'm not going to answer. You need to answer questions today, Norbie, not me. Furthermore, I sincerely hope when one of your friends other than Candi is charged that you won't defend him?"

"Probably can't anyway. You're safe, Rudy. One client out of the group is the rule. If another in the group is the perp, then, and you know I can't really imagine it right now, I would still have to protect my client, Candi. Don't get it wrong, Rudy. If I think you have gotten the wrong guy, I'll get my friend the best lawyer available."

"So again, what happened in New Hampshire?"

Norbie seemed to be conflicted. Finally, Norbie replied, "I can't remember who got the prize. Did you ask everyone?"

"No. Can't you remember? I heard there was a rift among the boys because the awardee shouldn't have been awarded the prize. By the way, just what was this prize?"

"I can't remember who got it. It wasn't me or Candi or Jack for sure. I can't remember for certain, but it was a big enough prize to cause dissension in the ranks. Probably it was some kind of knife. We were crazy over hunting knives, and my mother was totally against them. If that were the prize, then I would have been angry at missing out. But still, I would never have gotten the prize. I was never very good."

"What about Gerry Valle, Norbie?"

"What about him?"

"I'm pulling teeth with you, Counselor. What are his problems?"

"He has none. He never married. He never had kids. He's made a lot of money. He's achieved every single thing I ever heard him express a desire for when we were kids."

"So, you think just because he's successful, with no drain on him, that he's happy? Norbie, you know better than that. He has always loved women, so I'm told, so how come he couldn't get one to marry him?

"Easy answer, Rudy. It's because there was no woman who could meet his exacting standards, and who would put up with that shit? My experience is that women want to be noticed occasionally. Other than a perfunctory, 'You look nice.' Gerry doesn't do that. It's all about him, and he's smart enough to avoid the ones who just want his money."

"I heard, Norbie, that he had a fixation on his mother. Is that true?"

"True enough. My mom was a beauty, but she was my mom. I thought she was just a mom. She didn't play around. I didn't have to explain her actions unless she was mad at us for some stupid thing we'd done. I don't know the impact on kids who have mothers who were known to be over loving. Look, Winston Churchill had one of those mothers; didn't hurt him too much."

"You're rationalizing, Norbie. You know what I'm going to do."

"Captain, do what you have to do. I can't play a game with you this time. Life is not always the way we remember or want to remember it; we fool ourselves with our memories. Do your job, Captain. Make sure you do it right."

"Norbie, I couldn't agree with you more."

MCU Detective Toddington working with the other departments brought the requisite paperwork to the court to request searches. An unhappy judge snapped at the essence of the request for a search for a Bowie knife and high-end boots with minimal supporting evidence.

Toddington came away with search warrants only for the knife, for Valle and Cramer's places of work, their main cars, and their homes, offices, and any outside buildings attached or not attached. The last items were only relevant for Valle's home as Cramer lived in a condo. The warrant included storage at Cramer's condo. Within the hour the police were serving them. It was a big job and took until late that night.

The next morning found the detectives looking at the minimal spoils of the search. They had found eight knives, but only two long enough to meet the ME's description, and one was found in each home. The Captain sent them both for analysis.

Beauregard told his detectives he'd already heard from Cramer and Valle's defense lawyers, who were making threats. He also reported when Detective Toddington entered the Valle home, the back wall had an eight-foot-tall portrait of a beautiful woman. He was told by the cleaning woman who was there the woman was 'Mrs. Valle.' Ted asked if Valle were married.

The cleaning woman said, "Oh no, his mother. He loved his mother. They were very close."

The word of a search at a suspect's home was out on the street, and Cramer's wife called for an interview separate from Cramer's attorney. The Captain had conferenced with the Holyoke, Nonton, Springfield, and Wales Police departments. Boston's MCU said they'd call later. "There should be some news fireworks and maybe another attempt on one of the women late tonight. The pressure is on," the Captain said.

———————

Ginnie, Vic Cramer's wife, entered the major crimes unit. She presented herself to the Captain as a woman on a mission.

"Captain Beauregard, I remember you from the fundraiser. You were in the audience, and I thank you for your interest in my cause. I won't waste our time. The officers who searched our home found a knife. I am here to tell you I have never seen that knife before. If it were in my home, I would know about it, and I would have insisted the knife be removed.

"I asked Vic, and he said he did not know where it came from. I believe him. In three years, I have never seen Vic with a weapon. I am a recovering alcoholic, and I'm telling you now, Captain, I know when people are lying to me. Vic cannot lie successfully. He can bullshit as he says, but he can't lie. He's not devious. I trust him. Please don't ruin him. Vic is a good man, insecure but morally sound. He could never deliberately hurt any person; man or woman."

"Doctor Connell, the knife we found matches the marks on the murdered women. Where was your husband last night?"

"Why are you asking, Captain. I thought the attack on Ms. James occurred in the daylight? And that knife does not belong to Vic."

"Someone put the knife in your husband's briefcase where the officers found it. Where was there an opportunity for that to happen? Where was your husband yesterday, and doesn't he check his briefcase? It's important to tie down the timeline on when, if what you say about your husband is true – when was there an opportunity to drop a knife in his briefcase without his knowing about it? Doctor, this is very important."

"Vic was out and about. He called me at lunch and said he was hitting the Celtic Belles at two p.m., that the guys would be there. By guys I mean the Boys Club group."

"Do you know if they all showed up?"

"Well, I know he saw Jack and Gerry, and Myron because he mentioned discussing the murders with them."

"What kind of discussion, do you know?"

"Captain, I'm sick of hearing about these horrors. I hear so much about horrors I'm afraid I tuned Vic out."

After Dr. Connell left, Rudy held a meeting with his detectives. He opened the meeting with one question. "Motive. What's the motive? I have an idea and if I'm right, then protecting Martina, Lavender, and Valencia is not enough!"

Petra, Ash, and Mason knew the Captain had made a determination while Toddington seemed to just struggle to answer the Captain's question.

Ted said, "Captain, the mother fixation is strong. After seeing the idolization of his mother painting in Valle's home, I thought maybe that would be the motive. You know, without sexually touching these women, who ignored him, he would put them in the same place as his mother who also ignored him. But in thinking it over, he should have been freed by his mother's death. Instead, he really mourned her; at least he gave the appearances of mourning her. So why kill all these women? Maybe that isn't the motive after all."

Beauregard said, "I think we're close and I agree with you, Ted, but we're not quite there. Valle has been successful in every endeavor except one. He can't find a beautiful woman who doesn't want just his money but wants him. Why is he not successful? We've been told he's boring. Imagine knowing every one of his friends can get a beautiful woman but him."

Petra caught on. "You may be right, Captain, but why just these women? They can't be the only good-looking women he tried to get. Why, these women?"

The Captain shook his head and sighing, said, "What did all these women say about the other 'Brothers from another mother'? There was only one 'Brother' that the three women still alive always talked positively about, almost to the point of nausea. That was Candido Rodriguez."

Ash got it. "He wants to remove Candi and does it by trying to ruin him."

Mason really got it, saying, "Captain, he wasn't successful with Lavender yesterday, and we've got protection on all the ladies, so he can't reach them. You know who is at risk, don't you?"

Beauregard replied, "I wanted to hear how it sounded when I verbalized it. We're protecting the wrong people today, I think."

———

Norbie Cull was disturbed by the news of the attack on Lavender James. It was the final act that let his client completely off the hook, but something bothered him. He'd been thinking about his conversation with Beauregard and realized he had not been completely honest in his memories. *Valle and Rodriguez may have discovered girls earlier than the rest of us, but I don't think that's what's important. Although Valle may be OCD, I've seen him get dirty when we would fish or play. He'd get dirty when it was a requirement to beat any of us. He is and was the most competitive man I've ever met, and I'm a defense attorney. That says it all. Cripes, that says it all. How could I be so blinking stupid?*

Cull got to Candi's house just as the detectives pulled into the drive. All was quiet. They rang the doorbell with no answer. Norbie had tried to call but got a message back that Candi was busy with a 'brother.' Petra insisted exigent circumstances existed, while Mason back at the station, promised to get a warrant. Ash easily opened the lock, and they entered the home. They searched but did not find Candi. They did find two broken coffee cups and spilled coffee on the floor and rubber heel marks on the floor, but found no other mess.

Cull said, "I think someone was dragged out of here." They searched out by the front door and found Candi's cell phone in the flowers by the front door.

Ash played with the cell phone finding that it was on 'record.' It was difficult to be certain, but it sounded as if there was an altercation between two men, a crash with a broken cutlery sound, and someone huffing and puffing and swearing.

Nothing to do now thought Beauregard, *it's time to move and hope we're in time.* Accompanied by his detectives and Cull, they headed the mile away to Valle's house. Finding a black Mercedes Benz SUV parked in front, they noticed a 'two' on the plate.

Cull informed Beauregard, "When he was a kid, his mother always left the back door open for friends or in case the family members lost their keys. Gerry's a victim of habit. Don't break in, keep the cops all around but try the back door first. I think if we're to save Candi, surprise is the only way."

Beauregard agreed. And the back door was open!

Beauregard pushed Cull to the rear as they all filed quietly into the house. They could hear Gerry talking to Candi, but Candi's answers appeared muffled.

Valle was heard saying, "It's time, Candi-ass Candi. You, with your psycho pablum, making all the pretty ladies want you! You told me to get over my mother and find a wife, and then you fucked with me. Candi knows everything!!! What a bunch of bullshit you fed all the beautiful ladies, making them think you were God.

"Knowing that I was crazy over Janice, you told Devon to protect

Janice. She liked me, and you ruined it. I could have had a beauty for myself. You just couldn't keep your mouth shut, could you? You told Loretta she should move out of the area to a bigger city, that she had ambition and should go for the gold. She would have been happy here if you hadn't counseled her. You didn't care if I was hurt. Brilliant Candi. You could have shut up for once. No, you wanted to keep me out of the loop with the ladies. As long as you were happy, you deliberately pushed the ladies against me.

"You told Lavender her first duty was balancing her life and not to be overwhelmed by money. Like she needed to hear that! Tonya told you about the man at the lake. She never told you it was me. She was responding to me.

"You said anyone who was willing to keep a relationship secret was not for her future, that she needed to be up-front about life. You encouraged Lisa to think bigger than money or local guys. You set Valencia up to look for certain values - for what? She fools around with a married congressman after saying no to Devon. Serves him right for interfering with me and Janice! And what about Martina, you think you're her level? Oh, how you helped her cope with her history. She was lonely. Stupid, they are all stupid, beautiful women who don't know real value. You encouraged them in their stupidity and ruined everything. You're a low life who found a profession, which screws with people's brains. Well, it all ends here, buddy. I win."

By this time Beauregard and the others had entered the study where they found Candi lying on a rubber tarp tied and clearly compromised by a blow to the head, while Gerry, dressed in coveralls was standing over him with an industrial reciprocating blade saw in his right hand.

Cull moved in quickly and said, "Gerry, give it up. He's a brother. Where the fuck has your loyalty gone? He's not wealthy. His wife nags him. He's not someone to get even with. Get even with me. I'm going to turn my back on you and not defend you. I'll put a lien on all your assets for his widow. She'll own everything. Rodriguez will win that way."

While Cull was talking, Rudy and Ash moved forward towards Valle and Rodriguez. Valle was infuriated by Cull and started the saw. Cull laughed at him. "Got it all wrong again, Gerry! Candi is the wrong guy – I'm the one who told them about you. I broke the trust. You're going to die today."

When Valle lunged with the saw, Cull barely escaped. At that moment, Petra bolted and grabbed Valle at the knees, the saw flying in the air. It missed Cull by a hair but fortunately had an automatic turn-off. Lucky for Cull!

Beauregard said, "Thank OSHA for its standards, Norbie, or you would be cut up. Now, why the fuck did you think you're a police negotiator? If you were, the goal would be to de-escalate, not enrage the perp. Your gambit did work. However, you should remember this is not a courtroom. I don't like dramatics. You could have been killed. I hate civilians at my scenes; even you -- Cull."

Hours later at the station, the other detectives asked Beauregard when he first decided on motive. His answer was, "Per usual, I thought of it, rejected it as a possibility, thought it again, and it just wouldn't leave my mind until I finally had to throw it out to you. The appearance of high-end boots at the Lavender assault scene and the perp's movement beyond his planned order for victims convinced me. Valle is the only one who would have a planned assault and not wear old clothes. He also seemed in my mind to be the best possible choice as an impersonator of the young surgeon who tried to move Valencia. He could be a perfect actor. He is, after all, in addition to being OCD, narcissistic, and nuts; a sociopath, Sociopaths are famous for manipulating and when necessary impersonating. It's always the little things that bring you over the top. It was changing our concept of motive that did it."

The detectives were very busy getting ready for another big press conference outside their station. Ash was seen talking on his phone with whispered love speak to Martina while Petra was arranging a decorating conference with Lavender at her home for the next evening. Meanwhile, a persuasive Mason was on the phone describing to his cousin Latoya how he had protected Myron throughout the investigative process.

Beauregard was at peace. He called his wife, his parents, and his brother Liam to share the good news all the while thinking, *We can all be fooled by a sociopath. Even Norbie was fooled, and he is fucking smart and knew Valle forever.*

Acknowledgments

To my husband Joe for his unquestionable loyalty, kindness, and love.

To my children: The lights of my life.

To my grandchildren: Dream, Endure, and Prevail!

I am grateful for all technical assistance I received from my good friends:

Police Matters: Ret. Springfield MA Chief of Police Paula Meara and MA State Police Officer John Ferrara

Attorneys: Charles E. Dolan; Ret. MA Justice Joseph A. Pellegrino; and Raipher D. Pellegrino

Editors: I thank you for your support and counsel.

To all above: All errors on implementation are solely mine

Care to Review My Book?
(or "Honest Reviews Don't Kill")

Now that you've read the story to the end, I'd love to know what you think of it – and read your honest review about the book on Amazon, Goodreads or other major online book retailers where it is featured.

https://kbpellegrino.com/review-brothers-from-another-mother

Review some of my other books:
https://kbpellegrino.com/review-sunnyside-road
https://kbpellegrino.com/review-mary-lou
https://kbpellegrino.com/review-a-predatory-cabal
https://kbpellegrino.com/review-him-me-paulie
https://kbpellegrino.com/review-killing-the-venerable

Thank you for your interest in my books!

Kathleen

More Books by K.B. Pellegrino

The Captain Beauregard Mystery Series

Evil Exists in West Side Trilogy:
–Sunnyside Road: Paradise Dissembling
(Livres-Ici Publishing) 2021, (Liferich Publishing) 2018
–Mary Lou: Oh! What Did She Do?
(Livres-Ici Publishing) 2021, (Liferich Publishing) 2018
–Brothers of Another Mother: All for One! Always?
(Livres-Ici Publishing) 2021, (Liferich Publishing) 2019

–Him, Me and Paulie: Drugs, Murder and Undercover
(Livres-Ici Publishing) 2019
–A Predatory Cabal: Worm in the Apple
(Livres-Ici Publishing) 2020
–Killing the Venerable: It's Their Time!
(Livres-Ici Publishing) 2021

You can find K. B. Pellegrino's books on all major online Book Stores, such as Amazon, Barnes & Noble, kobo, and iBooks.

Bonuses, Giveaways, and Freebies

Free Chapters

"Sunnyside Road: Paradise Dissembling"
Download a free chapter of the first book in the Evil Exists in West
Side Trilogy
"Sunnyside Road: Paradise Dissembling" at
www.kbpellegrino.com/sunnyside-road/FreeChapter

"Him, Me, and Paulie: Drugs, Murder and Undercover"
Download a free chapter of the Captain Beauregard Series book #4
"Him, Me, and Paulie: Drugs, Murder and Undercover" at
www.kbpellegrino.com/him-me-paulie/FreeChapter

To access more freebies, visit: www.kbpellegrino.com/bonus

Follow K. B. Pellegrino

Join My Private Email List

To receive updates about books, new releases, upcoming events, or to simply keep in touch with me, join my private email list.

We do not release your information to any other vendors.
www.kbpellegrino.com/join-list

On my website at www.kbpellegrino.com
On GoodReads at https://www.goodreads.com/author/K.B.Pellegrino
On Facebook: https://www.facebook.com/kbpellegrino
On Instagram: https://www.instagram.com/kbpellegrino_author/
On Twitter: https://twitter.com/kbpellegrino